Advance Praise

"In Su Chang's hypnotic, transfixing novel, the reader shares in Lemei's fever dream of purges, kidnappings, and mob violence, followed by the waking horror that all of it is true. Daring and astute, *The Immortal Woman* goes beyond asking what people will do to survive. How will they live, with themselves and with each other, once the surviving is done?"

—Thea Lim, author of *An Ocean of Minutes*

"*The Immortal Woman* shocked me with its clarity and compassion. In this page-turning tale of a spirited mother and daughter, Su Chang illuminates a cruel chapter of recent history, exposing the generational scars inflicted by a dehumanizing regime. The result is a fierce, unforgettable debut."

—Alissa York, author of *Far Cry*

"*The Immortal Woman* reveals a *woman's* experience of revolution. Mothers and daughters suffer from mistakes and betrayals during the terror of the Tiananmen Square protests. In difficult migrations to a new country, a new culture, they try to leave behind a past that relentlessly torments them. But even a repressive regime cannot silence a woman's emotional truth, and Su Chang tells it in this novel. It's a book that makes our hearts bigger. Read it."

—Kim Echlin, *Speak, Silence*

"At once lush and heartbreaking, *The Immortal Woman* is a shimmering, exquisite story of two women finding freedom at the limit of ideological groupthink. A gorgeous, intelligent debut."

—Kathryn Kuitenbrouwer, author of *Wait Softly Brother*

"With vividly immersive, dreamlike prose, Su Chang unearths a dystopic period of one country's history and its far-reaching echoes, revealing seeds of brutality that feel frighteningly familiar in so much of the world today. Perceptive, mesmerizing, and open-hearted, *The Immortal Woman* is an urgent reminder that we must hold tight to our humanity, and our imaginations, at every turn."

—Jessica Westhead, author of *Avalanche* and *Worry*

"Few novels can give you the sense of the entirety of a time and place, but that is what Su Chang has accomplished in her debut novel. She captures the political and social world of two generations of women: Lemei and her daughter, Lin, the former a Red Guard leader while merely a student in 1960s Shanghai, and the latter who makes her escape to the free world decades later, only to discover that this world is not as bold and promising as she had imagined. But the real achievement of *The Immortal Woman* is not merely the social and political realities its author describes, but the depths of feeling she explores and articulates in response to these realities. This novel is a wonder to behold."

—Joseph Kertes, author of *Last Impressions*

"Su Chang's *The Immortal Woman* traces the threads of women damaged by history, carrying their wounds forward across generations to unwittingly warp their most intimate bonds. This tender and heartbreaking excavation forms a portrait of a mother and daughter fractured first by their past, and then again by the weight of dreams they could not live up to in the present. *The Immortal Woman* is a testament to the dangers of history, and the power of words to both wound and heal."

—Tessa Hulls, author/artist of *Feeding Ghosts*

# THE IMMORTAL WOMAN

# THE IMMORTAL WOMAN

*a novel*

# SU CHANG

ANANSI

Published in Canada and the USA in 2025 by House of Anansi Press Inc.
houseofanansi.com

House of Anansi Press is committed to protecting our natural environment.
This book is made of material from well-managed FSC®-certified forests, recycled
materials, and other controlled sources.

House of Anansi Press is a Global Certified Accessible™ (GCA by Benetech)
publisher. The ebook version of this book meets stringent accessibility standards and
is available to readers with print disabilities.

29 28 27 26 25    1 2 3 4 5

Library and Archives Canada Cataloguing in Publication

Title: The immortal woman : a novel / Su Chang.
Names: Chang, Su (Author of The immortal woman), author.
Identifiers: Canadiana (print) 20240489853 | Canadiana (ebook) 20240514343 |
ISBN 9781487013172 (softcover) | ISBN 9781487013189 (EPUB)
Subjects: LCGFT: Novels.
Classification: LCC PS8605.H35627 I46 2025 | DDC C813/.6—dc23

Book design: Alysia Shewchuk
Cover images: stock.adobe.com

*House of Anansi Press is grateful for the privilege to work on and create from the
Traditional Territory of many Nations, including the Anishinabeg, the Wendat, and
the Haudenosaunee, as well as the Treaty Lands of the Mississaugas of the Credit.*

With the participation of the Government of Canada
Avec la participation du gouvernement du Canada | Canadä

*We acknowledge for their financial support of our publishing program the Canada
Council for the Arts, the Ontario Arts Council, and the Government of Canada.*

Printed and bound in Canada

For my family

*An orange blob swayed on the match's phosphorous tip, its glow illuminating the dusky jungle of anatomy charts and skeletons. She opened the drawers; journal papers spilled out and beckoned the fledgling flame between her fingers. The fiery tendrils licked the byline—Hong Ting, MD—before caressing a page with a burst of energy. The flame sank into the flesh of the paper, a darkening stain percolating downward and fanning outward, until it clutched the wooden desk and devoured the dry fuel with a beastly hunger. The wood popped and crackled. She jerked her chair back and hopped aside, her heart thumping, her hands grabbing all they could reach—charts and jars and tubes, Caucasian masks, Asian masks. Feed the beast! Feed the beast! With each round of renewed fuel, the flames jigged and jived, a mesmerizing dance. She danced too, her silhouette on the wall a wild blurry dynamo, swelling, ballooning. The women burst in, shrieking. Ma's gnarled hands were on hers, wrestling, killing the beast. Strings of apologies leaped out of Ma's mouth, saturating the thinning air. She couldn't breathe; she had to fight back. But the doctor lunged at her like a White Bone Spirit, whiplashing her with shrill cries: "Psychos! You and your mother—you are both psychos!"*

PART ONE

# THE HAPPY GIRL

1954–1981

# 1

According to family lore, she was laughing the minute she was born, on the morning of New China's National Day in 1954. Naturally, her father, ever the faithful first-generation revolutionary, named her Sheng Hua (盛华), Glorious China. But nurses and doctors kept lingering by her mother's bed, clapping their hands over the giggling infant.

"Too much gas in her tummy!" one declared.

"Not to worry, just a happy girl, beats the whiny kind," another assured Yu Ma.

"A happy girl! A happy girl!" more exclaimed, marvelling at the baby's wide, glittering eyes that instantly transformed into Laughing Buddha crescents. The label rippled through the hospital like whitecaps across water. Within hours, her parents gave in, informing the birth registration officer of their daughter's name: Lemei (乐妹), the Happy Girl.

In primary school, she discovered her passion for Chinese classics—old novels and poetry her Ba used to hand her. But over the years, those books disappeared from the family's bookshelves, replaced by a four-volume *Das Kapital*, twenty installments of the Chairman's Thoughts, and a smattering of Soviet leaders' essay collections. While her Ba hunched over his desk, making copious notes in the margins of his new books, she retreated to the back stacks of her school's library, drinking in *Three Hundred Tang Poems* and *The Songs of the South*. Her classmates crowned her the Princess of Shijing, as she had the quaint habit of quoting the "Airs of the States" and "Court Hymns," often with a contemporary twist to lighten the mood.

In the last semester of primary school, an elegant Ms. May from the nearby middle school was parachuted into her classroom to substitute for the unfortunate Ms. Qu, who was exiled to the countryside to atone for her Kuomintang father's sins. Ms. May loved to put Lemei on the spot. When they dissected Lu Xun's works, she'd tap her on the shoulder and say, "Give us your take," after others had repeated quotes taken straight from the Chairman's praise for the revolutionary writer.

Lemei would say things like, "Lu Xun's *Ah Q* shines a light on the weakness of the Chinese psyche, and how readily we could all abandon our humanity." Her replies always sent a tight-lipped smile to her teacher's face, and once the class was dismissed and they were left alone, Ms. May's conspiratorial grin would blossom further. "You've got something special, kid. Keep on reading." She'd unlock a drawer behind her desk and take out a book—always wrapped in a handmade, nondescript dust jacket—and press it into Lemei's palm.

She followed Ms. May to Fengyang High in the summer of 1966, her head still swimming in her ancestors' songs and rhymes. Some might say her timing was impeccable, as the Red Guards moved into her new school merely a week later. More precisely, senior students from families of the Five Red Categories, her brother included, metamorphosed into Red Guards overnight. Lemei was still too young to join the Guard, though all her classmates were clamouring to become one. Of course she loved the Chairman too—she owed her entire life to him—but how someone like her brother could represent the Great Man was beyond her. At fourteen, two years older than her, Feng the Simpleton was all muscle and no brain. His plump cheeks were hollowed by a habitual sneer; his vacant eyes under those bushy brows never failed to nauseate her. He could be relied upon to crank out consistent Ds in all his classes, his poor grades a dependable kindling to ignite Ba's fury.

"In one ear, out the other!" Ba would bellow after every failed attempt to help Feng with his homework. Such occasions had become increasingly rare though; there was always something holding up her parents at their work unit. A struggle session. A self-criticism assembly. A big-character poster marathon.

Lately, Feng had grown bolder. He'd roar back at Ba, his eyes black and unyielding: "Homework is a waste of time anyway! Chairman has better things for us to do. Don't turn into the Old Guard they think you are!"

Ma had to deposit herself between father and son, by turns pleading and threatening, or all hell would break loose.

IN THE SECOND WEEK of September, the Red Guards kicked open Lemei's classroom door in the middle of Ms. May's poetry lesson.

"Class suspended!" a stocky boy spat, waving his meaty fist, his upturned nostrils flaring like a pig's snout.

Lemei recognized him right away as Feng's classmate, whose rural accent her brother loved to mock behind his back. Feng was in the mob too, his cheeks cardinal red, a blue vein throbbing with the metronome of excitement.

Pigface snatched the book from the teacher's hands. "Li Bai?! Chairman ordered us to strike down the Four Olds! How dare you still teach this trash from feudal China?"

"Chairman is a huge fan of classical poetry," replied Ms. May calmly. "He's an accomplished poet himself."

"See? Told you," the bully crowed. "A sneaky snake. She's a true People's Enemy. Lock her up!"

The mob, as if following the hands of a conductor, exploded in unison: "Lock her up! Lock her up!"

Feng pushed through the throng with a metal placard that read *Bourgeois Revisionist Element*. He hesitated for an instant so brief that only Lemei noticed, before plunking the placard around Ms. May's neck. Cupping his shaking hands, he froze in place, sweat running down his oily forehead. His nerves had ruined his first time in the spotlight as a Red Guard, and he knew it.

Pigface elbowed Feng aside. With a raised pinkie, he threw the book of poetry to the floor. "No place in our school for such garbage!"

*How original*, Lemei thought, *copy every overwrought move from a Model Opera.*

His followers stomped on the book, cracking its spine and muddying its innards. Lemei kept her gaze trained on Ms. May, hoping her teacher could read the support in her eyes, but her head dangled low under the weight of the placard. The plump crusader shoved Ms. May out of the room, raising his doughy double chin high like a royal executioner.

Lemei rubbed her eyes and wiped away hot tears. What now? No one knew how to react. A girl two rows ahead broke into sobs. Her desk mate shushed her and gave her the stink eye. "Yay! No more classes!" the usual rascals hooted and clapped, only to be met with more sobs. Lemei wanted to do *something*, at least find out where the Guards were taking Ms. May, but her body felt heavy and lethargic. She fought the sinking force of gravity as she rose from the chair, her heart hammering. Before her feet could move, a barrel-chested young man in an olive-green uniform sauntered in, flanked by Pigface and Feng.

*Just what we need, more second-rate actors.*

"Be seated. Quit the commotion!" Pigface was at it again. "Comrades, I give you Dashan, student leader from Beijing's 101 High School!"

Applause erupted like firecrackers. Xiaomin, her desk mate, tugged hard on her sleeve until Lemei sank back into the wooden chair.

"Comrades, we're here to spread the Chairman's directives outside the capital," Dashan intoned, his tongue-rolling Beijing accent thick and abrasive. "Situation here is dismal—Shanghai is moving too slow. We want to elevate the Shanghai Red Guards, light the fire of our Great Proletarian Cultural Revolution!" The Beijing leader gave Pigface a meaningful nod, sending him into a visible spasm.

"Take out your Little Red Book!" The young thug's voice was an octave higher than Dashan's, as if hysteria could mask its shakiness. "Time for a recitation contest. First place gets a merit point in his personal dossier!"

Her eyes glided to the copy of Li Bai's poetry still open in front of her, a drawing of a yellow crane tower emitting a forlorn glory. Xiaomin tossed the book under their desk just before Dashan's sweeping gaze landed on them. But the verse had already come to her, clear as an autumnal sky:

> My old friend bids farewell to me at Yellow Crane Tower,
> Amid April's mist and flowers, she goes down to Yangzhou.
> The distant image of her lonely sail disappears in blue
>    emptiness,
> And all I see is the Yangzi River flowing to the edge of
>    the ether.

*So that's it then; it's all over.* She shuddered, avoiding Dashan's glare. The barbarians were here to stay.

# 2

Ms. May was sent to the cowshed at the back of the school, which used to be an abandoned storage room. The Red Guards laid reed mats on the dank floor and threw all the unwanted "cow demons and snake spirits" in there to repent their wicked ways. For weeks, Lemei crouched behind the hibiscus bushes after school and watched her teacher's frail figure bending over the communal garden, pulling weeds or seeding vegetables. Ms. May was shrinking fast, her skin, loose and folded, hanging over her like a deflated balloon. One afternoon, she emerged from the shed with half her head shaved bald and the other half turned grey, a sinister half-moon, a humiliating crown for the devil. For the first time, she lifted her head and acknowledged her best student behind the bushes, with the same tight-lipped smile she used to reward her with in class. Lemei had to run away, her heart racing and clenching small.

She sought sanctuary in the narrow alleyway behind her apartment building, between the wisteria-covered walls. Sitting on her three-legged round stool, she buried her head in the last book Ms. May had lent her, her fingers tracing the tiny crimson stitches lining the dust jacket that concealed the book cover. *Sometimes, truth can only be preserved through deception*, her teacher had told her. Lemei had so many questions about the book, with its ornate illustrations and translated vocabulary. She sensed the lush terrain stretching between the lines—if only she could crack the codes—unlike the boundless desert her mind conjured whenever she walked by the new titles on her father's bookshelf.

"I knew I'd find you here," a voice boomed at the entrance of the alleyway, her brother's shadow looming large.

She peeled her eyes from the book and squinted into the setting sun. "Good afternoon to you too, Feng."

"What dirty book are you reading now? You're a diehard capitalist roader, aren't you?" he said, wiping snot on his sleeve.

"Clean yourself up. Ma's going to have an aneurysm looking at you."

"They're working late again. Aunt Fu sent a message."

*Not again.* Ma had long promised to make Lemei a copy of the apartment key so she could let herself in, but that damn locksmith just had to run into trouble with the Red Guards last week, yanked away from his dingy basement where he'd served as a longtime capitalist. Perfect timing. Now she was stuck in the back alley, talking to Feng.

Her brother sidled up to her and snatched the book from her hands, stripping off the dust jacket like a butcher flaying a carcass. "Tsk tsk, look at this cover—filth! American devils have no shame!" He looked indignant, but his eyes were fixed on the foreign lady's bare shoulders and the half-moons of her bosom. Lemei had peeked at that cover too; the lovers' passionate kiss had at once shocked her and tickled her insides, the pleasure on their faces a delicious enigma. But it had turned out to be a different kind of book. Instead of feeling disappointed, she sensed a mysterious rapport with Anna, the title character.

"Not American, Soviets."

"No longer our friends either!"

"Of course not. Find someone else to bother, will you?"

"So you can plunge back into the arms of this revisionist hooligan and his slut? No way. Time I gave that muddy brain of yours a deep cleaning!"

She wrenched the book from his grip, tossed it into her backpack, and got up to leave. He merely rearranged his limbs, his body morphing into a solid gate. She edged forward anyway. "What's with you today? Not enough teachers to beat up at school?"

"Say you won't read such drivel anymore! 'Opium for the mind'!"

"Whatever you say."

"Watch your attitude! You think you're above the law, little brat?" He flicked her in the forehead, sending her staggering backward. "If you weren't a girl, I'd have given you a nice beating long ago."

She steadied herself with both hands on the stone wall and breathed hard. *Come on, Lady Swallow, let's teach him a lesson.* She channelled the heroine from a bootlegged kung fu flick and lunged at her brother. They tumbled out of the alley and landed in the neighbourhood lane, his bear hands around her neck. Struggling for air, she stabbed her fingers into the hollow space above his collarbone, hooked deep, and gave a sudden yank. He fell away like a lump of dough.

"Leave me alone, freak!" She rose from the ground and slung her schoolbag over her shoulder. Onlookers were gathering around them, a cloud of grey-blue suits emanating an oppressive muskiness. Street fights erupted like wildfires all day, every day, but they never lacked an audience. Lemei pushed through the crowd and sprinted forward, dizzy with adrenaline.

"She's got a porno book!" she heard Feng barking behind her, followed by a stranger's stern voice: "Stop!" She turned and saw a young policeman glaring in her direction. Beside him, Feng's vengeful smirk.

Fright spurred her on as she led the officer through a maze of alleyways, broke onto Fuxing Road lined with French wutong, and pivoted sharply at the gardenia-scented Fengyang Road. It was there that a counterrevolutionary saved her. In front of the Shanghai Music Conservatory, an agitated mob were screaming obscenities at a middle-aged woman with the wrinkly, jaundiced face of a newborn, a pointy witch's hat balanced precariously on her head. Wielding a pair of garden shears, a rosy-cheeked girl of no more than eighteen slashed open the woman's frumpy grey pants and used her bare, cotton-white thigh as a spittoon. "Poison youths with your bourgeois music, this is what you get!"

Lemei slipped through the cheering throng, nimble as a baby eel escaping lines of fishnets. When she looked back, the policeman stood motionless, mouth agape, gawking at the sea of zealots.

He had forgotten all about the small fish Lemei.

# 3

Lemei found Wei, her partner in crime, after a night of unceasing dreams—a lone rose stood in the harsh desert wind, waves of sand rising and swirling and gushing over its stem until the red petals turned a desiccated brown. For Wei, it had been a night of looting. Wei was an enigma, her almond-shaped eyes perpetually tinged with demure mockery. Unlike most girls in their grade, who wore their hair in swinging pairs of revolutionary braids, Wei cropped hers short and neat above her ears, revealing a slim and pale neck. She exuded a boyish handsomeness, reminding Lemei of a camouflaged Hua Mulan. Her parents were doctors, trained in the US in the 1940s. *Idealists.* After 1949, they had answered the call to return to their motherland and serve their people. Upon arrival, they were swiftly entangled in wave after wave of political persecution. This time around, the Red Guards had picked a soggy fall night to ransack their home, taking the doctors into custody.

The next morning, at recess, Lemei fidgeted around the doctors' daughter, condolences stuck in her throat.

SU CHANG

"I know everyone's been whispering about me." Wei had broken the ice.

"Let them talk. All compliments! They say the Guards found more books in your parents' study than in Du Yuesheng's mansion."

"I can't imagine the gangster boss having much time to read."

"Are your parents okay?"

"They're both veterans by now. They'll survive."

"And you?"

"I'm fine."

"The Guards left you alone?"

"I'm nothing to them. Burning books all night long, they only scratched the surface." Wei chuckled. "It's my parents' revenge."

Lemei pictured the girl's sleepless night—huddled in the corner of her smoke-choked apartment, the hooligans rushing to and fro, carmine flames rising and crackling like a starving beast. But none of that had left a mark on Wei. She looked serene as usual, her eyes two deep wells, unfathomable.

"I'm sorry about all the books."

"Don't be." Wei tapped her temple with a finger. "All in here. I've kept them safe."

Lemei smiled dumbly. *Glad I've found you.*

WEI'S APARTMENT BUILDING stood across the street from the music conservatory. From her bedroom window overlooking Fengyang Road, she could see an endless parade of professors in daily struggle sessions. Two weeks after the Red Guards torched her family's library, she sneaked into the conservatory and found the vast campus deserted. The library, looted and vandalized a month ago, was a gaping wound beyond the grey wall. She tiptoed through the cavernous opening, stepping over the toppled shelves strewn across the floor, the smell of singed paper tickling her nose. But the Guards had done a sloppy job. In the dimly lit back stacks, layers of spiderwebs crisscrossed boxes of "bad element" literature: *Romance of the Three Kingdoms*, *Water Margin*, *Dream of the Red Chamber*, and translated works of European masters. Like a starving child facing a lavish buffet, she dropped to her knees and stifled her giggles, filling her backpack with weeks of supply. So when Lemei complained to her, in hushed secrecy, that she was running out of good things to read, Wei knew precisely where to take her. Later, they traded the finished books like two underground spies swapping codes for survival. Those nights flowed like a river, carrying them back to the cradle of their ancestors, to a place responsible for both the pride and the tribulations of their motherland, carrying them forward into a dream where they no longer needed to live like fugitives.

ON A WINTRY EVENING in 1967, Lemei dashed into her friend's apartment, offloading a heavy bag of books. The door slammed behind her, shutting out the wailing northwest wind.

"Freakish, this weather." She blew heat into her frozen hands. "The Dragon King has had enough—got to blow away all those big-character posters!"

The room was eerily quiet. A thin piece of paper, blotted and disembodied, loomed ominously under the only working light bulb. Behind it, an apparition, a bundle of shivering bones.

Lemei rushed to her friend but refrained from touching her, fearing a mere pat on the shoulder could trigger a disintegration. Instead, she took the paper gingerly. *Orphan, no legal guardians, state's custody*—the words rushed at her like hailstones. "When did this...?" She sucked in the cold air. "So sorry for your loss. Your parents are heroes, no matter what others say. They gave their lives to—"

"They aren't dead."

"They're not?"

"Just trying their best to protect me."

"Who? The state?"

"No. Ba and Ma. Look again, look at the bottom."

Lemei found a pair of elegant signatures standing shoulder to shoulder next to the scarlet seal of the Revolutionary Committee.

"So ... they've *abandoned* you?"

"You really don't understand anything, do you?" A chilling cackle. "Right, you're from the reddest family in town. Clueless."

She couldn't bear to watch her friend, the gentlest soul, turned bitter by a vicious letter, just as it was intended to do.

"First, a divorce, in case one of them gets out first. Now *this*. Severing all ties. Set me 'free' from their blackened history! Ha!" Her eyes shone with a crazed light. "Does it work? I'm still ordered to sit at the back of the class, aren't I? Unless it's a struggle session, then I'm centre stage, face to face with the cow demons. Killing the chicken to scare the monkeys—those shows are all for people like me!"

"Hey, let's get out of here." Lemei seized her friend's icy hand and started for the door. She knew what Wei needed—that bottle shaped like a lotus flower Ba kept in the kitchen cabinet. She'd seen Ba pouring Ma the magic juice whenever she was upset, and Ma mellowing after a single shot. But she'd have to act fast, before darkness swallowed her friend whole.

They turned the corner onto Fuxing Road, relieved to escape the direct confrontation with the angry Wind God. Posters blown from the walls littered the street, an off-white carpet stretching into outer space. Under the yellow streetlights, calligraphy strokes overflowed the pages like a tsunami of giant spiders. Wei was losing steam, losing command of her muscles and bones. Lemei felt the vibration of a blow, her friend's hand slipping out of hers, joints smashing into the ground. Boys' jeering and hooting drummed her temple as she turned. A pair of attackers—one tall and one stout—were clapping, their young, pockmarked faces vaguely familiar from school.

"Why do you swagger, huh?" the tall one barked at Wei. "We've had our eyes on you for weeks. Dirty seed from capitalist traitors. How dare you walk around like some kind of hero on these roads paved with the sweat and tears of our socialist workers?"

The stout one squatted down, running his filthy hand up and down Wei's neck. "Smooth skin, this one." He pressed his snub nose to her face, his lips brushing her cheek. "Smells nice too. Landlords' girls always smell better."

"Want a taste?" His companion smacked his lips. "Tonight's your chance!"

Lemei slapped the tall one across the face, her body shaking with a sudden recognition of evil. A black cloud raced at her. Upon impact, it was hard as a rock, her attacker's knuckle smashing into the bridge of her nose. The pain blindsided her and sealed her eyes.

"You want some attention too, don't you? With a pretty face like yours, better learn to lay low, or trouble will follow you for life." The tall one leg-tripped Lemei and pinned her to the ground, his hand clamping over her mouth. She opened one eye to a slit, only to squeeze it shut again. She couldn't watch the stout devil drag her friend to the nearby alley after shoving a dirty rag in her mouth. She forgot how to breathe, her body porous, heat escaping from her like water from a net. Judging by the thug's cry of pain and incessant cursing, Wei was putting up a fierce resistance. The sound of tearing clothes lacerated Lemei's insides. She wiggled her mouth until she could bite down on the thug's fingers—

"Let her go! I'll report you two! I'll crack your damn skull and feed your faces to stray dogs. Help! Help us!"

A worker's boot landed on the back of her neck like a boulder, squeezing her airway and extinguishing her voice. Eyes blurring under the searing pain, she waited for the final snap, the instant end. *Come on, put me out of my misery...* She heard a curious swooshing sound, a long stalk slicing the air and hitting the ground. Her eyes flew open just in time to catch the stout one buckling after the tall one, his fat face crashing onto the pavement at the mouth of the alley.

"Stay away from my sis!" a familiar voice thundered.

Tears gushed down her fevered cheeks, her freed body shivering. *Give them hell, muscle man.* She dropped her eyelids and let the inky cloud of oblivion envelop her.

SHE SAW THE SUNRISE, bright and innocent, from her own bed the next morning. *So it was only a bad dream.* She sighed with relief. But her spine creaked and moaned as she lifted her head. Bloodstained clothes were balled up at the foot of her bed like crumpled innards. *Shit shit shit…*

She pictured herself dangling lifelessly over Feng's shoulder, passing by Ma's petrified face. Holding her breath to stem the pain, she started toward her parents' bedroom, her untrimmed toenails scratching against the wooden floor in the eerie silence. Their bedroom door was wide open, the bed still made, their pajamas lying prostrate in prayer position. She let out the air in her lungs. Must be another emergency all-nighter at the work unit, struggling against some People's Enemy, freshly snatched out of a camouflaged existence among the People.

On the bookshelf, remnants of Ma's altar stood in serenity—white tea candles, a jade incense bowl, a black rock. Ma had packed away the centrepiece, a statue of the Immortal Woman cradling a lotus blossom and riding on cotton-white clouds. Lemei lay prone on the floor and peered at the locked metal box under the bed. She'd been ten, playing a game of hide-and-seek with Feng, when she discovered the figurine in that box. What a handsome saint—those elegant eyes and crimson lips, that elaborate crown woven with orchids and peonies. "Old trash!" Feng had muttered when he found her. Later that night, Ma had made them both swear not to speak about the statue at school. Lemei had felt an odd excitement, and a new sense of affinity—so Ma had a secret! She wasn't the spinning cardboard character she presented to the world! Since then, Lemei had liked to press her face to Ma's bedroom door whenever the scent of sandalwood and amber permeated their apartment. Through a slit, she'd see Ma lay out the prayer mats and kowtow in front of her saint, her face softening and transforming into a foreign terrain of devotion.

"Father in heaven!" Feng cried by the door.

"Good morning." She got up and smiled at him.

"What were you doing? Lying there like a ghost."

"Thank you for last night."

"Don't mention it." He waved, as though shooing away a dirty fly.

"How was Wei? Was she ...?" She couldn't bring herself to say the word. What exactly could a man do to a woman? Her only knowledge of the matter was a few vague references from history classes about the wartime horrors inflicted by the Japs.

"She's all right. Frightened. But nothing happened. I took her back to her apartment."

"I owe you one."

"You learned your lesson?"

"Yes, never to wander the streets after sundown again."

"And stay away from Wei."

"She's my friend."

"The Chairman taught us, the first step of our Revolution: differentiate between the sneaky enemies and ourselves!"

*And talk like a cheap mannequin.*

"I can't abandon my friend."

"Her own parents did," Feng sneered.

Blood rushed to her temples. "What do you know about her parents?"

"Everybody knows. Her whole family's on the blacklist. You're a counterrevolutionary if you still hang out with her."

Her gratitude melted away like a fast-retreating glacier. "Is that a threat again? You know, those are getting old."

"Take it however you want. Remember—you got lucky this time. They could've targeted you too."

"They wouldn't dare. Our Ba is revolutionary royalty. First generation. Gassed by the Japs three times. Lived in stinky caves in Yan'an. Those pimple-faced thugs wouldn't dare touch me!"

"Watch your tongue. You're not immune." Feng suddenly gazed at her with an expression akin to sympathy. "Be humble, and ... just be careful, okay? The tides are turning."

He tossed a packet of biscuits into his pocket. "Gotta go. Political study with Dashan this morning." He darted out the door without looking back, his bag flapping behind him like a white sail.

"Weirdo." A chill started in her gut, slowly looped around to her back, and spread into her extremities. The world dimmed, the floor beneath her breaking and turning into floating ice, steep black walls of a fjord pressing at her. Any minute now, a maelstrom would come out of nowhere and gulp her down, leaving no trace of flesh or bone to prove her existence.

# 4

## SPRING 1967

Lemei ran feverishly from school, lines from the Little Red Book buzzing in her ears like pesky bees energized by the warming season. She ducked under the stone awning of her apartment building, slipping into the mouth of the damp stairwell. Closing her eyes, she willed silence to overtake her, but blocky quotes and slogans resumed their attack. She let out a cry and dashed up the stairs.

She found her mother in the kitchen, hunched over the empty counter. What was Ma doing here at this early hour? Her stomach growled on cue. "Special day, Ma? I'm famished. What's for dinner?"

Ma's face was wan and sullen, like a wilting plant that needed urgent watering. "I'll get to it. Still some green beans and rice. Tomorrow I'll go to the ration station."

"Is Ba coming home tonight?"

"No, work's keeping him," she mumbled and turned away.

"It'll just be the two of us then."

"Where's your brother?"

"Camping out at school."

"With all the Red Guards?"

"Only the fanatical ones." Lemei snorted. "Call themselves the Torchbearers."

"Since when?"

"Last night. Said he'd crash at their tent for a few nights. Guess he's finally making the move, climbing up the ladder." She pictured the Torchbearers in their makeshift camp on the northern edge of the school, a bunch of brainless boys wielding paintbrushes and loudspeakers. Eyebrows knitted, they seemed to be locked in a perpetual debate about what nasty title was best bestowed on which teacher, a pathetic exercise only insecure boys would indulge in.

"You should talk to him, Ma. That group's up to no good."

"You know how stubborn he is. Too much pent-up energy. Let him be." Ma splashed soy sauce into the wok's greasy belly and stirred the green beans with vehemence.

"You know what the Torchbearers are known for, right? Sneaking into the cowshed at night and beating up teachers while they sleep. They're ... *terrorists*!"

Ma spun around; her lips twitched. She plopped a plate of rice and beans in front of Lemei, but her eyes sailed past her.

"So you'll talk to him?"

Ma merely sighed, still failing to focus her gaze on her daughter.

"Is something wrong? You're scaring me."

Ma pushed the plate under her nose.

"No, tell me what's going on first."

"Revisionist, they kept calling him."

"Who? Calling whom?"

"The guards at the Cadre School. 'Jing Hu, Rank 13, Revisionist,' the brats kept on yapping."

"Start from the beginning, Ma. I'm not following."

With her chopsticks, Ma picked out two glistening green beans and shoved them into Lemei's mouth. When she spoke again, her voice was high-pitched and vindictive, as if to punish her daughter for her incessant questioning. She offered up frivolous details—her long bus ride to the top of a dirt road, the beige Soviet-style low-rises, the hordes of midges hovering over the walls. The muddy ocean less than a kilometre away, endlessly repeating its charge-and-retreat dance, washing soot and clay onto the deserted beach. The city's largest cowshed, whose underbelly her father now called home. Lemei's overactive imagination filled in the rest—the black mould coating his cell, the high-voltage ceiling lights that blasted all night long, the watered-down soup after a long day of struggle sessions. She wanted to ask how, and why, but she held her tongue; Ma's anemic face was showing signs of a full-blown storm.

She hid from her mother after dinner, and in the days that followed, dodging the bull's eye of her sorrowful wrath. In her lucid dreams—when they were not nightmares about her father—she begged for the return of her old Ma: famously mild-tempered, her voice rarely rising above the rustling of a willow, her small frame fitting snugly in the crook of Ba's arms.

·   ·   ·

AUNT FU PAID THEM a visit two weeks later. Lemei lingered and breathed nervously as the two friends locked themselves in a silent embrace. Their eyes were burning red when they retired to Ma's room. Lemei curled up by the closed door, cringing as Ma divulged her plethora of "women's problems." The hormonal imbalances, the heavy periods, the frequent migraines, the misdirected Chi. Fu hmmmed and ahhhhed, a constant string of sympathy. "Don't know if this helps, but I did inquire about Lao Jing," she said finally.

"Tell me, tell me!"

"No one wanted to talk, but Secretary Wang owed my Lao Zhao a favour. I asked him over for tea. He said Lao Jing's downfall was his habit of voodoo worship."

Ma's gasp rushed through the wall, hitting Lemei with heat. "What nonsense!"

"Does he really keep a shrine at home?"

"Not his. It's mine, my ancestor."

"You know it's all just an excuse, right? Cadres at his rank have been on the precipice since last winter. Lao Jing's an easy target too, going after those fake productivity reports, making himself an enemy ..."

"I'll turn myself in tomorrow, tell them everything."

"That's crazy talk! You want to be thrown in the cowshed too? What about the children?"

"I can't just sit here and do nothing!"

Lemei heard stomping footsteps and jostled to her feet. Ma's ghostlike face appeared in the doorframe, her eyes steely like carving blades.

"Go fetch your brother. Tell him to get his ass back here this minute. Tell him I'm not kidding around this time!"

"Yes, Ma!" Lemei pulled on her shoes and darted out of the apartment.

AT SUNDOWN, FENG WALKED through the door, dragging his feet and a mile of dirt behind him. His plucky mask crumbled the instant he saw Ma. Lemei had avoided looking at their mother too. Age had caught up with her in a single week after years of slacking off, casting a web of grey crevices over her face.

"So you've done it," Ma said, her voice barbed. "You've ratted us out."

Tears welled in his eyes. An apology stuck in his throat.

"You unfilial, unworthy seed," Ma snarled.

Feng opened his mouth, but no sound escaped.

"Running around like a rabid dog, bringing pestilence to our house. What do you have to say for yourself?!"

His face shifted, hardening. "It's *your* shrine, isn't it?" he said at last. "*You* are the one responsible for his downfall. Don't you pin this on me."

Lemei couldn't help it. She slapped him on the cheek, her palm smarting. "Traitor! *You* told the thugs about the shrine. Now Ba's taken away, probably being tortured this very moment. And you have no remorse?"

His eyes flitted between his sister and his mother, as though forming a coherent picture—a hostile family that stood in the way of his great potential.

"I don't care what you two think of me. I'm leaving anyway."

"Yeah? Where to, big shot?" Lemei snorted. "You think you're not stained by your own confession? Must be tons of demerit points in your dossier!"

"Heading to the countryside. I'll be a big fish in a small pond. Dashan promised me."

"No, you're not, son! It's all a trick."

"I *want* to go."

"Every time they can't feed all the mouths in the cities, they do this..." Ma's voice broke.

"I have to go."

"Don't be the fool they want you to be. The city wall is invisible, but it's there, and it's *impenetrable*. Our Shanghai hukou—"

"Is a badge of shame."

"No, it's a *shield*. Don't listen to their words—their poison!"

"It's already settled."

To Lemei's shock, Ma lunged at Feng and clasped him in her arms. "Whatever lies they're telling you now, they won't let you back into the city, do you understand, son? Don't leave Shanghai. I beg you..."

Feng didn't fight Ma, his body pressed against hers. But Ma must have felt a heavy sense of futility, felt him slipping away, or she wouldn't have burrowed her head into the crook of his neck and shed her elegiac tears.

SOMETHING'S WRONG WITH ME; *I'm rotten to the core*, she thought often now. She wasn't a non-believer—she came from the reddest pedigree, after all—but hard as she tried, she couldn't keep a straight face through all the political studies and struggle sessions. She wanted to poke those around her: *You can't be serious!* But they were—they were as serious as surgeons doing open-heart operations, or petty shop owners counting every penny at the end of the day.

At least Feng was a pure-minded true believer. Ba would be so disappointed in her if he knew how she really felt. Why couldn't she be upright in her thinking? Perhaps Ms. May was indeed evil; perhaps those illicit books had bewitched her and poisoned her blood.

By the spring of 1968, she lived in a surreal state of anarchy. Fights broke out at all hours—between groups that each claimed absolute loyalty to the Chairman, and accused the other of being a pack of wolves in sheep's clothing. In his metallic voice every morning, the faceless radio announcer intoned: "The Chairman fully supports the rebels!" But rebels against whom exactly? The teachers? "Old Guards" like her Ba? A boring life where teenagers weren't constantly gouging each other's eyes out? Nobody knew the answer anymore; adults were too busy proving they were the ultimate rebel, gyrating wild-eyed to the revolutionary anthems. She mimicked them with an impure heart, learning the mannequin-talk, the art of substituting Little Red Book quotes for everyday vernacular. So when news came from the school cowshed that Teacher Li, their flamboyant math teacher—the one who liked to prance before the blackboard with chalk in hand and spin a victory samba whenever a student answered a question right—had been found dead in a pool of cold blood one morning, a correct quote flashed in her head just in time: *Communism is not love; Communism is a hammer we use to crush the enemy.* Numbly, she listened to the hushed chatter at school:

"I thought the Red Guards watched them like hawks. No sharp objects."

"A toothbrush, apparently, sharpened over weeks. Teacher Li opened his veins with it."

She pictured her teacher's warm, rollicking body oozing red-purple liquid and deflating into a mushy sack. Waves of nausea lapped over her, a slimy taste on her tongue. But there was no visceral pain, her empathy cells burned out after too many trials. The revolution had made her stronger.

When the music stopped in the summer that year, as abruptly as it had started, it seemed that the band of rebels could not stop spinning. But the Great Helmsman had had enough. The puppets had done their job and now were nuisances, even threats. The same radio announcer trumpeted the New Order on repeat: "Urban youths need to take root in the country, experience the working life, learn from the peasants ..."

She didn't get to see her brother leave. On that starless night in autumn, she was caught in the grip of a recurring nightmare—Ba's leg shackles tolling a slow cling-clang, his oversized shirt soaked in blood, his former intern towering over him with an oily sneer and a shiny whip. When she woke in a cold sweat, darkness glued her eyes. She heard a pot hissing on the stove, a sharp, bitter smell assaulting her nose. *Visiting day.* The only day of the month Ma would put on a patch-free shirt, before embarking on the two-hour bus ride to the Cadre School with her home-brewed concoction. And she, the dependent child, would be denied again, per the visitation policy. She scrubbed her nose until her skin turned hot and raw, but she couldn't scrub away the revolting smell. Ba would remain an abstraction, a hologram evoked only through the tang of turmeric, dandelion roots, and an assortment of weirdly named medicinal herbs.

Meanwhile, Feng and the entire Torchbearer gang were sardined onto a train, heading for the western frontier, bringing the Chairman's good tidings to the remote mountains and villages. She only heard about it the next morning, in the schoolyard that had slipped into an uncharacteristic hush. The younger Red Guards, with their cheeks burning crimson, stood in perfect formation in olive-green uniforms, listening to the sinister whistling of the wind.

A man in his late twenties with triangular eyes and lopsided lips grabbed the loudspeaker at centre stage. His Yangzhou accent, whiny and jarring, tickled her insides. "Young comrades! Some previous Red Guards overstepped their boundaries. From now on, all Guards work under the tutelage of the Workers' Propaganda Committee. I'm your committee leader, Changshen." His beady eyes scanned the crowd at his feet. "People from my hometown wield three famous knives—a kitchen cleaver, a pedicure blade, and a shaving razor. I'm the son of a butcher and a barber. In the fifties, when you Shanghai people still had lard in your noodles, I ate tree bark and clay. I'm here to safeguard the dictatorship of the proletariat!"

She watched the new leader pontificate, spit flying through the gaps between his yellow, crooked teeth. Was he made of steel or sand? Would he harden or be blown away when the wind shifted next? When the younger Guards chanted the slogans, parroting Changshen's every word, their voices sounded limp and meek. What good was it to occupy the golden throne when the best foot soldiers had evaporated into thin air?

# 5

## MARCH 1969

Shrieks tore into her ears from blocks away. A wall of stench sucker-punched her in the face as she turned into her neighbourhood off Fuxing Road. Boys, sniggering and muttering obscenities, slouched in a semicircle facing her building, facing a brown-striped fox flower kitten nailed to the wall through its four limbs. It twitched and spasmed, staring straight ahead with menacing green eyes.

A dart flashed through the air and pierced the creature's belly, penetrating its flesh with a corking sound. The kitten wailed; the crowd cheered.

"Savages! Stop!" She stomped her feet, but no one bothered to look at her. The urge to inflict pain was too absorbing. One by one, the boys sent darts flying, slicing open the cat's furry neck within seconds. Blood gushed onto its chest like a fresh coat of paint.

"Bastards, scram!" She grabbed a thug by his shoulder. He turned, snot dripping down his chin. It was the neighbour's boy.

"Yang? What the hell are you doing? Do your parents know you're skinning a cat alive?"

Then she remembered. Yang's parents were locked up in the Cadre School too.

"Lemei!" he piped up brightly. "Come taste the cat soup tonight! Shanshan's cooking."

"Cat soup? Are you insane? What's for dinner tomorrow? Rat stew? Cockroach noodles? That cat's probably crawling with parasites. You'll all be shitting worms for days! Just...*scram*!"

The others edged closer, shoving her, the fun-spoiler, out of the circle. Shanshan, the older boy, leered at her chest with an idiotic grin. She hunched instinctively and wrapped her arms around herself. The world shimmered and swayed before her eyes. She was sinking, her straitjacketed body undulating in the waves of dirty hands.

"Lemei." A voice behind made her jump.

"Aunt Fu! What brings you here?"

"Come with me. Your Ma gave me the key..."

"Finally, an adult. Look at this... this mess."

The woman flinched at the sight of the bloodied cat, but only sighed. Putting her arm around Lemei, she pushed her out of the crowd. A cloud of snickering rose behind them, turning up the heat inside Lemei. Not even an adult could discipline those barbarians! She had to retreat, defeated, with a near-stranger. They climbed the four-storey walk-up in silence. Fu's hands were shaking when she turned the key. Once inside, she locked Lemei in a suffocating embrace. "Everything will be all right."

"Those evil boys..." Lemei wriggled out of her arms.

Fu twisted her lips into a squiggly line and broke into tears.

"Aunt Fu? Where's my Ma?"

"At the Cadre School ... I'm sorry. I promised I'd be strong for you."

"So they got *her* as well?"

"No." The woman inhaled sharply. For a moment, she blinked at her and looked lost. "No. It's your A-ba."

The apartment started spinning, the floor rippling like water. Lemei stumbled back and leaned on the wall, shutting her eyes. The hooting started anew downstairs; she needed to go and yell at the boys. Fu would be gone in a minute, along with her sinister agenda, the ominous message she carried. But her voice loomed—"passed away," "last night." *Gone. Dead. No more.* Lemei tried to dodge the words like bullets in the dark. They penetrated her skin, ripped apart her flesh and veins, ricocheted in the hollows of her chest.

"Your Ba's a hero, and you're a hero's daughter."

She panted. The thugs cheered louder and louder in her ears.

"I mean it, I really do." Fu wouldn't let up.

"*Stop* it!" Her dam broke. "That's the kind of bullshit people always say—"

"Not in your Ba's case, he's a true—"

"*Go. Away.* If he's such a hero, why was he treated like a criminal?"

"Someday history will clear his name."

"What's the bloody point then?"

"Your Ba's soul will stay with you. He'll watch you grow."

"Lies, lies, all lies!"

"No, no, a superhuman like him won't just disappear ... He's made of steel. What they did to him, anyone else would've—"

"So he pissed them off, and they killed him?"

"Child, you can't say things like that out there."

"But was that what happened?"

"Not exactly."

"So there's truth to it."

"Lemei..."

*Damn you! Can't say this, can't say that—are you even telling the truth? Did the Revolutionary Committee send you here to mess with me?*

Her eyes darted around the room and landed on a pile of homework from Ba. He'd never let bad handwriting slip; he'd come back and make her rewrite it. *You just wait!* She wanted to throw the stack of calligraphy paper in the woman's face. She wanted her face—her mask—to shatter into pieces. She wanted to smash down the door and slink into a different universe.

"You must be hungry. I'll make you something to eat." Fu's hand was on her cheek. Just like that, she was yanked back into the drab, cruel, ordinary universe. The boys outside had gone quiet. Yellow dots of light emanated from neighbouring buildings. She wondered how many families were having the same conversation tonight. If she walked the streets, would anyone pause at her distress? Or would they stare at her with vacant eyes, their faces cold and wooden, locked in their own tragedies?

The sweet and garlicky aroma of zhajiang mian wafted into her nose. It was Ma's favourite dish to make, and a popular one with Ba. He always wolfed down his first bowl and begged for a second in a theatrical pledge, eager to meet Ma's proud, smiling eyes. The aroma of normalcy, so incongruent that it made her queasy and weak. She slumped into a chair.

"At least tell me what happened? Ma said your husband was in the same cell as Ba."

Fu hunched over the stove, a dish sizzling in the silent void. Then she turned, holding a plate of golden-brown noodles like strands of charred intestines. Nausea struck Lemei.

"Your Ba got sick. Cirrhosis. His belly blew up like a melon. Hepatitis."

*Hence the home-brewed concoction. Ma said it was only dietary supplements. Lies, lies.*

"We all thought he'd get proper treatment soon, but..."

"They refused to treat him."

"They put him in solitary confinement instead."

Her mind raced to Ba's single cell, with oily paste smeared on the window so no daylight could possibly seep through.

"That's murder, wouldn't you say?"

The woman rubbed her face and sighed.

"Give me some names. The murderers..."

"Shhh! However we feel about it, we can't use those words, okay?"

"One. One name."

"I don't know any."

"What about your husband?"

"Lao Zhao wouldn't know either."

"Why are you all protecting the murderers?!" She flung her dish to the floor; the plate skidded the length of the dining table, splattering brown bean paste.

She turned away from the woman's crumbling face. Fu was kneeling now, scooping up julienned carrots and noodles. Lemei had to cover her nose and drag her spongy legs to the open window. Black clouds clustered in the night sky. She was determined to sit on Ba's lap, his body emanating a mellow, enveloping heat, and play a game of finding shapes in the clouds. At first, all she would see was cotton candy, but Ba's ink-stained, elongated fingers would guide her eyes—a long-winged phoenix here, a staff-wielding Monkey King there. *Stay with me, Ba, sit back and relax, don't you go anywhere.* She felt a cold, devouring hollowness. Fragments of her father rushed at her from the clouds—his handsome smile bracketed by laugh lines like long parentheses, his serious face that concealed his pride when he checked her homework, his dreamy eyes when he kneaded Ma's shoulders at the end of a long day.

Ba with a melon belly, surrounded by thugs with fiery hair.

The crucified kitten bobbed to the surface of her consciousness—its droopy eyelids, the rivulets of blood draining down the wall.

She'd find those thugs. She'd make them bleed and die a slow death.

WHEN MA ARRIVED HOME at two in the morning, Lemei met her quivering eyes and read her entire harrowing journey from the Underworld. She took the urn from Ma and squeezed it to her heart, sensing the ashes tumble toward her and climb up the interior wall that separated the living and the dead. Even at fifteen, she knew that funerals were prohibited for disgraced prisoners from cowsheds, especially an intransigent one like her Ba. Just as she'd imagined earlier that night, as she'd leaned on the windowsill and waited for Ma's return, young men in perfectly fitted Mao suits had long before carted the body away with maximum efficiency.

By the time Ma appeared at the Revolutionary Committee office, the shiny urn had been waiting for pickup for over an hour. Ma signed the release form with cool serenity, fully aware of the guard watching her every move, every facial expression, searching for signs of discontent. In the end, the guard extended his hand and murmured condolences, for a brief moment acting like a world-weary proprietor at a funeral parlour.

On the bus home, a clearing briskly materialized around Ma. Death is contagious; no one wants to take a risk. The bus groaned and rumbled through the dimly lit arteries of the diseased city, the unsettling silence in its belly contrasting with the shouts and fights outside. A baby-faced Red Guard stared at the urn in Ma's shaking hands, eyes pensive and on the brink of abrupt change, like the lull before a child's tantrum following a game gone awry. Ma shot the girl a piercing glare, swallowed her bitter cackle, and redirected her gaze outside the moving bus. Under the moonless sky, agitated faces flickered behind the miniature windows like warrior shadow-puppets.

Later, mother and daughter lay in bed in fetal position, the urn nestled in the hollow space between them, its exterior washed over and over by their salty tears. The world, with its mad proclamations and convictions, fell away. Their home-grown madness simmered and swelled and roared and fell silent, gearing up again, going on and on in the deep freeze of the spring night.

# 6

On the eighth morning after Ba's passing, someone pounded on their door, insistent and urgent. Groggily, they scrambled out of bed, bracing for the worst, and found a girl with bouncy pigtails and flushed cheeks, a smile of embarrassment clinging to her lips.

"My family runs the phone booth in the laneway."

"Of course, you're the youngest daughter," Ma rasped. Grief had sanded her vocal cords raw.

"A message for you, Auntie. The Revolutionary Committee at the Statistics Bureau offer their condolences. They respect the tradition of seven days of mourning but need you to report to work today. The revolution must go on. That's what the man said before hanging up." The girl exhaled the string of words without a pause for breath.

Ma nodded faintly as the girl bounded away. She shifted stealthily across the apartment, eyes ravaged, back curved in a new hunch. Rooting around in the kitchen cupboard, she found two packets of sesame seed biscuits and tossed them at Lemei. "Have some fuel. I'll be at work." She shuffled into the bathroom and closed the door behind her. Water gushed out of the groaning pipes. The staccato of her sorrow escaped the sound of the torrent, seeping under the door, tapping Lemei on the temples. Out of Ma's shadow, the urn shone sinisterly in the middle of the bed.

*I won't survive being left alone with this.*

Lemei wolfed down the biscuits and found a more solid footing on the floor. Still light-headed, she plodded down the stairs and onto the streets of Shanghai.

Her legs threatened to give way after five blocks. At the intersection of Huaihai and Taikang roads, she stumbled into a theatre. Scenes from Old China rushed at her. A screening of a Model Opera was underway. White-masked capitalists whipped labourers with sadistic delight. Girls and their widowed mothers shivered on snow-laden streets, until cadaverous labourers, in an act of true proletarian love, piled on them their tattered coats. Young wives faced off with Nationalist soldiers, while their husbands were hauled away to the front line. Darkness encased the earth until an auspicious sun rose on the horizon. Hundreds of lithe young women streamed onto the screen in long, flowing blue dresses and floral headpieces. The golden fans in their hands glistened like the feathered trains of exotic peacocks. In the next ten minutes, they arranged themselves into endless formations of sunflowers—blooming in slow motion, or in complete blossom. Sometimes they stood still for the audience to take in the full glory; other times they gyrated frantically to match the swelling anthem about a magnanimous saviour. "All will follow him like sunflowers turning toward the sun!" the chorus sang. By the time the music came to its jarring crescendo, all around her the misty-eyed audience chanted, "Long live the Chairman!" The most beautiful dancer received the final close-up, flashing her strenuous grin under a rising sun, which in turn swiftly eradicated all the shadows of the land.

She didn't wait for the credits to roll before dodging out of the theatre.

"Lemei!" The whiny Yangzhou accent she dreaded at school boomed behind her. She turned and saw Changshen perched on his bike and squinting at her. She'd been caught skipping school, along with the political studies, by the leader of the Workers' Propaganda Committee no less. Fear parched her throat and pumped strength into her legs.

"Wait, don't go! Just a quick word!" The Yangzhou devil blocked her with his bike. "Would you come to my office first thing tomorrow morning?"

"Yes, sir!" she replied reflexively, standing up straighter.

"Splendid!" He smiled, an eerie, bashful smile. He pedalled away, humming the theme song from the movie. She dashed toward home, adrenaline thrashing in her veins.

THE NEXT MORNING, AT the office of the Workers' Propaganda Committee, she couldn't believe Changshen's proposition. *Leader of Fengyang High's Red Guards.* The highest honour any student could ever dream of. Changshen had never been more congenial, his triangular eyes collapsing into slits, as if his own life depended on her agreeing.

"I'm flattered, sir."

"High time for a female student leader! You'll be a shining example of our commitment to gender equality!"

"That's great, really, but I'm not sure I qualify..."

"Why not? To be frank, we're tired of all that violence in the past. The Cultural Revolution has entered a new phase.

A young woman like you can bring a more nuanced leadership style to the Guards. You saw that star actress in the movie yesterday, single-handedly propping up the sky?"

She peered at him, looking for a hint of anger, but he was impossible to read.

"Don't you want to be like her?"

"I do, sir." She shifted in her chair, the cold metal cutting into her hip bone. "But surely others are more worthy? Someone who's been in the Guards for months..."

"That's for my committee to decide, isn't it?"

"I'm a total rookie."

His smile froze. He kneaded his eyelids. "Comrade Lemei, I have a feeling you're declining the committee's invitation. Got something against the Red Guards?"

"No, no! Just don't want to step on anyone's toes." Her voice shook, and she hated herself for it. "Others may not appreciate an outsider like me parachuting in from nowhere, that's all."

"All the guards are under the leadership of our committee. They'll welcome whoever we choose with open arms!"

She was running out of excuses. Declining the offer would make her an instant target, a counterrevolutionary. But joining the thugs, the enemy? She'd never be able to look at herself again.

"My father..." A last-ditch manoeuvre. "You may have heard. I'm not... *clean* enough."

"Ahh, I did hear." His gaze, strangely wounded, bored into her. "Between you and me, I thought the Revolutionary Committee at your Ba's work unit went overboard."

"But there must be demerits in my personal dossier because of him."

"He's paid the ultimate price, hasn't he? Atoned for his sin." Changshen jiggled his legs, his patience wearing thin.

"I should check with my mother. Still early days of mourning for her."

"The news will cheer her up greatly, don't you think?"

Yes, Ma would be relieved. *But I will have to live with this, not Ma, not anyone else.*

"Let me talk to her first. I don't want to surprise her at such a difficult time."

"Okay!" Changshen pounded a fist on the desk. "You have twenty-four hours, Comrade Lemei. We await your positive response by tomorrow morning."

"Thank you, sir."

She rose from her chair, sensing the heavy weight of his gaze. She half expected him to break into a guffaw and the real chosen Red Guard leader to storm in and throw her into the cowshed. Instead, Changshen closed in on her, his breath hot and sour on her face. "Do keep in mind, young comrade, your Ma's still here. You don't want to cause any more trouble for her, like you said, at an already difficult time." His face morphed into the evil capitalist from that Model Opera, a weasel of a man.

*A ticking bomb in a candy wrapper.* She gritted her teeth and nodded in obedience.

SHE ARRIVED HOME TO find Ma cradling the urn in a lotus position. A single tea candle emitted dim light from the altar, spreading a flimsy scarf of yellow over her shoulders. The statue of the Immortal Woman was still missing, replaced by a supersized portrait of the grinning Chairman. When she heard her mother speak, it was like eavesdropping on her stream of consciousness. Ma had received a call from Changshen, a mix of condolences and motivational slogans, of congratulations and threats.

"Take the offer."

"You want me to join the enemy?"

"Save yourself."

"And *you*."

"Yes, if that's not too much to ask."

*Yes, it is.*

"They'll treat you well."

*Like a pet canary in a golden cage*, she wanted to hiss at her. *Well-fed and groomed but never free again.* But she merely plopped down beside Ma, folding her legs into her chest and nodding shallowly when her mother said, "There is no other way, and you know it."

# 7

On the third day of Lemei's tenure, at recess, Wei slipped a copy of *The Kreutzer Sonata* into her pocket. "Banned in Russia," she whispered. "About a man's jealous rage. Can't say I understood it. Talk to me when you finish."

A loud bang made them jump. A rickety bike crashed through the school gate with a clown perched on top of it, a cigarette dangling from the corner of his crooked mouth.

"What the hell is *he* doing here?" Wei murmured.

"Wrong school!" a boy shouted from the far side of the yard, followed by a nervous titter.

"That's Lang, Red Guard leader at Weiyu High," Wei whispered.

"I'm aware," Lemei whispered back, her heart thumping.

Lang threw the bike aside and swaggered toward Lemei, flaunting his tanned skin, muscled shoulders, and a leaf-like scar under his right eye. He dragged his feet with a cockiness that made him indistinguishable from a member of the youth gang that had capitalized on the chaos and prowled the streets day and night.

"Tsk tsk, look at our pretty doll." He spat his cigarette butt in her face.

"We're both student leaders, extend some basic courtesy." She kept her voice calm.

"Ha, *student leaders*. Are all the men at Fengyang High sissies? Letting a little girl take charge? How pathetic!"

Ball players halted mid-step and hopscotching girls froze in their squares. Even the buzzing flies seemed to retreat to the far walls.

"Go back to your juvenile detention," she hissed and turned away.

He yanked at her shoulder. "What did you say?"

Hair rose on her back: a lioness puffing up her mane at the battle cry.

"You don't want to fight me." She lowered her voice. "It hasn't been a good week."

"Oh, yeah? Tough-mouthed too. I like it!"

A blow landed on her jaw, scorching her bones. Wei's squeal somersaulted in her ears. Heat pushed and pounded her chest, begging for release. Lang looked the part, like one of those thugs she had pictured at Ba's cowshed, a cold-blooded animal who derived pleasure from inflicting pain. She wiped off the blood trickling from her mouth. *Stay alert, you know the drill.* Years of fighting with her brother had been a training camp for this moment. Another mammoth but stupid boy, oblivious to his blind spots. She dodged his frontal attacks with nimble steps, her mind seeing his moves in a familiar sequence before they materialized. *You fight just like Feng. You boys don't use much imagination, do you?* When he made the mistake of reaching for her collar, she seized his hand and rotated it toward his arm, locking his wrist. He shrieked like a dog in heat. *Don't cry, I'll put you out of your misery.* She pulled his elbow forward and away from his body, ducked under his arm, and pinned him onto a patch of dirt with one clean leg-trip.

A collective gasp rose around her. "The girl can fight!" Her schoolmates chanted her name as they kneeled to restrain the intruder.

"Look who's a sissy now!" Wei hollered at Lang, who lay spread-eagled under the weight of a human pagoda.

"Get off our turf, you clown!"

"Or our lady boss will whip your ass!"

Lemei didn't let go of Lang until Changshen stormed out of the building and lifted her off the ground. "My office!" he barked at her.

But she couldn't stop smiling, as Lang hobbled out of the school gate with his fat invisible tail between his shrivelling legs.

"HOW COULD YOU BE so reckless?" Changshen slammed his office door behind them.

"I'm sorry. I'll write a self-criticism. But I had to teach him a lesson."

"You *had* to?"

"Those young Guards from Weiyu High have been at our gate every morning. I'm sick of their gawking and finger-pointing, like I'm some kind of exotic animal," she blurted, bracing for his wrath.

He edged closer with a first-aid tray and gestured for her to sit down. "You're a curiosity to them, yes." He dropped his voice, like an older brother softly chastising his treasured sister. "But in a few days they'll get bored and find something else to fuss about."

She was tongue-tied, puzzled by this man and his seesaw-ing moods. He dabbed blood off her cheek with a cotton ball, his hands shaking and his triangular eyes downcast. A pulsing, sour heat radiated from him, from the deep centre of him where a watery heart beat and beat. She felt cold and feverish at the same time, a cramp in her stomach. He placed a bandage next to her lips, his fingers grazing the contour of her chin. When he lifted his eyes, she was scalded by the longing in them. She shot from her seat, knocking the metal tray to the floor, and started for the door.

"Promise me you won't fight again," he pleaded behind her. "Leave the fighting to the men."

THREE DAYS LATER LANG returned, bringing an entour-age—boys with scarlet armbands and timorous eyes. Changshen and his committee men poured out of their smoke-filled office and planted themselves at the gate.

"Looking for the girl leader," one boy piped up.

Lang opened his mouth too. "An eye for an—"

Changshen lunged forward and swung an iron rod at the back of Lang's knees, over and over, like bludgeoning a stray dog. Bones yielded under his savage force, a hideous chorus of cracking and snapping. Lang's friends dispersed at the sight of the crazed workers' leader. Two, unlucky, were recap-tured and made to watch the whole ordeal. The young thug, eyes and mouth curved into three shocking Os, collapsed to the ground, his wails ricocheting between the four walls of the schoolyard. When Changshen was done, he threw the rod at the fence, waved airily at his right-hand man, and stomped away, his face reddish-purple, nostrils flaring like a ruffled camel's. His underling dropped a stretcher by the pair of boys. "The hospital's a couple of blocks away. Get him out of here and never return. Or else!"

"Curiouser and curiouser," Wei whispered to Lemei as they witnessed the gruesome scene from their classroom window. "I always thought student Guards were mere pawns in a proxy war, fighting for their workers' committees. After all, students' lives are much cheaper. Guys like Changshen wouldn't want to get their hands dirty. Guess I got it all wrong."

Lemei flinched at the sight of Lang's dangling trousers as his friends hauled him onto the stretcher, his flesh and bones mushy inside the bloodstained fabric. The workers' leader appeared before her mind's eye with a sad grin and wounded gaze, churning her stomach. She felt hopelessly out of her depth; even her books couldn't help her now, not in the face of a man holding a bundle of desire in one hand and a lightning bolt of violence in the other. And how rotten was she to have attracted such a man?

That evening, she dashed home and stripped off her clothes, plunging into a wooden basin of icy water. Willing the cloak of rottenness to fall away, she scrubbed herself ruthlessly until patches of skin burst. Afterward, she wiped off beads of blood and prayed, huddling by the Immortal Woman under Ma's bed:

*The seed of desire, let it perish, let it perish in the cold soil of my neglect.*

THE RUBBERNECKERS FROM OTHER schools vanished after that morning. With the external threats vanquished, the Workers' Propaganda Committee and the young Guards returned to battling the internal enemies—the bourgeois thoughts lurking in the minds of the students, and the cow demons lurking in the shed. To Lemei's surprise, she was not bad at her job. Years of reading illicit literature had filled her head with beautiful turns of phrase, hollow but emotive, critically useful at rallies. The struggle sessions against teachers were still hard to bear, but she adapted as well, imagining herself as a character in a stage play, her words and posture merely an actor's craft.

Two weeks into her job, she convinced Changshen to let her lead the procession back to the cowshed after the struggle sessions. Only then, when she was alone with the teachers, did she tear away her mask. She sat with her prisoners, cross-legged on the reed mats, and passed around mint-scented healing salves. She whispered her apologies and watched them shake their heads like rattle drums.

"We've never been treated better." They told her about the beatings they had endured at the hands of the previous Guards.

"Please, spare me the horrors," she implored them one day. "Tell me something else—what will you do when you get out of here, when the revolution is over?"

"Are we allowed to dream?"

"I insist."

"I'll give my mother a proper burial," the music teacher said, nodding pensively.

"Have a fine day with my son," murmured the art teacher. "Him doodling on his notepad, me sipping tea and watching him. Quiet street outside our window, everyone minding their own damn business."

"I want to hug my brother and sister," whispered the history teacher. "Their confessions landed me in here, but how I miss them."

"What about you?" Ms. May asked her.

Lemei held her favourite teacher's hands, once silky smooth, now covered with torn calluses. *Leave* was the only word stuck on a loop in her head.

"Be a writer," Ms. May pleaded, her eyes liquid, earnest. "Write what you see, what you *feel*, in and out of this godforsaken cowshed. Don't let the madness go on in vain."

# 8

Lemei lost contact with Ms. May after her release from the cowshed in 1971. Rumour had it that she'd escaped to the rugged, windswept terrain of Qinghai to become a nun. Lemei thought it befitting her character, like a lotus flower growing out of the mud but unsullied. Remembering her teacher's dream for her, she carried a notebook in her pocket and wrote whenever she could in her last year at Fengyang High. Of course, the act of keeping a notebook was a risky business. All it took was a single power-hungry Red Guard—any of her underlings—to discover her secret. They'd relish reading her private ponderings before hauling her into the maze-like underbelly of a detention system, letting her marinate in her own tears and filth, to meet the same fate as her father.

But she kept at it. The blank pages served as her punching bag, her pillow to scream into, her refuge from insanity and self-pity. After briefings with Changshen, words would gush out of her like an evening tide, banishing the shame caked all over her. He made his intentions clearer with each passing day, whispering directives from his higher-ups into her ear like sweet nothings, his leg brushing hers. She knew he was trying hard to impress her, straining, in vain, to speak Standard Mandarin instead of his Yangzhou dialect that the locals loved to ridicule. He insisted on shaking hands at the end, squeezing the fleshy inside of her palm. She hated his odour, the shape of his eyes, and the coveted ration ticket he always left in her hand. But the sorrow in his gaze pained her too; she felt like a stony-hearted pharmacist refusing to dole out the life-saving elixir.

Only her written words cocooned and massaged her conflicted heart. The heroine of her novel-in-progress tried on different tones and gestures and masks of practised detachment. Of course, there was no chance of ever publishing the book, even if she managed to finish it one day, but she dreamed on. She would seal the five-hundred-page manuscript in a redwood case, a time capsule, and bury it near a site of cultural significance, perhaps Ming Emperor's tomb or the Forbidden City. Dynasties rise and fall. Children from the future, passing their ancestors' graves, would dig holes for worms and locate the unexpected. They'd read her book without the police hot on their tails. They'd cry for more, burrow into the earth searching for sequels, and go home broken-hearted but inspired to write their own.

Daydreaming sustained her through the last year of high school. But in reality, her writing remained mere fragments of rants and sentimentalism, a reflection of the bouts of anger and grief assailing her. So in the late spring of 1972, when she graduated from Fengyang High (and, to her great relief, was automatically discharged from the Red Guards), she did the same as every young person and took a number in life's waiting room, praying to be called by a benevolent receptionist.

By July, boys in her grade had been assigned to steel plants or cement factories, labouring by the blast furnaces or rotary kilns. Several went to petrochemical factories, churning out plastics, pesticides, detergents, and would later perish in their early forties from a dizzying array of cancers. The lucky ones, those with connections to the Inner Party, snatched assignments in the "light industries"—cameras, radios, watches, fountain pens, glassware. Girls were absorbed into the vast textile sector, except for a handful who had won life's lottery, escaping the monotonous assembly lines for the greener pastures of the "cultural sector."

It was the summer of ceaseless murmurings—

*Did you hear? Bo got into the No. 2 candy factory!*

*That brat?*

*His Ma died just in time for him to take over.*

*Must've died young?*

*Diabetes. She enjoyed those discards too much. The only fringe benefit at the candy factory sent her to her grave!*

*Heard about Xiaoyu? She was going to waste her life away like the rest of us, but the little missy had the good sense to sleep her way to the top!*

*So it paid off? Letting that wall-eyed uncle from the committee put his paws on her…*

*They're sending her to the Theatre Academy. The slut's going to be our next People's Star!*

Lemei dodged the gossips, but they followed her stubbornly: at the lines for breakfast buns, the morning bus, the soy sauce shop, the grain ration station. Chatter about young people's assignments hovered above her head like a cloud of midges fanning their gossamer wings. She was surprised to hear the collective tone shift, the *impure* thoughts cropping up stealthily among true believers, the buzz from the growing Imposters' Club, but she wondered more about her assignment letter. What was the holdup? Even Wei had received hers two weeks before and now reported to work as a cleaner at the steel plant. On the weekends, Wei would show up with a half-bottle of baijiu she always managed to lay her hands on. The first time they tasted that devil's juice, they threw up all over the kitchen floor and burst into hysterics. They'd since learned to embrace the initial shock and the reliable after-effect, the glorious tranquilizer for their starved minds.

One Saturday night, Wei was sitting in Ma's favourite bamboo chair, her bleached khaki pants chafing the edge of her seat. "Still no news, eh?"

"Nothing. Zilch. Starting to think they've completely forgotten about me."

"Impossible. You're the Golden Girl of the Revolution! You know your problem? Too many talents. They don't know where to place you in our Great Socialist Utopia to max your contribution!"

"I wish they'd just let us ... *apply* for something."

"Tsk tsk, Comrade Lemei, that's the bourgeoise in you talking. We aren't like those capitalist countries. We young people are *not* a commodity—we're a *national resource*!"

"Someone's been paying attention at political studies. You think they'll let you join the Party as long as you talk like them?"

"No, no, I don't have such grand delusions. Just look at the purgatory they put me in. Join the Party? Not in a million years."

"Still so bad?"

"It's been great. It provides me with a deep sense of

accomplishment—whenever I wipe up the piss and shit and return the toilets to factory mode."

Lemei watched Wei chuckle and toss down a shot. She didn't want to show her proud friend any pity. She filled their glasses instead, shoved Wei's into her hand, and clinked them. Cicadas chorused begrudgingly in their late summer ensemble. The harsh liquor slithered through their veins, melting away the weight they each carried inside. But the moment of peace was fleeting. Soon the clock would strike ten and, like a ritual, Ma would march into the living room and slam a chamber pot by Wei's feet. "Time to sleep," she'd say in a brittle voice.

Ma's aggression used to embarrass Lemei, so much that she once flung the chamber pot in her direction, narrowly missing her. She'd pick fights with Ma immediately after her friend was chased away. "Who sent her?" Ma would exert herself in a high pitch. "What information was she fishing for? They already took our men. Now they're after you and me too?!"

Only then would Lemei back down, recognizing her mother's wounded tremor, the sick person behind the valiant mask she wore all day. She'd remember the willowy beauty, the child whisperer. Sympathy would roll in on a wave and extinguish the flame.

AT THE START OF August, a letter from the principal's office summoned her back to Fengyang High. She ascended the spiral staircase of the administrative building, the four-storey French-style villa sighing in her presence. *Shhh, you survived.* She glided her fingers over the ugly carvings the Red Guards had left on the once-ornate wooden banister, the cherubic angels with their eyes gouged out and noses chiseled away. She reached the top landing and pushed on the office door. As it swung open, she shuddered. The room swelled with heat, a rusty ceiling fan twirling like a ballerina gone mad. With clenched teeth, she nodded at Changshen, who was squatting in the principal's mahogany chair, a clown on the throne of a learned man. His usual green khaki shirt drenched in sweat, he fanned himself with a propaganda pamphlet.

"Been a while," he said, his voice razor-scraped.

"So it's *you* who summoned me here." Seeing him after a month produced that familiar sensation in her—a mix of nausea, pity, and a suppressed urge to strike.

"Sounds like an accusation. I thought you wouldn't come if ..." He trailed off, flicking a beetle from his knee. "I under-stand you still don't have your assignment letter?"

She stood motionless, waiting for him to unfurl his proposition.

"What would *you* like to do with your life, Lemei?"

"Serve the people, however the Party sees fit."

"I thought you wanted to write." A muscle twitched around his lips. Was he suppressing a smirk? Had he seen her scribble in her notebook? She clutched at the hem of her shirt, her palms turning clammy.

"I can help you with that, you know." He took off his sweat-soaked khaki, revealing a round gut barely concealed by an undershirt. He ambled toward her, his triangular eyes rocks of burning coal. She turned, but he pounced at the door and swung it closed with a bang.

"You didn't even say a proper goodbye. For those thugs I fought off for you, for all those ration tickets, for the days we worked shoulder to shoulder, you didn't even say a proper goodbye."

"I'm sorry. Good—"

"Except I don't want a goodbye." He clasped her hands and leaned in, the stench from his nostrils searing her face. "You want to write for a living, am I right?"

"If that's the best way to serve the country."

"Can't you see I'm your friend? That I only want to help you?"

"Thank you, sir," she said, trembling.

He bared his teeth, a wild dog ready to quench its thirst with blood. Then his lips moved in and glued onto hers, kneading, chewing. A briny, rotting vortex sucked her in, first her mouth and nose, then her eyes and her entire sheath of skin, lubricated with sweat and saliva. She forgot how to breathe, her mind an empty theatre dimming into black, row by row. He was sinking with her, purring. She didn't register his loosening grip until her index finger popped free, a tiny motion breaking the curse. She wriggled both hands out of his and dealt a heavy blow to the cavity of his chest. As he fell away, he never opened his eyes, as if clinging onto the grand vista behind his lids. She flung the door open and staggered out.

# 9

## 1975

1,200, 3,300, 7,800, 15,000, 20,000, 50,000, 80,000, 120,000, 200,000.

The climbing numbers hit her like a train of bullets. She stole a few deep, painful breaths and glanced at her colleagues. *Mimic your pack, don't stray.* She straightened her spine, discreetly wiped away the water rising to the corners of her eyes, and applied herself squarely to her notebook again.

Investigation Day 2. Tropical cyclone, 62 dams gone, 7 metre flood, Henan, Yellow River Valley. ~~1,200, 3,300, 7,800, 15,000, 20,000, 50,000, 80,000, 120,000,~~ 200,000 dead.

Facts, no matter how damning, could be contained, sealed, and buried. This cloistered conference room would be their final resting place. A veteran reporter was chain-smoking and coughing on the other end of the phone line, cutting in and out, blaming the connection. She wondered if he was crying. Her pen kept on moving, recording the sound bites, welcoming them to their silent grave. *Liberation Daily! Iron rice bowl! Sure worth the wait!* Her mother's shrill excitement for a job with security replayed in her ears, always at the most opportune time, her overdue assignment letter— Changshen's gift—fluttering in Ma's hand like a captured dove. *What were we celebrating, Ma? I'm the voiceless writer covering up the truth. Are you happy now?*

After work, she took the slow bus home, eavesdropping on fellow passengers, a clandestine survey of the damage she had done. Five months ago, it was her shameless praise of a once-denounced cadre, suddenly tapped by the Chairman to be the new VP. Point by point, she had reversed every condemnation her paper had piled on the man in a previous editorial. A bald-headed worker on the bus had pulled out both articles and noisily compared the two. "Incredible! Just say every sentence again, but backward, I can do this job!"

Two months ago, it was her sneaky attack on the long-suffering premier, via a battle cry against the Duke of Zhou, the premier's namesake from the eleventh century *BC*. She had holed up at the ancient archives of Shanghai Library, collecting incriminating evidence.

"The duke's been dead for three thousand years. Can't we leave a skeleton out of this?" she had complained to Lao Chen, her senior editor.

"Madame Mao ordered it."

"She ordered an insinuation?"

"Insinuation is our job."

When the piece came out, people on the bus took to calling her—the faceless reporter—the Gravedigger, and she could only duck her head and nod along. She almost missed her early days on the job, when she was still on probation, flitting from desk to desk, hovering over the real reporters and serving up clay pots of Yellow Mountain Peak, Iron Goddess of Mercy, Lushan Cloud. "Are you hydrated enough? Caffeinated enough?" Mindless work, but at least her conscience had been clean.

Near the entrance of her neighbourhood, she bought a stack of joss paper from an old lady with knobbly hands. At home, she took a bite of a vegetable bun on the kitchen counter and spat it out immediately. Appetite, gone. Sense of taste, gone. Her comeuppance. She locked herself in her room and folded the joss paper into golden lotuses. At midnight, she sent them all into a rippling river of fire in a metal basin. For the silent dead. And for herself, cutting ties with another shitty day.

Still, she couldn't sleep. Gurgling sounds of drowning sloshed against her eardrums, suckling babies swept away from their mothers' arms until they were bobbing white dots on the distant horizon.

ON FRIDAY MORNING, day four of the investigation, a hoarse voice broke through the scratchy phone line in the conference room. Behind it, a cascade of barking orders.

"I knew this would happen someday," a man breathed laboriously. "Remember all that steel production during the Great Leap Forward? Deforestation, land degradation followed. I couldn't stop them. I've failed." His voice collapsed into sobbing spasms.

"You were the project's chief engineer back in the fifties. Did you inform the local officials?" Lao Chen asked.

"Why do you think I ended up in this godforsaken labour camp? I told them it was suicidal to build dams in that area, let alone so many. They promptly packed me away to the hinterlands. 'Stinky Rightist,' that's my label."

*Stinky Rightist.* That'd been her father's label too. Another bullheaded intellectual believing his facts were above the shifting winds.

"You've got to tell the world what happened," the prisoner pleaded. "Hold those imbeciles accountable—"

"Does that mean we can quote you in our article?" Lemei cut in.

A gasp from the colleague next to her.

"Yes, and please tell everyone I'm sorry."

"Thank you for speaking to us, Comrade Nin. Goodbye." Lao Chen slammed the handset back into the phone's cradle and fixed his eyes on Lemei. "Please leave the room, comrade."

"Editor, I didn't mean to—"

"You need a refresher."

That afternoon she was placed on a week-long leave for political studies. Eight hours a day, she stared at a droopy-eyed Teacher Shen, who pontificated on the role of a "cultural worker" during the Great Cultural Revolution, white foam bubbling at the corners of his mouth. At "recess," she drafted and revised her self-criticism, as a dusty fan whirred in the stifling heat. She had to apologize for straying from her pack, but it'd take a dozen failed attempts for her to get it right. The key to a successful self-criticism, the kind that'd lift Teacher Shen's droopy eyelids, was to erase herself thoroughly from the pages, to replace every thought of her own with the right quotes from the Little Red Book. That way, not only would she prove herself a devout student of the Chairman, she'd also have written a piece unassailable by mortals.

Still, she held out a sliver of hope, stubborn and impure as she was. Night after night, she combed her newspaper for any hints about the collapsed dams. But no ink was spilled; the lives of her countrymen were cheaper than the beached whales in America and the panda royals in captivity. Someone with upright thinking and capable hands had taken over her notes—watermarked *Top Secret*, taped and sealed in manila envelopes, and buried under a bureaucratic pyramid. She'd have to wait for a quarter of a century, long after the bodies had crumbled to dust, long after the human cells had dispersed across the universe and recycled into roses and cacti, birds and reptiles. Only then would she find a terse article in her paper's *Science* section describing the failed dams for the first time. It was a once-in-two-thousand-years natural disaster, the article would insist, an act of God sprung upon puny mortals, and not a darn thing could've been done to prevent it.

# 10

## 1976

For over a year, she had been stalking a gnome at Xiangyang Park.

One night, after a senseless fight with Ma, Lemei had bolted out of their apartment and tramped aimlessly around the neighbourhood. On Huaihai Road, the dome of the Orthodox cathedral loomed ahead under the moonlight, desolate and forlorn. She felt a Pavlovian urge in her groin. When the large public toilet by Xiangyang Park was built in 1950, directly opposite the cathedral, most expats were of the opinion that it was the Communists' way to humiliate them. *Shanghai is no longer your playground!* the urinals solemnly declared. When Lemei was a child, Ma used to take her to the park on the weekends, and every time she'd send her to use the toilet.

She raced to the unlit entrance of the public toilet and smashed into the solid chest of a brawny man. She apologized and saw him exchange annoyed looks with his companion, a small man no more than four feet tall. The two muttered obscenities and strode away. As she relieved herself, she heard the pair's voices on the other side of the wall, one octave apart and spiced with intrigue. She finished her business quickly and pressed an ear to the concrete.

"Hong Kong first, it's a must."

"How long's the wait?" asked a reed-thin voice.

"Depends. A year at most, likely four to six months."

"That long?!"

"Takes time to get you a spot to Guatemala. After that, you can practically walk to Mexico. We'll have a Texas-bound van waiting."

She tiptoed out of the toilet and hid around the corner. The pair was stretched out on a bench obscured by a thick camellia bush, far from the lone streetlight. To her surprise, the thin voice trickled from the big-chested fellow. And the small man, with his deep throaty drone, was the mastermind: "You get a choice of three cities. In all three, I've got relatives running restaurants. You can go straight to work."

"Any way it can be cheaper?"

"I'm not selling cucumbers, brother. I'm walking if you plan on haggling."

"It's just ... twenty thousand is steep."

"Cheapest you can find in the whole Middle Kingdom. My bro in Fujian charges thirty thousand apiece."

*Holy!* She jumped. It'd take thirty years on her current salary to gather that kind of money.

"Talk to your Ma again. Your granddad didn't transfer all that money abroad for nothing. I bet he's rolling in his grave, screaming, 'Give the boy a goddamn chance!'"

"Ma says ten thousand tops. She needs the money too."

"Keep working on her. Worst case, you get me fifteen now, then I'll have to siphon ten out of your restaurant wage once you're on dry land."

She tried to piece things together: landlord's progeny, Old Money, overseas assets, probably transferred just before 1949. The whole country was sealed up to high heaven; only the Old Money could buy themselves a crack and slip out of purgatory unnoticed. The rest of them must keep on toiling! She touched the ration tickets in her pocket, flames of jealousy licking her heart. Briefly, she moved in the direction of the police station, a sense of injustice egging her on, until clarity skidded down her spine like quicksilver. *A crack is a crack!* She pivoted and headed home instead, in a hopeful, giddy haze.

After that night, she came to the park often, searching for the mysterious gnome, who reminded her of the Earth Spirit from old legends, whose magic power could bail any hero out of their conundrum. At work, as typewriters clacked and teleprinters dinged, she floated away from tall stacks of propaganda and glided toward the mountain range of Guatemala, the vast Mexican desert, the sun-bleached Texan ranches, the Golden Gate Bridge, soaring, soaring.

But Ma's face would appear like a hot air balloon on the horizon. Lemei would flutter and thrash before crashing back to earth. The giant balloon loomed over the wreckage, casting a crater of a shadow: *You ever think about me, this frail bag of bones? You want to drag me into your suicide mission? What if your Ba's spirit comes back? What if Feng comes back?*

*All I ever think about is you!* she imagined hissing at Ma. *Can't you see I'm drowning here?*

. . .

WHEN THE ANNOUNCEMENT OF the Chairman's death rolled in on the radio waves on a grey, drizzling day, she went out into the street and let the surge of mourners engulf her. She watched those around her put on fierce, *competitive* shows of public mourning. They swayed and huddled, kowtowed and prostrated, howled and yowled. Some begged the Chairman's spirit to stay, to "shower them with another day of sunlight and raindrops." Others raised their fists and vowed to stay loyal to his Thoughts and Theories, to defend him until their own demise. At the gate of the music conservatory, a young girl rolled her eyes back and convulsed in a prolonged fit, while her mother pranced around her like a stilted exorcist.

But their hearts were not in it, she was convinced, as the force of the crowd propelled her down the streets, the smell of tears and nervous sweat filling her nose. *It's only a herd mentality at play.* Later that day, she experienced it first-hand at her newspaper's memorial. In the beginning, no tears were forthcoming. *The old bastard finally croaked* was all she could think. But once the anguished notes of the dirge blared out of the boombox, and others in the rally—her colleagues—wailed with such depth and devastation, saline streams leaked out of her eyes, clearing away any remaining resistance. Once she was at it, she couldn't stop either, a new understanding solidifying in her skull: the sky had fallen! Gone was the dynasty's Founding Emperor, who had held the Middle Kingdom in his palm. Now warlords would turn their whimpering into battle cries! Bloodbaths must follow a strongman's demise—wasn't that her people's unbroken curse?

The ensuing months went by in a quick succession of surreal dreams. The Gang of Four, aka Warlord (Pack) #1, put the nail in their own coffin by plotting the downfall of the Chairman's handpicked heir, a broad-faced Chairman lookalike whose frigid smile failed to conceal his urgent lack of intelligence. When the four evil spirits were hauled away to rot in solitary confinement, crowds poured into the streets again and exploded into song and dance. This time, *happy* tears would not stop flowing. Next, the righteous heir, aka Warlord #2, ordered himself a haircut identical to his heaven-bound Political Father and vowed to mimic the late Chairman in every possible way. In article after article, Lemei's paper peddled the new Paramount Leader to an increasingly suspicious public. But the doppelganger's trump card of being the chosen heir was only a liability in the hearts of the masses—the pretend true believers. Whenever he struck a pose imitating the Chairman over-looking Tiananmen Square, his people vomited in their mouths and cracked private jokes about the vacuous Party hack. The righteous heir had the good sense to concede one wintry morning, like a bowing chess rookie, even airlifting Little Deng, aka Warlord #3, out of the purgatory he'd long dwelled in. The country's most prominent Rightist strode into the limelight, his miniature physique, intense gaze, and broad forehead reminding Lemei of the mastermind at the park.

She trained her eyes on the grainy photo of the rising star on the front page of her paper. *Another Earth Spirit? Will he be our true saviour?*

. . .

THE FOLLOWING SATURDAY, Wei arrived at their baijiu session wearing a gloomy face. "Everything all right?" Lemei asked. When Wei didn't answer, she soldiered on, nudging away her unease. "Did you read the editorial in the *Daily* yesterday?"

"I stopped reading that paper of yours a long time ago. No offence."

"No offence taken. But *this* you've got to see." She plopped Friday's paper before her friend. "A miracle. *Liberation Daily*, the Central Committee's mouthpiece, is praising the Democracy Wall in Xidan!"

"Didn't think I'd live to see this day."

"Right? Listen to this: 'People have legitimate reasons to worry about corruption, unemployment, officials' special privileges'—mind you, those things, up to a few weeks ago, didn't even exist in our socialist paradise."

"Guess Little Deng is winning. So your paper's ditched the lame-duck Chairman's heir?"

"You know how the game's played! It's all about Little Deng now. But he seems like the real deal; he wants *reform*. Look here, front page: 'One hundred million Chinese still have little food to eat.' That's the kind of statistic they used to cover up, for thirty, fifty years! Maybe, just maybe, I can be a real journalist with him at the helm, not just a parrot for the Politburo."

"I'm happy for you. It's about time," Wei said with reddening eyes, and poured Lemei a shot.

Lemei tossed it down, feeling her insides dissolving. Trilling vocals seeped from behind Ma's closed door and hovered above their heads.

"Sounds…*feudal*." Wei chuckled.

"Amazing how quickly the radio station ditched the Model Operas and revived our ancestors' repertoire."

"You know this tune?"

"With the pipa, the wailing, it must be 'Princess Zhaojun Going Out of the Fortress' again."

"I'm impressed."

"Heard this tune a dozen times in the last two days. Ma's been obsessed. She grew up on this stuff. When she was a little girl in the thirties, her whole village used to gather under the stars, watch the wandering opera troupe paint their faces and sing their hearts out. I think even Ma, our revolutionary widow, has been starved for some *real* opera. And I'm just grateful she leaves us alone."

"Yeah, I sure don't miss the chamber pot."

They giggled and ate the tea leaf eggs Ma had prepared in the morning, the salty browned egg whites melting on their tongues. But Wei's sorrowful gaze made a swift return.

"How was your week?" Lemei asked cautiously.

Wei shook her head. A shy glance, a sharp inhale.

"What is it?"

She paused again, kneading the hem of her shirt. "I found two girls kissing in a bathroom stall last week."

"*No!* You didn't!"

Wei's face crumpled. "Yeah. Hard to believe," she murmured and lowered her head.

"Girls at your steel plant are bold!" Lemei blabbered on, unnerved by her friend's shifting mood. "They can go to prison for it. Or the loony bin. Did they seem crazy? Did you report them?"

"I'm not the Thought Police." Wei's voice had dwindled to a whisper.

"How terrible you have to endure such indecency." Lemei pressed a hand to Wei's shoulder, feeling her friend's body tense up under her touch. "You'll be out of that hellhole soon. The universities are reopening. Little Deng isn't kidding around. He wants gaokao back—meritocracy! Our ancestors' system! Nothing to do with the political class you come from. With your smarts, you'll be among our first batch of homegrown PhDs—teach at a university! Wouldn't that be grand?" She raised her glass for a toast. "To our very own *professor*!"

Wei froze, unmoved by Lemei's cheery attempt. Dark shadows pooled under her eyes.

"Hey, what *is* it?"

"I've been meaning to tell you ..."

"What?"

Wei cleared her throat, making up her mind. "I'm ... *leaving*."

"Leaving? You found a better job somewhere?"

"I'm going to America."

Lemei's hands wobbled, spilling liquor all over her lap. "Damn prankster, how much did you drink?"

"I only found out this week myself. Little Deng opened the Great Wall, and my application suddenly went through ..."

"What application?"

"My uncle. Runaway seaman in the fifties. Docked at San Francisco Bay with his cargo ship and decided to sneak away to the underbelly of Chinatown. Unlike my naive parents, he never bothered to look back. Married some American prostitute, got his citizenship and her syphilis. He considered it a fair trade."

"So he's like, what ... sponsoring you?"

Wei nodded. "Didn't think it'd ever go through. A pipe dream. Then, boom, my visa's here. Guess Little Deng doesn't want people like me to stick around any longer."

Pressure built steadily behind her eyelids. Her bosom buddy, her lifeline, soon to be gone.

"I heard America's scary," she muttered, like an insolent child. "White people chew up the blacks and the yellows without spitting out the bones."

"Lemei."

"Have you even met this uncle? Sounds like a seedy character to me. There's this bootlegged book about the San Francisco Triads you should read..."

"I'm so sorry."

*So you're abandoning me. Where's Ma's chamber pot when we need it?*

"I promise I'll come back and visit..." Wei was weeping now.

*Weakling, traitor.* Lemei couldn't bear the sight of her. "Go, go, I can't..."

She watched Wei scramble to her feet and head for the door, her frail physique dissolving into the dark stairwell. She slumped to the floor. Princess Zhaojun was singing a mournful song from Ma's radio, her voice snaking down Lemei's throat and stirring up a thick dust of sorrow:

> *It's a setting sun outside the Great Wall*
> *I'm scared to hear the falcon scream*
> *Still a long way to go ... Send my message to the*
>   *Han Palace*
> *Who will come to pick up my bones?*

Was the song for her or her friend?

That evening, Ma never re-emerged from the land of emperors and concubines, of red-faced warriors and white-faced clowns. High-pitched spike fiddles and beats from percussion blocks suffused the air well into the night. Stranded alone in the land of the Ordinary, Lemei tossed and turned in bed, haunted by her selfishness. Was Wei supposed to wither away by the stinky toilets? Hadn't her doctor parents' wasted lives taught her enough? She only fell into a shallow sleep when the sun was on the horizon, streaking muted pink across the sky. In her dream, Little Deng and the gnome from the park were working out a deal about her future. She towered over them like a dim-witted giantess, unable to fathom the decision on her fate.

# 11

## *Changshen*

### 1981

Even after five years, dead fish still made him squirm. Hundreds of them lined up with their bulging, despairing eyes, mouths wide open, as if they were incredulous at their untimely deaths and horrified by their afterlives. For ten hours a day every day, he suppressed nausea and descaled those strange creatures of the sea, scalping open their fleshy white bellies, reaching into the slimy cavities, and pulling out the pink guts and translucent balloons. A clean, decapitated shell was his final product, passed onto the next workstation. At the end of each day, he'd wash the floor on all fours, scrubbing away blood and innards, so that he'd have a spotless station to return to the next morning. He knew it was futile; the floor would be covered with filth as soon as the new day began. But besides cleaning, he couldn't think of another way to preserve his last shred of dignity.

He knew he was one of the lucky ones. As a "running dog" of the Gang of Four, he could have been thrown in jail or shot point-blank when the Cultural Revolution ended. Instead, he got his precious anonymity on the assembly line of a fish jerky factory. Each day, he left work at seven, dragging his empty, sore body the three kilometres back to his basement bachelor pad. He'd pass a newspaper stand and buy a copy of the *Liberation Daily*. At home, he'd fix himself a plain white bun and a small plate of fermented tofu, and search the paper for Lemei's article. He'd savour every word, sometimes looking up unknown phrases in a beat-up dictionary. He'd cut out her article and plaster it on his wall with the rest of them. He used to line them all up around his bed, pretending they were personal messages from her, imagining her whispering the words into his ears as he drifted to sleep. Now that there was no more space by his bed, articles proliferated beside his dining table, above his cupboard, around his stove. He was proud of her. He could still picture the first time he'd noticed her at a school rally all those years ago, and how shocked he had been by the familiarity of her beauty. Those wide, feline eyes, that delicate button nose, that upturned chin, even the small red mole above her pouty lips, all of which had reminded him of the village belle he'd long lost. After that, he had lingered outside her classroom, watching the sunrays pirouette on the back of her silky black braids, like he'd done in his boyhood, sitting behind his village love, dumfounded by her perfection. Now, alone in his subterranean existence, he couldn't wait for their nightly reunion.

If he was lucky, she'd come into his dream as his new bride. It was always a summer night, lavish with the heady scent of gardenias. Faceless guests would cram into their apartment bearing wedding gifts—a double-happiness pillow, a jade spittoon, a dozen red-dyed eggs, a pair of thermoses adorned with blooming peonies. Lemei's mother would splurge on a queen-sized quilt with a coveted dragon-phoenix pattern. After a toast, everyone would sit down to a feast—braised pork balls, Kung Pao chicken, mapo tofu, golden crispy spring rolls, complete with dowry cakes and sweet lotus-seed soup. The guests would eat ravenously, oily sauce dripping from the corners of their mouths. They'd grow tipsy on three bottles of baijiu. But his focus would be squarely on his bride—in her perfectly fitted Lenin tunic and a knee-length crimson skirt, a belt accentuating her hourglass figure. He'd pray for time to run faster so they could be left alone. When the clock struck midnight, the guests would bow their drunken heads and take their leave, shouting a mix of revolutionary slogans and obscenities into the dark night. Shivering, he'd usher his bride into their bedroom and under the dragon-phoenix quilt. He'd cradle her soft body, purrs escaping his throat. He'd slide his hand under her skirt, feeling her silky-smooth thighs with his fingertips. Almost always, his dream would crash to an end then, and he'd wake in despair, sticky liquid running down his legs.

On Sundays, when he didn't have to work, he'd hide inside the musty stairwell across the street from Lemei's paper, knowing she'd been working on weekends ever since her best friend had left. In the beginning, when he was still foolish and brave, he'd approached her at the gate. She'd run the other way as soon as she spotted him, ignoring his pleas to hear him out. He'd seethed and remembered their first and only kiss. For a few seconds on that sweltering August afternoon he had tasted euphoria, chewing on her supple flesh and fuelling himself with a confidence he'd never known in this life. When the village belle of his youth left him for a Beijing soldier, he had been a nobody. But staring down at Lemei then, he was convinced he could give the girl whatever she wanted, if only she'd let him.

Now, he was back to square one, a nobody once more. He had to be content with watching her from afar. He soon learned the pleasure of stalking, the power of being the one in the shadows, of stripping agency from the one under the sun, as he balanced her distant, figurine-like body on his palm and kissed every inch of it.

WHEN THE LETTER FROM his village elder arrived in the spring of 1981, he sensed the noose of his old life tightening around his neck. His mother had late-stage stomach cancer, the ancient man informed him in his chicken scratch, and as her only child, and a son, no less, he was duty-bound to shepherd his mother through the last leg of her journey. For days, his terminally ill Ma, ensconced in a wheelchair and smiling feebly, beckoned him in his dreams. Despite a coveted Shanghai hukou awarded to him at the start of the Cultural Revolution, he knew he'd forever be an outsider in this metropolis, labouring for the rest of his life at the fish station and languishing in the underground hole he called home. He didn't want to admit it to himself, but once he returned to the verdant fields of his childhood, he would not find the strength to leave again.

Two weeks later, he went to the Shanghai train station and bought a ticket for the next outbound Sunday express to Yangzhou. That night, his dream began mercifully in the privacy of their wedding chamber, his body intertwined with Lemei's. When the explosion of pleasure sent him reeling and gulping for air, he clung to her like a resolute pilgrim. The treacherous world dissolved as he traced her naked contours with his fingers, fascinated by every little detail. How impossible it seemed, to harbour a feeling so intense yet so private, without the zeal of the loudspeakers, posters, slogans, rallies. No wonder romantic love had to be vilified as bourgeois drivel, the archenemy of the revolution.

The next day, a Saturday, he couldn't focus at work, the scenes from his dream playing on a loop. He sensed that the consummation was a goodbye, his brain finally giving up the fight against itself. *Tomorrow morning, I'll be gone*, he thought with surprising calm. After work, instead of heading home, he wandered the city in a trance, taking in the last impressions of the neon lights and French villas. When his feet carried him to the entrance of her paper, the sun had dipped below the horizon. He wasn't sure what he was doing there. He patted the train ticket in his pocket. *Guess I'll bid farewell in person*, he decided, and caught the door as a newspaper man left the building.

He climbed the five flights of stairs he'd only seen from outside the glass wall, ducking his head whenever someone passed him on their way down. When he reached her floor, he sneaked into an empty meeting room. She was saying goodbye to a colleague on the other side of the thin wall.

"Getting late, time to close up," a baritone urged.

"Almost, editor. I'll lock up. You don't need to wait."

"Take a break tomorrow. See you on Monday."

He listened to the footsteps vanishing down the stairs. Soon there was only the sound of a grandfather clock tick-tocking unremittingly toward the day of his departure.

*It's now or never.*

He tiptoed to her office, pushed on the wooden door, and poked his head in. The room was dusky. A narrow shaft of weak light filtered through a tiny window near the ceiling. She sat beside a mustard-coloured lamp, besieged by towers of books and papers. She was holding a thick tome with both hands like a studious pupil, her eyes downcast and lashes quivering, her lips moving along with the text. His heart raced. She hadn't changed at all, the bride from his dream. He shuffled his feet nervously, creaking the floorboards. She lifted her eyes and let out a shriek. The book in her hands fell onto the desk with an echoing thud.

"What are you doing here?" she barked.

The aggression in her voice shook him. He regretted coming here, their tender love shattered into pieces by cruel reality.

"I mean no harm. Just want to say goodbye. I'm going home."

"How did you get in? Did you break in? Anyone still here? Hello?"

"I only want to talk—"

"Get out now, before I call the police."

"Lemei, for old times' sake—"

She shot up from her chair, and in no time pushed the door against his shoulder. Pain flooded him.

"My Ma's dying!"

"Leave! Leave!"

He couldn't stand the madwoman in front of him, so unlike the perfect lover who had visited him night after night. Scorching heat pulsed and expanded in him. He swung the door open and seized her arms.

"Listen to me! I'm going back to my village to take care of my dying Ma."

"Let go of me, you thug."

"I never told you how much you look like my first love ..." He stared down at her scarlet face as she twisted and writhed in his grip.

*Not this time, not again.*

"Do you ever listen? I said I'm going back to the countryside. I've devoted all my best years to the revolution. Do you know, they abandoned me like a dog in 1976? And you, you always treated me like a mortal enemy."

She spat in his face, but he barely noticed. He stooped to kiss her and was bitten on the lips. The jolt of pain only fanned the flame in him. "Shanghai missy, you always thought I was beneath you, didn't you? You think I'm a dirty country bumpkin. After everything I've done for you! You wouldn't have this cushy job without me."

With her arms bound by his strong hands, she kicked his knees and shins. He collapsed on the floor, hauling her down with him. A lotiony smell rose from her heated skin. He wanted her skin to be on his own, so her sweet scent would infiltrate his pores and become a part of him. He wanted to take her back to his village, to his mother's deathbed. He could no longer hear the screams blasting his ears. Instead, he embarked on a search mission for the bride who frequented his dreams—the red moles on her clavicle, the pink orbit of her areola, the smooth curve of her marbled thigh. He was climbing a mountain with a heavying load, and he could go no further. A violent spasm roiled through his body. He shuddered and relaxed his grasp on her.

Suddenly, savage curses inundated him. He saw her tattered blouse, a droopy breast hanging out of her bra, blood trickling down her naked legs.

"I … I'm sorry … Let me take you to a doctor …"

"Get the fuck away from me!"

Fury had mangled her beauty. She seized the hefty dictionary from her desk and clobbered his head with it, cursing his mother, his eight generations of ancestors. His beloved had been subsumed by a raging beast, with a bruised, fiery face and a determination to kill. He gathered himself from the floor and ran for his life.

# 12

She huddled on the cold concrete floor all night, shivering, tendrils of blood drying on her thighs. In her wrath-induced haze, she saw herself hunt him down and twist a pair of scissors into his stomach, wounding but not killing him. She'd tie him to a chair, take her sweet time shearing open his pants and cleaving off the flaccid root between his legs, luxuriating in his pleas for mercy. Hungry dogs would gather and fight over the bloody stub. Later, she fell into a numb paralysis, dipping in and out of a nightmare: a dark and mossy cavern, oozing viscous tar, blackening the walls of her mother's house.

In the morning, she dragged herself in the direction of the hospital. She stopped cold at its entrance, suddenly debilitated by the thought of suspicious eyes, a formal registration and ID check. She shuffled past the Soviet-style beige block and wandered aimlessly, until the Shanghai Library loomed ahead under a cluster of black clouds. In the history stacks, amid tales of palace intrigue among emperors' vying concubines, she found her ancestors' recipe.

Later, she roamed the dim rows of the apothecary,

gathering saffron, deer musk, and persimmon pedicels into crinkled brown bags. The ancient granny at the checkout counter mumbled condolences and a prayer, without lifting her grooved eyelids. "Bleeding will atone your sin" were her parting words. She didn't know if she should thank or spit at her, so she merely nodded and scurried back to her office. In the kitchenette, she ground the stems and poured the mixed powder into a pot of boiling water, digging her fingers into her wrist to stop it from shaking.

When the brew cooled, she took a tiny sip, the bitterness making her gag. But she tossed down the entire potion, nose pinched, without coming up for air. She ached for the red deluge to cleanse her from the inside out, to flush out the dirty seed that toad had left in her. Thunder rattled her ears. Rain tumbled out of the clouds, beating on the windowpane, erecting a moving grey curtain, shattering the solidity of roads and buildings, bodies and faces.

PART TWO

# THE
# AMERICAN
# DAUGHTER

2000–2001

# 1

The girl in front of her twisted and turned in the window seat, staring out into the clouds, her left eye smeared blood-red from too much crying. Lin had been watching her long before this. At the departure gate, the poor thing had sobbed into her mother's arms in a theatrical spasm that made fellow travellers giggle under their breath. A hint of jealousy bobbed in Lin's chest. A healthy dollop of grief would be appropriate right now.

Or sheer terror.

After all, she was flying into the unknown without a parachute. Instead, she sank into an enveloping wave of relief, grinning at the thought of putting six thousand miles between her and her past.

What a fluke it had been—to be paired with the rural boy, to have him do the heavy lifting while she collected the golden ticket. She'd seen the boy around in her neighbourhood, emerging with his migrant worker mother from the underground bomb shelter beneath Building Number 5.

She'd even pulled him out of the school bullies' slimy hands a few times. But she hadn't given much thought to the gossip about his "freakish" talent. So when their principal declared her and Dali the Emerald Girl and Golden Boy of their high school ("one English prodigy, one math genius!"), she hadn't allowed herself to believe that they'd indeed be this year's winning combination at the international math competition. Now, with an exhausted fondness, she remembered those final hours of the competition, when she raced to translate the fifty-page report into foreign codes, straining to follow the plot twists, to stay true to the exquisite treasure map Dali had laid out with symbols and formulae. Her apartment floor was dusty when she dropped to her knees and kissed it, after the results were released, Ma weeping next to her and looping her arms around the waxy statue of the Immortal Woman on the family altar.

A whirlwind of good luck had followed—a math scholarship to an American university, a student visa to the Promised Land. Dali had received the same offer, but last she checked, he wasn't coming. Money problems ran deep in his family, like the underground hole he and his mother called home. *Thank goodness*, she only admitted to herself now, dodging shame. The boy had inched closer and closer each day during their four months of training together, his sidelong glances tender yet dagger-like, until his fevered heartbeats had drummed in her ears.

The elderly flight attendant doddered in her direction, collecting trash row by row. Lin reached into her pocket and patted the pebbles, cool and smooth on her fingertips. She'd carried them for years, given them names and infused them with personalities: *Felicity. Tranquility. Lucky. America.* Her mouth tingled, the stone's grainy and metallic taste springing to her tongue. She tapped their rigid surfaces one last time and scooped them out of her pocket, stretching her hand toward the half-smiling flight attendant. The stones plunged into the deep pit of the garbage bag, their final thuds exciting her. *I'm done with you little devices of torture!* Her mother's downcast face flashed before her; she waved it off like swatting a fly.

Inside the plane, it was eerily quiet; apparently, it was three a.m. California time. Beside her, a plump man in a teal business suit snored, his stubby lashes trembling with each heavy exhalation. She opened the blind halfway and let the sun's rays cocoon her. Closing her eyes, she welcomed the rare sensation like a long-lost friend: this heated brightness, this red-orange cloud nudging away the greyness that had become her undertone. Rich aromas of Shanghai's street foods—fried pork buns, sesame balls, green onion pancakes, tofu flower soup—slithered into her nostrils from a decade before, when Laolao used to take her for long strolls crisscrossing the city's narrow alleyways, teeming with life. They'd stuff their bellies with a dizzying array of finger foods, stagger to the Marx and Engels statue on the luxurious lawn of Fuxing Park and collapse there, giggling and basking in the afternoon sun. Pleasures so simple that they had to be rooted out like weeds, when English and Olympic math classes butted onto her calendar with annihilating pomposity. Those excursions were too "irresponsible" anyway, Ma had told them. "Can't you see the freckles blooming on the girl's nose?" Ma had glared at Laolao.

"Are you seriously declaring war on freckles?" Laolao shot back.

"You bet I am," Ma said, still feeble from the most recent bout of her mysterious malaise.

Laolao sighed, her eyes resting on the umbrellas standing sentry behind Ma, their wide spectrum of colours puzzling her. "Those are for ...?"

"For Lin." Ma hadn't missed a beat. "To match her outfits every day."

Those damn umbrellas, they didn't age well. This morning, as she scanned her childhood home one last time, they had sprawled on her bed like spidery aliens, their skeletons half-crumbled from too much use. A ghostly figure had flickered before her eyes—her younger self strolling the city streets, her white mask of a face obscured by the shade. "The child's looking too pale, not right!" Laolao used to complain, directing her worried gaze toward Ma, who would grin dreamily at Lin, as if admiring a marble sculpture she'd laboured over her entire life.

"We're an hour away from touchdown, ladies and gentlemen." The captain's booming voice jolted Lin from her trance. "The weather in Los Angeles is clear and sunny, with a high of seventy-seven degrees this morning."

She straightened up and peered out at the cotton-quilt clouds and the blue streaks of ocean shimmering beneath.

So this was it, the Golden State. She had made it to the other side of the Pacific Ocean.

LAX REMINDED HER OF the old train station in Shanghai, before the migrant workers tore it down and built a glistening new one, all in four months—the no-frills design, the dimly lit low ceiling, the earth-toned columns and floors shrivelling in their ripe age, the mix of urine and sweat making her woozy. After sixteen hours of flight, following a decade of throat-scratching longing—*This is it?*

She trudged with the crowd toward the exit, pushing the giant suitcases Ma had packed for her. Outside the sliding door, scenes of syrupy reunions sprang at her. She held out her name plaque feeling like Andersen's match girl. At last, a woman shrouded in a plain brown shirt and wrinkled khaki pants hollered at her. "Lin! Aunt Wei here!"

Lin hesitated and took out the photo from Ma. It wasn't a perfect match, not even close. The young lady with gemstone eyes and a full head of lush hair had dwindled into an androgynous figure in a buzz cut.

The woman rushed toward Lin with a hunchbacked gait and spat out rapid Shanghainese. "All grown up! Your Ma's so lucky!"

"Hello, Auntie. Good to finally meet you. No, no, let me—"

But the woman had already dragged away the heavy luggage and Lin had to hurry to catch up. In the parking lot, Wei loaded the suitcases into her trunk with the fluidity of a stockboy, and gestured for Lin to get into the passenger seat. Turning on the radio, she steered the car toward the Pacific Coast Highway without uttering another word.

Lin squirmed behind her seat belt, straining to make out the torrent of foreign words sputtering out of the stereo.

"Pesky commercials!" Wei palmed a button, turning it off.

Here was Lin's cue to break the ice. "I've heard so much about you, Auntie. Ma says you're a woman of letters, whip smart, the most promising student from her high school."

"Try to make me cry, kid?"

"What? No, no, sorry. Just that Ma talks about you like she's a big fan. Says you studied literature, and then switched to computers. Says you have the brain to do everything well!"

Wei laughed bitterly. "I'm not sure about that. I had to switch majors, no choice."

"Why?"

"Had to feed the beast, this constant hunger in my belly. Study literature? A dead end. My friends here told me a long time ago: 'Switch to something practical!' Oh, I just had to be stubborn."

"*I* think it's admirable, to hang on to your dream."

"You know what a student loan is? Five nights a week in Chinatown. All that dishwashing and floor-mopping could hardly cover the interest, let alone pay down the principal. I sobered up eventually. Took me too long."

Lin's back muscles clenched. This sounded nothing like the America Ma had waxed lyrical about in her bedtime stories. "So, are you still in IT?"

Wei shook her head wistfully. "I work for a Chinese company now, a large grocery chain." She tapped the stereo button again. Bossa nova and a reedy female vocal suffused their fast-moving metal box, nudging at Lin's disappointment.

"A rare Chinatown company. Good benefits, good health insurance. I'm very grateful," Wei said emphatically, putting a lid on the Q&A.

Lin kept her mouth shut for the rest of the drive, focusing instead on the syncopated thumping on the radio, as their beat-up Ford Taurus glided past stretch after stretch of pristine white-sand beach.

. . .

LATER, AT THE EL Dorado dormitory that resembled a gauzy resort for the working poor, with its dirty pool and plastic plants, Wei unloaded her luggage and pressed a scrap of paper into her hand. "My number. Got to head back for the evening shift. Call me if you need anything."

"Come in for tea—" Lin started, but Wei had already jumped back into the driver's seat. With a final wave, she pulled out of the parking lot, taking with her the last cord of Ma's maternal protection. Lin watched the car retreat and disappear at the end of the street, loss ballooning in her chest.

Ma called when she was knee-deep in unpacked luggage. "You made it, kiddo. Congratulations."

"It's past midnight in Shanghai. Can't sleep?"

"Guess I won't sleep for a while. But don't worry about me."

They talked about the greasy airplane food, the view of the Pacific Ocean on the drive to school, the new dorm. Awkward pauses shushed along the thousands of miles of wire between them.

"You're American now," Ma said after a long silence.

"Am I?"

"Make friends with laowai, learn their ways. Soon you'll be one of them."

"Sounds easy."

"Nothing worthwhile comes easy."

"I know…" She didn't like where this was going.

"The easiest path is to find the nearest Chinatown and hang out with the newbies like yourself. Is that what you want? After all the work we've done?"

Lin held the phone away from her ear. Her body felt lethargic, like a well-trained dog ready to capitulate to her irascible master. But she wouldn't give Ma the satisfaction, not today. "I just got here. Can't even tell night from day yet."

"Of course, get some rest. Take good care of yourself, okay?"

"You try to get some sleep too."

"Don't forget the sunscreen, hats, or umbrella. And Dr. Hong's magic cream twice a day."

Lin hung up, pretending not to hear that last command.

THE NEXT DAY, she defied her mother with a vengeance. She went to a nearby Kmart and giddily handed over a fistful of greenbacks in exchange for a lady's cruiser. She pedalled up and down her new town, from the UC campus to the treeless Girsh Park, to the commercial district with big-box stores and potbellied laowai hoisting themselves in and out of their Hummers. She followed Hollister Avenue, pivoted at San Pedro Creek, and kept pushing ahead until she reached the small but stately airport with its quaint red-tile roofs and white stucco walls. The midday sun scorched her pale skin, her cells humming a sweet song of freedom. At night, she traced the glowing red patches on her nose and forehead, and gave her mirror image a high-five.

# 2

The linear algebra professor stood before the chalk-board, scanning the room with a bored face. He wore old-fashioned round spectacles and a flowing white beard so extravagant that the class had dubbed him Headmaster Dumbledore. All around Lin, arguments over the latest scandals of the Clinton White House and Brad Pitt's love life were approaching a fever pitch. She'd read about Clinton and Pitt too, but she wouldn't risk speaking up again; she'd done enough damage in the short span of four weeks. When she fell off her bike one evening she'd screamed, "I've got a concoction!" into a concerned bystander's face. At a meet-and-greet party at her dorm she'd told a sympathetic blonde how "flag bastard" she was about the dirty common areas, before butchering a joke about her future "knight with shining arms." She'd promised one teacher that she'd "dart all the eyes and cross all the teeth" on her assignment. She thought she'd digested the many idiotic American idioms, but they inevitably slipped out the wrong way when it was showtime (why not "hitting the head on the nail?"). Her new tongue could never catch up with her thoughts. Even with her polished American accent—fruit of her decade-long labour—she knew the game was over whenever she made one egregious mistake. She couldn't stand seeing another pained face suppressing a guffaw as she unwittingly played the part of a fool, an *alien*.

"Hey, mind if I join you?"

She pivoted toward the familiar voice with a rush of joy that surprised her. "When did you get in?" she asked, looking into Dali's smiling eyes.

"Last night." He sat down beside her, smelling like the salty ocean.

"Thought you weren't coming."

"I thought so too, but Ma said I had to. Now she's got a big loan to pay off. The woman's a saint."

Dumbledore cleared his throat, signalling the end of the break. He launched into a baritone monologue on vectors, subspace, matrix, transformation. What wonderful labels, words from a sci-fi novel Lin would have readily devoured. But instead, the words stood guard at the gate of an extraterrestrial world, barring her entry. Dali, however, nodded the whole way through, making throaty sounds of pleasure whenever Dumbledore completed a proof, as if he were listening to the most fascinating tale, with a grand finale that brought him instant satisfaction. When the clock on the wall struck eleven, marking the end of the lecture, Lin exhaled the bottled heat from her lungs.

"That wasn't so bad, was it?" Dali said.

"Bit hard to follow," she muttered.

"Yeah, I learned this stuff back home, but now it's in English, lots of terminologies to catch up on."

"You've learned this already?"

"After our competition. I found a textbook in our school library."

"Wow."

"The good thing is, this prof writes a lot on the board. Formula is the universal language."

Lin gnawed on her lips.

"What do you think of the homework question?" he asked innocently.

*No clue*, she wanted to say, but her cheeks started to flare.

"I can only work out part of it in my head," he chirped on. "Need to write it all down. The eigenvalue here is a red herring. I think he's trying to trick us." Dali chuckled.

"You work so fast."

"I can give it to you for proofreading afterward." He looked at her intently, letting his offer linger between them.

"That's all right. I'm sure yours is correct. See you next time." She shot up from her seat and dashed out of the classroom. She ran all the way to the library. Huffing and puffing, she constructed a pagoda of reference books from the stacks. She dove in, searching for clues to the homework, her pulse drumming with despair. The formulae pirouetted across the pages in a cruel tease. She didn't leave the library until closing, but all she had to show for it was a jumble of math sentences and half-logic, each step a leap of faith from the last.

THE NEXT DAY, DALI found her behind the math stacks. "There you are. I've been looking all over for you."

She moved away from him, averting her eyes.

"Can I study with you?"

"I prefer to study alone. Can't focus when others are around."

"Fair enough. Here." He shoved a slim notebook into her hands. Before she could protest, he had vanished like a spring lark.

She scanned the notebook. His lecture notes, a neat combination of math and Chinese, read like a mocking rebuttal to the incoherent heresies with which she populated her own. At the back, there was the solution for yesterday's homework, all twenty-six lines of pure elegance. She clutched the page to her pounding chest and looked around like an amateur thief, shivering, cursing.

This went on for weeks. She switched floors in the library, but Dali always managed to find her and deliver the lifeline. She was sinking deeper and deeper into a muddy pit, and he was still grinning. When he appeared in front of her two weeks before the midterm exam, she seized the notebook he placed on her desk and threw it in his face. "Get out of here!"

"Shh, it's a library."

"Stop whatever you're doing."

"Just some lecture notes."

"And solutions to the homework! You want me to be taken down to the academic integrity office, tried by the tribunal?"

"A proof is a proof, not much variation."

"Why are you doing this?"

"I ... don't like to see you struggle." He eyed her timidly.

She covered her face so tears wouldn't escape her palms. "I can't do this. My brain doesn't work this way ..."

He waited patiently for her heavy breathing to subside. "So what?"

"Leave before I scream."

"You're not very good at linear algebra. Not the end of the world."

"Easy for you to say. That classroom is like a paradise for you."

"I'm not good at English. You win some, you lose some. Teacher Wu used to read all your English essays to us. All I felt was despair. My stiff tongue can never crank out your kind of elegance."

"That doesn't help an iota in algebra class."

"Wrong. Algebra is a language too."

"Bullshit."

He plopped down beside her with a steely determination that silenced her. "Don't get bogged down by symbols and formulae. Let's start with two stocks." He drew on her notebook. "Here's a little secret: linear algebra is simply a mini spreadsheet." He reeled off a string of market signals ("Rogue CEO! Hiking interest rate! Xerox eclipsed by emails!"). "How do you update the stock portfolio?" He stared at her before answering his own question. "Use matrices! Right?"

She nodded mutely, suddenly scared of this new version of him. He hopped out of their carrel and came back with a bouquet of Crayolas. He launched into multicoloured graphs of eigenvectors and eigenvalues—words that had taken on a mystical dimension in her mind. For the first time, she noticed his taut biceps and strong jawline, his rural shyness overwritten by a commanding confidence. The disjointed concepts that had long terrorized her now slowed their frantic gyrations, their chilly abstraction taking concrete shape in his warm tone. She watched in amazement as the deflated terrorists fell into the neat slots of a solved puzzle with final bows of obedience.

"Wow, that was ... was a ..." she stuttered, tears of relief coursing down her cheeks.

He leaned into her; their knees touched. But he must have seen the shock welling up in her eyes, for he stopped short of brushing her lips. Murmuring apologies, he scurried away.

THE NEXT DAY, HE approached her gingerly at the library, wearing regret in his sober eyes. He deposited a boulder-like backpack between them, a silent oath to keep his distance. She let him stay that day, and the days and weeks that followed. With a touch of giddiness, he lectured and graphed, analogized and metaphorized, pulling her, with all his might, out of the murky water of an assortment of math subjects.

At night, Ma's long-ago warning peppered her dreams. *Stick with laowai! Those who look like your people—resist, resist! I've seen sons betraying fathers, lovers backstabbing each other. You never know where another Chinese stands. Stick with laowai!*

"It's only Dali!" she cried out in her sleep. But she felt trapped too. He tailed her everywhere, in classrooms, tutorials, lunch breaks, shutting off every chance for her to make a new friend, a *local* friend. She might not be ready to fly, but to be hijacked into a two-person canoe, cast away on a foreign sea? American peers nodded at them with nauseating politeness, giving them a wide berth from across a poisoned moat. On the rare occasion they conversed with the locals, the Americans enunciated every syllable, loudly and slowly, their eyes shining with earnest sympathy, treating them like defenceless toddlers. *I'm not stupid!* she wanted to scream.

*I've read Dickens and Jane Austen!* Instead, in his rickety, accented English, Dali replied dutifully on behalf of them both. She cringed on the sidelines, watching him trip over his syllables and smile apologetically, and sensed the Americans' sorry gazes bearing down on them—the ocean-doused FOBs who had no future on the New Land.

THE DAY AFTER THE last final exam, her roommate, Regina, a charcoal-haired, olive-skinned Mexican-American beauty, knocked on her door and invited her to a birthday party. Regina was into polyamory ("Not illegal here, trust me honey!" she'd told Lin with a mix of pride and pity). During her first week in America, Lin had stumbled on a mound of naked flesh in their shared living room, and stared into three pairs of ravenous eyes reflecting the moonlight. She had shrieked and shrieked, rousing the neighbours. Despite Regina's profuse apologies the next morning, Lin had avoided her at home and on campus ever since, unable to forget the image, or the smell of fermented fruit that had hung in the air that night. Regina, oblivious and exceedingly positive, still waved at Lin whenever they crossed paths at school, but the minute Lin saw her approaching on a skateboard like a wild manga spirit, she'd run the other way, as if the moral corruption were airborne and contagious.

So it was a surprise that she found herself standing behind Regina's crew of boyfriends and singing "Happy Birthday." The curly-haired boys grinned ear to ear, circling the scantily clad, bejewelled birthday girl, who blew out the candles in one long, sensual breath. Tequila shots sailed around the room, echoed by obscene in-jokes. Lin hovered on the periphery, pulling on her too-short tank top, unsure where to stand or sit, and what to say. She feared that Dali's broken English would tumble out of her mouth as soon as she opened it, and she'd instantly morph into a party clown with rainbow hair and a ballooning red nose. She didn't last long, slipping into her bedroom without saying goodbye. She crawled under her blanket and buried her head beneath the pillow, ostrich-style. High-pitched laughter pierced her ears. Glasses clinked and clanked, and later shattered into pieces. Her room shook with the thumping music from the other side of the wall. *They've taken a page from the gulag!* A headache climbed the back of her scalp and radiated down her neck. She imagined her nerves stretching and snapping like silly putty.

Later that night, she found scraps of fragmented sleep in between the moaning and groaning outside her bedroom. A stinging sensation spread down her torso, like an army of small pins marching under her nightshirt. She splayed her fingers and stroked herself, spasms of electricity jolting her. Breathing jaggedly, she chased the high, the unattainable, growing fierce, ruthless. Heat and tremors rose between her thighs, until a wave of warmth gushed out of her, flushing away remnant strands of thought. Her perennial bedfellow, the long figure of loneliness, folded back into the crook of her arm. She fell into a merciful oblivion.

The next morning, she called Dali and said she needed a break from him.

"What happened?!"

She switched to English, erecting an instant wall. The foreign words felt heavy and sluggish on her tongue, like a long-lost friend hesitant to give the relationship another try. "I can't live in a vacuum anymore," she said.

She couldn't explain to him how exposed, how *naked*, she felt speaking Chinese in a sea of English speakers. Or the message she had received growing up—incongruous and incessant—that America was her true home. Instead, she had become fearful of Americans, their wild-doe eyes and tall noses, the exaggerated geometry of their Caucasian masks. She could no longer look at her flat features in the mirror, her Asian mask, without panic shooting up her throat. How could she ever become one of them?

"Did I do something wrong?" he whined in Mandarin.

"It's not you. Just respect my wishes, *please.*"

She hung up; the pitiful register of his voice was driving her crazy. She plunged into bed and stared at the grey sky, her brain lured into that great Chinese tradition and national pastime: seeking patterns among the clouds. *So what's the plan*, the cloud elephant snorted at her, *now that you've chased away your only friend?*

*Mind your own fat trunk!* She turned away from the window and thrashed about in bed. Her stomach growled, a cavernous pit. She remembered she hadn't eaten since lunch yesterday, and even then, it was only a Subway sandwich, which, like most American food, seemed to glide right through her body and leave no memory behind. She tiptoed to her door and opened it a crack, bracing herself for the obstacle course of worn-out flesh after a night of debauchery. Takeout containers, broken glasses, and rumpled blankets littered the living room, but no one was there. The door to Regina's bedroom was wide open, her bed tidy and abandoned.

She ventured into the kitchen and opened the fridge. Half a chocolate cake—*Regina* still intact in blue icing—made her mouth water. She dipped a finger into its soft shell and brought the moist chocolate to her lips. The rich flavour burst onto her tongue, the sweetness sharp and nauseating. Instant warmth expanded inside her lungs. She rummaged for a knife and cut herself a paper-thin slice. The chocolate and buttercream flowed down her throat, a divine concoction, flooding open tiny doors on the elusive path to euphoria. Another thin slice. Another, another, the knife's edge drawing dangerously close to the *R*. The perfect half was folding like a Mandarin fan, but she couldn't stop inhaling the little pieces of heaven; she needed this nascent fire in her to keep on burning. When she could no longer slice the cake without destroying Regina's name, she forked out the middle layers like a mad archaeologist. The top layer soon threatened to cave in, and she had to halt the excavation. A final glance at the precarious structure—her handiwork. Just like that, the blissful bubble popped, and shame bulldozed over her. She darted back to her bunker and dove into bed, smearing dark brown icing all over her virgin-white sheets.

# 3

At a College Democrats meeting, she scored her first American friend.

For weeks, she had lived at the mercy of endorphins and exhaustion, zigzagging across campus nightly to exorcise the emptiness inside. One evening, she stumbled into the back of an auditorium, into a sea of young, enchanted faces under banners and signs and portraits. A spirited Ken lookalike was campaigning for a seat in the House of Representatives. In a casual polo shirt, his brown curly locks pulled into a ponytail, he cracked jokes and shook hands with the students, a far cry from the scripted, geriatric Chinese statesmen she'd only seen on TV. The floor shook and the room throbbed; applause and raucous chants filled her ears. Her feet took her to the front row as her lips moved to match the chorus.

She could feel her mother in this crowd. Ma used to school her on American politics regularly. On CCTV's world news, Ma had watched greybeards duking it out in front of the camera. The Americans' voices were drowned out by the news anchor, but that had only stoked Ma's obsession.

"Can you believe it? Two men—two political parties—opposing each other on national television for the whole world to see!" A beam of longing light had shone through Ma's pallid face. "I still remember that Reagan fellow at the debate—piercing gaze, iron jaw, looking like a king. But he was only a Hollywood B-lister, someone who used to feed chimpanzees onscreen! And a divorcé! If *he* could be the leader of the free world, anyone could!"

The young Lin had laughed, studying Ma's dreaming face, imagining a devouring crowd and an adrenaline-pumping auditorium like the one she now found herself in.

Lin's tribal instinct kicked in as soon as the girl president took the stage alongside the candidate. She had a small round face evocative of the Chinese South, framed by a neatly cropped pixie cut. Her black eyeliner and blond highlights added hipness to her natural look of innocence. She spoke with an impeccable American accent, about education funding, abortion rights, and support for local unions. Lin was used to seeing Asians keeping their heads down and doing the gruntwork. She never knew an Asian could pluck attention and adulation from a sea of blue-eyed, golden-haired followers.

She lingered in the auditorium afterwards, waiting for a chance to worship the girl president up close. When the crowd dispersed, she sucked in the sweat-scented air and climbed up to the podium.

"Hi, I'm Mei." The president extended her hand right away. "Welcome to College Democrats."

"I'm Lin."

"I noticed you in the audience."

"You did?"

"Yeah, Asians always stand out. There're just so few of us in this room. Are you an international student?"

Lin nodded. *Found out in two seconds. Time for a wardrobe change. Or a tongue scraping.*

"It's great you want to get involved in American politics."

"I'm just curious. The system's so different here."

"Where are you from?"

"China."

"Gosh, must be such a culture shock for you! Hey, why don't you come grab a bite with me? I'm craving some bubble tea. I know a place with deep student discounts."

Lin smiled incredulously, dumbfounded by her good fortune.

A MONTH AFTER THEIR first meeting, she was invited to the girl president's dorm. They'd been sharing weekly meals at Hakka Café after the College Dem meetings. Mei would order for two: scallion pancakes for Lin, beef noodle soup for herself, and two red bean bubble teas. Lin suspected that she'd become the girl president's pet project, as she settled on the tatamis by the same low table every week, watching Mei explain how the political system worked and how grassroots campaigns could make a difference in local elections. Mei wore an aura of big-sister smugness that sometimes got under her skin. Lin almost walked out one night when Mei casually mentioned her birthplace of Taiwan and Lin naively called her a "fellow Chinese," only to face arched eyebrows as if such a suggestion were ludicrous. But Lin knew she *reeked* of insecurities and friendlessness, and she couldn't possibly walk away from the prospect of an American friend. So week after week, she returned to her listening mat, letting Mei's odd blend of foreignness and familiarity push and pull at her, luring her into submission.

*What is this?* Lin felt the force of the scene as she stepped into the dorm room—Mei grinding an inkstick, thick, buttery, velvety-black liquid sprouting on a well-used stone. The sweet scent of sandalwood and pine trees tickled her nose. Mei's brush pirouetted on the paper—dip-glide-slide, dip-glide-slide. A famous poem from Du Fu materialized stroke by stroke like magic.

"You've got some skills." Lin marvelled at the elegant seal script. "As my mother would say, every character has a spine."

"I don't exactly know what I'm writing. I left Taiwan as a baby. But the characters sure look pretty, don't they? Like paintings. This is from years of lessons and practice."

*Show off.* Lin bit her lip. A stinging ache rang through her body. Her own calligraphy set, shattered and defaced, circled her head like a UFO. She hastened away from the desk and was confronted by Mei's bookshelf instead, lined with translated Chinese classics—*The Analects*, *Water Margin*, *Romance of the Three Kingdoms*, *Dream of the Red Chamber*. Like a cornered child, she grew insolent. "You insisted you're not Chinese. What's with this obsession with *my* culture?"

"Hey, you're the one who refuses to practise Mandarin with me! Who replies in English every time I try to speak *your* mother tongue!" Mei said with a teasing grin.

Lin wanted to wipe that smirk off her face. *You don't know where I came from.* She saw her preschooler self circle Ma's desk and mimic her every move, wishing to harvest Ma's energy so her own brush could traverse the page like a graceful figure skater on ice. Those calligraphy lessons had been the start of her training, to adopt her mother's will, to scoop up Ma's hopes and desires, pretending they were precious pearls instead of tapioca balls.

"You see, you mainland Chinese often have this problem. Your government's done a fantastic job," Mei chirped.

"What's *that* supposed to mean?"

Mei put down her brush and looked at Lin intently. "Maybe the time's come for you to think for yourself. Culture, nationality—do they have to be equated? Can I feel connected to my heritage without signing on to a political system?"

A simple provocation. No one had laid it out like that for her before.

"You can talk pretty, but deep down you're just a separatist," Lin muttered.

"And you look cute when you're mad." Mei winked at her and went back to her calligraphy.

IN THOSE DAYS, Lin was still the dutiful daughter who took her mother's calls twice a week. "How's the melting going in the Melting Pot?" Ma's demand reverberated in her skull: *Become an American!* Lin had known this was her ultimate mission since she was seven, when Ma returned home from the asylum, swaying, frail, weightless like a hologram. The higher-ups had stripped Ma of her news reporter duties and demoted her to the paper's embryonic advertising division, little Lin had overheard Laolao telling a friend. Was that why Ma had been locked away in the asylum? Was that why she thrust a fistful of pills into her mouth before every meal? Lin had been too scared to ask the older women. Ma's energy ebbed and flowed, but on good days, she stayed out well after work, attending workshops offered by the city's first American ad agency and bringing home stacks of prints and VHS tapes that she studied feverishly into the night. Her windowless working closet was strictly off limits to Laolao, who loved to rail against the danger of Western values corrupting the minds and souls of the younger generation. But Ma welcomed Lin into her tiny hollow, now plastered with images from an alien world.

"You're looking at some classified materials, kiddo. That means top secret. So don't go about broadcasting it at school, promise?"

"Are those like ... national secrets?"

"I suppose you could say so. Our leaders don't want the masses to see them. They don't exactly, well, reflect socialist values." Ma chuckled.

Lin couldn't decipher the images. A woman's triangular back, with jeans pulled halfway down to reveal her snow-white flesh and the label of her underwear. A bejewelled blond beauty with a milky mustache, striking a power pose. A long-haired, olive-skinned man crouched on a white-sand beach, watching Lin so keenly that she had to look away.

"Do you know what it says here, Ma?" She pointed at the English caption underneath the man's funny pose.

"Yes, they gave us the translation at the workshop. 'The fragrance for men, created for the pleasure of women.'"

"What exactly is the guy selling?"

"Perfume."

"For men? Why do men need perfume? And why does he look like a lady?"

Ma laughed, tilting her head back like in the old days. "That's the whole point, a kind of gender reversal. To subvert a classic cultural trope and create something fresh. Just like what the product itself is hoping to achieve."

Of course, that kind of talk went right over little Lin's head.

"Who would've thought advertising could be such a frontier, a place for rebels?" Ma murmured, her eyes fixed on the pictures.

"Ma? I don't understand what I'm looking at."

"Freedom, kid, freedom. This is America. A different way of life. How lucky we are to get a glimpse of it."

Drug shortages plagued the early years of Ma's illness, and every so often she would have a spectacular relapse, carving bloody stars and moons into her arms with scissors and razors, flinging pieces of her skin like a trail of breadcrumbs across their living room. Her other favourite pastime was to raid the family bookshelves, tearing up their ancestors' classics while mumbling, "Liar, liar, pants on fire!" a chant Lin recognized from Ma's American poster featuring a long-nosed Pinocchio.

One night, in the middle of Ma's rampage and Laolao's threats to return her to the asylum, Lin pulled Ma into her working closet, shutting the door behind them. She slid a VHS tape into the player, and the theme for *The Magnificent Seven* swelled in the air. They had listened to this tune over and again, huddling in this cramped closet, as if the cigarette commercial were a portal to religious transcendence. They had *worshipped* the Marlboro Men, picturing themselves gallivanting across the vast prairie, gusty wind on their faces, the horses' velvety coats under their palms.

Lin held and rocked Ma's shivering body, whispering into her ear: "I'll be American one day, I promise, I promise,

I promise." Ma's crazed eyes bore into Lin until the sweet spell seeped into her bloodstream. The straining muscles on her face softened and her eyes shone with heartbreaking hope. Outside the closet, Laolao's cursing and sobbing faded, like a distant storm retreating into the dark mouth of the horizon. Little Lin had found the key to Ma's recovery.

# 4

## 2001

A week before the Mid-Autumn Festival, she received a party invitation from the Chinese Students Association. Surprised, she threw the letter into her bottom drawer. On the night of the festival, she went to bed early, only to count three thousand sheep with swelling agitation. The bright full moon behind the curtain taunted her: *Living precariously, Scaredy Cat? Come on, your Ma's not watching!* She covered her face with a pillow, but mooncakes assaulted her in the dark, red bean paste oozing out and smearing her. At nine, she shot out of bed, defeated, rooting around in her closet for her navy-blue dress.

The party was in full swing when she arrived. At the entrance, she sidestepped a young man teetering diagonally with half-closed eyes, a shot of baijiu balanced perilously in his hand. Sappy Mandarin songs blared out of a karaoke machine in the far corner. Small groups dotted the room like islets, each with a leader pontificating in the centre.

The boy at the registration desk studied her with curious eyes. "First time? Want me to show you around?"

"I'll be all right, thanks."

She bought a club soda at the bar and wandered toward the nearest islet. A tall, lanky young man with black-rimmed glasses was speaking in an accent she recognized, a Shandong dialect similar to Dali's.

"Stick with us! Trust me, we know the hidden minefields. We'll save you tons of time and headaches. Some profs you must avoid at all costs; some are sympathetic to international students, some are extra cruel. And a handful are downright racist. We have a list of them all. The trick is to work efficiently, get in and out quickly, like a sharpened knife in a good butcher's hand." He tried to demonstrate the dubious metaphor, spilling his drink. "You see, a degree here can lead to an H-1B, and after that, a green card. After *that*, a glorious life awaits!"

Lin chortled a little too loudly. Something about his brash manner rubbed her the wrong way.

The Wise Guy screwed up his eyes and scanned her from head to toe. "Anyway," he continued, "as I was saying, white kids sometimes stay here for five, six years. They like the *experience*. They lie on the white-sand beach daydreaming, *philosophizing*. They go surfing. They go marching in the streets for this and that. Gay rights, animal rights, weed, hookers, the planet. The whole world is on their shoulders—if they don't act, it'll crumble! Too many superhero movies growing up! You and I don't have that kind of leisure. You and I need to focus on what matters. We go for degrees that *deliver*. That's why we're successful. That's why, in a generation, their offspring will be serving ours. They call us the 'model minority' for a reason, right? Go check out those new Chinatowns in Silicon Valley, in New York City. You never have to speak a word of English there. You can be with your own people, be who you are, and still bask in all the luxuries of the world. That's the glory, the *freedom*, I'm talking about! You with me?"

Cheers broke out from his audience. The Wise Guy studied Lin from the centre of his islet. She gave him a faint nod and turned her back. He had made his pitch, but she had heard something else—a tormented soul grappling for happiness (*Fuck the imperative of fitting in!*). "Yeah, yeah, rebuilding the Old Kingdom on someone else's land, brilliant new idea," she mumbled under her breath and walked away.

Settling in a corner, she nursed her club soda and scanned the crowd. She was keenly aware of her position: on the sidelines, looking in. Her default position.

The Wise Guy plopped down beside her. "I could tell you weren't too convinced by my message."

She shrugged.

"I'm Yangyang. Bioengineering, fourth year." He took her hand and shook it, startling her. "Full disclosure, I've noticed you on campus for a while. You're friends with that Taiwanese girl from College Dem, right?"

Uneasiness crept up her spine. "You keeping tabs on us?"

"No, no. It's just…" He inched closer and nudged her shoulder. "Got a thing against Chinese students or something?"

"What? Of course not!" Her mouth was dry, but her hands felt clammy.

"You seem to avoid us."

"I'm … shy. School's super busy."

"Good. 'Shy' we can fix. Stick with us, okay? Trust me, you don't want to be like Du-sha."

"Who's Du-sha?"

"Lin?" Behind her sounded a familiar voice. "It's really you! I didn't think you'd come!"

The Wise Guy got up and patted Dali on the shoulder. "Hey buddy, good organizing work! You know her?"

Dali nodded, his gaze burrowing under her skin.

"Ahh, is this the girl you've been telling us about? Silly me, never put two and two ... She's all yours. Sit, sit. Tell her about Du-sha. And ... be a *man*." He winked at Dali before ambling away.

"Who's Du-sha?" Lin switched to English as soon as Dali sat down.

"Never mind Yangyang, he can be intense," Dali said in Mandarin. "Wow, has it been almost a year? How have you been?"

"I'm fine."

"How's your math?"

"Getting by." Her math scores were sliding south without his help, but she couldn't tell him that.

"You know I'm always here to help."

She nodded. "How are you?"

"I'm okay now. Had a rough patch when you ... *abandoned* me."

"I'm sorry. I didn't mean to hurt you."

"Thankfully I found CSA. It's great to be part of a community again."

"Good for you."

"I was elected treasurer last month."

"Right up your alley."

"I do … miss you. Can we study together sometime, or have lunch?"

Her body tensed, but she felt him holding his breath. "Maybe lunch sometime."

"Yeah? Great! You should join CSA too. We have lots of events like this."

"I need to explore a bit longer … by myself."

"Lin, we take good care of our own. Yangyang's a great example." Dali dipped his head at the Wise Guy, who was observing them from half a dozen seats away. "He's graduating next summer but already landed a job in Silicon Valley. Some CSA shi-xiong recommended him. His offer comes with the whole package—signing bonus, stock options, immigration lawyer. You and I can have those too. Lin, we could have a good life together."

This was all going at lightning speed. She racked her brain for an exit strategy. "I don't think we want the same things."

"Aren't you lonely? Away from your own people?"

"I've gotta go."

"Don't be like Du-sha," he muttered darkly.

"Who *is* Du-sha?"

"This junior girl in engineering, set her heart on dating white boys. Don't be like her. I've seen my fair share of character assassinations around here. It can get ugly."

Her chest grew heavy. He edged closer. "Lin, why are you speaking English to me?"

"I need to practise more."

"You don't find it strange?"

*Yes, damaged goods, steer clear.*

"Yangyang says you think the same way as Du-sha."

"What have you been telling him? He's never even met me before."

"He's a keen observer. He says girls like you think Chinese men are beneath them."

"Nonsense!"

"Then join the CSA. And stop pushing me away."

Yangyang locked eyes with Dali and gestured for him to make a move. Dali tossed down his drink, its pungent smell burning her nose. "Let's just be ourselves and be happy. I can save you ten years of struggle. Give me a chance." He pressed a hand on her bare thigh and squeezed it.

Something exploded in her chest, flinging the room into a wild spin, voices around her warping and dilating. She pinched her eyes shut, her throat seizing up. "Are you okay?" Dali's hand was on her shoulder now. She clutched it and dug in with her fingernails.

"Get the fuck away from me!"

"Oww, miss!"

She opened her eyes. The boy from the registration desk stared at her, petrified, his arm in her hands, raw with claw marks. She jerked back, letting him loose. The whole room was quiet, all eyes on her. Dali and Yangyang had retreated into the shadows.

Later, on the online forum frequented by mainland students, the night's events were told and retold in a competition of creativity, new witness reports materializing like cheap cards in a magician's hands. She had her own designated thread. A little attention from the "it" boys of CSA had sent her into a downward spiral and a public breakdown. How could she ever recover from that? Someone had penned a sexual history for her—a sweeping, sordid tale involving a string of imaginary white men. *Whore! Racist! Traitor to the motherland!* Bystanders threw virtual eggs and tomatoes.

Two weeks later, Dali approached her at the school cafeteria, apologizing for his behaviour at the party but denying any involvement in the smear campaign. She felt woozy again, certain they were onstage under a blinding limelight, beyond which people were pointing and laughing. She dropped her burger and fries and ran all the way back to her dorm. Only in her tightly enclosed bedroom, curtains drawn, did she find some relief. So she hunkered down there, nursing a silent, lacerating scream.

# 5

A week later, Mei dug her out of her mole hole and dragged her to the College Dem meeting. "Enough! Quit feeling sorry for yourself!"

The night's speaker was an ashen-haired, mixed-race former Wall Street banker, who in his retirement had become one of the biggest local donors for the Democrats. He spoke movingly about his mother's childhood in Taiwan and lathered praise on a list of lawmakers who were hawkish against mainland China. The girl president nodded beside him with a cheerful, canine obedience. During the Q&A, Lin stared at the audience's microphone in front of the stage, feeling as if she was standing on top of a skyscraper. She pictured leaping off its edge in a suicidal arc. *Bye-bye, Mei, it was never meant to be.* She seized the mic and lashed into the banker, calling him a quisling, a Judas, a filthy separatist. Panicked, Mei paced the stage, barking at the IT guy to cut the mic, before escorting the speaker out of the room, apologizing all the way. The young men and women, her beautiful, mostly white comrades in American democracy, closed in on her, shaking their fists and mumbling obscenities, their steely glares demanding that she scram.

She staggered out of the auditorium, sensing the demon hot on her heels. When she reached her empty dorm, it swept her into its powerful grip. She tore into the fridge and pantry, hunting for fat and sugar that could bring a fleeting moment of relief. She found half a lasagna in a baking pan, pasta in a Tupperware, and a container of leftover Chinese takeout. She dug in with all her fingers, sauces dripping onto her shirt, the floor. As food slid down her throat, her brain fired rapid pleasure signals, penetrating the thick fog of numbness. The adrenaline rush from committing the clandestine theft only added to her excitement.

The next morning, she found little white flags all over the fridge. One stuck to the seam of a takeout box read *Don't touch me*; another pinned to a yogurt container was marked *Leave me alone*. In every drawer she opened, white flags stood sentry, sometimes with hand-drawn eyes on them, monolid and sinister, glaring straight at her. She fell backward, gasping, her skin crawling with humiliation. She imagined Regina making these tokens of silent protest well into the night, cursing her terrible luck to have to live with a freak. Lin scurried back to her room and dialed the number for Student Housing. "I need to move out immediately," she told the lady on the phone. "No, I'm not asking for a different suitemate. Just let me give up my room!"

Sight unseen, she took the first apartment she could afford in the classifieds—a basement unit eight blocks from campus.

. . .

IN HER SUBTERRANEAN DWELLING, her dreams took her back home. She stood amid the rush of travellers at Pudong Airport, wobbly and disoriented like a foreigner visiting Shanghai for the first time.

Ma came to her rescue, collecting her against her shrinking frame. "Welcome home, child," she said, studying her. "Hard life in America? Your face's getting dark. Need a refill of Dr. Hong's cream?"

Her skin prickled with a familiar resentment. *It's the Golden State. Live a little!* she wanted to say, but she knew she'd regret it. How could she forget her place in this family? The Perfect Daughter. The only person in the world who could keep Ma sane, if only she'd just try harder.

At home, Laolao's mouth-watering pork dumplings mellowed her. She carefully retrieved her mother tongue from the dim recesses of her memory. But words jammed in her mouth, her jaw stiff and gelatinous at the same time.

"Talk to me, kid. I've waited a thousand days for your return," Laolao begged, massaging her jaw like kneading dough.

Eventually, words and phrases and sentences sputtered out, prompting Laolao's happy claps. But her mental gymnastics instantly kicked into high gear, translating every word back to English in real time.

A faceless gatekeeper floated outside the window, behind him a tacky archway draped with the star-spangled banner. He was watching her, keeping score, ready to disqualify her at every turn: "Loyalty! That's all I ask. Prove it!" he barked. "Not good enough! NEVER good enough!"

Ma shot from her seat and slammed the window shut, the sudden motion jolting Lin awake. Her mother's lament seeped out of her dreamscape: *Was I naive? Didn't think I'd lose you ... What do I have left without ...*

*You can't have it both ways!* She gritted her teeth in the dark. *You wanted this. I was only your pawn, remember?*

Vengefully, she flicked on the light and pulled the *Dictionary of American Slang* from her drawer. *So dead in here tonight. I'm jonesing for a coffee. I want to bring my A-game! She ticked me off. She got my goat. She ground my gears. She drove me up the wall!* She spat the string of nonsense at the mirror, rolling her tongue and stretching her chin, scrunching up her nose like an agitated American teen. Tone, check. Facial expression, check. Body language, check. She prayed for the black magic to rise, to give this new creature the upper hand, so she'd never have to slither back into her old skin.

LORELAI GILMORE AND HER eccentric entourage moved in with her. Lin had found them by the curb, like a litter of stray cats. Since then, with the help of an old VCR the landlord had left behind, the warm glow of Stars Hollow reigned in her eight-by-ten basement bedroom. In the mornings, as the sun struggled to penetrate the single window near the ceiling, she woke to the humming of the theme song about an unconditional friendship.

"This adult stuff is hard, isn't it?" Lane, the token Asian, sat by the foot of her bed, holding drumsticks and studying her with a knowing smile.

Lin rubbed sleep from her eyes, remembering the dread of having to step outside and face the world. "I don't wanna go to class today."

"Of course not." Lorelai sashayed in, strutting her

hourglass figure and balancing an oversized coffee mug in one hand. "I don't like Mondays, but unfortunately they do come around eventually."

Lin nodded at her and shuffled to the fridge. She opened it and basked in the glory of its emptiness.

"Looking great, sugar!" Babette's raspy voice rang in her ears. If Lin closed her eyes, she could even feel the older woman squeezing her shoulders. Sometimes, at Green Thumb, the small grocer around the corner, she'd sense Babette's plump presence, trailing her down the aisles, huffing and puffing. "Drop that Pop Tart, sugar. Try a tomato, they're better than sex!"

Life was more bearable with them in the house. Lin could listen to Lorelai for hours—her made-up problems, her make-work projects, her make-do boyfriends.

"Sorry, pal." The American beauty winked at her. "You know my babbling capabilities have no bounds."

Occasionally Lin would get annoyed with her, gawking helplessly at her perfection. "Just look at you! I mean, just ... *look*!" she'd bellow. "There's a long line of women and men waiting for a chance to be your friend or be your date. Who in your shoes wouldn't be peeved constantly?!"

But most of the time she didn't want Lorelai to stop. She wanted her and her gang to fill her ears and eyes and the hollow inside. When she cooked dinner after a trip to Green Thumb, careful to purchase only a day's worth of groceries, she'd eavesdrop on the feisty Paris and chuckle to herself as the gutsy gal bit the head off her unwitting interlocutors. She'd watch the bantering between Lorelai and her daughter Rory, America's New Sweetheart, while savouring her portion-controlled meal, dragging it out with fork and knife like a dainty socialite (no more stabbing chopsticks!). She knew the demon was still prowling, perching on the windowsill, biding its time. But was it really there if she didn't acknowledge it? She turned up the TV volume, repeating lines of dialogue, until she was in the airy living room of a Stars Hollow residence, chatting with the townsfolk like she'd known them her entire life. She had found her people, reality be damned.

Of course, there were nights when nothing worked. The demon lunged at her in full view of Stars Hollow's residents, chasing her out the door. Her feet would carry her into the bakery a few blocks away, and she'd race home in a giddy haze with an eight-inch celebration cake. Like a devout worshipper, she'd kneel in front of the buttery beauty. The world stood still. Voices, in her mind and on TV, screeched to a halt. Her fingers sank into the soft and moist interior as her high-strung head melted away. Her hands and mouth worked in a swift, hypnotic dance, until the buttery beauty turned into dust on her sacrificial bed, or a new sensory signal managed to slip through—an accidental glance at the mirror, her zombie-like eyes glaring back, chocolate cream trickling down her chin like oxidized blood. The voices would return like a flash flood:

"I've made a list of enemies," declared Paris. "And I'm adding your demon to my list."

"You have so many years and screw-ups ahead of you. Get used to it, kiddo," Lorelai advised.

She'd snivel into Lorelai's arms and mumble to her roomful of imaginary friends, "I'll beat it someday, that demon. Beat it to a pulp. I'll find a town just like yours. I'll slip into the throng on Central Plaza and fit in there, like a simple piece in a jigsaw puzzle. My past, locked in a safe and cast away to sea, will never return to haunt me."

"That's dark," Lorelai intoned. "But hey, solidarity, sister."

PART THREE

# PANDEMONIUM

1988–1989

# 1

SHANGHAI

O n a crisp Sunday in the autumn of 1988, Lemei opened her apartment door to find a familiar apparition. Her mother had taken little Lin to the communal bathhouse for a much-needed shower. She was left alone, staring up at the stranger.

"Hey, sis." The ghostly figure gave her a soft punch on the shoulder. The muscles around his mouth twitched; his restless eyes darted between her and the floor.

She drew a breath. A mosaic of images bobbed to the surface of her memory, infusing the bony frame before her with flesh and muscle. Once a boulder of a man, now pared down to essentials. "Is it really you?" she asked.

"Have I changed that much?"

She punched his chest in return, to gain a sense of solidity. Her vision blurred. "So you aren't dead after all."

"Sorry to disappoint you, sis."

"Cut it out, you cold-hearted brat. How long has it been? Nineteen years?"

"Going on twenty…"

"You couldn't have written a single letter? A telegram? Ma wrote you every month for three years. Did you ever reply? Who gives you the right to show up like this when it finally pleases you?"

He stared at his shoes. "I'm sorry. You're right. I'll leave."

She seized him by the arm. "You're not going anywhere. No way I'm letting you vanish on us again! Come in. Ma will be back soon."

"No, no, no. Not yet. I need to talk to you first. Let's go somewhere." Feng looked at her entreatingly, his facial twitches starting anew. He resembled someone from Madame Mao's Model Opera, a stock character who stood on the wrong side of history.

Her heart softened. "All right, lead the way."

THEY TROD SIDE BY side on Huaihai Road, the same strip they'd traversed daily in their adolescence. Instead of the big-character posters that used to cloak the street, an assortment of advertisements now covered the walls and telephone poles— women's heels, men's hats, infant formula, magic deodorant. Feng led her to a hole-in-the-wall Lanzhou noodle joint. A tanned young man in a tall white cap stood behind the counter, doing acrobatics with a lump of dough. His hands worked in rapid flourishes, twisting, stretching, folding the dough into strands, launching them into the air. *Thud, thud, thud*, the sound of noodles slapping against the board bounced between the four walls. Lemei felt her neck stiffen.

Feng poured weak barley tea for them both, his hands shaking so much that half spilled on the table. "Shit," he cursed quietly. "Useless shit."

She studied his face, taking in the marks etched by time and a harsh life. Two decades stretched between their youth and the present, elastic and fragile like hand-pulled noodles.

"When did you get back?" she asked, keeping her tone casual. The old Feng wouldn't have appreciated any whiff of pity.

"A month ago."

"A month! And you're only coming to see us *now*?"

"I wasn't sure if I should ... I was busy looking for work too. It's been tough."

She swallowed her anger, recalling an article her youngest colleague had pitched at the staff meeting about the impossible job prospects for the sent-down youths upon their return to hometowns—how a stint in the countryside was supposed to be a prelude to leadership, but instead, the loyal foot soldiers of the revolution had been forgotten, relegated to the bottom of society. The article was rejected outright.

She took a sip from her cup, a bitter taste permeating her tongue. "Where have you been staying?"

"An old classmate let me crash in his spare room."

"I see ... Well, you made it back. That's the most important part. They should've let the sent-down youths return to the city long ago."

"How's Ma? Is she well?"

"All right, but come see her yourself."

"I was the one who told them about the altar, the goddess," he said suddenly, a tremor in his voice. "It was all me."

"Huh?"

"We broke into the school cowshed one night. Dashan shoved an iron rod in my hand, told me to beat up Ms. May.

I couldn't do it. He said I failed the test, said my heart wasn't with the revolution ... I had to give them *something*, or they'd never trust me again. I had no idea they were after Ba ..."

"I know, Feng. It was so long ago."

"I didn't send a single letter ... I tried to write, but everything sounded like an excuse ..."

"Brother." Lemei reached across the table to steady his hands, alarmed by his gritty skin. "It's all in the past. Times have changed. Even Ma's altar ... Do you know, her patron saint's back? Now standing side by side with the Chairman and Little Deng. Old religions are all the rage again. Have you seen the potbellied businessmen clamouring to get into Jing'an Temple on Sunday mornings, throwing hundred-yuan bills at the incense station?"

"Ma will never forgive me."

"Silly, she's long forgiven you. She's shed too many tears for you. She misses you."

He only stared at her and shook his head.

"We have a new family member now," she blabbered on. "My daughter, six years old. You've got to meet her. What about you? Any family?"

His face, a robust maze of wrinkles, seemed to crumble further. "Sis, I need to borrow some money."

*Ah, so that's the reason you wanted to see me.*

"How much?"

"Five hundred? A thousand, if you have it? Just enough to tide me over for one more month. Things are getting expensive around here."

"True." She nodded. At home, they'd had to stretch three meals out of two lately, and she'd heard the numbers in hushed conversations at her paper: *20 percent for pork and 17 percent for cabbage.* Readers' letters were piling up on reporters' desks, demanding to know when they'd finally do their job and write about the rampant inflation. "I'll get you something," she said. A headache climbed the back of her neck amid the thudding noises from the open kitchen.

"I'll pay you back. They told me my assignment letter is coming. I was so close to getting a job at the radio factory last week, but you know how it goes, the manager's nephew got first dibs."

"Yeah, damn nephews. Have you tried other ways? A few guys from Fengyang High have quit their state jobs and opened their own companies. A labour market is coming. Not everyone has to wait for an assignment letter anymore, thank heavens."

"What guys? Who are you talking about?" He pounded a fist on the table, startling her. "Sneaky snakes! Why wasn't I smart like them, sis? I did everything the Chairman asked of me, and more. Didn't hide a single book under floorboards like those damn rats must've done. They told us learning was poisonous, a waste of time, didn't they? They filled our heads with Old Marx and the Little Red Book—no space for anything else, anything useful. So what do they expect from us now? A labour market, like what the capitalists have? Is that a joke?"

She leaned into him. "Shh, not so loud." He was flustered, his face deep crimson, reminding her of his first time in the spotlight as a Red Guard. The old Feng—those eager eyes and ruddy cheeks, that loud mouth at political rallies, ready to defend to the death every word ever uttered by the Chairman.

She was now in the presence of a stranger.

"Let's go home," she whispered. "We can go to your place if you like."

"No liquor at home." He hollered at the server to bring two cups of baijiu. "I need this. Look at us—me and my little sister reunited, twenty years later. We're celebrating!" The young cook lifted his eyes and stole wary glances in their direction. Lemei was suddenly grateful for the camouflaged soundscape he had created for them.

The baijiu burned away Feng's rage and turned him into a chatterbox. He told her about the country rodents the size of baby pigs, the endless stomach ailments, the backbreaking farm work, the tiny straw shack he called home, the freezing nights he huddled beside the communal kitchen stove. But there were also the Shanghai-style rallies he brought to the village in those early days, the awe and admiration bestowed on him by the villagers.

"And I had a girl," he said bashfully. "Daughter of the village head. A country girl, but prettier than any Shanghai missies. Smart too. Taught me how to drive a tractor." His eyes glistened with a Milky Way of memories.

"Good for you! You brought her back? There's now special Shanghai hukou for spouses of sent-down youths."

The young cook had disappeared from behind the counter and the silence was jarring. Drip, drip, drip, strings of pearls rolled down Feng's cheeks into his cup, diluting the liquor.

"I don't care for the city," he hissed at last. "I'd happily stay by her side for the rest of my life. Hauling manure and planting rice by day, warming her bed by night. Poor, honest living."

"What happened?" she whispered.

He squeezed his eyes tight, but tears kept flowing.

She gulped down the futile words at the brink of her throat. Instead, she locked eyes with the server on the far side of the room and gestured for another round of baijiu.

AS SOON AS SHE got home, she told Ma about Feng's return, and his treasured country wife who had died from a hemorrhage in a late-term miscarriage. Ma dropped her glass, staggered to her room, and howled behind the door. She re-emerged an hour later holding an envelope thick with cash, her cheeks bright red and blotched with white stains. "Give this to your brother. Tell him to come home for dinner tomorrow. I'm making mapo tofu, his favourite."

That night, Lemei dreamed she was back in the kitchen of the empty newsroom, staring down at the yellow concoction in her hands, its pungent smell nauseating. Resolutely, she tossed down the poison and waited. As usual, her body responded with defiant stillness. She was dealing with a fighter as stubborn as herself.

*I can't win.*

*Why punish the innocent?*

She made up her mind and let her body drop, let it swell and contract like a rubber sack, the earth shattering beneath her. The creature moved across the folds of her insides and exploded through her tattered flesh. It wriggled on her belly and zigzagged toward her breast, shedding its bloody membrane along the way. Within seconds, it latched on, lips pumping rhythmically, a greedy little alien determined to turn her blood into a spring of life.

Hot tears seared her face. *I'll love you, and you'll love me, and we'll be enough for each other*, she chanted.

She woke with the chant on her lips, cupping her sagging

breasts, the strange awe still coursing through her body. She wished her sister-in-law had lived to experience it. She was never one to believe in karma, but her heart clenched small— *That poor village girl. Was she paying for my sin?*

WITH SOME ARM-TWISTING, Feng arrived the next evening, trembling like a pupil meeting the headmistress for the first time. He had on a clean white shirt and a pair of ironed slacks, but nothing seemed to fit him now that he was skinny and big-boned at the same time. His thinning hair was washed and brushed to one side, leaving wide bald patches on the other, reminding Lemei of the yin-yang haircut Ms. May had to endure at the hands of Feng and his goons years ago. She swallowed her disgust.

When Ma emerged from the kitchen, drying her hands on a greasy apron, Feng tumbled to her feet and kowtowed.

"My son! My son!" Ma broke into spasmodic sobs, sinking to the floor to caress her long-lost child. Little Lin gaped at the grown-ups before bursting out crying too.

Lemei picked up her daughter and rubbed her back. "Hey, you guys are scaring the kid. It's a happy time! Let's get on with the feast."

They helped each other up, stumbled to their seats, and sat down to mapo tofu and copious pork and chive dumplings. Feng dove in ravenously, stealing sheepish glances at the rest of them every time he wolfed down a dumpling without chewing.

"Slow down, son. No one's competing with you," Ma chided softly, piling more food onto his plate.

A pang assailed Lemei, at this scene from light-years ago, this illusion of turning back the clock.

. . .

FENG VISITED MA FREQUENTLY after that, but Lemei
didn't see him often. In the early months of 1989, things at
the newspaper were heating up. Workers of all stripes materialized at her office unannounced, their faces distorted with
indignation: *Why do Party officials still buy everything at the
pre-reform prices, and we, people on a fixed salary, have to pay
the much higher market price?* People had no idea where to
air their grievances, treating her paper like a police station
or a mayor's office.

Lemei took dutiful notes—the mass layoffs courtesy
of the economic reform, the piling medical bills thanks to
privatization, the escalating market rent as subsidies from the
revolutionary era ran out. Later, in staff meetings, she eagerly
presented her notes and volunteered to interview the officials
to get their side of the story, pitching an objective article.
But she had the feeling their senior editor was no longer
there. Lao Chen's face grew longer by the day, like a baboon
in distress, a stark contrast to his almost jovial demeanour
in those earlier, heady days of the reform.

"I've heard you all, comrades," Lao Chen intoned after a
round of pitches one morning. "A lot is going on, a lot is at
stake. It's a confusing time, I admit. But our job at the paper
is to direct the people to the right attitudes and opinions, to
our socialist values."

"But, editor, those who came to us want nothing more
than to *uphold* socialist values," Lemei said, measuring every
word. "The two-tiered economy has thrown them off. Sooner
or later we'll have to address their concerns. We may be their
last resort before they do something radical."

Lao Chen closed his eyes, his brows knitted into a triangle. "You may be right. Those Democracy Salons at the universities ... not entirely unthinkable they could get out of control."

"If people feel their voices are not heard, they'll have to take matters into their own hands," she echoed.

He let out a sigh. "All right. Write a first draft by Monday, and we'll talk again."

"Thank you! Thank you!" She nearly hopped on the spot.

But Lao Chen had already retreated back to his world. Taking his golden fountain pen out of his breast pocket, he scribbled in frantic strokes with the air of a judge penning a life-altering sentence.

# 2

L emei descended the stairs of her apartment building
in slow steps, her head hung low. She had woken with
a hollowness in her chest again, a new daily ritual.
One month had passed since she'd submitted her article,
and Lao Chen had fallen into radio silence. Some days she
moped behind her desk and fantasized about walking out of
the paper for good, smuggling out her rejected articles and
plastering them all over the walls of Nanjing Road.

On the landing of the second floor, a long shadow
awaited her.

"Hey, sis!" Feng looked withered as usual, a wintry tree
with bare branches, but his eyes sparkled with a new, hungry
energy.

"Hey, coming to see Ma?"

"Yes, but I want to have a quick word with you first. Been
a while."

"Sorry, I'm late for work. Catch up tonight? I can come
to you."

"Sis, real quick." He tailed her down the stairs. "Several buddies of mine—all sent-down youths from Shanghai—are heading to Beijing soon. You know, to support the student movement. I want to join them. More bodies, more voices, right? I thought of you. You're a big-time journalist at the *Daily*. If you could lend your pen to our mission..."

She stopped cold. "You sure that's a good idea?"

"All for a good cause."

"Things are heating up quickly there."

"Just think about it, will you, sis? Search your heart."

She mulled over a firmer rejection, but she heard him say, "You know where to find me when you're ready." Then he dashed up the stairwell, his footsteps stirring up a cascade of metallic echoes.

On the bike ride to work, images from the Party's last *Internal Reference* report spilled over her eyes. One black-and-white photo had especially rattled her. A student leader wearing a kamikaze headband roared into a megaphone while floating on top of a sea of waving, scrawny arms. Seeing it again in her mind's eye, she felt light-headed. She hopped off her bike and leaned on it, waiting for the dizziness to pass.

Was this 1989 or 1966? That picture could well have been from her Red Guard years.

*Don't flatter yourself! You only had borrowed slogans. That young man was wailing words from his heart, the words of freedom.*

How would that feel exactly? she wondered. And could it last—at the very feet of the Dragon Throne?

She straightened up and walked her bike to Tibet Road. A crowd lingered on People's Square and swarmed around a commuter bus. The driver was berating a circle of students in rapid Shanghainese, his face and neck red like a newly plucked chicken. "You stupid eggs! Haven't you learned how to puncture tires? One jab in the front tire, the bus is fucked. Why are you poking all over? It's not a voodoo doll!"

The youths giggled. "Sorry, uncle, we'll do better next time. Can we give our speech now?"

Commuters disembarked from the marooned bus, some stomping their feet and spitting at the colluding driver and students.

"Damn pesky rats, I'm late for work!"

"You want to rebel? Go to the capital!"

"We don't need your kind in Shanghai!"

But more were streaming toward the bus. "Fudan students are giving a speech," they murmured to each other and plopped down by the wrecked tires, watching the students unroll their banners and transform the bus into a podium.

A petite girl in a white blouse and a magenta ruffled skirt climbed to the top step of the bus and surveyed the crowd with a surprising air of authority. "Thank you all for coming. We're here to show solidarity with the students on Tiananmen Square," she announced into the megaphone, her voice soft but firm. "We must pressure the Shanghai government, and the Central Government, to reverse *People's Daily*'s verdict in its April 26 Editorial, incriminating our movement…"

Lemei glanced at her wristwatch. Ten minutes until the morning staff meeting. *Silly children, look at this mess.*

She elbowed through the paralyzed traffic, toward a narrow opening on People's Square. By the time she'd wrestled her way onto Fuzhou Road, she was five minutes late for her meeting. She got on her bike and pedalled feverishly, her brother's righteous tone ringing in her ears. That warmongering fool! He had to stay in perpetual struggle to be happy. *What's wrong with a normal, peaceful life, Feng? What's the point of protesting anyway? Those young ones have no memories of the past, but we should know better.* As she parked her bike and flew up the three flights of stairs to the office, she reminded herself that she was now a duty-bound mother. Her family depended on her to stay calm and stay put.

Her colleagues were in such a heated debate that no one seemed to notice her sneaking into the conference room. She slipped into the seat beside Chun, a quiet junior reporter on the politics desk. "What's going on?" she whispered.

"*People's Daily.* The whole team have dissented," Chun whispered back nervously.

"We really haven't shown any moral courage since the start of this crisis," brayed Min, a recent recruit and the new firebrand of the office. "Now even *People's Daily* has come out against their own editorial. Time for us to take a stance!"

Rumour had it that Min was a remote relative of Wan Li, the vice premier. If it was true, he must have thought of himself as invincible. He reminded Lemei of her young self before her father perished—hot-blooded and foolish, squandering his good fortune, oblivious to the shifting winds.

"Watch your language, Min. This doesn't reflect the *Daily*'s official position. It's only the staff there," intoned Ke, Lao Chen's longtime deputy. Lao Chen himself brooded in silence, puffing compulsively on a cigar, his face half-hidden behind a cloud of smoke.

"It's the paper's entire team of writers and editors! What else is there?" exclaimed Min.

"The whole team can be replaced overnight! Our country

has no shortage of talent. All of us are disposable." Ke uncoiled that last word emphatically while scanning the room.

"So to save our jobs, we resign ourselves to being the biggest cowards? We should start calling ourselves the *Illiberal* Daily!"

"Out of line, Min!" Lao Chen pounded the desk with his inkstone.

"I'm sorry, if I may ..." Lemei interjected, sensing a rare window of opportunity. "Perhaps there's a middle way. For us not to be on a collision course with the hardliners but still save our integrity. That article I submitted on inflation and the ills of the worker class in the Reform Era—it has voices from both sides. Beijing students have been airing the same complaints for weeks. The article can't possibly be construed as radical at this point—"

Lao Chen put up a hand. "The timing's not right."

"Even Secretary Zhao has called for a reassessment of the Party," she entreated. "His May 4th speech—"

"Which reads like his political swan song," Ke sneered. "Or maybe a suicide note."

"How dare you!" Min hissed.

"All that's to say—it's a hyper-sensitive time right now, comrades." Lao Chen sounded exhausted. "Let's not forget the Chairman's words—'a single spark can ignite an entire field.' Now's not the time to light a spark."

"But editor—" Lemei whined.

"No more. Surely, you all understand—the ultimate arbiter is not in this room. Now excuse me, I have an important call." Lao Chen signalled for Ke to hand out the day's assignments and briskly left the room.

. . .

SHE SULKED AT HER desk, listening to the crackling sound of a remote speaker outside her window, and the murmurings of hundreds of distant voices. She'd never lived near the central power of Beijing. Shanghai, her hometown, was a pragmatic city, almost single-minded in its pursuit of profit and wealth since Little Deng's reform. Ideals and passion, the overwrought performances of their northern compatriots, often came as a shock to the practical sensibilities of her fellow Shanghainese. But even *her* city was pulsating with an anxious, restless energy lately. And here she was, the bigwig reporter, trapped like a toad at the bottom of a well.

That afternoon, a dishevelled woman appeared at her office with a near-naked infant crying at her breast. Lemei sat motionless, unable to move her pen to write down another account of lost jobs and corrupt bosses. *It's all futile*, she wanted to tell the visitor.

The mother looked at her askance, suddenly exploding: "Disgusting, you call yourself a journalist? Clutching your iron rice bowl, not giving a fart about the rest of us! Look at my baby! What chance does she have, born into a society of spineless people? You don't have children, do you?" Then the woman spat and stormed out in a huff.

Lemei nodded reverently in her direction. "I deserve all your blame." Pacing her miniature office, she felt ancient. Fifteen years of *Internal Reference* stood sentry on her bookshelf, an impenetrable wall. A blue spine, out of place, protruded at the edge and beckoned her.

*Lu Xun.*

The last time she had read his works was the summer after graduating from high school. She opened the book and leafed through the pages, her adolescent handwriting leaping at her from the margins and making her squirm. A sentence was underlined twice in bold red: *I have a dream that I will fulfill, and nothing else will distract me from my path.* She dropped the book as if scalded. How ludicrous. No wonder her young self had been smitten with him.

On the bike ride home, she passed a stalled streetcar, its overhead cable disconnected from the wire like a long braid swaying in the wind.

"*I* cut the braid!" a boy with flushed cheeks declared to the onlookers, his shiny eyes begging for admiration.

Did the boy fashion himself after the revolutionaries of 1912, abolishing the Qing dynasty's favoured pigtails? Another reincarnation of the past, a bygone dynasty re-enacted, and round and round we go.

Commuters were gathering for a new series of student speeches, flapping their bamboo fans vigorously. A doddering old man with white hair shooting out of his nostrils collected donations in his hat. "So damn hot and humid. Let's buy the kids some ice cream sandwiches."

Lemei was in no mood to stay, to look into those youthful faces with their suffocating ardour and conviction. But she emptied her wallet into the old man's hat, a capitulation.

*How far I've missed the mark with my life.*

From the top of the streetcar, a young man's voice came through the megaphone: "Lies written in ink cannot disguise facts written in blood!" Another line from Lu Xun, gashing into her like a direct accusation. She hopped onto her bike and pedalled furiously away.

She was breathless when she reached Feng's temporary apartment. As her hand hovered over the door, her courage waned. "Give it three more days. If nothing changes…" she murmured, and turned to leave.

The door opened behind her. "Hey, sis. I won't bite."

"Watching me from your peephole?"

"Come on. Even Tuzi is doing something about it."

"Tuzi? The yin-yang head barber?"

"The yin-yang head barber turned owner of a popular hair salon on Huaihai Road. You know his new gig? Giving free haircuts on the Bund to whoever's willing to hear the students out. It's time, sis, for all of us to do our part."

Her defences melted. "All right, tell me about your plan," she said and entered his apartment. A pungent smell—an odd mix of ink and chili pepper—filled her nose. The kitchen counter was shrouded in a thick layer of red dust.

"Since when are you a fan of spicy food?"

"My country wife…"

She regretted the question, sensing the quickening of tears in his chest and an urgent need for distraction. "You did all of this?" She pointed at the stacks of pamphlets lining the walls and the half-written banners littering the desk.

"Embarrassing, I know. You'd produce much, much better results. Wish I'd taken calligraphy class, or *any* class, more seriously back in the day. Feels like drawing water from a dry well. But I try… I've got to at least try."

A wave of shame rolled over her, threatening to drown her again.

"Not bad at all. It's all about getting the message across, isn't it? So, what's the goal?"

"My friend drafted this." He uncoiled a poster with a list of pleas—from more abstract ones on democracy and freedom of speech to practical requests for jobs, housing, and curbing inflation.

"Basically what the students have been demanding for weeks," she said, resisting him still. "But those things don't come easy..."

"The kids in Beijing really need our help, sis. They've got youth, energy, drive, but they're new to the struggle. We have experience. We've done it so many times—the organizing, the speeches, the banners, the whole shebang."

"I'm not sure there's much we can offer. We've fought our battles. Now it's their turn. We're no longer young..."

"How could you...?!" His face twisted. "They're not just fighting for themselves, you know. They're fighting for us too, the generation forgotten, abandoned. They're fighting for the children, for your little Lin. Don't you want her to grow up in a free country?"

She studied her brother's earnest face. She had forgotten how persuasive he could be.

"Every movement needs a megaphone and a sharp pen. You've got the pen, the platform. Help us, sis. It's *your* moment too."

"It's not like I can decide what goes in the paper."

"You're a big-shot reporter. Sure beats our group of nobodies."

She tried to remember the young Feng, with crazed eyes and flexed muscles, always ready to take down a counterrevolutionary. "You do realize you're asking for things you used to fight against, right? What happened to 'do-whatever-the-Party-asks-us'?"

"Oh, yes, I've gone to the dark side, and it's been exhilarating." He winked, a mischievous smile blooming at the corners of his mouth. "Come join us."

FOR TWO WEEKS, LEMEI treaded softly at home, cooking dinners after work, taking little Lin to the park so Ma could get some respite. She did all the bedtime duties, singing and bouncing Lin on her lap, lying by her side until she fell asleep. She was mesmerized by her daughter's sleeping face, the way her eyes moved behind the lids when she was dreaming. "There's a life, different from mine, that Ma will fetch for you," she whispered to her child. "Even if it means going to the moon and back."

A negotiation was ongoing with her senior editor. She had to seize the upper hand she'd gained the hard way—from months of notetaking and research that had gone nowhere. Lao Chen, for his part, was in a rush to send a reporter to cover the ever-changing "frontier," as he called it. He'd have preferred someone with a track record of loyalty and stability, but Lemei had volunteered so fiercely that he'd agreed to take a chance on her. "You were the Golden Girl of the Revolution, after all," he said, as he patted her shoulder and handed her the assignment letter.

On May 17, 1989, she boarded the Shanghai–Beijing Express with her brother by her side. She had finally told Ma about the reporting trip the night before, without mentioning her travel companion and downplaying its significance ("Only a routine trip. I won't go anywhere near the protest."). As the train pulled away from the bustling Shanghai station and chugged toward the rice paddies of the countryside, her heart galloped. Her moment had arrived.

She'd see history unfolding up close. She'd finally be a real damn journalist.

Outside the window of the moving train, the sun sank swiftly over the edge of the earth, and vacuumed away the speckled hope dancing on the rippling fields only a moment ago.

# 3

Shouts from outside rumbled through their shuttered windows in undulating waves. She pressed a hand to Feng's forehead. Damp, but no longer burning like before. Squatting by the sofa, she watched him sleep like an innocent child, wisps of hair falling over his quivering eyelids.

*Time to get back out there.* She sighed, straightening up. She couldn't shake the feeling that the universe had undergone a seismic shift in the interstices of time since she'd closed the door behind them, hoisting her brother's frail body onto the sofa. This last oasis, this dank room she'd been renting as a makeshift office, would be annihilated by the New World Order the minute she stepped outside. Nonetheless, she had a job to do. As she moved toward the door, pain shot up from her wrist, her body lassoed by a death grip.

"Where are you going?" Feng groaned.

She looked down at his pale, gaunt face. "I need to go back to the Square."

"I'm coming with you."

"You're in no condition to go back. You fainted out there." She shook off his hand and took a plain bun out of her bag. "Here, have some food. Sorry to break it to you, but you're too old for this. Your body can't take another round of hunger strikes."

"Solidarity with the students!" He raised a fist.

"You can show solidarity without killing yourself. Just eat the damn bun."

He tossed the bun on the floor and scanned her up and down with a sudden recognition. "What the hell are you wearing? Army uniform?"

"What do you care? I've got to go. You stay here and get some fuel, okay?"

He shot up from the sofa and tugged on her shirt with surprising strength. His face contorted eerily, morphing into a stranger's. "I won't let you walk out of here and steal my thunder again!"

"What in the world are you talking about?"

"You know what I'm talking about! People stole from me all my life—my youth, my school, twenty years of my life! Look at me, already an old man. You little bourgeoise highbrow, your belly pampered by clean water and Shanghai rice—you haven't changed a bit. *You* are the biggest thief!"

"What did I steal?"

"My big break! *I* was next in line to lead the Red Guards. You stole that away from me, Miss Big Shot."

"You've got to be kidding me! Who was bent on going to the countryside? Ten thousand horses couldn't pull you back from that damn cliff! I had nothing to do with it. I don't have time for your nonsense!" She slapped his hand off her belt and made for the door.

He clung to her from behind in a tight embrace, suddenly shaking. "I've always wanted to be a soldier, sis. Not a farmer, not a worker, but a soldier. In the village, if it wasn't for my darling girl, I'd have gone with the paramilitary. I'd be a soldier by now ..."

"What do you want from *me*?!"

"Let me wear the uniform for a day. You have the camera, take a picture of me so I'll have proof."

"I need the uniform today!" Lao Chen's stern warning rang in her ears: *Little Deng has given his edict. Wear your army uniform and press badge if you don't want to be mistaken for a counterrevolutionary.*

"It's the least you can do, you dirty thief!" Feng's voice hardened again.

She struggled out of his arms. "Fine, suit yourself!" She unbuckled her belt and threw it at him. In a minute, she'd stripped off the uniform and put her regular clothes back on. "Hope you're happy, nutcase! Stay here and play your dress-up."

"My picture?"

"Later! If I still have film left. Don't leave the apartment—that's an order!" She grabbed her Nikon and ran, unable to stand another minute of his madness.

"Yes, ma'am!"

When she turned for a final glance, Feng was in a perfect salute, his eyes shining earnestly under a soldier's cap.

. . .

SHE FLEW OUT OF Damucang Hutong and headed south on Xidan Street. The world had indeed altered irrevocably during the hour she'd been inside. The smell of sulfur assaulted her nose and stung her eyes. The sound of bullets firing into the air—unthinkable even a few hours ago—made her shudder. Only days before, she had been filming the students sharing tea and breakfast buns with PLA soldiers. The young soldiers had smiled self-consciously, their faces beet red, while the students chanted, "People's Army is for the people!" But that friendliness between the two sides had decidedly evaporated.

Civilian crowds were streaming out of every hutong and alleyway, marching toward Chang'an Avenue, their faces sombre, devoid of the frenzied but hopeful excitement of the recent past. "Protect our children, erect the barricade!" they shouted. She followed the throng eastward toward the Square, talking to the protestors, snapping photos. Beside her, a group of women in their forties strode in silence, their nightgowns flowing in the wind, tears coursing down their beautiful, lined faces. A dozen locals in their pajamas and bamboo slippers climbed to the roof of a deserted bus, waving banners that read *No killing of peaceful protesters!* The crisp breeze carried snippets of speeches from the centre of the Square, young voices imploring each other to stay strong.

"Coming through, coming through!" A middle-aged man pedalled full-force on a three-wheeled bicycle cart, charging down Chang'an Avenue against the tidal wave of the crowd. Four men flanked the wooden cart, yelling and diverting traffic.

Lemei dashed to the party of five and hollered over the great din: "Anyone hurt?"

The pedaller's gaze, bottomless and blank, sailed right through her.

One of the running men, with a bushy, unkempt beard, pointed at the group's leader. "His son got shot! My daughter saw him west of Xidan."

"Can I help?"

"Come along!"

"What was his son doing there?"

"Putting up barricades, him and his friends. The army's closing in. Several kids were shot at Muxidi. We can't let them get any closer!"

A hefty cloak of futility shrouded her: a human chain of flesh and blood, against tanks and machine guns. *Retreat, retreat!* she wanted to scream, but more were overtaking her, turning westward and joining the search for the boy. They were racing in the direction of the army now, the sound of gunfire, not unlike firecrackers, bouncing off the buildings. A burning bus a few blocks ahead lit the evening sky, licks of red flame flaring up, hissing and crackling, a raging fire beast. The pedalling father breathed heavily, sweat raining down the sides of his face. He flung his shirt off; his back muscles strained with each push. She snapped a photo of him from behind—a moth flying headlong into hellfire. She took a few more, until the pedaller collapsed in her lens, his rickshaw slumping to one side.

"My son!" The father darted toward a body on the steps of the Cultural Palace of Nationalities. Others were already tending to the boy, wrapping shirts haphazardly around his wounds to stem the bleeding. The father hoisted his son into his arms, raced back to the rickshaw, and laid him on the wooden cart. A shrill cry leaped out of her throat as Lemei caught a glimpse of the bloody mass.

"Union Medical," the bearded man ordered. "Go north on Huayuan."

"It's full. I just came from there," someone said.

"Try Tongren Hospital."

"Also full!"

"Union Medical is still taking patients for emergency surgery!"

The grieving father stood motionless, scanning the crowd with confused, bloodshot eyes. Lemei rushed to his side. "Comrade, let's try Union Medical. It's the closest, right by where I'm staying. I have a phone there, can make calls to other hospitals if needed."

They lifted the father onto his bike and pushed the rickshaw up Huayuan Street. It was impossible to look away now, with the boy's cheek touching the back of her hand. He couldn't be more than fifteen or sixteen, full-lipped and baby-faced. Blood had soaked through the white shirt around his neck. She counted an additional five bullet holes on his torso and wondered if anyone had checked his pulse, if they were all acting out of wishful thinking. They passed her temporary apartment and reached the entrance of Union Medical. The air was putrid, the metallic smell of blood mixing with the stench of urine and feces. Disfigured bodies lay strewn across park benches and wooden planks, surrounded by floating faces of shock and despair. Injured youths huddled together, dazed and silent. On the west side of the entrance, middle-aged volunteers were forming a line to give blood. An elderly nurse with hollow eyes approached their rickshaw as if ascending from the Underworld, her fingers alighting on the boy's wrist.

"I'm sorry, he's dead," she said matter-of-factly, running her hand over the boy's half-open eyelids. "You can take him in and wait for a morgue space, but we can't guarantee a spot tonight."

Colour drained from the father's face; his eyes rolled back. Bystanders rushed to support him, but he shoved them away and keeled over by his son, letting out a yowl so wild and raw that Lemei cowered. He buried his face in the boy's neck, shoulder, torso, his lips dripping with his son's blood. He seemed to want to absorb his child back into himself. Feeling like an intruder, she shot furtive glances at the father's contorted face, his jerky sobs echoing in her skull. Her chest pounded, on the verge of explosion. A few steps away, the bearded man sank to the ground, rubbing his face so hard it turned purple.

"Murderers! Down with the Fascists!" someone bellowed.

She edged toward the bearded man. "Shall we inform the mother?"

"She passed away when the kid was four. It's just him and his Ba..." He choked on his words.

"Down with the Fascists!" The chants were gaining momentum. Passersby poured in from every direction, kneading the father's back, murmuring condolences in his ears. Several attempted to break the seal between father and son, to no avail. An image flickered in front of her eyes, of her little Lin lying on the rickshaw, bleeding her life away. She knew the father could never survive this. Even if he did, he'd grow into a bitter old man, gnawed away by guilt, wishing for the rest of his life to switch places with his child.

She raised a fist and joined the chants.

. . .

AT THAT MOMENT, A soldier appeared like a phantasm in an ill-fitting uniform, standing a few metres away, arms stretched wide, an idiotic grin on his face.

"Take a picture, take a picture!" he shouted at her, like a comical figure from a low-budget school play, bursting at the seams of his costume. The pant legs and sleeves, too short for his physique, revealed his bare calves and forearms.

The crowd stood in stunned silence.

"Pig!" a young woman spat, breaking the spell. A stone whooshed past Lemei and pierced her brother's left eyelid, blood cascading down his cheek. Shocked, he was rooted to the spot wearing a frozen smile, a grotesque scarecrow.

"Feng, go home!" she screamed, but her voice was zapped by the cacophony surging around her.

"Kill the Fascist! A life for a life!" The crowd charged at Feng, hurling bricks and rocks. She saw him snap to attention and dart out of Damucang Hutong, pivoting sharply to the right.

"Shit!" She grabbed the nearest man by the sleeve, who was swinging an iron pipe. "Don't ... That guy ... the guy in the uniform is innocent!"

"Accomplice bitch!" He scowled at her and struck her head with his pipe. She collapsed, a sharp ache climbing the base of her skull and spreading across her scalp. Bracing for more, she wrapped her head in her arms. But the attacker, chasing after the crowd, showed no further interest in her. Lemei struggled to prop herself up, the black cloud in front of her eyes blinding her. Sirens, gunfire, shouts, and cries clashed in her ears. She crawled to the side of the alleyway and tried again to stand up, steadying herself against the jagged stone wall. Her legs shook but didn't buckle. Head still throbbing, she rode a wave of adrenaline and thrust herself forward.

On Xidan Street, a new tide of protestors engulfed her. She craned her neck and spotted the bearded man at the tail of a group, disappearing into Tangzi Hutong. Like swimming up a roaring waterfall, she elbowed through the crowd with all her might. More rickshaws carrying the injured tore into the traffic and swept her sideways. She dodged them clumsily, losing her balance, and bounced between pockets of protestors. By the time she entered the west end of Tangzi Hutong, she knew it was too late. A fetid smell smacked her in the face. Bone-chilling shrieks penetrated the booming chants of the mob.

"No, stop, stop, please!"

A tightly packed throng filled the narrow and winding hutong, an impenetrable artery. She saw a leaping fireball from afar, a charred, agonized face flickering in and out of the carmine blaze.

"Stop! Water! My brother! Not a soldier!" She squeezed her way in, begging incoherently, her pleas met with more curses and chants. "Kill! Kill!" Rocks whistled unremittingly over her head and landed in the flames.

She inched closer to the front, watching the fireball crumble against the brick wall after a final screech. Feng's face had been reduced to a fleshy surface with gaping craters. A row of white teeth glowed, shrouded by the blackened skin. Her stomach heaved, sour liquid rising with alarming speed and projecting out of her mouth. Her knees wobbled, but she aimed at the white teeth and hurled herself toward him. Grasping hands pawed at her shoulders, a searing pain. She fell backward into a net of flailing arms, crisscrossing her body, pinning her down on the cobblestones. Hollowed faces with bloodthirsty glares, demons of pandemonium, descended on her. Black currents closed her burning eyes. Then the earth broke apart and devoured her in a pit of complete darkness.

THEY STRAPPED HER DOWN on a gurney for the night, and the day after, in the cramped hallway of Union Medical. She retched into a bucket over and over, her throat inflamed and raw as though scraped by sand. The smell of open wounds and bleeding flesh made her gag for a long time after, but her belly was so empty that nothing would rise up anymore. Every few minutes, a mangled mass would pass her by, carried on a park bench or in friends' arms. Someone would yell for doctors and nurses and break down when none could be found. Medical workers periodically emerged from surgeries, dazed and bone-tired, wringing their hands, pleading for patience and order. The floor was slick with blood, the hallway filled with anguished cries. But she couldn't close her eyes. Lurking behind her eyelids was something more gruesome—the charred remains of her own flesh and blood, crammed away in a mortuary cabinet two storeys below her feet.

*Am I the murderer?* The question haunted her. She asked for a pen and paper from a nearby schoolgirl who wore a single eyepatch. Inhaling sharply, she began to scribble, her head hammering, her body pricked by thousands of needles.

*Write it down. Write it all down.*

It was the only way to outrun the paralyzing guilt, and the unshakable feeling that her brother had perished in her place.

# 4

JUNE 24, 1989

SHANGHAI

From the window of her tiny cell, she could see a murky river forming on the street. The rain had poured unrelentingly for three days. "There's a hole in the sky!" the nurse had said this morning, cackling. Lemei stared into vast sheets of rain, wondering if the streets of Beijing were equally flooded, if heaven was in cahoots with the powerful, flushing away human blood and remains into the sunless underground sewer system, leaving the city swept clean of incriminating evidence.

The lady next door was at it again, pounding the wall between their cells—*boom, boom, boom*—like gunfire. She had to get out of here. But would they ever listen to her, after everything that had happened last week?

What a total disaster—a breakdown at work in front of Ke. But it couldn't be helped; sooner or later they'd have found an excuse to send her here. Just look at the way they had watched her since she returned from the capital—the sideways glances, the mid-sentence silence whenever she walked into a room. They'd only been biding their time before she cracked.

*Haven't I conceded enough?*

Her heart contracted as she recalled Ke's twisted logic. After reading the first draft of her article he'd said, "If it's civilians slaughtering each other, there's no moral to the story. Got to be civilians against a soldier."

"But my brother was not a soldier, had never been a soldier," she'd argued, as if the truth mattered.

Four drafts later, Ke was still not budging. "If a soldier was killed as a direct consequence of a civilian casualty, the story is still not good enough."

Her most recent draft had looked like a grisly battle-ground under his red pen.

"Too much moral ambiguity! Our country can't afford that right now. We need absolute moral conviction at this critical juncture."

"What exactly do you suggest?"

"Get rid of the part about the boy. Make your position clear. It's a story about an out-of-control mob savaging our PLA soldier, an unarmed one at that."

"That'd be an outright lie."

"Not a lie. A partial truth, if you will. If you still want to pass the censor..."

"I can't do that."

"Let me remind you, we didn't ask for this article. You insisted on writing it. Lao Chen offered you a sick leave, but you came back."

"I need to tell this story right. I owe my brother that much."

SU CHANG

"Look, I'm sorry about your brother, but now's not the time to let your emotions get in the way."

"Just one true story."

"Lemei, you don't seem to understand the kind of responsibility our paper has in this urgent battle of hearts and minds."

"I've been a good foot soldier. One damn true story, that's all I'm asking. I beg you..."

"Pull yourself together."

"Let me talk to Lao Chen."

"He's in political studies with senior editors across the country." Ke sighed grimly. "Even that cocky editor at *People's Daily* has been sacked. No one's safe now!"

"Editor Wu?"

"Who else?" Ke snorted. "Calls himself the ethnographer of the Square, amplifying students' voices... Damn arrogant fool! Just two weeks ago, they were turning a blind eye to his little rebellion. Now? He's looking at a minimum of five years. The wind has shifted. The hardliners are winning. Let's not get caught in the crossfire!"

From the shadowed corner of the editor's office, Feng lifted his head, wearing that silly grin of his. Her big-boned, bull-headed, star-crossed kinsman. The brother she had a hand in killing.

"Pull my article then," she snapped. "Don't even bother running it." She nodded at the ghost that had not left her side.

"Is that a threat? We need a piece for the Politics section. It's the eleventh hour!"

"I won't put my name on this draft anyway. My brother lived his whole life as a pawn of the system. For once, he wanted to be a human being. You want to turn him into a pawn even in death? Over my dead body!"

"What about tomorrow's paper?"

"I don't give a damn! Find some other liar to fill the page. What's the point of a paper if we just lie through our teeth, day in and day out?"

Tears flooded her face and neck. Staring at her editor, she saw the reflection of a crazed woman in his eyes.

That was all he'd needed to pull the trigger, calling security first, then an ambulance to the city's infamous psychiatric ward, all the while flashing her—his disobedient underling—a menacing, bulldog-like smile.

AT ELEVEN, a pretty nurse came to inject her with a drug cocktail, the second dose of the day. As if on cue, her head throbbed, liquifying. At lunch, the same nurse brought fried pork and pudding on a tray. Her stomach churned; she rubbed her nose harshly. Three weeks. She couldn't expel the stink lodged deep inside her nostrils, the smell of charred flesh.

"Please, I told the doctor, I can't..." she begged the nurse, pointing at the meat.

Eyeing her with annoyance, the nurse dumped the pork in her oversized garbage bag and stomped out. For the next hour, Lemei gaped at the translucent jelly and the pool of thin drool dripping and accumulating on her plate. Her hand shook so badly that it could no longer complete the intricate operation required to bring the dessert to her mouth. So she slouched in a trance, watching sunrays penetrate the surface of the pudding, illuminating the many shades of pink.

The days when she made jellies with little Lin rushed back to her. It was their spring tradition. She'd take Lin to the Botanical Garden, where the cherry trees showered them with light pink petals. The child would gather the fallen flowers in her chubby fists and, with a triumphant smile, deposit them into her silky sack. Once home, they'd bury the petals in clear jelly cones—glass-like mini-towers entombing the cherry blossoms. Her little daughter, ever the sentimentalist, would study their creation for hours, refusing to consume the treats, as if she could intuit, at her tender age, the intimate connection between beauty and mortality.

BY THREE IN THE afternoon, her headache had mercifully subsided. She had one hour to herself before a third dose of the drug cocktail. She took out a notebook from under her pillow. Last night, she'd attempted a self-portrait on its cover; it had turned out to be a tousle-haired she-monster, baying into the wind. She turned to the first page: *Diary of a Madwoman*—hats off to Lu Xun's masterpiece. She flipped ahead to her last entry:

> *Twenty years since you killed my Ba and stole Ma's soul I forgot it all I'll pay for my amnesia*
> *What good is our ancestors' grand old civilization? Analects Tao Te Ching Doctrine of the Mean The Great Learning thousands of years of pretty words destroy them all! Start afresh from a new mould*
> *Should've gone with the snakehead if only I'd kissed his dainty feet and begged for a spot on his freedom ride*

She winced and crossed out that last sentence, her mother's wails suddenly ricocheting in her skull. After her return from the capital, Ma had climbed into her bed night after night, clasping her hands in the dark, desperate for an earthly tether. When the sun filtered through their windows in the morning, Ma's black, vacuous eyes would deflect all light, like levees that contained an ocean of grief. She had made Lemei promise in front of her father's urn that she'd never leave her side again. "Otherwise," she'd hissed, "you can collect my bag of white bones upon your return."

Had Ma been sleeping at all since she was carted to this loony bin?

The words in her notebook seemed childish now, bursts of incoherent thought in fitful strokes, clashing and breaking into each other.

She tucked the notebook away, but not before adding a single line:

> *Too late for me but not for Lin save her save the children*

PART FOUR
# LOVE, ILLUSION
2004–2011

# 1

## *Lemei*

It was supposed to be a different kind of day.

Lemei paced her low-ceilinged motel room, revisiting the whirlwind events. Lin had been radiant this morning in her Oxford cap and gown, a magenta Hawaiian lei around her crane-like neck. But she looked nervous, her eyes downcast the whole time she was on the commencement march. By the time the graduates sat down, a dozen rows ahead of the family seating area, the salty ocean air was pulsing with jubilation. Young men and women hugged and babbled with overwrought gesticulations. Uncertainly, Lin had scanned the crowd around her, and then stared down at her hands.

*So what if she's not the most sociable.* Watching her daughter, Lemei had to suppress the uneasiness creeping up her spine. *Don't compare. Americans are famous for their flamboyance. We Chinese are reserved, after all.*

After the speeches, the graduating class lined up to receive their diplomas from Chancellor Yang. Every newly minted graduate bowed and beamed at their robust band of cheerleaders, who hopped with their funny hats and party blowers, making a big fuss. Lemei teared up, moved by the community spirit. Then it was her daughter's turn; Lin nodded at the audience, a hint of a smile blooming around her lips, but it quickly withered and died a premature death. Not a single student made a peep. A jolly song blared from the loudspeaker like a mockery, while a smattering of applause came from the family section, polite and distracted.

Lemei felt her temples throb. "Congratulations!" she wailed in Chinese, her raspy voice zapped by the music. Lin had already walked off the stage. The next kid was up, rousing the crowd as usual. A white mother turned and studied Lemei with curious eyes. Sweat slithered down her back, soaking the dress suit she'd ordered for the occasion, one that had cost her three months' salary. With a quivering hand, she shielded her eyes from the mercilessly glaring Californian sun.

LATER, SHE FOLLOWED HER daughter in search of a place to eat. The student village of Isla Vista simmered and swung in the heat. Raucous bravos and demands for shots filled her ears. Young graduates, clutching beer bottles and cocktail glasses, staggered sideways and crashed into them, apologies coming on strings of giddy laughter. In front of every restaurant, long lines of sunburned and fatigued families waited their turn to celebrate their progeny's milestone. It seemed like an impossible mission to find a seat anywhere. Lemei had in fact anticipated this and made a dinner reservation at Madam Lu's China House, but Lin had vetoed it as soon as she heard the name.

"My guidebook gave the place rave reviews," Lemei insisted.

"Too expensive."

"That's the whole point! This is a once-in-a-lifetime occasion. We've got to celebrate in style. Ma's treat, of course."

Lin shook her head resolutely. She led Lemei to a hole-in-the-wall taco shop, a cheap haunt for college kids after drunken late-night parties. A desert landscape and sombrero-clad guitarists beckoned from a faded mural.

"They offer student discounts here. This may be the last time I get to use it," Lin said airily.

Lemei bit her lip. *Compromise. Don't make a scene. It's her big day.* She hung her head and tailed her daughter to the only table inside. Grease and brown sauce stained the plastic chairs. She bunched a ball of napkins from the counter and scrubbed. Beads of sweat covered her forehead; the stains seemed permanent. She felt the futility of her actions, but it was the only thing she could do to make this absurd situation a tad better. The owner glanced at the standing pair askance.

"Ma, sit down!" Lin hissed, forcing the napkins out of her hands and pressing her into a seat. Lemei pictured the stains infiltrating the fibres of her fancy dress pants, a permanent mark on her precious possession.

Her daughter flipped through the menu. "Okay if I order for you?"

Lemei nodded. A rhetorical question since she couldn't read the menu. "But no—"

"No meat. Of course, I remember."

Lemei eked out a smile of gratitude. *She remembers. A taboo from a past that should've been long forgotten.*

"I've never had Mexican food before. This'll be an adventure," she said, reconciling. "Quite a ceremony back there. I'm so proud of you."

"Thanks, Ma. Means a lot to me, you flying all this way."

"Nice to finally see your school, your teachers and classmates. See you in your element."

They spoke politely and cautiously, like diplomats representing different nations at a peacekeeping summit. When their tacos arrived, they ate slowly as if to prolong the silence. Lemei chewed the oversalted mushroom taco, the raw cilantro and chili powder too potent for her palate. She picked out the red onions and laid them, one by one, on her plate like sacrifices.

"I didn't know your chancellor was from Chongqing."

"Yes, Chancellor Yang is well-loved here."

"A Chinese immigrant like yourself. Now in the highest echelon of American society. How very inspiring!"

"I suppose that's the American Dream you always talked about."

Lemei eyed her daughter carefully. Lin had said those words without a hint of sarcasm. "So you still believe in the American Dream?"

"Sure."

"Good! Today's the first step, a big milestone. Cheers to you, kiddo!"

They clinked glasses and sipped on the ice water. Lemei was invigorated by the chilled liquid. "An applied math degree must be popular in the job market. We all know

American kids can't do math," she said, chuckling.

Her daughter studied the eviscerated tacos on her plate and said nothing.

Lemei weighed her words and mentally rehearsed a casual tone, fending off the hunch that something sinister was about to pounce on her. "So... what's next? Which American firm will have the honour of enjoying my brilliant daughter's service?"

"I don't know."

"No? I thought international students only have a year to work? On the postgraduation visa?" She rummaged through her bag for her little notebook. It was almost exactly four years ago that she'd consulted a Shanghai lawyer about Lin's student visa, work visa, and of course, the most coveted green card, planning years into the future. She flipped to a page with copious handwritten notes. "Practical training on an F-1 visa, maximum twelve months. Your clock's ticking, kid."

Lin pursed her lips and shifted in her chair.

"Was the job market bad this year? Maybe you should apply for more positions. Now's not the time to be picky."

"I did... and there *was* an offer."

"There was? Where?"

"Bank of America in LA."

A boulder fell off her chest. Lemei let out such a hoot that the owner rushed out of the kitchen. "Everything okay?" he asked with a look of alarm.

She beamed at the stranger and spat out the few English words she knew. "Bank! Offer! Woohoo!"

"Ah, congratulations!" The owner gave a thumbs-up, clearly amused by her little performance, and went back behind the curtain.

"Ma, slow down. Something else came up."

"Does Bank of America sponsor your green card?"

"I don't know. Probably H-1B first, and then...potentially, yeah."

"Remarkable. Americans will do anything for talent. Chinese, Mexicans, Indians. Doesn't matter. If you've got the skills, they'll let you stay. What a system! That's why countries like ours have brain drains." She squeezed her daughter's hand. They had made it. The Grand Plan she'd been orchestrating for fifteen years had reached its triumphant finale.

Lin raised her voice. "Can you just let me explain the situation?"

"What is it?" That creepy feeling made a swift return.

"I'm not taking the offer. I'm moving to Toronto next week. A theatre there is putting on a play of mine."

The news blew over Lemei like a desert wind. Her head spun; her sight dimmed.

"I need to be there for the rewrites, rehearsals, things like that..."

"What play? What are you talking about?"

"I picked up a creative writing class at the start of my fourth year. It sort of...*saved* me. I felt lighter, like myself again. I've been working on this play for the whole year."

Her brain was spongy. "How did you find the theatre? In Toronto? Where's Toronto? Isn't it in Canada? You're moving to *Canada*?!"

Lin giggled.

*How dare she laugh? Unfilial daughter, everything's a joke to her!*

"Yes, Ma. Toronto's the largest city in Canada. This theatre put out a call for scripts online. I sent them my work and it got picked up. A miracle, like winning a lottery ticket."

"Having an American bank sponsor your green card is like winning a lottery ticket!"

"You don't understand—"

"You're *not* throwing away your future, for some little … *play*! If you must, go there for the summer, do your fun thing, and come back to your real job."

"It's a year-long mentorship program. I don't think Bank of America can wait that long."

"Then call the theatre, tell them you're not coming. Trust me, it's not worth throwing away your entire American Dream for a play. Those two things are simply not comparable."

"Maybe not to you, but to me …"

"How will you survive there, in … *Canada*? You don't even have legal status. Be a starving artist? Live on the street? I sure as hell won't sponsor you!"

"I have a visitor's visa. The theatre will help me find an apartment. They even offer a small stipend. Ma, do you know how incredibly lucky I am? A no-name writer like me. They receive hundreds of submissions every year!"

"What do they see in *you*? Something's fishy here. Is your English really that good now? You're an immigrant!"

"Right, immigrants have nothing unique to say."

"Knock it off, you and your sarcasm. You can write on the side. Hold down a real job first. Get your green card first."

"Opportunities like this are extremely rare. I may never get a second chance—"

"Think clearly, Lin! What happens after this little play? Your time here will run out. The Americans won't let you back in—what will you do then?!" Her voice cracked. Nothing seemed to get through the thick skull of her stubborn mule of a daughter.

"I'll cross that bridge when I come to it."

"Impudent child! You're a math major! All those years of hard work—you'll let it all go to waste?"

"All sunk cost to me. How long do I have to throw good time after bad? I've always wanted to write. You know it, Ma. I used to be such an avid reader—novels, poems, I *inhaled* them all, until you put a stop to it." Lin drew a sharp breath. "Never mind, let's not go there."

Pain lodged behind her eyelids. "Of course, *I* am the villain."

"Math was only supposed to be my ticket out. I'm not banker material. I want to be a writer, like *you*!"

"Well, *don't*!" Lemei cringed at the shrillness in her voice. She stared at her daughter as waves of queasiness washed over her. A silent blizzard of words clogged her throat.

*Your Ma, this so-called writer, a gigantic failure. Never wrote a single piece with substance, with TRUTH.*

*Your Ma only had one dream and you're crushing it to a pulp. Well done, you unfilial...*

The room was boiling and spinning. She threw a ball of bills on the table and staggered out. Her vision was blurring fast; her legs wobbled and swayed and gave out beneath her.

SHE TOOK THE LAST Greyhound bus from Santa Barbara to LA, her head pounding the whole way. She had promised her daughter she'd rest at the motel after her dizzy spell, but she couldn't stand the silence and loneliness, not after what felt like a mortal blow. How had she missed this?

When was the last time they had really talked? And how could they talk, with all the treacherous minefields and hushed taboos?

When she showed the address to the cab driver at LA's cigarette-littered bus terminal, the middle-aged Latino man eyed her suspiciously. After a ten-minute ride, passing a long parade of low-rises with ugly, stained facades, she found herself in front of a dilapidated three-storey walk-up. Shuffling her feet on patches of dry, withered grass, she scanned the complex. There were a dozen units in the building, stacks of newspapers and old toys cluttering the tiny balconies, the railings leprous with old orange paint. Holes dented the brick veneer, revealing the mustard-coloured wood structure underneath. A middle-aged couple plodded out of the building to take down the laundry hanging between two saplings, their complexions melding seamlessly into the misty dusk. She was startled when they said hello to her, and practically ran up to the second floor. She knocked on the door that had the number 6 on it. No response. It was resolutely dark inside the apartment.

"Wei, you there? It's me!" Her knocking grew desperate.

Number 5 opened the door a slit. "Wei's still at work," a young Black woman said in a tired voice. "Come back later."

Lemei leaned toward her. "Where ... she work?"

"Chinatown."

"I go there?"

"Who are you?"

"Best friend." Lemei rooted around in her bag, producing a picture, a notebook, and a pen. "This, us!" She handed the photo to the neighbour. Under the dim corridor light,

SU CHANG

the woman examined it and looked at Lemei uncertainly.

*I know, it was a lifetime ago. Who are these fresh-faced girls grinning shoulder to shoulder?*

"Come back later." She tossed the photo back to her.

"*Please.*" Lemei edged closer and gesticulated with the pen and notebook. "Where she work, write, write."

The woman sighed. She scrawled the name of a store, even scribbled a small map. Then she swiftly closed the door.

Lemei walked down the street and pivoted left after three blocks. Her ancestors' golden imperial gate rose before her like a mirage, with its glazed, wave-like ceramic tiles and arched roofs. So this was Chinatown. She thought the place looked gaudy and cartoonish, like the entrance to a theme park. Behind the gate, bold colours filled her vision. Bright red lanterns, lacquered benches, shiny pavilions with raised curves, fortune tellers perched on high towers—it was like the set for a period movie. The aroma of familiar spices hung in the air and made her stomach growl.

She circled a block three times until she recognized the face behind the checkout counter at a grocery store, with open access to the street and boxes of fruit spilling onto the sidewalk. An incandescent light bulb dangled above Wei's head, highlighting the hardened lines on her forehead and a pair of pursed lips. The short hair of her youth had morphed into a buzz cut. With her flannel, button-up shirt, washed-out jeans, and heavy boots, she could easily pass for a small-framed, middle-aged Asian man. Lemei watched as a large manager type pulled her friend to the side and hissed at her. Wei bent her head, beads of sweat accumulating on her forehead. She nodded non-stop under a rain of spit, her body minuscule in the man's shadow. The manager let her go

178

at last. She bowed at him and staggered back to her station. The customer at the front of the line, a South Asian man with a blond mohawk, shot her dagger eyes.

"Sorry, sorry," Wei said.

"Just hurry up!"

"Sorry, sorry." She kept her eyes low, her hands working in an amazing rhythm.

Wei had made only three trips back to Shanghai since her emigration to America, the last one being ten years earlier. Lemei had heard fragments of her life, but not enough to stitch together a coherent narrative. When Wei had first returned in 1981, after five years of radio silence, she was only one course shy of graduating with a comparative literature degree, but she'd decided to start all over with a computer science major. "I was stupid, too idealistic," she'd told Lemei. "CS is the way to go, the *future*."

On her second visit in early 1989, she was jubilant, feasting with Lemei during the week-long Chinese New Year celebrations. She had secured her first job in Silicon Valley. "Micro-freaking-soft! Still pinching myself every morning!" Cup after cup, Wei poured baijiu down her throat like water. Lemei had to push Yu Ma's handmade dumplings on her friend, just to slow down her drinking.

The mood of her third visit in 1994 was more sombre, but there was no sign of a downtrodden life. She still came to Lemei's apartment bearing gifts from America—vitamins for Yu Ma, a Nordstrom hat for Lemei, a GAP woollen scarf for Lin. Lemei had been jealous of her friend's good luck—to live freely in the Promised Land she'd yearned for all her life. She had imagined her lifestyle: lunches with American co-workers, shopping sprees at luxury brands, vacations on white-sand beaches by the undulating sea. After almost thirty years, Lemei was sure her friend could switch between cultures effortlessly, like slipping in and out of different outfits. Now, watching Wei from the sidewalk of Chinatown, she was peering into a parallel universe.

AT ELEVEN, THE BURLY manager informed the shoppers of the store's closing. Wei dabbed her sweaty face with a handkerchief and quietly collected her belongings. Lemei tiptoed into the store and tapped her friend on the back. "Surprise!"

Wei spun around and screeched, a strained, happy sound.

The embarrassment on her friend's face gnawed at Lemei. "I'm sorry I didn't call ahead."

"Thought you were arriving Saturday."

"Yeah, schedule change. I can sleep on the couch."

"No, no, of course you'll take the bed." Wei volunteered a hug. "Welcome to America, my friend!"

They locked their bony, shrunken frames together, feeling the sting in their eyes. *Finally, finally, finally.* They deserved a moment as long as eternity, but the manager needed to close up. At the sound of his dry cough, they wiped away the tears and straightened their spines.

"So, hungry?" Wei asked.

"Famished."

"Let's go to my buddy's restaurant. Best Shanghai noodle soup in town, slow-cooked all day long." Wei pressed a hand on the small of Lemei's back and guided her outside.

At the noodle joint, they each held a warm soup bowl to their chest, breathing in the aroma of chili bean paste and rice vinegar. The aroma of home.

Wei took a long sip from her bowl and smacked her lips like the girl Lemei remembered. "*This* can heal wounds."

"I went to your apartment first. Your neighbour told me where you work." Guilt still sloshed around her chest.

"Tanya?"

"Didn't get her name. A Black lady."

"Probably Tanya."

"Do you ... like living there?"

"The government helps with the rent. I was lucky to find a place so close to work."

"Aren't you afraid? Living among the Blacks?"

Wei chortled, a condescending sound, as if a fatuous child had spoken. "Black people are not the problem, my friend. Poverty is. Good thing we're all poor there. Nothing to be afraid of. When I first came to America, I was afraid like you. Back when I was delivering Chinese food, I did get mugged a couple of times by some Black brothers."

"Wow. When was that?"

"'84, when I graduated. I was a delivery girl for five years, before my Microsoft gig."

"I had no idea."

"I remember going into that Microsoft interview paranoid, thought I'd never scrub the fish-sauce smell off my skin. Anyway, then I met more Black people at work, and in my neighbourhood. Most are the friendliest folks you'll ever meet. Saved me a few times too. You'll see. I'll introduce you this week."

Lemei took a bite of her imitation fish cake, feeling like a simpleton who had never seen the world. She had so many questions, but had suddenly lost the courage to ask any.

"So, how was Lin's graduation?"

"A disaster."

"What happened?"

"The kid wants to move to Canada."

Wei raised an eyebrow. "Really? That's great."

"Is it? What's good in Canada?"

"What's *not* to like? It's a nicer America, with fewer guns and free healthcare. You've got a wise daughter."

"Hmm ... Canada ... Don't know anything about it." She looked up and realized her friend had stopped eating, a large pile of glistening noodles still in her bowl, untouched.

"Don't like the noodles?"

"Oh, I do. I *crave* them in fact. But I shouldn't. Why do you think I put up with that bully?"

"The Popeye at your store?"

"More like Bluto, not a nice guy. The company's decent though. A rarity in Chinatown. They pay my medical bills. You know, America's only a land of freedom if you're not sick."

"You're sick?"

"Diabetes. Diagnosed too late. My kidney's already damaged. If it was up to my doctor, I'd be on celery sticks and oatmeal for the rest of my life. I do cut down on the white flour though, don't want to be on dialysis. But once in a while, I crave a big bowl of noodle soup from home."

"Ahh ... I'm sorry." For a moment she was at a loss for words. "Is drinking out of the question too?"

Wei winced, as if the mere mention of alcohol caused her pain.

"Last time you were in Shanghai, didn't you say you had joined some Silicon Valley startup?"

Wei narrowed her eyes as though recalling the Stone Age. "Dot-com bubble. The whole company burst into flames.

They didn't pay us much, you know; all our fortune was tied up in stocks. *Looked* like I had a million bucks for a few weeks. But—poof! Money on paper, easy come, easy go."

"What a roller coaster. Why didn't you go back to Microsoft?"

"A miracle I even lasted five years there. Never learned how to kiss my manager's behind, or backstab, or self-promote. Not with my funny accent and yellow face. Ever heard of stack ranking?"

Lemei shook her head, a simpleton again.

"Never mind. In any case, they wouldn't take me back, and honestly, I don't have the stomach for more bloodbaths at annual reviews."

"Sounds rough."

"Welcome to America. After the startup, I applied for almost two hundred jobs. The whole industry had tanked. Plus, there were kids from Stanford and Berkeley and Princeton hungry for the same jobs. Not a chance for this Chinese grandma with a CS degree from a community college."

"You regret making the switch? From literature?"

"Didn't have a choice back then, did I?"

"Did you want to be ... a writer?"

"Sure, I had my pipe dream."

"That's what Lin wants to do."

"I see. Little Lin wants to be like her mother."

"I wish she didn't. Words are useless, meaningless, can't change the world a bit." Her chest clenched again.

"Is that really true?" Wei said carefully. "All those years we sneaked books around. We were crazy about them ... Yes, I know, that terrible job you had at the newspaper ... But remember, Lin has escaped; she's in a different world. And Canada! Well, sometimes I wish *I* could move to Canada." She poked her noodles with chopsticks, eyes ravenous.

"What's stopping you?"

"Oh, the usual. Love interest, long story."

"Who's the lucky guy?"

Wei dropped her chopsticks and looked intently at Lemei, a mix of disappointment and amusement in her pinched smile.

"Not a guy, a gal."

Her face tingled with heat. Memories of confusion from her youth flooded back to her. What an imbecile she had been! Or was it prejudice that had blinded her?

She wished she had baijiu to blunt the edge, to dull the humiliation eating away at her heart.

THAT NIGHT SHE LISTENED to a baby's wails and its mother's pleading, again and again like a mantra: *"Please, go the fuck to sleep."* Sleep was doing a sneaky dance, escaping from under her nose, tantalizing her. The mattress squeaked and whined every time she changed position. She remembered their last conversation before Wei emigrated to America, the year the Cultural Revolution ended. She understood it now, and the icy loneliness her friend must have felt in her bones. Wei wasn't just up against the Big Men in their cloistered chamber of law, or doctors behind the inventory of mental disorders—she wasn't even seen by her best friend. No wonder she'd had to run away.

But to what? This prison cell of a place? She scanned the bedroom—the low ceiling, the four bare walls, the bad paint job. The iron bars guarding the window, obscuring the view of a strip mall behind the building—not that it was much of a view. She sat up and let her feet touch the cold concrete floor, and then, the hard edge of a bottle in her bag. She'd asked Wei to make a pit stop at Albertsons on their way home, pretending to look for a toothbrush. She knew it was bad form to drink alone, but what if it shut down her overactive brain? The burn made her eyes leak instantly. The liquid snaked its way down, seeping into her blood, coating her insides with a layer of warmth. Her tongue, after a few seconds of numbness, could discern the grainy, woody flavour, even a hint of sweetness. She twitched and sighed and at last melted into the dark night, her friend and daughter joining in for a slow waltz. No more fighting or bickering. No more secrets.

She didn't wake up until noon. The empty whisky bottle stood on the nightstand like a monument of shame. Still drowsy, she hid the bottle under the bed and left the room. Wei fluttered between cupboards in the kitchen, her thinning hair spiky and shiny with mousse.

"Morning!"

"Sorry I overslept. Going to work soon?"

"Two hours until my shift starts. I usually head out early to stop by my girl's place." Wei tapped a large Tupperware full of soup dumplings and juicy pork buns. "She works overnight, so she's going to bed right around the time I go to work."

"You made all this for her? What a lucky girl. Tell me more about her!" Lemei said, grinning overeagerly.

*Pathetic. A sorry attempt to compensate for my years of bigotry.*

"Yeah, I'll have to fill you in. More like an ex. It's complicated. Meet me at the store tonight, and I'll take you for the best dim sum in Chinatown."

With Wei gone, Lemei roamed the streets of downtown LA for the better part of the afternoon. She was stunned by the pervasive rundown houses, the graffitied walls, the ubiquitous iron bars on windows, the homeless men reeking of urine and cigarettes, the drug addicts on the sidewalk boring into her with their leery, bloodshot eyes. She was dizzy with disappointment, feeling cheated and swindled, her whole life built on a deception.

At the dim sum joint, she slumped into the seat next to Wei, bowing her despondent head. "Where's the glamour? This is Los Angeles, home of Hollywood, no? What a dump."

"That's America for you. The uber-rich and abject poor drawing breath side by side."

"Where do the rich people live?"

"In the suburbs, behind tall gates and security guards. I'll take an afternoon off this week and we can go for a ride. West LA is nice, lots of mansions. We can't go near them, but we can gawk from afar."

"Those downtown streets, don't they remind you of Old Huangpu back home?"

"Yeah, the slum."

"Remember those families crammed into tiny alleys? All gone now, the alleys turned into eight-lane expressways. Those families moved into brand-new skyscrapers, private kitchen and bathroom and all."

"Tsk tsk, who'd have thought our Lemei, the ultimate America-lover, would someday praise the New Capitalist and look down on the Old?"

"Trust me, no one's more surprised than me."

"So, you regret sending your daughter here?"

Lemei considered the question, suddenly less straight-forward. She shook her head. "No. Folks back home still go missing after saying the wrong thing. Like my neighbour Yang, remember him?"

"The mousy little boy who used to follow us around."

"Yes. Ratty-looking still, and not the smartest either. He posted something online under his real name. A knock on the door in the middle of the night. He was invited to 'tea' by the police and didn't resurface for two months. His Ma freaked out, pestering anyone with any sort of connec-tion. Finally, he came home and threw his computer in the garbage chute. Last time I bumped into his Ma, she said he's now a Buddhist apprentice at Jing'an Temple."

"Didn't know Jing'an Temple was such a hotbed for dissidents."

"More like social discards. 'Still craving freedom? You're not meditating enough!'"

"Ha! My girl's also into meditation. Reads tons of self-help books, all telling her to meditate more. Same kind of idea: 'No money? No problem. Find your inner peace. Desire's the root of all your suffering.' This whole 'Zen' thing is having a huge comeback."

"Tell me more about this mysterious girl of yours."

"It's complicated."

"What's her name?"

"Cindy."

"You want to marry her? Are you allowed here?"

"Not yet. But earlier this year, that San Francisco mayor issued thousands of marriage licences to people like me. They're fighting it out in the court right now. People are cautiously hopeful. Probably just a matter of time."

"That's *great*!"

"Yeah," Wei muttered, looking down at the wontons on her plate.

"So what's the problem?"

She shrugged.

"Tell me."

"I'm just...not sure she's equally committed," Wei said haltingly. "She's moody, we've been on and off for four years. I know she still calls the ex she left behind in China. I think there's another woman in Monterey Park too..."

"Oh." Lemei felt her smile slipping from her face.

"But I like her so much, you know?" Wei shot a look at Lemei, a tremble in her voice. "When she's nice to me, she's everything I've ever dreamed of—pretty, witty, a golden voice. She's been through a lot. The poor thing got here through a Fujian snakehead."

"You mean she's illegal here?"

"Of course part of me knows she's probably just using me for a green card, waiting for gay marriage to be legalized. Fake marriages for green cards happen all the time."

Lemei looked into her friend's eyes, a lump in her throat. "Wei, don't—ever—let her take advantage of you, promise me?"

"That's what I tell myself. But taming the heart is another matter, right? Then again, look at me, I've got nothing to lose. Why not take a risk for love?"

Wei chuckled, wrinkles reconfiguring sharply on her face.

ON THE EIGHTH DAY of her visit, she made the mistake of drinking early. Every night, she had waited to hear her friend's steady breathing before cracking open a bottle and

188

boozing herself to blissful oblivion. Her body had adapted surprisingly, her hangover never apparent by noon, when she re-emerged from her room. But that afternoon, her imminent departure burrowed into her head like a bloodsucking tick. *One sip, just to quiet my nerves.* The fuzzy cocoon ensnared her instantly. She stopped drinking only when Tanya began a yelling match with her boyfriend, banging on the thin wall that separated their apartments. "Shit, shit." She shoved the half-empty bottle under the bed and rushed out the door for the goodbye dinner.

The sky was dusky grey, a crescent moon tearing at the edge of the clouds. She ran, tripping on her own feet, her head stuffed with cotton balls, until she saw the store and the incandescent bulb illuminating her friend like a tarnished halo. It was Saturday night. The place was packed, much busier than the other days she'd been there. Shoppers of different shades of skin sauntered around in unifying T-shirts and jeans. Her inner propagandist rolled up its sleeves and sang: *Ah, the Melting Pot in action; ah, the harmonious coexistence; ah, the nation unparalleled in its embrace of immigrants!* She leaned against a telephone pole, the warm liquor still waltzing inside her, and closed her eyes.

A woman's scream wrenched her from a lucid dream. Petrified, she saw Wei lunging toward her in slow motion. A few steps in front of her, a sandy-haired man in rags was piling up plums in his arms. He took a big bite of one, a teasing smirk on his grimy face.

"Put them down!" Wei roared, landing on the thief's back and clutching at the fruit.

The man turned and spat the half-chewed plums in Wei's face, dark juice running down her cheeks like blood. A stream of insults sprang out of his tainted mouth. Lemei caught the few words she could understand: "dirty," "Chinaman," "fuck," "go back," "chink" ("a special racial slur reserved only for us Chinese," Wei had taught her just two nights ago). Perhaps mistaking Wei for a man, the scoundrel moved rapidly. A punch, a push, a violent shove; he sent blows to her head, all the while using her as a spittoon.

Lemei's vision swayed, sights and sounds from a bygone era tumbling by. Thugs yowled in her ears, egging her on. Her best friend, as usual, could not defend herself, and it was Lemei's cue. She spotted an empty ceramic vase by the banana crates. Holding her weapon with one hand, she elbowed through the crowd thickening around the pair. *Incoming, incoming, leader of the Red Guard!* She hurled the vase at the thief with all her might, watching it shatter into sharp, glinting pieces on the back of his head. He plunged to the ground, whimpering and groaning. She closed in on the intruder and mapped out the sequence of moves. *Strike when the iron is hot!* She raised one arm, but a shooting pain reverberated from her shoulder blades down to her core. A bear paw seized her, a pair of chilly handcuffs restraining her wrists. She was spun around like a wooden doll. A heavy-set policeman glared down at her, pointing and yelling, spraying a mist of spit on her face. She couldn't understand a word he was saying.

"Don't know," she tried in English. She turned toward Wei and asked in Chinese, "Am I under arrest?"

A burn on her cheeks stunned her. The officer, eyebrows arched, cupped her face in his meaty palm and continued to holler in gibberish.

*Why don't you save your garlicky breath?*

Lemei stole a glance at her friend and saw the gratitude in her eyes, like in the olden days. Liquid pooled around Wei, her blood mixing with the Californian plum juice into a silky, crimson rivulet.

TO LIN, SHE NEVER uttered a word about her week with Wei—not about Wei's noncommittal dream girl, or the fight at the store, or the eyewitness reports that had set her free. Her friend's parting words pained her long after she left: "Don't worry about me. Nothing our time in the sixties didn't prepare me for!"

When Lin hugged her goodbye at LAX, Lemei clenched her teeth and breathed through the ache lodged deep in her shoulders. She even managed to squeeze out a faint smile. She left without giving Lin her blessing, but she didn't question again her daughter's imminent move out of America.

# 2

## *Lin*

### TORONTO

I rma, the artistic director at Fox Theatre and a longtime
transplant born in East Berlin, was a workaholic who
never stood still. She wore an efficient crew cut, save
for a puff of golden hair that spiked up like a crest. Her eyes
shone with intelligence and anxiety, behind a pince-nez
that gave her the air of a retro academic. Irma seemed to do
everything around the theatre. For the current season, she
was the director of a mainstage show, the producer of a new
works festival, the mentor of writing fellows, and seemingly
the go-to person for all lighting and sound questions at Fox.

"This is what it means to be in the theatre—a jack of
all trades! Money's always tight. We give everything we've
got," she said in her signature rapid-fire style on Lin's first
day. "Mainstage this fall: John Logan's *Red*. Know anything
about it?"

Lin shook her head, embarrassed.

"Come to the rehearsal anyway," she commanded. "All part of your initiation into the magical world."

That afternoon, Lin sneaked into the rehearsal hall in the middle of a scene. On the small, rickety stage at the front of the room, a balding man playing a painter of some stature was berating a young assistant, who hung his dejected head during his master's tirade. Then the young man lifted his eyes, and in a first timid then emphatic voice responded to the master's burning inquiries. He was no empty vessel for the elder's monologue; he had a vision of his own. Lin was struck by the liquid melancholy in his eyes, framed by those bouncy golden curls. She felt dumb, gawking at him like that, as he experimented with subtle shifts of emotion in his lines. The older painter barked an order at him. On cue, the young man dipped a thick brush into a bucket of paint and swept it across the empty canvas. He moved fast, suddenly a modern dancer, paint dripping and splashing, an extension of his arm. All Lin could do was stare and stare at the profile of his concentrating face, the primal expression on the verge of masculine violence. She gasped with relief when he finished, plopping himself on the floor with a thud.

The lights went up. Irma clapped her hands and patted the young Apollo on the shoulder. "Nicely done! We can all sleep well tonight!" He bowed his head at the beaming director and got off the stage. Scanning the room, he rested his eyes on Lin. She spun around, her heart pounding.

"Hi there," he said, already towering over her.

The intensity of those baby blues. The impossibly long lashes. It was all too much at such close range.

"You must be the new writing fellow. I'm Sasha. Pleased to meet you."

She shook the warm hand he offered. "Yes, that's me. How did you know?" She couldn't stand her wobbly voice.

"Irma warned us. She has high hopes for you, but don't let her dictate your work." He dipped his head toward her, the faint tobacco scent on his breath searing her face. "Would you come to my party tonight? Meet the gang? Irma won't be there, but all the important people will be." He winked, seeming to enjoy his effect on her. He jotted down an address and pressed the paper into her sweaty palm, his baby blues unrelenting.

"What should I bring?" she managed to say.

"Absolutely nothing. Just your beautiful self."

He winked again and strolled out of the room.

SASHA LIVED IN THE basement of his mother's rowhouse, with a separate entrance from a stamp-sized backyard garden. When Lin arrived, the "older painter" was alone at the top of the stairs, puffing smoke. Voices and music rose from below him, signalling a teeming underworld. Her whole body screamed *Run!* but the actor put a firm grip on her arm.

"New blood! Nice to meet you! I'm Vlad. Come meet the gang. We look scary, but we don't bite." He put out his cigarette and escorted her down the narrow staircase.

The basement was surprisingly spacious, its walls lined with shelves of books. More books spilled onto the floor in stacks, used as stools by the partygoers. Chatty men and women sprawled across a double bed in the corner. Sasha, in a yellow tank top, sat cross-legged on the floor, a bottle of vodka in hand, arguing with someone who looked vaguely familiar from Fox.

"Hey, you came! Welcome!" Sasha piped up as she entered the room. "Everyone, meet our new writing fellow—Lin!"

The room went quiet for a moment before greetings rushed at her from every corner. She gave a shaky wave.

"Come with me. I'll make you a drink." Sasha got up and gestured toward a breakfast bar with tall stools.

"I don't really... drink," she said, but she followed close behind him.

"You don't? Time to get started then, now that you're a writer." He turned and flashed her a smile, blowing away her good sense again. "I'll make it weak. We can all use a bit of social lubricant when we enter a new group, right?"

His hands moved in a blur, chopping strawberries and lemons into little chunks before mashing them to a pulp. Crushed ice, a splash of vodka, a vigorous shake. "Here, sip on this, slowly. You'll feel better, trust me." He nudged her with his bare shoulder. Wispy hairs stood tall all over her body. She sipped hard on the cocktail, desperate to focus on the stinging sensation unfurling on her tongue.

Sasha pointed at his friends from Fox one by one: "Alex, Igor, Adrian, Mikhail, Anastasia, Katina, Paulina." She repeated each name three times in silence, an old trick for memorization, and for regulating her heartbeat.

"Very attractive bunch indeed," she said. Then it dawned on her. "Everyone here is... *white*?"

"Irma didn't tell you? Fox was founded by Russian Canadians, and until recently, we've stayed very close to our founding community."

"She didn't mention it at all."

"The board hired her two years ago, our first non-Russian artistic director. The plan's to move away from Russian-facing programming, to be more inclusive and diverse. Irma takes her job very seriously."

"Hence, me."

"You're our key to a larger world," he declared, impersonating Obi-Wan Kenobi.

"Some big shoes to fill. I had no idea I was such a trailblazer."

"No pressure. Your presence alone is already helping Irma. You're ticking the diversity checkbox, bringing in the grants, even if the whole show is a colossal failure. Which, of course, it won't be," he added quickly.

She didn't like the sound of this, but he was saluting her with a flourish and a grin. She couldn't care about anything else.

"I'm a total newbie," she muttered after a pause.

"Irma digs newbies. She fancies herself an experimental theatre creator. You'll fit right in."

Even in his smooth low tenor, the hint of sarcasm singed her.

LATER, THE FOX GANG talked about the shows in the new season.

"I still can't believe the Great Reformer greenlit it. She *despises* shows with mainstream accolades," said Paulina, a striking raven-haired beauty.

"Sasha and I worked on her for a good four months. Two public polls. In the end, the audience picked the play. Democracy prevailed!" Vlad raised his glass at Sasha.

"I'm afraid money prevailed, old pal," Sasha said. "Fox needs at least one mainstream show a year to fill the fiscal hole, from all those 'experiments' Irma constantly puts us through."

Lin's cheeks were aflame. She was clearly one of those *experiments*.

"The play is the best of both worlds," Sasha continued. "It's about a Russian painter—immediately a crowd-pleaser with our longtime subscribers—but it's also about avant-garde art and written by a gay playwright. Irma couldn't resist *that*."

"Why are *you* so attached to the play?" Mikhail asked.

Sasha turned pensive, his fingers tracing the feminine contours of his ocean-blue vodka bottle. His voice was wistful when he spoke again. "Rothko reminds me of my old man. I want to get closer to him, observe, dissect, so I don't turn into him someday." He smiled enigmatically, scanning the room before locking eyes with Lin. "Enough about me, let's hear everyone's favourite movies and books so far this year. Starting with our new writer." He winked at her.

"Me? I don't know." Her heart raced anew. "Hmm, I'm following this writer-director couple. They're working on a trilogy about Asian girls and women, the second one just came out a few weeks ago—*Foolish Ant*, I think it's called. About their daughter who lives in Boston and struggles with her identity. Her mom is Chinese and her dad is Japanese—"

"And look what they did to me!" Igor hooted drunkenly from the far side of the room, lifting up the corner of his right eyelid and pressing down his left, before collapsing into a pile of books.

Lin lost all her words; her vision blurred.

"Shush, you alcoholic! Are you five?" Sasha yelled at the bleary-eyed offender.

"Yeah, shut up!" others joined in.

"Sorry, what did I say?" Igor murmured, already half-asleep.

"I'm so sorry." Sasha looked at her guiltily. "He's always been an idiot after a few drinks. Never mind him, please go on."

"Not much to say. A slow art film, you have to watch it to get it." She drew in her knees so she wouldn't shiver, averting her eyes from Sasha, from the pity written all over his face.

The conversations meandered from movies to books. She half listened, questions popping in and out of her head. Sasha and Vlad were loyalists to German literature, especially Hesse, Mann, and Remarque. *Was Igor bullied or a bully in his childhood?* Katina and Paulina were disciples of Proust and George Sand. *The mean gestures—were they such playground mainstays that he could go on autopilot years later?* Everyone read the contemporary Americans too, and religiously followed the *Times'* Sunday book reviews. *Was everyone else thinking the same, still too sober to let their animal selves show?* Several times, the Fox gang called on her to give an opinion on a book, and she could only offer an empty stare. She felt it, their disappointment circling her like a flock of vultures: *She hasn't read anything! Calls herself a writer—what an imposter.* Sasha saved her every time, steering their attention away. She ignored his concerned gaze as the popcorn-like questions inundated her.

At the night's end, when everyone had drifted past alcohol-fuelled euphoria toward a state of catatonia, Sasha rubbed his face and inhaled deeply. Like a stealthy nocturnal predator, he crawled at a measured pace toward Paulina, who was drinking by the bed. He put his mouth to her ear and whispered, making her giggle. His mouth was seeking something else, inching closer to her flaming lips. She pushed him away with the graceful arc of her long white arms. But he wouldn't give up; he was begging now. She tapped a finger on his nose as if scolding a wayward child. He protested in Russian, louder, whinier. She gave him a final smile before rising to gather her purse at the door. Sasha stared at her back, a possessive stare, but she was gone in a flash.

Lin felt her heart seize up. Time to go. She stepped over the sleeping bodies on the floor, past Sasha, pretending he wasn't there.

"Hey, don't go yet."

"It's late. I have an early meeting with Irma."

"I'm really sorry about Igor. What an asshole."

"He was drunk."

"Still, no excuse."

"Anyway."

"Wait, just a minute."

He went into the kitchen and came out holding a large cloth bag. "Take some books, whatever you want." He pressed the bag into her hand. She let her eyes feast on him— chiselled chin, broad shoulders, sculpted chest—her desire mixed with a lurch of anger.

*Don't be so smug. I was a bookworm too. Ma and I used to read loads of books together.*

As if on cue, Ma's shrieks echoed in her ears, followed by the sound of snapping and smashing, and the sight of her treasured books shredded into a mountain of jagged flakes, shimmering under Laolao's broom.

She shoved the bag back at him. "Recommend something for me."

# 3

## *Lin*

Her play, about a Chinese-American mathematician whose AI invention was wreaking havoc in her immigrant community, had hit a solid wall. The ever-productive Irma had scrawled notes on every page of the current draft. "My preliminary suggestions. Mull them over. Write a second draft," she had ordered.

Most days, Lin huddled in a small office next to the rehearsal hall, staring at the director's notes, too paralyzed to make a move. She wriggled and writhed. She paced the room. She typed on her computer, only to delete everything. She tried writing long-hand and soon filled the trash bin with discarded scenes. Irma had asked for a structural change, even a genre change. Lin felt like a mother whose baby had gone in for a routine checkup and come away with a mandatory multi-organ transplant. Every afternoon, the actors gathered in the room a thin wall away and filled her ears with pre-rehearsal chatter. She gave up on writing a single decent line of dialogue. A family of sparrows was building a nest outside her window, carrying twigs and leaves in their beaks, fluttering to and fro and flaunting their freedom. A curious young one knew how to get on her nerves, peeking in at her as if visiting a prisoner through the small window of her cell, until she tapped on the glass and shooed it away.

When the bell chimed, she'd walk into the rehearsal hall, defeated and ashamed. She needed more than a room of one's own; she needed an urgent transfusion of talent! She'd watch the actors show off their craft, teasing and taunting, egging each other on—like in a team sport—to sink deeper into their characters' skin. She'd grow jealous, feeling like a lone, deflated buoy bobbing and sinking in the vast ocean, drifting, drifting.

AT HER NEXT MEETING with Irma, Lin admitted she was making zero progress and had started dreading her daily writing sessions. Irma waved away her concerns as if swatting a pesky wasp.

"Thinking, not writing, is part of the process. All writers go through it," she said in her hard-sounding German accent, which emerged whenever she was stressed. "Don't worry about the daily word count or silly things like that. Think big-picture."

"Can we talk specifics? You wanted me to flesh out the AI tool as a character, a moving, talking being, but that changes the integrity of the play, in my humble opinion."

"I think it'll indeed be wonderful to hear more from Oracle Eve herself. I have an actress in mind already. We're blessed with some excellent modern dancers in our company. She'll add a much-needed visual dimension."

"But this is not a song-and-dance piece. Nor is it a fantasy. The show may look prettier with a dancer, but it dilutes the harshness of the story, which is deeply rooted in realism." She'd been rehearsing this bit and was relieved it came out in one piece.

Irma cocked her head to one side and watched Lin with a taut smile, amused by her little rebellion. "Are you enjoying *Red*?"

"Yes. It's coming together nicely."

"Do you know why a guy famous for his floating, coloured rectangles still inspires and invigorates decades after his death? Because he *refused* to settle for 'realism.'" She spat out the last word like it was dirty. "You know what he called himself? A *mythmaker*."

Irma leaned in and hissed, "That little emptiness you felt in your belly, that emptiness that drove you to write in the first place, where did it come from? A lack of mythology of our times! If I want realism, I'll go read a newspaper. Give us a Greek tragedy. Give us not a modern software, but a goddess imbued with humanity's folly. Blow things out of proportion! Give us ... *drama*." Irma's laser-green eyes burrowed under her skin, digging for an affirmation.

Lin nodded hastily and looked away. She left Irma's office unconvinced. But the director, with her strident voice and air of determination, was not a force she wanted to reckon with. She rewrote the play scene by scene, religiously following the notes, a mechanical exercise not too different from the math drills she had endured in her youth. She plowed forward, dared not to look back and read what she had written, as if the act of rereading and reflection would shatter the illusion of progress.

She settled into a routine: rewrites in the mornings, auditing rehearsals in the afternoons, and at night, she curled up in bed and devoured borrowed books from Sasha. In between, she watched the delicate mating dance. Paulina relished the role of a tormenter, playing hot and cold, keeping Sasha on a leash. After rehearsals, Sasha would search for Paulina in the audience, his puppy eyes pleading for her approval. When she flashed him a thumbs-up, he'd leap into the air like a prepubescent boy, shamelessly shedding his cool-guy persona. Lin took it all in like a soldier, until pain and embarrassment swelled in her chest and chased her out of the room.

But wasn't she doing the same, with her feverish nightly reading? Books had become her perfect pretext to see Sasha. At first, her visits were formal and brief, like a transaction at a local library. But lately, he'd bring out tea and cookies, eager to exchange book reviews with her. "You're such a fast reader. Do you ever sleep?" he asked. "How wonderful to have someone new to discuss books with. People don't read anymore—you're a rare gem."

The admiration in his voice sharpened her senses. She'd suddenly notice the fireflies crisscrossing through the bushes, the trees rustling, the dim stars hovering above their heads, the whole world in cahoots to make the night flawless for them. She had never been one for fairy tales, but she was willing to give anything a try now. She imagined herself a noble girl under a heavy spell, only steps away from her saviour-prince. She met his glistening eyes, her thoughts taking on a hypnotic quality. *Come on, see me. Eyes like yours are meant for seeing through the fog of a spell. I'm your destiny, can't you tell?*

She slept poorly. She'd finish reading at three a.m. and drift into a slumber, only to be haunted in her dreams—at first, by the many fictional characters leaping out of the pages, and then, with increasing frequency, by Sasha and Paulina's marble-like faces. She weaved in and out of their dance of seduction, admiring, marvelling, boiling with despair. In a recurring act of violence, she'd claw into Paulina's face with her serrated fingernails and rip off her skin. "Look! Only a mask!" she'd proclaim to Sasha. The terror on his face contorted his beauty as he plunged toward the girl of his dreams. She'd catch a glimpse of the uneven flesh jutting out of her rival's skull, before springing up in bed with a soaked nightshirt.

One morning, still groggy from a restless night, she started constructing her own mask. From the bottom of her suitcase, she retrieved a heavy box with a velvety blue exterior. Her mother's parting gift from China, chock-full of cosmetics patented by Dr. Hong, including a thirty-page illustrated guide on "How to Make Your Own European Face." At Ma's insistence, the doctor herself had offered Lin a complete tutorial. The young Lin had witnessed her laborious but astonishing transformation, how her eyes lengthened and enlarged, how her bones rearranged themselves under the shifting lights. "I specialize in optical illusion!" Dr. Hong had declared like a true magician. "This box is a portal to a new life." The young Lin had been repulsed by the affectation in the doctor's voice, and the foreign veil she was peddling. *A mask is a shield.* She heard her Ma's voice now. *Why do you think the Russian girl is winning?* Lin sighed, nodding, capitulating.

She dabbed the magic cream with her pinkie and

massaged it into her cheeks and forehead, picturing her yellow pigmentation disintegrating. The rest of the procedure was perilous. The mascara dripped and flaked. The fake lashes slanted askew. The promised European smoky eyes turned into Beijing-opera diva eyes, terrifying in broad daylight. The highlighting cream on her nose and chin gave her the greasy look of a circus clown. She washed everything off in a tizzy. But in the ensuing mornings, she tried again and again, until she got the hang of the delicate operation, even catching a hint of her rival in her own reflection.

She debuted her painted mask at an afternoon rehearsal, feeling like a naked fool. Irma glanced at her disapprovingly, but she had too much on her plate to offer a critique. From the stage, Sasha squinted in her direction and raised an eyebrow. He made a beeline for her after rehearsal, where he'd compulsively shouted out dozens of pseudo-synonyms of *red*, from *pomegranate* to *lobster* to *Santa Claus* to *Chinese flag*.

"Aren't you all dolled up today? Special occasion?" He gazed into her eyes, which were camouflaged behind blue contacts. A new excitement shone on his face.

"No, unless you call our book exchange tonight a special occasion." She raised her chin, feeling her power grow.

"I find myself looking forward to our book discussions these days," he whispered. "Come by at nine. I have some classics to give you. More challenging than what you've been reading, but I think you're ready."

"That's a bit condescending, isn't it, Professor Sasha?"

"Sorry, that came out the wrong way. You have a knack for literature ... You're the writer, after all."

She enjoyed seeing him flustered. In a different world,

a hierarchy-free, raceless, or simply *blind* world, she'd have dropped the conceit and told him how grateful she was for the books, for making her read again after a long, barren passage of time. But *this* world allowed no margin of error. She bit her lip and hung on to her slim upper hand.

He followed her to her office. "How's the writing going, by the way?"

"It's coming along. Almost done with my second draft. I have a meeting in two days with Irma to present this." She tapped the new printout on her desk.

"May I read it?"

She grimaced at the thought.

"I know her taste. I can help you prepare for your big meeting."

She studied his earnest face. Her script *could* use a fresh pair of eyes. She'd been labouring over it for so long, a slave to Irma's demands. She felt distant from it, the way a new mother must feel, holding her baby born from a surrogate's womb.

"All right. You have four hours. I need it back tonight."

"Glad to be of service." Sasha picked up the script and gave her shoulder a gentle squeeze, his thumb grazing the edge of her clavicle. Lin held her breath, goosebumps flaring across her body.

LATER, SHE FOUND SASHA brooding under the moonlight. The mixed scents of roses and angel's trumpets permeated the air, baked in the unseasonable heat of the fall night. A slanting red maple from the neighbour's yard formed a loose canopy over the garden.

"Sorry I'm late." She approached him, unsteady on a

pair of stilettos. She'd spent an hour remaking her face and getting comfortable in a plunging V-neck dress. She'd rehearsed her sashay in front of the mirror too, but at show-time, she was still a nervous wreck.

"You ... Fantastic ..." His gaze made her insides turn.

She gestured at the manuscript in his hands, trying to maintain her composure. "So, the script?"

"Right, I'm reading it for a second time."

"What do you think?"

He opened his mouth, but no words escaped.

"Come on, I can take it."

"Well, how do I put it ...?"

"Put it in the honest way. How will I improve if I can't even count on my beta reader?"

"Right, okay, here it is. I find it ... confusing. It started out promising; the juxtaposition of conflicts and tenderness between the mother-daughter pair was intriguing, and *real*. Then the Oracle leaped on the scene. I'm not too hot on this dancing queen of a character. Seems to make a caricature of herself. Am I reading fantasy now? A sudden break from the first half, shattering the contract with the audience. As a whole, it felt incongruous and unbelievable."

Her eyes filled. He was spot on, and she had known it all along, but she'd still wished for a miracle.

"I'm sorry, was that too harsh? I don't mean to hurt your feelings. Many good scenes here, definitely salvageable. Two voices seem to battle on these pages. In fact, I can see Irma's fingerprints all over the second half. Am I right?"

"Irma wanted a Chinese Greek tragedy. My original story was too small, too inconsequential for her."

"Did it feel small to you?"

"No."

"Then why the hell listen to her? Why care so much about what *she* thinks? What's art if the artist can't even listen to the voice in her own head?"

"Because she's my mentor? The director of my play? Because I'm so green and insecure that I can't trust that little voice in my head?" she yelled, crying, sinking into stupidity.

"Art *is* subjective. No one else can be an expert on *your* story. *You* have to find a way to tell it. Irma's a veteran, but she's been wrong before. Her avant-garde impulse to bring hybridity into every project can sometimes ruin a solid human story like yours."

He passed her a tissue. "I know how hard it is to stand up for yourself. There's so much bullshit in theatre. I learned the hard way myself—Irma benched me all last season because of our artistic differences. But she's not a monster. I ended up going to her office hour every week, asking her to hear me out, and eventually she did. And now we have more mutual respect in the rehearsal room."

"You and I are different. I don't have the same ... power."

"Why not?"

*Are you truly so clueless?* She held his gaze. A Roman statue of a man, godlike, every bit a representative of the mainstream. Versus her, a slant-eyed yellow immigrant from an enemy state, at the mercy of visa sponsors.

"Do you know why I read so much?" His voice softened. "I read for self-preservation."

So he had read her mind. He sipped on his tea, closing his eyes. "I'm sure your journey has been hundreds of times harder than mine. But believe it or not, I was once every bit the outsider."

She shook her head. She could laugh.

"When Mom and I immigrated here, we lived in a housing project near Jane and Finch. A poor, rough neighbourhood, and I was the only light-skinned kid in my class."

"Goes to show the racial disparity of this town."

"No doubt about that. But I did catch a glimpse of what being a visible minority is like. I was ten, scared of going to school. I couldn't even tell my mom because she was always working."

"Where was your dad?"

"Stayed behind in Moscow. He was a painter of some fame in his younger days, but he couldn't sell enough art to support us. Abusive toward Mom too. By the time our Canadian PRs were approved, he was in and out of psych wards."

*Psych wards.* She wished it was a foreign concept. "Sorry to hear," she muttered.

"Boys that age were cruel. They ganged up on me, calling me names. Bumpkin, honky, commie, white trash. Didn't help that my English was so poor. Mimicking my accent was their favourite recess game."

"You don't have any accent now."

"I was *obsessed* with getting rid of it. Scrubbed my tongue every morning. I used to lock myself in my room and flip through the channels. I wanted to be Zack Morris, Dylan McKay, Joey Russo. I copied the way they talked, the way they threw their heads around. I avoided other Russians like the plague, even my mom, so I could quit speaking the language."

Lin swallowed a gasp. He might as well have been describing her life.

"For the entire first year, not a single kid played with me at recess. I was anxious all the time—depressed too. My English teacher took pity on me and gave me a box of books. That was it. I was hooked. All those characters became my friends. So these days, when Mom asks me to get rid of some books, I tell her, how can I abandon my bosom buddies?"

"So you're a survivor too," Lin mumbled, feeling his irresistible, magnetic pull. A young Apollo with a traumatic past. Her last defence was crumbling.

She made the first move, seeking and finding his lips in the shadows. They tasted salty and she wondered if she was doing it wrong. Nonetheless, she chewed on them greedily. She'd watched enough American damsels on TV who succumbed to the call of their hormone-soaked bodies. She could do this too, her old self be damned.

"I've always wondered how it'd feel..."

He pressed her shoulders back. "It can't be?"

"Yes, my first kiss."

"I'm flattered but—"

She cupped his face and dove back in. His body stiffened briefly before reciprocating, his tongue searching for hers in a frenzy. They twisted and writhed in a tangle that sent torrents of heat through her. His pale skin gleamed like porcelain in the moonlight. She was awestruck, boiling, panting, tuned into the heavy breathing of a young god.

SHE'D NEVER THOUGHT SHE had it in her. The tease, the deliberate holding back, the art of seduction. Part of her intrigue, she would learn the hard way months later, was her resistance to plunging into bed with him. His image flashed before her eyes every night like an alluring, unrelenting phantom. She'd knead her sex until her body trembled and imploded, exorcising him. But whenever they were alone together, fear and shame stood by her like a pair of stern chaperones, slapping his hands away from the mystery between her legs.

Her elusiveness excited him at first. He'd show up at her small apartment bearing new books and a bouquet of handpicked wildflowers. They'd lie on her cheap rug, talking about books, rehearsals, Irma's mood swings, scenes she was revising. He must have thought of every evening as a new, promise-filled beginning. He'd pull her onto his lap, his lips, soft and moist, landing on her eyelids, moving slowly to the tip of her nose, her cheekbones, her neck. She'd drive her tongue into his mouth and let it roam. Without undressing her, his hands wandered down her spine, squeezing her buttocks, tracing the length of her thighs. He'd suck on her lips, harder, stronger, until she couldn't help but grind against him. But the chaperone sisters would cough loudly, bringing in the big guns—her prune-faced health teacher from her Shanghai high school. "Complete celibacy before marriage!" she barked in Lin's ear, ushering her back to her straitlaced adolescence. "A woman's virginity is the most precious gift she can offer her husband. Do you know how painful the hymen repair surgery is?" She was instantly reduced to her teenage self, revisiting the only sex ed she'd ever received—a shocking, no-nonsense video on the anatomy of the penis, after which she'd joined the entire class of girls in a sob fest.

"Sorry, I'm not ready yet." She'd push Sasha away, retreating with the laughing chaperones. His eyes would snap open, pleading, but the night was over.

. . .

THIS SADISTIC DANCE WENT on for months. Sasha's patience waned. He began turning up late to their dates, empty-handed, avoiding eye contact like a schoolboy who'd been wronged on the playground. She ceded new territory to placate him but resisted his ultimate quest. One night, he was thrusting himself up and down the length of her body, fully clothed, when he stopped cold and studied her, his golden hair licking the tip of her nose.

"I can't do this anymore," he muttered. "I've tried to put myself in your shoes, to make this work, but I can't."

He hopped off the bed, aggrieved and defeated, and strolled out of her apartment.

She was invisible to him again. At rehearsals, he spoke his lines in an agitated voice, his posture onstage resembling a wounded animal's—prowling, sulking, prone to impulsive attacks. Irma loved it, this sudden edginess in her leading man. He renewed his longing looks in the direction of Paulina, who coolly returned his gaze, a callous smirk twisting her glossy lips.

Lin felt pain drilling into her bones. At night, insomnia plagued her. She tossed around in bed, searching for a strand of his flaxen curls, sniffing for a remnant of his scent on her pillows and sheets. She stared at the ceiling in the wee hours, fearful of closing her eyes, or the images of the golden couple would engulf her—their naked white flesh clashing, clashing, his exhilarated face, her red lips sucked pale by his passion.

# 4

## *Dali*

Dali arrived at the computing lab at seven on a Saturday morning. He sipped on loose-leaf long-jing and breathed in the stale air of the mercifully deserted room. He had a ton of assignments to catch up on, but the nerves he'd suffered all week had abated. His brain was ready to function again, now that his supervisor had left town for a conference-slash-vacation.

Unlike the other research groups in the math department, Dali's had no other Chinese students. He had missed the PhD application deadline the year before, after five months of unsuccessful job-hunting. He'd begged the department chair to look at his file and his impeccable math scores. But even with the chair's blessing, Professor Winkelman was the only one willing to take him on.

"No, no, no, no, no." His shi-xiongs at the Chinese

213

Students Association had shaken their heads gravely, as if he were a lamb offering himself for slaughter. "Avoid Dr. Quasimodo at all costs. He's got a baaaaad reputation."

Dali had thanked them for their concern and quietly accepted the offer. He knew what his CSA friends didn't. For five months, he'd witnessed dozens of HR ladies shift uncomfortably in their chairs, studying his moving lips and struggling to decipher his words. Most, with a patronizing smile, had thanked him for coming in. The more helpful few had told him how hard it was to understand him, and that communication skills were crucial, even for the technical positions he'd applied for. A middle-aged Indian lady had clasped his hand at the end of an interview and whispered like a benevolent aunt, "I know it's hard for you to be away from home, child, but you've got to get rid of all that mud in your mouth." He'd known he couldn't land a job by the year's end, when his OPT visa would expire. It was time to seek shelter at school again, from the watchful eyes of the immigration officers.

"But shi-xiongs sure had a point," he murmured to himself in the empty lab. His eyes landed on a thick report and his heart ached anew. He tossed the stack—a whole month of hard work—into the waste bin, but it was too late, his humiliating presentation from the day before already wheeling through his mind.

Quasimodo had been in a particularly uncharitable mood. Instead of focusing on the report itself, he had dwelled on Dali's *v*'s and *w*'s, *l*'s and *r*'s, mimicking his lengthened vowels and laughing callously.

"'Harro Amellica! I rove you, Amellica!' Our little Chinese brother here thinks he's speaking English. Shall we break it to him? Do you think he can *surwive* in the *vest*?" Quasimodo had addressed the other two graduate students in the audience. An eerie, creaking sound echoed against the four walls as he straightened his hunchback.

Dali's group mates stared blankly ahead, batting their long, blond lashes. Dali had no illusions that they'd stand up for him. Those spineless underachievers. They were only happy that their volatile supervisor had found an outlet for his wrath.

His inbox dinged. A new email from his mother with the subject line: *Lin's number.*

*Thank you, Ma*, he mouthed at the screen. His mother must have called Lady Lemei on their old rotary phone from the underground bunker, her fingers splayed at the base of her chin, reciting the script he'd fed her—two empty-nesters bonding over their loneliness.

At seventeen, he had followed his mother from their small coastal village by the Yellow Sea to the Grand Shanghai. That was almost six years ago now, and he remembered the first few nights in a windowless migrants' hostel where his mother feverishly filled out applications for jobs the locals would never touch, where he'd wake up to the stench of stale urine from the communal toilet and the crisp swish of his mother's pen under a dim lamp. But within a week, like a miracle, they were greeted by Yu Ma, the departing VP of a residential committee in the old city centre, who offered his mother a full-time job as a neighbourhood sweeper, over the scores of min-gongs vying for the position. The silver-haired, bespectacled granny had called around on their behalf for subsidized housing too, but that didn't go anywhere due to their lack of Shanghai hukou. The city's skyrocketing rental market was out of their reach, so Yu Ma took them to a witch-like neighbour with black-ringed eyes and even rows of gold teeth who had recently converted a series of Cold War–era bomb shelters into apartments.

"The ventilation here needs some work," Yu Ma had said, sniffing the musty air and pacing the stone-carved, cave-like dwelling. She'd asked the landlady a long list of questions, ensuring the electricity, plumbing, and sewage system were all in good order. She'd held his mother's hands and told her it was only temporary.

His mother had nodded eagerly, as if she'd won the lottery, her wide grin making Dali uneasy. "Why are you so nice to us?" he asked Yu Ma tactlessly, prompting a gentle swat from his embarrassed mother.

The granny cast a warm gaze upon him. "Because when I was your age, your grandma was my playmate. You and I are from the same village. Can you believe it?"

His mother gasped.

"Everyone called me Little Swallow when I was young."

"Ahh, Grandpa Yu's daughter! We've heard so much about you. Small world!"

"I had to do a double take when I saw your home address in that big pile of resumés. Our village is tiny—I've been in Shanghai for fifty years, never met a fellow villager until you two came along."

"Do you prefer our village or the Grand Shanghai?" Dali asked bluntly, turning away from his mother who was shushing him with a finger raised to her lips.

"That's a hard question," the granny said, patting his shoulder. "I miss our village a lot. It comes to my dreams all the time. But I suppose I was lucky, got here before the

Liberation, when the city border was still porous. Got my Shanghai hukou through my late husband. By the time of the Great Famine, I tried moving my parents here too, but there was already this impenetrable wall—invisible, but with barbs and thorns! This city is like a fortified island. Shanghai folks don't know how blessed they are! Others bang their heads all their lives trying to get in."

His mother nodded like an obedient pupil. "I knew it wouldn't be easy, but I had to at least give it a try, for the boy's sake," she said quietly, squeezing Dali's hand.

"You are one brave woman, Qin. Don't be a stranger, okay?" Yu Ma piled a hand on top of theirs as if the three of them were in a team sport. "I'm at your service whenever you need it."

A few days after, Lady Lemei had visited them on behalf of her mother, and offered Qin a contract to clean their apartment once a week. Qin would arrive at a spotless home week after week, and instead of scrubbing the bathroom, she'd spend the hour chatting with Yu Ma over a fragrant pot of Dragon Well, recounting stories from their island village, the land of their shared ancestors. She'd return home giddy and gather Dali in her arms. "We couldn't repay that family's kindness in eight generations! What dumb luck we have!"

*Do you still feel lucky, Ma?* He stared at the email with Lin's number and pictured his mother in her underground bunker, messy haired and dirty cheeked, newly released from a long day of physical labour. He suppressed a pang and whispered another *thank you*, forcing himself to mimic his mother, who was forever grateful.

. . .

THAT EVENING, HE REHEARSED his lines over and over before dialling her number.

At his greeting, Lin sounded alarmed, tearing open the scabbed wound in his heart. *I'm not the predator you think I am*, he wanted to yell at her and hang up the phone with dignity, but the vulnerable undertone in her voice made him pause.

"You can't still be mad at me. You know in your gut that I had nothing to do with those online posts. I could never do something like that to you."

"What do you want, Dali?"

"I need your help." His voice broke first, followed by the brave facade he was clinging to. Words tumbled out of him, flushing away his prepared script, airing months of frustration that had been festering inside and poisoning him. The monstrous American professor, with his unremitting mockery and public humiliation, had dismantled his self-esteem brick by brick. Depression, which Dali didn't have a label for until this moment, had been breathing down his neck night after night, whispering and questioning why he was still hanging on to life.

"I'm so sorry." Her voice was desolate. He suspected she could relate to his misfortune. "But how can I help you?"

"Tell me the secret to your success. How did you eliminate your accent so thoroughly?"

She laughed, a harsh, edgy sound. "Pebbles."

"Pebbles?"

"All part of Ma's Grand Plan to mould me into an American. She used to take me to this deserted beach just outside Shanghai. I can still picture those shipping containers, so colourful, stacked up by the bay, waiting to be deployed to some mysterious destinations. There was my Ma, placing the pebbles in my palm. She said orators from Ancient Greece used to hold pebbles under their tongues when they practised speeches. The pebbles force the tongue to move more, to be more flexible."

He drew a breath. "And you tried it?"

"Had to spit them out right away at first. The chafing— too painful. But Ma insisted on doing it with me, until I could repeat every word on my *Crazy English* tapes, yelling for hours into the wind with stones in my mouth. My tongue would go numb ... I wouldn't even notice the bleeding."

So Lady Lemei *was* sick, he thought. The rumours about her on-and-off "crazy spells" were true.

"But it worked wonders. After a few months, I sounded just like the woman on the tapes."

"So you'd recommend it?"

"Oh, I wouldn't wish it on my worst enemy!" Lin chuckled. "There's no shortcut, Dali. You just have to *adopt* the language, feel it, live it, sink yourself into it. Practise, practise, and more practise."

He switched to English. "Can I ... practise with you?" He held his breath.

A long pause. A TV murmured in the background.

"All right, English only."

"Deal!"

They fell into a brooding silence again. His cheeks were heating up, the foreign words from his mouth grating even to his ear. They flung him back to his first day at his Shanghai school, listening to his new teacher reading Lin's English essay in a singsong lilt and feeling ashamed that he couldn't understand most of her turns of phrase. The min-gong school he'd attended before had resembled a raucous daycare rather than an educational institution. He had sunk into his chair and let the musicality of her composition, the cadence of her ideas, wash over him. He found himself waiting for her outside her classroom after school, wanting to catch a close glimpse of Yu Ma's granddaughter, the girl who could weave magic with words. But the school bully had spotted him first.

"Country boy! How was your first day?" he hollered with a menacing smirk on his face.

"Fine," Dali muttered, triggering hoots of laughter from the bully.

"I *love* your accent! Where are you from? Let me guess, Heilongjiang? Tibet? Inner Mongolia?"

"Shandong."

"Ah, of course. Your parents are min-gong, right?"

Dali weighed the word on his tongue: min-gong. Peasant worker, filthy migrant.

"How did you wriggle your way in here?" The bully wouldn't let up. "You should go to school with your own kind. There's one under the highway by Xinzha Road."

Dali dreaded the crowd that was assembling around them. He imagined putting the Shanghai brat in a choke-hold and politely telling him that the school had recruited him for his special math talent, that he'd been able to do long division since the age of five, that he wasn't a freeloader— his mother paid three-quarters of her salary for a spot here, which was free for the locals. But how could he, and what was the point of explaining to the arrogant imbecile towering over him?

The bully edged closer, pinching his nose. "Shanghai schools are for Shanghai people. I'll have to ask my Ba to write to the principal. Can't let our school be contaminated by rural riffraff!"

"Are you finished, Tan?"

His heart raced at her voice. Lin stepped into the light from the shadows of her classroom, an oversized schoolbag slung over her shoulder, a faint blush imprinted on her porcelain skin. "How did *you* wriggle your way into our school?" she asked the bully calmly. "I thought everyone here was smart."

The bystanders giggled. The bully's face turned crimson.

"Leave him alone, or I'll tell Teacher Wang you've copied my homework a dozen times this semester," Lin said, before nodding at Dali. "Let's get out of here."

He followed her through the school courtyard and up the four flights of stairs to the library, away from the bully's whisper-shouting behind them ("Fatherless freaks!"). She was shaking and fighting back tears, but he dared not say a word. At the top floor, she signalled for him to stop at a study cubicle. "Don't let those idiots get to you," she said without looking at him.

"I won't," he replied, hoping it was a conversation starter. But she'd already walked away to a cubicle on the far side of the empty floor. He spent the next two hours stealing glances at her concentrating face—the girl with the magic, teleported to another planet by a pyramid of books. He wondered if he could ever bridge the distance between them, if one day he could travel across the galaxy to reach the orbit of her star.

A woman's shrill cries punctured his ears, shattering his reverie. A couple on TV had started a fierce quarrel on the other end of the phone line. He couldn't understand the allure of this language that had conquered the world.

"Why don't you leave your program if it's causing you so much pain?" he heard Lin whisper in the foreign tongue, softening the soundscape.

*Because I want to find my way back to you, when I become a doctor, a* somebody. "I don't want to go home, don't want to let my Ma down," he said instead.

"Yeah." Her hollow voice conjured an image of untethered water reeds. "It's like we were born unwanted. Can't stay, can't turn back."

He listened to her quiet breathing and dreamed of transporting himself across the four thousand kilometres to her doorstep. *I go where you go*, he'd coo in his broken English, channelling Stands-with-a-Fist. She'd like that, a reference to an American classic. Perhaps she'd finally understand what he had always wanted to tell her: against a cruel, capricious world, a lover is a sanctuary. And it seemed they both could use one right now.

# 5

## *Lin*

### MARCH 2005

She lost her virginity on the night of the spring equinox. *A time for renewal and rebirth*, she had written in her secret letter to Sasha, after weeks of tortuous, sleepless nights. She reread that letter over and over before slipping it inside his locker, each time shushing the raucous Opposition: the chaperone sisters, the Prune-Face, her former self.

He tailed her to her office after rehearsal. "You don't have to do this. I'm sorry if I was pressuring you." But the luxurious light emanating from his eyes couldn't lie.

"I've made up my mind. I'm ready."

"You may regret it later. I've been thinking, I do like you, but our backgrounds are too different. Let's just go back to being friends."

"Meet me at my place tonight."

"I don't think that's a good idea."

"Nine o'clock. I'll be waiting," she said slowly to keep her voice steady, masking her desperation.

AT NINE, HE WAS a no-show.

She changed out of the dress she had worn on the night of their first kiss. She was a woman on a mission, sliding into the silk interior of her family's heirloom: her grandmother's wedding qipao. She had never tried it on before, as it was strictly reserved for the wedding night. But she understood perfectly its alluring, suggestive power—the high mandarin collar, the knotted buttons in a neat, slanting line from neck to underarm, the long slit on the side, at once concealing and revealing a woman's leg. Her reflection in the mirror smiled at her coyly, her breasts swelling under the body-hugging fabric, a golden peacock wrapping its fluorescent feathers around her swaying hips.

*Tonight, I will be your bride.*

She cloaked herself in a trench coat and hailed a taxi. Her heart slammed into her rib cage as she stood outside his basement apartment, watching the amber light from his window dissipate into the night's mist. She sucked in the chilly air, expunging fear from her lungs, and descended the stairs. When he opened the door, she walked past him without a word, the air thinning rapidly. She reached the centre of the room and let her coat drop. He gasped, covering his mouth.

"Are you so scared?" she asked.

He drew near her, his eyes flickering in the dark. "You're the sexiest thing I've ever seen."

"All yours." She ran a finger down his unshaven face.

He wrapped his arms around her and lifted her off the

floor. She listened to his solemn steps and pictured herself as a piece of fragile art in a gallery, cradled by capable hands. He laid her down piously, an offering on his altar. Pressing his hands to the silky contours of her qipao, he massaged her breasts, his fingers lingering in the hills and valley before skidding along her bare arms. A string of giggles escaped her throat.

He paused. "Are you all right?"

"Yes. Just ticklish. No one's touched me like that before."

He closed in and licked her earlobe, his tongue reaching into her ear cavity. Thousands of pleasure alarms went off in unison, sending her panting and grasping her rising, stiffening breasts. His hands glided down her waist and traced the slit on her qipao. With a theatrical flick, he tossed the flap to one side, unearthing her legs.

"Open them for me," he intoned, ripping apart her lacy underwear.

Her stomach roiled, his lips on her sex, spasms rippling through her body. She cast her arms about and dug her fingers into the bedsheet, petrified. "A flood down here," she heard him say, and squeezed her eyes shut. *Too late to back out now.*

"I could lick you all night long," he moaned.

"Take me," she demanded. She needed to concentrate; this was what she wanted.

With one hand, he unbuckled his belt and opened his fly, his erection long and robust as a drawbridge. His other hand wrestled with the knotted buttons on her qipao. "So many damn little buttons." He chuckled at his clumsiness.

*The genius of anticipation, my ancestor's wisdom.* She sensed the irony of her pride and swallowed it.

By the time he freed her from her armour of seduction, he was a starving animal at her throat—firing her up too. They battled in torrid entanglement, seeking dominance and submission, burrowing and sinking into each other with their teeth and fingers. When he finally entered her, shattering the thin layer of membrane that'd held both her shame and her honour, she flinched, blindsided by the pain. He clasped her to his chest, moving glacially like a true gentleman. *You are free, you are free, you are free*, she chanted in silence, until a wave of genuine emancipation sprang out of her heart. She wrapped her legs around him and gritted her teeth, pushing him deeper into her with the bottom of one heel. She was impaled on the obelisk of the Athenian god, her life hanging by a thread, but she was *free*.

His thrusts grew urgent and decisive, his face painted with a thick coat of anguish. "Don't stop," she egged him on. He was boiling, expanding, filling every nook and cranny. With numbing endorphins, she could focus on the enveloping heat that was burning through sheets of ice from her decades-long solitude. Then he trembled violently in her arms, pulling himself out just in time. His seed slipped down between her breasts and pooled in her navel. She was suddenly shy, pulling up the blanket to cover herself. A salty, alkaline smell suffused the air.

"My baby," he whispered in her ear. "I think I'm in trouble."

*You have no idea.* Gratitude flared from inside out in the form of goosebumps; her molecules humming a song of liberation. She smeared his face with wet kisses.

. . .

LATER, SHE WATCHED HER young god sleep, a smirk curling around his pouted lips. His long lashes fluttered with each breath, pulsing the air, sending furtive messages from his dreams. She smoothed his golden hair and traced the terrain of his face. He was her destiny; she was sure of it. She had been transfixed by this face all through her girlhood, thousands of miles away in her mother's working closet. In Ma's treasured posters, the white faces had stared down at her in solemn silence, like statues of deities in the cavern of a sacred temple. She'd spent her entire formative years admiring, romanticizing, *worshipping* those faces. Long before she could articulate it, she had understood what such a face symbolized: beauty, power, and, ultimately, freedom. Sure, there had been a long line of schoolmates who were the subject of her secret fancy—boys descended from her own ancient tribe. But this, this frightening desire still ebbing and flowing inside her, was entirely foreign. A desire reserved only for white flesh.

# 6

## *Dali*

**D**ali listened to Lin's voicemail greeting, pleasant and distant and robotic. Sighing, he hung up without leaving a message and scanned the auditorium. Students were streaming in from all three entrances. *CSA's favourite speaker is back!* declared a scarlet banner, slightly off-kilter on the stage. Underneath the banner sat the day's guest of honour: Dr. Li, a silver-haired, professorial type in his fifties, with intense eyes behind modern, spindly glasses. He was a senior researcher from China's Academy of Social Sciences, now on a fellowship at UCLA. Dali remembered the first time Li had come to deliver a speech—how his sizzling energy and rallying allure had dazzled the audience. Hearing him talk, Dali had felt heavy with pride, picturing the torrential Yellow River rushing and roaring with the ferocious lifeforce of his motherland.

Zefan, the new CSA president, had dashed onto the stage and asked for Dr. Li's autograph like a fanboy cornering a celebrity. "What an orator!" he declared at the executive meeting later that night. "We've got to invite him back. Conversations with students. Debates! We'll run it in the American style!"

Dali had admired the new president's enthusiasm, though he was a tad wary of CSA's increasingly political undertone. He missed those halcyon days of simple camaraderie, of holiday feasts and festivities. But he was only a grandfathered treasurer, without the ambition and zeal that could match CSA's new blood. So when Zefan proposed inviting the Hong Kong Student Association to the debate, Dali had nodded blankly and said aye.

Now Zefan and Denise Lau flanked the Chinese scholar onstage. Denise, the purple-haired president of the Hong Kong Student Association, wore a sombre face that declared her readiness for a pre-emptive strike. After a round of introductions, she jumped into the fray with a staccato of Cantonese-accented Mandarin. "Dr. Li, I read in an online profile that your father died in a cowshed in 1969."

Zefan raised a hand, like issuing an objection in a court of law.

"Relax, buddy." Li patted him on the shoulder, evoking a few laughs from the audience. He turned toward Denise with candid eyes. "I see you've done your homework. That's correct."

"My grandma met the same fate during the Cultural Revolution, which prompted our family's secret passage to Hong Kong. My mom went through a period of deep hatred for the government after my grandma died. Was that your experience too?"

"It was a challenging time for me indeed."

"So it's quite a one-eighty—what you do now?"

Li nodded pensively. "It's been a long journey. After high school I was assigned to a tire factory. Mindboggling, backbreaking work, ten hours a day. The *smell* ... pungent chemicals, probably shaved a few good years off my life. But when the universities reopened, I took the first gaokao and, miracle of miracles, Beijing University accepted me."

"PhD in history," Zefan chimed in proudly.

"I did my bachelor's and master's at Beijing U, and my PhD at Cornell. Seven years at Cornell was long enough to cure my illusions about America."

"Can you elaborate on that, Dr. Li?" Zefan seized the opportunity.

"This may be a generalization, but Americans are some of the most arrogant people."

Denise snorted. "America is the most powerful country in the world! Power breeds arrogance. We'd be the same if we were at the top."

"Maybe, but that still doesn't make it pleasant. And for all the talk of democracy, it's rather hypocritical to pinch your nose and look down on everyone else, isn't it? When I was a student here in the nineties, I tried my best explaining to my American profs and peers. Seemed to me they never really thought about other people's experiences—I mean, *historical* experiences. Always quick to judge others based on their own values, the values of their 'founding fathers.' So I asked them, how would your system fare if I judged it based on Confucian values?"

"Good question! How did they respond?" Zefan prompted.

"They just stared at me like I'd asked the most idiotic question."

"But perhaps their political system *is* superior, as are their underlying values?" Denise retorted. "Maybe the old Chinese sage is indeed out of touch with the modern world?"

"You've been in thrall to America for too long!" Zefan snarled at his Hong Kong counterpart. Offstage, the audience murmured their opinions in a low hum, picking sides.

Li smiled at Denise warmly. "You're not alone, my young friend. Many Chinese intellectuals have worshipped America, my old self included. But times are changing. Let me ask you this: Would you at least entertain the possibility that most of our people actually *like* the system we have? Or at least prefer it to its alternatives?"

Denise shook her exquisite purple head.

"All right then, a bigger question: How did America get here? Some say it can trace its way back to the Dark Ages, the endless battles between the Vatican and the British Empire. A line from the long-suffering thinkers in the Dark Ages to the intellectuals of the Renaissance, the Enlightenment, the struggle against the dogma of theology, the celebration of humanism, so on and so forth. Then somewhere along the way, a band of English separatists, *hotheads*, clamoured for complete autonomy. For that, they needed a colony in the New World. So they did the dramatic crossing of the Atlantic, the *Mayflower*, braving the storm and all that."

"Wow, you know your history so well, Dr. Li," Zefan cooed. His fanboy puppy-dog eyes made a swift return.

"I could go on all day. But here's the bottom line: the American system is contingent upon their unique history. So is ours."

"But aren't you saying, in comparison, the Chinese system is backward, because we never had the Renaissance or the Enlightenment?" Denise asked, pouting.

"Not backward, just different. Tell me, what's the one consistent way to achieve political mobility in China?"

Denise stared blankly at him.

"Young friend, you need to read more Chinese history!" Li tilted his head to the other side. "Zefan, what did I tell you about my daughter's job?"

"She's a civil servant at the Treasury Department."

"How did she get the job?"

"Civil exams."

"Exactly! Our ancestors' civil exam system has been in place for two thousand years. That's the linchpin of our politics."

"What about the Mao era?" Denise asked darkly.

"That was a humongous outlier, yes, but since Chairman Deng, we've been going back to our roots. Ironically, we've got a system that the Americans should appreciate—meritocracy! How do our cadres advance? The gruelling exams first. Only the top *two percent*, only the brightest, the most diligent, can make it to the *bottom* of that hierarchy. Then you move up the ladder one rung at a time, spending years at each level. By the time you reach the top—*if* you reach the top—you won't look like some photogenic young man anymore, but you'll have a deep reservoir of experience, you won't make rookie mistakes. *And* you can think long-term, instead of being bombarded by the noise about your next election. My young friend, you honestly think our system doesn't have some serious advantages?"

Denise hesitated, her hand scribbling on a notepad, likely sketching out a counterargument. Zefan filled the vacuum and declared Li's victory. "Well said, Doctor! People who blindly worship the West should all hear you talk! We'll take a break now. When we return, Dr. Li will tell us about the recent developments in Sino-US relations, and how we overseas Chinese can do our part to uphold the dignity of our motherland!" He raised his hands above his head and clapped like a zealous disciple. His passion was contagious; the crowd responded with cheers and applause.

Dali sensed the Mother Yellow River roiling in his blood again. He rose from his seat and exited the auditorium. Out of habit and a new-found urgency, he dialed Lin's number again. After six weeks of silence, he prayed for a miracle. His heart sank when the call went to her voicemail once more. He wished Lin were here to meet Dr. Li. Whatever her malaise was, he was convinced it all stemmed from one knotted root: her fevered, unrequited love for the West.

# 7

## *Lin*

### 2006

S he lay sedated on the operating table, the doctor's voice flickering in and out like echoes from a tunnel. Her mother, in cerulean scrubs, stood shivering by her feet, a bundle of nerves. The surreal, painless sensation of cold metal slicing open her skin, sticky liquid running across her cheeks and congealing on her earlobes, her mind going dark like a drawn curtain.

She woke days later, in a black, airtight cocoon, looking out through a peephole. The warped face of a young nurse zoomed in, faded out, and reconstituted again. Slowly, her body lightened, her skin peeled away layer by layer. "Ta-da!" the nurse exclaimed with a final flourish. Her cocoon was gone; the adults in the room were gasping.

The doctor staked a mirror in front of her. "Like it? This skin, tsk, tsk, translucent baby pink, all that dull crust of yellowness—gone! The contours, oooooh, perfection. Chin, sharper! Cheekbones, higher! Nose, slimmer! Eyes? Mew, mew, feline!" the doctor barked cheerily like a car parts salesman.

"What an American beauty!" Ma cried out in relief.

Applause thundered in her eardrums.

"I don't recognize—" she started.

"Doll, I kept your beauty mark here, and those delicious freckles, a secret map to your past." The doctor winked and beamed, a grotesque, line-free grin. "You're welcome! Enjoy! Enjoy!"

The pretty stranger in the mirror, locked in a staring contest with her, sent shivers down her spine. The icy cat eyes stabbed at her, shattering her fortress and plunging her into a sobbing spell, straining and rupturing the tiny scars until beads of blood trickled out of every corner of her new face.

BREATHE, BREATHE.

She lay in the blue moonlight, bathed in cold sweat, incredulous. The once-recurring nightmare, long buried, had hunted her down.

She was thirteen when it all started, following an after-school trip to Dr. Hong's private practice. Hong Ting, a former military doctor famous for repairing five hundred soldiers' faces after the 1987 Black Dragon wildfire, was Ma's classmate from Fengyang High, the daughter of a pair of widely revered chemistry teachers at their school. They had lost touch after graduation and reconnected at a school reunion two decades later. That afternoon at the doctor's office, Lin was left alone with her homework while the two old friends retreated to the inner sanctum. Around her loomed a dusky jungle of white skulls, human skeletons, and startling anatomy charts. The two women whisper-shouted, the desperation in Ma's voice percolating through the wall. Lin made herself small and pressed an ear to the door, trying to decipher the source of Ma's anguish.

"You're not well, Lemei."

"I'm fine. As long as you help me."

"You know I'd do anything for you. My parents wouldn't have survived that cowshed if you hadn't been the Red Guard leader. We forever owe you."

*"But?"*

"As I've said many times: it's not your life; it's hers."

"The kid will be American. Her future's entirely there, in the West."

"She'll do just fine."

"I'm not naive. God knows I *love* America, but it's a racist country, I know that. Can't take any chances. You heard about that poor guy in Detroit? Died before his wedding. Some whites cracked his head open with baseball bats just because he was Chinese."

"Don't send her there if you're so afraid."

"Staying is not an option. Not after my Ba, after Feng."

"Every family suffered back then."

"You didn't see what I saw ... the pandemonium, the ghost haunting me ever since ... She *has* to leave. Too late for me, but not for her."

"I just can't do what you asked."

"Sure you can, you're the miracle doctor. I can't let her be ostracized. To be human is to be tribal, and too many tribal qualities are merely skin-deep, as you know far better than me."

"Take my magic box, my gift to her."

"Do more!"

"You're not thinking clearly. You're teaching the kid to hate herself."

The two women were speaking in code, but Lin had understood them. The room was suddenly frosty. She wrapped her arms around herself but couldn't stop shaking. *So Ma is still sick.* Despite the peace that had descended on their home after years of her outbursts, despite the measured tone Ma employed to address the world, to signal normalcy.

*YOU'RE REGRETTING IT NOW, aren't you?* A voice rose inside her, Ma's voice. *I was right all along, wasn't I?*

Lying on her sweat-soaked sheet, she clawed at the black void. *Away! Away!*

*I only wanted you to be normal. Imagine being able to fit into any crowd, to move freely around the world. Imagine your white boy seeing you not as some exotic prey, but as an equal partner in life. Imagine that.*

*You don't know him! He'll come back,* she argued weakly. *Away, away!*

But their disastrous date from the week before was already replaying in front of her eyes. She cringed at the drama, the fatuous, loaded dialogue, the pattern that had become entrenched between them.

"I'm going away with my buddies for the weekend."

"Can I come with?"

"I need to blow off some steam."

Her cold stare, her wounded gloom, her screaming inside: *Don't you understand I became your bride that fateful night of the equinox?*

Her bitter accusation: "It's only a game of cat and mouse for you, isn't it?"

"No, of course not," he muttered, and gathered her in his arms. In her bed, he undressed and kissed her and came quickly. He snored so loudly that she couldn't hear herself weeping. She didn't sleep all night, huddled beside him and dreading the first light of day. She rose early to remake her mask, so that she could sit by his head with a painted face, wringing her hands until he woke up.

"What are we doing?" Her attack, swift as usual. "Why don't you announce us to your friends? Why keep us under the radar?"

His eyes, filmed with sleep and alarm. "Calm down."

"You're ashamed of me, aren't you? What *am* I to you?!" Her yelling at his vacant face, at his broad back as he fled from her bed.

*You're regretting it now, aren't you?*

She got out of bed and plopped down before the mirror, studying her naked reflection and seeing the numerous ways it deviated from white "normalcy": epicanthal folds, narrow eye fissure, flat nasal dorsum, retruded mandible— the list her mother had researched and repeated for years until Dr. Hong married a geriatric German and emigrated to Europe. An inventory of undesirable traits that needed urgent elimination.

*I was right all along, wasn't I?*

She clawed again at the grim voice, shaking, breathing laboriously. *Got nothing to do with me. He's not ready, or maybe he's a dud. Behind all that perfection,* normalcy, *maybe he's just a dud to balance things out! It's got nothing to do with me...*

But she couldn't fool herself.

. . .

IN JUNE, SHE RECEIVED a surprise call from Ma in Shanghai. They hadn't spoken for months.

"I have good news for you," Ma said, an icebreaker that rang like a mockery. "I've been in touch with an old friend on WeChat—a classmate from high school, a math whiz in the old days. Taught himself calculus and algebra when our teachers were hauled out of the classroom for struggle sessions. He went to Canada in the nineties, got his PhD, and worked for some big banks. He's now striking out on his own, setting up a data company in Toronto. I've been telling him about you. He called yesterday and said his company is looking for bilingual talent and he'd be happy to interview you."

The message swam into her ears and bounced around her skull.

"Still enjoying Toronto?" Ma asked, a hint of alarm creeping into her voice.

"Yeah, yes."

"So you want to stay?"

She pursed her lips so she wouldn't burst into tears.

"Lin, what's going on?"

"I'm workshopping my final script next week. Don't have the mental capacity to think about other things right now."

"Okay, all right." Ma's dark tone returned. "I'll WeChat you the contact. Introduce yourself when you're ready. But hurry, the world won't keep on waiting for you."

THERE WAS NO RED carpet or balloon arches at her play's single-night workshop production. The mother instinct

239

she had toward her creation was long gone, lost in rounds of mechanical rewrites based on her director's vision, until she could no longer recognize this play with her name still attached. A month before the premiere, the lead actress Fox had borrowed from an Asian actors' collective buckled under the double whammy of overwork without pay. Irma couldn't find another Asian in town to fill the role, but she was a woman ready to turn any challenge into an opportunity. She planted Katina in the lead role and ordered the whole cast to don masks redolent with symbols from Greek mythology. It was the Great Greek Tragedy she'd wanted all along. Lin had scoffed at the idea when Irma first proposed it at the staff meeting, but she was too numb to fight. Sasha, to his credit, eviscerated the proposal: "Brilliant! Now it's race-free, ethnicity-free, and facial-expression-free!" He called it the biggest sham in the history of Fox and stormed out of the room. Irma looked shocked, but Lin was used to him fleeing the scene.

So it was with an odd sense of vindication that she read, in a popular online magazine, the single review of the workshop production the morning after the show: "The director lost me at the masks. An incongruent, farcical, mock fest of a should-be important political story of our times." She remembered the reluctant smattering of applause, the baffled murmurs as the curtain dropped, the pity and embarrassment on people's faces when they offered her their brief and obligatory congratulations. She remembered searching for Sasha in the small audience and not finding him there. "Time to go," she said to herself, and powered off the computer.

That afternoon, she packed her laptop and her original draft in a cardboard box and tossed the mountains of revisions into the trash can, filling it to the brim. She said goodbye to the bare walls of her office of eleven months and slinked away. The golden sunlight outside the theatre gave her instant jitters. The neighbourhood buzzed with early summer excitement. The pink magnolia tree across the street bloomed blithely, little tots dancing under its vast canopy and stuffing their tiny hands with fleshy petals. She reached into her pocket for the folded letter from the Government of Canada, informing her of the expiration of her temporary visa. She recited those courteous words of eviction once more, and for the umpteenth time visualized her life back in Shanghai. A chill crept up her spine. *Nah, no way.* She sucked in the scented air, opened her WeChat contacts, and made the call.

# 8

## *Lemei*

2011

When Dali came to visit all the way from America, bearing a deluxe package of American ginseng and bottles of vitamins, Lemei barely recognized him. The pale, scrawny neighbour's boy had grown into a handsome young man with glowing, tanned skin. Clasping his hands, Lemei and Yu Ma studied him from head to toe. "Looking good, son!" they gushed in unison.

"Thank you, Granny, Auntie. Long time no see. Ma sends her warmest greetings to you both."

"How *is* your Ma?" Yu Ma asked.

"Not in the best shape. She works too much. You know how stubborn she is."

"Yes, yes," Lemei mumbled, remembering Qin's despair from a year before, and how, for weeks, the word *cancer* had clanged in her head like a gong. She had promised Qin she'd

242

keep the diagnosis a secret from Dali, so he could focus on his studies.

"Almost done with your PhD?" Lemei changed the subject.

"Oh, I quit."

"You did?"

"Yes. I now work for a consulting firm promoting Chinese culture in North America."

"We all thought you'd be a math prof at an Ivy League."

"I still like math, but I've found my real passion. I'm much happier at this job, helping our own people."

"Does your mom—" Lemei started.

"Good for you, child," Yu Ma cut in. "You made it in the white man's land. Your Ma's blessed. All her years of hard work paid off."

*Did it?* Lemei wondered. All that sacrifice so her son could become a ... propagandist?

Dali grinned at the elderly woman, a little too brightly. "Speaking of which, this Sunday at the Exhibition Centre, my boss and I have organized a commemoration for the Burning of the Summer Palace. One hundred and fifty-first anniversary this year. Granny, Auntie, you both should come!"

An excuse was on the tip of her tongue, but Lemei heard her mother say, "My daughter will go support you. My legs are too stiff to go anywhere now. I'll be rooting for you from my couch, child. You're on to great things!"

LEMEI REGRETTED COMING HERE. On the podium, a droopy-eyed, geriatric historian droned on about the atrocities committed by the Anglo-French troops during the Second Opium War, how it'd taken four thousand white men three whole days to destroy the "Garden of Gardens" and all its exquisite artworks. Decades of propaganda had eroded these shocking facts into platitudes that even grade school children could casually recite. When the scattered applause after the talk faded, Lemei was ready to sneak out.

"Auntie, you made it!" Dali caught her by the sleeve and slid into the empty seat beside her.

"Sorry, I was late."

"Good timing. My boss is next. See, that's him, Dr. Li, a senior researcher at both the Academy of Social Sciences and UCLA. He goes back and forth between the two countries," Dali said, his eyes shining with admiration.

Lemei scanned the speaker, unimpressed. Another brainwashed pseudoscientist, throat and tongue of the Party.

"We are in for a treat, trust me," Dali whispered.

Presently, Dr. Li dove into a passionate account of China's triumphs since 2008. He was blessed with a booming voice and an animated mien, his native Shanghai accent hinting at an intimacy with his listeners. The sleepy audience came alive with oohs and ahhs.

"You've all heard about Lehman Brothers? The flagship Wall Street firm that went belly up in 2008? Six hundred *billion* dollars in debts! Last year, their entire trove of world-famous art went up for auction. Like tearing down a giant, limb by limb. What else happened in 2008? The most *glorious* Olympics party the world has ever seen, am I right?" The crowd hurrahed as if seeing a dolphin jump through a ring. "My colleagues in America all said to me—only China has the deep pockets to put on a show like that now! Listen to that, comrades: the tide has turned. We used to look up to America, envious of its wealth. Now we're the envy of the world! Turns out Chairman Mao was right—America's really just a paper tiger!"

Lemei rolled her eyes.

"Something else for you to think about," Li continued, riding the crest of the wave. "Ten years ago, if a Chinese kid showed up at the American Embassy for a student visa without a full scholarship, the officials would turn up their big noses. Didn't matter if the kid had been admitted to an Ivy League. Now? American universities *beg* our kids to join them. Our kids are the single group keeping their schools afloat!" Dr. Li pumped a fist in the air. "What about other industries? How did GM stay in business last year? By leaning on the Chinese market! So did Boeing, Starbucks, Gucci, Nike. Comrades, just as the Western Empire plunged into the worst financial crisis in history, we alone stood tall in the storm, propping up the world economy!"

The audience went wild, clapping and cheering. "Isn't he just fantastic?" Dali beamed. Lemei cast curious glances at the neighbour's boy. How had a stint in America turned him into such a flag-waver?

Dr. Li sipped some water and surveyed the elated audience with a look of satisfaction. Sweat ran down his chin. He whisked his thick bangs to one side, revealing a jagged scar, like a centipede perched on his forehead. His bangs fell back swiftly, burying the centipede like quicksand.

*I've seen him before, but where?* The question pestered Lemei for the rest of the talk. When it was over and the enthusiastic applause had subsided, she tailed the line of fans at the podium.

"Dr. Li." She offered her hand when it was her turn. "Enjoyed your talk."

He shook her hand, confusion descending on his face. "You look familiar. Have we met?"

"That's what I'm trying to figure out. Which grade school did you go to?"

"Changle."

"High school?"

"Fengyang High."

"Me too! '66 to '72. You?"

Dr. Li drew a breath. "Old Father in Heaven! The Red Guard leader! You were the almighty, the *Queen*!"

Heat climbed up her cheeks. "Lemei. Pleased to meet you."

"Li Ming."

"So did we meet in school?"

"You wouldn't know me. I was a year behind you. But you knew my father. He was the math teacher for your grade."

A tsunami of memories hit her. Of course, badass Teacher Li. This was the son of the most stubborn prisoner of the school cowshed, who had refused to confess his crime or denounce a single family member or colleague, who one chilly spring night had pierced his veins with a sharpened toothbrush. And merely a day after his demise, three acne-faced hooligans had battered the fatherless son with bricks, crushing his skull, a waterfall of blood cascading down his face. Lemei had stumbled onto the scene with her brother—still a year before his exile. Within minutes, she'd convinced Feng to save the class enemy's son. She'd watched her mammoth brother tower over the young thugs, pick them up one by one, and fling them out of the way like garbage bags. She had been so proud of her brother, her unpredictable, perennial frenemy. Afterward, she'd searched for the boy on campus, witnessing his centipede of a scar maturing through various shades of red until it blended into his face as a permanent feature.

"Of course, it's *you*!" They grasped each other's hands, tears surging in their eyes. Two children of the revolution, two survivors.

AFTER THE EVENT, at the private and exquisitely decorated Lotus Court of the Imperial Palace Restaurant, Li and Lemei exchanged pleasantries and caught up on their families—he was widowed, with an adult daughter now working for the government.

"I can't believe you never married!" Li exclaimed. "You were the dream for so many—"

"Don't embarrass me, please," she cut him off softly, her fingers tracing the trail of scars on her arm. *You didn't know the years when I slipped in and out of the psych ward, blending right in with the crazies.*

It dawned on her that she was with a near-stranger, and a senior Party cadre no less, the likes of which she'd despised all her life. What was she thinking? A happy reunion? How could she get out of this?

"Which American city is your daughter in?" he asked.

"She's moved to Canada. Toronto."

"Ah, America's little brother. You're so brave. I could never send mine away. I knew I'd lose her. Plus, there are plenty of opportunities here at home now."

Her heart seized up. She could read between the lines: *Abandoned in your old age. If only you had more faith in your motherland.* "Let's not talk about my daughter," she said.

He nodded hastily. "Right, kids have their own lives. No point in us meddling in their affairs."

They sat in awkward silence. She racked her brain for an excuse to leave.

"What was my dad like in the classroom?" he tried again. "Do you remember?"

That hit a soft spot in her. "Yes, very well. Animated, enthusiastic, a high-pitched voice, wide gesticulations. Such a gifted teacher. He had the ability to make any topic fascinating, even to a hopeless case like me."

He grinned. "You and I were in the same boat then. Ba did everything to lure me into math. It almost would've worked if I hadn't had my nose in illegal novels all the time."

"Where did you get your supply?"

"Theatre Academy. You too?"

"The music conservatory."

"Ahh. Great minds think alike!"

The door flew open. Mapo tofu, golden glazed egg rolls, and soup dumplings sailed onto their table.

"You said you don't eat meat. These are all vegetarian. Dig in!" he urged.

Lemei chewed the marinated tofu, salty spice exploding on her tongue. She let her guard down a notch. "Was it hard, when your dad ..." she asked cautiously.

"Worst nightmare of my life. I was only thirteen, hated everything around me—the school, the other kids, my Ma."

"The Revolutionary Committee?"

"Absolutely, and that ugly what's-his-face ..."

Her pulse quickened.

"Changshen!" he remembered. "Dirty toad. I cursed him thousands of times!"

*Changshen is long dead*, she almost said. Throat cancer was his comeuppance, a mere three years after he moved back to his birth village. But she couldn't bring herself to utter his name.

"And the Party?" she asked gingerly, and regretted it right away.

He held her gaze. "Yes, the Party. I know what you're thinking. I get asked about this a lot."

He called for a bottle of Grand Dragon Dry Red. The frail-boned waitress with gash-like lips uncorked it and poured them each a generous glass, before retreating and closing the door discreetly.

"Good wine. They gave me a tour last summer at the vineyard in Yantai. It was impressive. I'm not an expert, but I used to work odd jobs at vineyards in Ithaca. I can tell a good bottle from a mediocre one. And this stuff is *good*, even though the brand is still so young. Try it."

"Oh, I know nothing about wine," she said but took a sip. All she could taste was bitterness.

"You see, I spent seven years at Cornell, to learn the American way. It was quite an education, all right. Let's just say it cured me of my obsession with the West."

"What happened?"

"Well, nothing explosive, just the daily grind. You turn on the TV every morning and see the clowns talking, the cults and fake gods, the obscene rich and abject poor, the school carnage, and you think to yourself—so this is supposed to be the pinnacle of human civilization? The best system in the world?"

"There's no perfect system," she mumbled.

"No, there isn't. But look at Obama. He's quite an orator,

isn't he? But is he good enough to be the leader of the 'free world'? What was his last gig? Community organizer. It's like airlifting the head of our residential committee to the Politburo. You know, Obama's really struggling to get things done right now, and somehow everyone's surprised! The American election is a giant beauty pageant. Our model, hands down, is a lot more reasonable."

"What *is* our model?"

"Based on civil exams, our ancestors' system."

"Is that really true? What about nepotism? Patronage? We inherited those from our good old ancestors too. Plenty of officials climbed the power pyramid by kissing the right behind."

"The older generation of cadres, yes. Civil exams were only reinstated in '94. Give it time. But shouldn't we talk more about the advantages of our homegrown model? If we want to improve, it should be a matter of reform, not revolution, right?"

Her hands shook. "I never said anything about revolution."

"Not you, but some have, especially since the Arab Spring."

"What's that?"

"You don't read *Internal Reference*? You work at *Liberation Daily*, no?"

*Barely. Advertising is just about as far from the high perch of the news desk as you can get.*

"Took an early retirement last year, no longer among the 'chosen people.'"

"Ahh, so you haven't heard about the Jasmine Revolution." Li sipped his wine and eyed her with a hint of disappointment.

The name sounded familiar, something she'd overheard from young people in her neighbourhood. She once saw a flyer soiled by dirty footprints in her building's stairwell, a protest at People's Park stamped garishly across the page. The murmurings had faded within a week.

"Don't know much about it," she said. "In any case, must've been a tempest in a teapot."

"Well, if the secret police hadn't been on top of it."

"Of course, the secret police. Did anyone get beaten up?"

Li grimaced. "Unfortunately, yes."

"So, the same old story."

"What happened to our Red Guard Queen? You were always a big-picture thinker! You know what happens to those countries that get swept up by the Arab Spring? Wreckage, death, economic collapse, displaced lives, all-out civil wars. Do our people want the same? Do *you*?"

Her stomach roiled. She'd definitely tasted meat and lard in that last bite of dumpling.

"I got to read memos from WikiLeaks," Li continued, "about the CIA's role in training the Arab Spring leaders. Yes, the Party can be paranoid, but is it so crazy to suspect one goal of those protests was America-instigated regime change?"

"Sounds like a conspiracy theory to me. All I know is political reform is overdue here."

"Oh, I agree. Wholeheartedly."

"Do you really?"

"Yes. And most people do too, other than the few hardliners who still see Mao as God. But most people also understand what's at stake. Look at our GDP growth for the last decade. As long as this Party continues to deliver the

material goods, its tacit agreement with the people won't
be broken."

"But for how long? The economy can't be on the upswing
forever. People are utterly sick of the corruption, the smog,
the polluted waters."

"If you ask me," Li edged closer and whispered, "we need
a stronger leader at the top. The current one is too weak. I've
got high hopes for the next president."

"The princeling."

"Yup. The princeling who was down in the gutter,
resurrected, ground his way up the chain of command over
decades. He's built himself a network. And of course, there's
his pedigree—his dad, after all, was buddies with Mao back
when the Communists were still guerrillas. They conquered
this land *together*!"

"Watch your language, Doctor."

"You know what I mean. The princeling has the kind of
audacity we need. The current president is plebian. Xi, on the
other hand, is Red Aristocracy! He's got a birthright! He'll
get rid of the corruption, the interest groups."

"Or he could go the other way, concentrate power in his
own hands, be an emperor in the truest sense."

"What if he's the Sage King, huh? Our people always
prefer a Sage King to a bunch of warlords vying for power.
Any cursory reading of our history will tell you that."

"So back to a monarchy then. What a step forward."

"No, no, I bet he'll push for *more* reform. He's got all the
political capital in the world to do it."

"I'm not so sure."

"Only time will tell, isn't that true, my friend?" He winked
at her coyly, the fatherless boy from her adolescence once more.

The gash-lipped waitress rushed in to stack the empty plates, her eyes downcast and her face expressionless, an efficient robot that couldn't wait to go into sleep mode.

"Well, looks like they're closing soon. We can't solve all the world's problems in one sitting! We'll have to meet again." Li laughed, rising to help Lemei with her chair, a thorough gentleman. His hand brushed away a strand of loose hair from her shoulder. "Can't believe I found you. At Fengyang High, I used to worship you from afar."

Heat rose to her cheeks, her heart thumping. *What's wrong with me? I'm fifty-eight, an old woman.*

"I'll call you, okay?" he said. "We have so much more to talk about."

She nodded and fled the room, before the colour on her face spread like wildfire and made a total fool of her.

SHE COULDN'T SLEEP THAT night, Li's illuminated face flickering in the shadows. No doubt she admired him—a man of the world, a fair-minded intellectual, a rare, candid interlocutor. But she was scared, and humiliated. His earnest smile at the end had sent her heart fluttering as if she were a pubescent girl again. She had long sworn off men, the memory of violence lodged deep in her cells. She couldn't imagine, let alone trust, a tender alternative. After Feng, after years of outbursts and pills and relapses, even her mother had agreed a husband was no longer in the cards for her. Decades had passed her by like a ruthless, rushing river. Now, at her ripe age, was the Universe playing a cruel prank on her?

Li kept his promise and called often, always from the road, mostly from the other side of the Pacific. *Silly me,* she chuckled to herself, *he's an eagle who can't be caged.* His disembodied voice, his humour and erudition nonetheless buoyed her spirit. She found herself mulling over his words when she was alone, even on issues where they didn't see eye to eye. And she couldn't help holding out a sliver of hope whenever his baritone came on the line—low, intimate, and road-weary. She pictured him under a yellow-tinted hotel lamp in a lonesome foreign town, speaking to her over a glass of cognac and heading to bed thinking of her.

She was alarmed when he first invaded her dream a few months later, his wrinkles whited out by silver moonbeams. His lonely grin disarmed her as he stooped to kiss her, jolting her awake. She leaned on the bedpost and listened to her racing heart, blaming her solitude for fast-tracking their inchoate relationship. Later, on her calls with Lin, she thought of telling her daughter about Li, but how could she, her feelings still straddling fantasy and reality? Worse, a thick dust of guilt accumulated in her chest as she waited for the many awkward pauses to pass, knowing her own view of the world was shifting, glacially but surely, bumping against memories of her beloved dead, betraying her daughter.

Sometimes the silence on their calls grew so unbearable that Lin would charge into a seemingly random topic, something she'd read about China, and their conversation would veer rapidly into dangerous waters. Lemei found Lin too unforgiving in her critique of the motherland, too gullible in her faith in her adopted country. She was losing her only child to a belief system behind which a vast network of writers, pundits, politicians, and strategists laboured around the clock, a belief system she herself had once preached but no longer held fast. The pain would stab her heart until she had to call it quits, leaving them both stewing in unaired arguments. When she hung up the phone with a sigh of relief, she'd remember Li's anecdotes from his student years in America—the slights and condescension he'd endured as a yellow-skinned alien at an Ivy League. The fire in his belly to rise to the top.

"That was when I abandoned my worship on the altar of the West. Instead, I reconnected with my Chinese identity," Li had told her.

"Can't you just be ... *you*? A citizen of the world?" she'd asked innocently.

"You have no idea. When a Chinese lives in the West, he's always a rep for his country, perpetually asked to pick sides. I've seen my peers choose the other side and lose their way. Their disdain for the political system made them disavow their cultural and national roots. They grew adrift, rootless, lonely, schizophrenic even. Is it really worth the price?"

She wondered if Lin had experienced any of that, and if she had pushed her daughter onto an impossible path for survival. On those nights, she'd capitulate in her dreams, letting Li undress her and enfold her body from behind. Her heartache would soften and fade, the syncing of their heartbeats mesmerizing, this metronome of love that had long eluded her.

# 9

## *Lin*

Things Lin would always remember from the early years after Fox Theatre:

DR. WANG. A rotund man with a kind, avuncular face and bushy sideburns like those of the Meiji warriors of Japan. She suspected he had been one of Ma's secret admirers in their youth, as he talked about her and their shared school days in that nostalgic, rose-tinted way. When she first met him, he studied her face as if searching for signs of the beauty he'd once idolized. Lin was grateful for the job, and the cocoon of security it offered her. Math wasn't her first love, but she came to appreciate its strangely healing presence like a sturdy, unsentimental domestic partner—the cool logic, the bulletproof procedures, the rigid order that defied life's uncertainty.

THE WORKING GIRL. Most of the time she was alone at the office, a two-bedroom suite on Queen West, up a squeaky flight of stairs from a movie rental place that was slowly going out of business. The rancid smell of old paint, mixing with the exhaust from the Thai restaurant next door, lingered over her desk like a stubborn fog. Dr. Wang came in only once or twice a week. He was on the road a lot, courting prospective clients, selling their half-baked math models. The two other employees, Jake and Drake, worked from home outside the city.

Jake, a fifty-year-old former insurance broker with a jet-black toupee floating like a central island on his bald scalp, had reinvented himself as the Data Guy. He was an odd combination of a geek and a social butterfly, who seemed to genuinely enjoy schmoozing with the myriad data vendors, riding the waves of the Big Data Revolution. "Data is the new oil!" he liked to remind the rest of them on their weekly staff calls—long before that line had become a cliché—as he reported the next novel data source on the horizon.

Drake, a twenty-nine-year-old PhD dropout from McGill, with the long flowing beard of a Zen Master, was her official mentor and, later, her covert competition. Lin worked her way up from an apprentice (cleaning, coding, wrangling data) to the custodian of half their models. When deportation or starvation were her only alternatives, she found it possible to dive into the mighty tomes of textbooks and lap up new algorithms of machine learning, to keep running in a field that leaped forward like a spooked bunny. Often, she'd wake from a slumber at her desk late in the evening, the model still churning away on the harshly lit screen, gorging on a batch of new data for nutrients and insights.

She liked it better at the office though. An army of cockroaches had descended on her apartment building, and sometimes she came face to face with the stragglers in her cupboards, their black triangular eyes and striped antennae nearly touching her nose. She didn't tell anyone about it. She was biding her time and proving her worth.

THE TAMING OF THE DEMON. One night, alone with a looming deadline and an impenetrable project spec scattered on her desk, she felt a tightness that blanketed her neck and jaw and throat. Her palms sweated; saliva churned on her tongue. She'd had her usual bowl of Pad Thai merely two hours before, but her stomach was growling, a once-familiar growl that was sinister and smug and made her heart race. In the presence of her dream man, who had occupied every inch of her psyche and hyper-alerted her to any risk of body disfiguration, the demon had stayed away, quietly playing the waiting game. Now she felt the rush of air around her, the demon circling. She'd half anticipated its return and done her research; she had to launch a counterattack, pronto.

Dashing out of her office and down the stairs, she ran two blocks west on Queen to the new health-food store, piling chewing gum and bottles of bitter melon juice into her cart. For the rest of the evening, she kept her mouth busy and tricked her brain with the imitation flavour of a pack of Trident. When that wasn't enough, she sipped on the bitter juice that numbed her palate. She let out a sigh of relief when the growling and sweating ceased, the air still and calm once more. She had escaped capture for the night.

In the days that followed, she added more ammunition to her arsenal. She learned to dispel the mirage of a chocolate cake with imagined toppings of rotten fruit. She jumped into an icy shower at the office, letting the shock reset her fevered mind. Some nights, when nothing was working, she went for runs under the yellow streetlamps in Trinity Bellwoods, ignoring the homeless man jeering at her from his battered sleeping bag, calling her the "crazy China doll." Loop after loop, her body boiled, and the demon, clinging to her failing system, would eventually recognize her kamikaze resolve and flee the scene.

It visited her less and less, until one evening she looked up from the technical mumbo jumbo and realized she hadn't felt its presence for weeks, even months. She patted herself on the back and smiled. It was a small win in the eyes of the unafflicted, but a big win for her. It felt good to know that she could still win.

THE WORKING GENTS. Vlad bartended two blocks away from her office, at a rowdy dive bar near the city's mental hospital. It took her a year to find out. She was racing to catch the last bus one night when he called to her from inside the bar, a stack of plastic chairs in his arms. The next evening, she stopped by for a proper chat. He told her about his new girlfriend, about Irma and Fox.

"Sasha has started working around here too, at that Starbucks by Trinity Bellwoods Park." He peeked at her uncertainly.

"He and Paulina...?"

"They're just friends."

"You mean they never—doesn't matter."

"They dated for a few months after you left but broke up a long time ago. You know, I've always rooted for you guys."

"It's all ancient history."

"Anyway, I'm sure he'd be happy if you popped by his shop and said hi sometime."

For a week, she steered clear of the park. At work, instead of researching hierarchical clustering, she studied Starbucks's all-day breakfast menu with an itchy, achy heart.

One morning, she found herself loitering by the bench outside his coffee shop, wearing a baseball cap and a pair of oversized sunglasses. When Sasha emerged from behind the curtain inside the glass wall, she gasped and giggled and leaked tears, disappointed at her underage-girl-spotting-pop-idol performance. But she couldn't look away. Those baby blues, the laugh lines bracketing his sensual mouth as he bantered with customers and made their drinks. The pesky young women lingering at his counter for an extra minute of flirtation.

Back at the office, she signed up for a speed-dating club. She needed to scrub his image from her mind. She needed other faces to overwrite his, other voices to drown out the sound of her frantic heartbeats. Even as she loitered at Sasha's window day after day, laughing and crying behind her dark shades, trembling like a drug addict getting her fix.

THE REAL ORACLE EVE. When the nameless credit risk software she'd laboured over for five years finally spelled out the neat predictions that made her boss swoon, she heard herself cooing her name: Oracle Eve. Dr. Wang, in his charitable offer to provide Lin with a legal status in Canada, had unwittingly turned her into a character from her own play. On the day of the big reveal, she paused for suspense, a perfect showman, before clicking the magic button on the keyboard with a flourish. Rainbow-coloured Lorenz curves sprouted and bloomed on her screen, her new curve diverging from the benchmark like a fearless foal galloping ahead. Jake and Drake cheered from the monitor screen like spectators at a horse race, their glitchy voices cascading, their faces a wild, exhilarating distortion.

"Wow, that's a thirty percent improvement from the old risk model!" Dr. Wang exclaimed. "Well done, team! This is going to make our competitors shiver!"

Then, a wink at her and a more personal note: "You've made your Ma proud, Lin."

"You're most welcome. Thanks for the opportunity," she said politely, returning his smile.

It was just what the doctor ordered: work as her refuge, an antidote to the muddy quagmire of her heart.

THE NEW APARTMENT. When the big bonus arrived in her bank account, she broke the lease on the cockroach-infested apartment near Lansdowne. Dr. Wang rented a U-Haul and moved her to a two-bedroom suite with a stunning, unobstructed view of Lake Ontario, apologetic the entire way. "I had no idea you were living in such abominable conditions," he mumbled with the regret and distance of a child protection agent. After the boxes were unloaded, he pressed a wad of cash into her hand. "You've been working hard for years. Throw yourself a housewarming party, a proper one! That's the Canadian way. Also the Chinese way—bad luck to enter a new home without friends and a lavish feast."

That weekend, with catered sushi platters, artisanal cupcakes, and swinging music, the old Fox gang gathered in her living room. She had gone to Vlad's bar to invite him. "Only me and my girlfriend? What about the rest of the gang?" he'd asked. "We've all missed you."

"All right, but no Sasha or Paulina, please," she insisted.

But Sasha came anyway, tailing the group with a bottle of champagne and a hangdog look. "I'm sorry, I know I wasn't supposed to..." His voice cracked. "Just wanted to see how you are. You look good."

She had to excuse herself to scream into a pillow in her bathroom.

They avoided each other for the rest of the evening, hiding behind the gang and feigning interest in other people's lives. She gave a tour of her new building and the actors oohed and aahed ("A rooftop pool!" "A yoga and spin studio!" "Was that really your doorman in the fancy three-piece suit?"). Around her marble kitchen island, the group closed in and offered their congratulations. Sasha sulked in the background, though he was the only one she could see.

"You've made it, Miss Lin!" Mikhail raised his glass of bubbly. "I hope you'll remember us theatre paupers. Come back and visit often!"

"And deliver us from our purgatory! We've got a season subscription just for a woman of your stature," Vlad teased.

She looked across the room and locked eyes with Sasha. The pot lights cast on him a bronze sheen, rendering him a Roman statue in a museum's exclusive corner. He raised his glass and mouthed a silent congratulations. She had to look away.

THE NEW BEGINNING. After the housewarming Sasha called often. Books, plays, theatre gossip—the tried-and-tested topics to lure her in. She spoke coolly and never let the calls spill over half an hour. After a while, he dropped the highbrow pretension and grew more candid. He wasn't doing well. His relationship with Irma had never recovered after the fight over Lin's play. He was auditioning for other theatres, even five-second TV commercials. "Landlords don't care about your artistic differences with your director." He chuckled bitterly.

"Don't you live in your mom's basement?"

"Still need to pay rent. She's not made of money."

Lin bit her tongue. She didn't want to offer help. Not yet.

She got off the phone and returned to her desk. She'd been writing a play based on their first attempt at love, and she kept evading the ending. *Whatever you two had, where do you go from here, Lulu and Alex? Use your imagination, find a way!* She was tired, her day job only six hours away, but her body buzzed and zinged with hopeful suspense. Unlike life, anything was possible in a script, especially the first draft.

*Give us fresh material! New inspiration!* Lulu and Alex demanded from the page. *All we do is hide from each other.*

"Spoiled brats!" she cursed them as she dragged her exhausted bones to bed.

The next time Sasha called, Lin said yes to his repeated request for a coffee date.

He gulped. "Did you just say yes? What's changed?"

"Beats me," she said. *Anything for art.*

She picked the swanky coffee bar in her building for their meeting—*a field trip*, as she was determined to call it. Sasha's hair was longer, golden ringlets bouncing on his sculpted chest. New lines ran tastefully across his forehead, accruing mystique, a ridicule of time.

"This place reminds me of that espresso bar we went to once," he said, smiling at her, warmth pouring out of his eyes like bedtime milk. "Remember we made up an entire skit about that pretentious La Marzocco machine, the long-nosed talking robot?"

She tittered and burned in her seat, digging her nails into her locked hands.

"I was quite shitty when I was young, wasn't I?" he murmured.

*Lulu, meet the new Alex. Hope this is enough inspiration for you.*

"I wasn't so wise myself." Her voice came out wobbly.

*Pull your fucking self together.*

THE FINALE. For five months, she let her "research" continue, one platonic date at a time. In mid-spring, six years after he took her virginity, Sasha pulled her in and kissed her good night at the end of a date, his languid arms looping around her waist under a blossoming lilac tree. She didn't fight him. His tongue tasted hot and sweet like the perfumed flowers over their heads.

The next day, a Saturday, Sasha gathered the whole gang, including Paulina, in his basement. He called Lin "my girl" and wouldn't let her leave his side, his arm draping territorially around her shoulders. "Get a room, you love birds!" Vlad hollered at them, feigning annoyance. Paulina nursed her drink alone in her favourite corner. From time to time, she lifted her beautiful eyes and scanned Lin from head to toe as if she'd never seen her before.

"I have something to show you." Lin winked at Sasha once the guests had cleared out.

"Aren't you full of surprises these days." He grinned dumbly, his face flushed from too many drinks.

She took the script out of her bag and placed it in his hands. "It's a short one, but I thought you might be interested in playing the leading man."

The clouds in his eyes dissipated. He scanned the cover and flipped through the pages. "You wrote this? How? When did you find the time?"

"Sleep is overrated."

"I thought you quit theatre. You're a data scientist now."

"Hustling multiple careers is a defining feature of our times."

"You're a wonder, you know that?" He pulled her onto his lap and planted kisses on her neck and bare shoulders.

"There's more. Drum roll, please ... Come on, work with me here!"

"Okay, okay." His lips shuddered and twisted, producing an impressive sound cloud. His hands moved in the air, clanging an imaginary cymbal.

"We are ... going to ... SummerWorks!"

"Holy crap! Are you serious?"

"Yup, got the acceptance email two days ago, my Leading Man."

He drew her deeper into the cavity of his chest, the stubble on his chin chafing her forehead. "I can't believe it. I ... *love* you," he said shyly, gazing down at her as if searching for approval.

*Lulu, do you like this new ending?*

She smiled back at him, mischievous, hunger roiling through her.

He hauled her over his shoulder and marched toward his bed, his blazing eyes both savage and saintly as he laid her on the white sheet. With a tremor in his hands, he removed her clothes and stared with renewed wonder at a terrain he was once familiar with. His lips were tender as silk, slowly and methodically traversing every inch of her nakedness. He was a man on a mission, determined to put her pleasure above his own. His mouth pulled and pushed tirelessly, until she juddered along the length of her spine, the afterwaves buoying her on a river of oxytocin. He grinned with pride, his lips glistening.

"Would you like to taste your sweet, sweet cunt?" he whispered, biting her earlobe.

She giggled, until she saw the seriousness in his eyes as he dove down and gnawed on her lips, the alcohol on his breath stinging her. He let his erection linger between her thighs, long enough for the flame in her to soar close to explosion. Then he thrust into her with a soldier's resolve, his moaning throaty and husky, drowning out the silly creaking of the bed. She squeezed her eyes shut, her head buried under his heaving, swelling chest. Pain rolled over her and flattened her insides. She'd forgotten this middle part, pleasure receding and teetering on the edge of torture. *Do I actually want this? Maybe not...*

Black clouds before her eyes parted. Tiny faces burrowed out of obscurity, porcelain-white, perfect symmetry, merely a hint of exoticism. She gawked at them in the shadows: faces with no basis for shame or fear, faces to be loved and desired across the galaxy. Their children's faces. Pain and pride lost their currency; she couldn't nudge away a sudden gratitude for his generosity, for the rich gift he'd bestow on the creatures of her womb. She could do this, mating as a sacrificial act, of self-destruction, of erasure, like a mother spider thankful to be eaten alive. Her orgasm, explosive and blindsiding, coincided with his. She knew it happened, right then and there—her female anatomy, once prey now predator, dark pathways and deadly viscosity snaring and locking his seed, the most coveted treasure there was.

PART FIVE

# THE SAINT
# RETURNS

2012–2013

# 1

## *Lin*

### 2012

The baby's kicks woke her from a shallow sleep. She had known it was a girl long before the doctor confirmed it. "Shhh, go back to sleep, tiny princess." She patted her belly. The grandfather clock upstairs sent out a faint, metallic wave of the Westminster chime. She rubbed her eyes and strained to make out the time on the nightstand: three a.m.

A musky smell hovered in the air, the smell of sweat glands and hair follicles, of bodily collision. She winced at the sight of her heirloom qipao crumpled by the bed like a discarded skin. She had been radiant in that qipao tonight, despite her protruding belly, but not enough to brighten their desolate city-hall wedding with Sasha's mother and her befuddled date from eHarmony as sole witnesses. Lin remembered the strangely acidic perfume on Nadya's extended nape as the older woman gave her a stiff hug, like a giraffe necking for dominance, her eyes steely when their heads parted. And later, Sasha's hairy hands, undressing her in this dingy pit of a basement. His hurried breaths, the impatient rearrangement of her limbs, his mechanical thrusts and fast release. His kiss on her forehead, distracted and distant.

"Will you snuggle with me?" She hated the begging in her voice.

"People are waiting upstairs."

"But we just made love. Does it mean nothing to you anymore?"

"I don't want to fight, not tonight." He put his clothes on swiftly, an act of escapology. "Get some rest," he muttered, and dashed up the stairs.

The cavernous basement closed in on her, plunging her into the murky bowels of a sinister beast, ready to grind her bones to dust. Sasha had insisted on spending their wedding night here, despite all the posh decorations she'd set up at her condo.

He'd cut her off when she mentioned her place as if she had suggested Chernobyl. "I want to have a drink with my friends in the open air, in my garden. Is that too much to ask?"

She had grown used to his accusatory tone. He was still capable of moments of tenderness, but his sense of entrapment seethed like a hidden river of molten rock. He blamed his drunken stupor for her current *condition*. But most of all, he blamed *her* for not doing her part.

They had gone back and forth on the decision to marry. She'd thought their success at SummerWorks, and the favourable reviews he'd received as the male lead, would placate him once and for all. The chatter at the show's afterparty had given her false confidence. "A patron *and* a writer—you've hit the jackpot with that girl!" Vlad had patted Sasha on the back, and Sasha had looked at her with those liquid, dreamy eyes.

But as her belly ballooned, his moodiness had returned with a vengeance, poisoning the air and keeping her on her toes. On good days, he'd crack open a bottle of Smirnoff and speak of their shared future in a remote but plausible way. Other times, he'd brood and sulk, complain about everything and nothing—the commute between her place and his theatre, her long workdays and lack of vacation time, how disrespected he felt when she paid for everything.

A flash of anger would seize her. "Get out, buzz off, leave!"

"What about the baby?"

"She doesn't need an ungrateful scumbag for a father!"

He'd stomp out and disappear for days, until she composed her regrets and apologies in a blur of voicemails, and sent them off in five-minute intervals: *All my fault you are far from a scumbag I overreacted as usual I love you I can't live without you we belong to each other the baby needs you come back now.* He'd resurface eventually, like an underfed dog, licking his wounded ego and her naked back under her sheets. Lather, rinse, and repeat.

In the end, she suspected the memory of his volatile childhood locked him in a chokehold and squeezed a nod out of him. They were lying in bed one night, after sex. The tip of his Marlboro lit up and dimmed with each drag he took, smoke rings hanging above their heads like speech bubbles. "I've always wondered who I'd have become if my parents were still together," he lamented. "Would I still be floundering in theatre, wasting my good years playing messed-up people?" He stroked her belly and sighed, as though resigning himself to the Goddess of Fate. She held her breath, sensing a breakthrough, slippery as quicksilver. Then he put out the cigarette and addressed their baby for the first time: "What should we call you? So many pretty names for little girls."

Bouts of laughter from the garden, interspersed with strings of rapid-fire Russian, cut short her memories. She pictured Sasha in a boisterous debate, surrounded by admirers and alive in his element. Abandonment carved a flaming gash inside her. She was being punished, his frequent reversion to his mother tongue the latest tactic to alienate her, to strand her in a no man's land. She covered her head with a pillow, despair expanding and crowding out her innards. She dug her fingers into the bedsheet, slashing it with her nails. Cries leaped out of her throat, the sound of a slaughterhouse cow. The merry racket went on and on outside.

*Lulu, meet the new Alex. Lulu, do you like the new ending? Lulu, what the fuck were you thinking?*

EXHAUSTION SALVAGED HER AND she drifted in and out of sleep, the boundary between dreams and reality fluid and oscillating. When the dusky sky turned pastel blue, she saw her grandmother perched on the windowsill, a petite, birdlike creature, her face lean and pale, her eyes moist.

"Laolao?"

"My child, you're a woman now," she rasped.

"I can't go on," Lin said in Chinese. The sound of her mother tongue did not make her cringe this time.

"You have to. You love him, right? That white boy?"

274

"I don't know anymore. I booked the first available date at City Hall, before he could change his mind." She chuckled. "How pathetic."

"Now's not the time to be doubtful."

"He's a year younger. 'Subtract ten years from a young man's age,' you used to tell me."

"Boys do ripen slowly. But you two have so much life ahead of you."

"I can't go on, can't go on." She repeated the words like a mantra.

"You have to. Even when they killed my beloved, I carried on."

"I'm not you. You're a woman of faith."

"You don't get to choose anymore, child. From now on, *she* will decide for you."

The elder's eyes betrayed her melancholy. Her thin arms stretched like elastics to bridge the space between them, until her skeletal hands rested on Lin's swelling belly.

The baby kicked again under her touch, resolute, ominous.

# 2

## *Dali*

Under the white hospital linen, his mother lay still like a desiccated mummy, her cheeks gaunt and sallow, retreating into her skull. Her closed eyelids, bluish and translucent, hovered below her creviced forehead like thin layers of ice.

"I'm sorry, I should've called you earlier," Lemei said, standing beside him. "I didn't think she'd go downhill so fast."

"Not your fault, Auntie," Dali replied without meeting her eyes. "Thanks for all your help." He knew his Ma wouldn't have been admitted to Ruijin Hospital, the city's best oncology department, without the Shanghai lady pulling strings. After thirteen years in Shanghai, his mother, a menial labourer, still didn't qualify for a city hukou. She had taken a precious hospital bed from a more deserving local, all thanks to Lady Lemei's mercy. But he hated being reduced to a charity case every time he returned to his adopted hometown. As bad as it was in America, at least it was an equalizer: Chinese—urban or rural—all belonged to the same alien class. He hated Shanghai for its snobbishness. He only wanted to be left alone with his mother.

"She's been in a coma for three days. The doctor's unsure if..." Lemei trailed off. She squeezed his shoulder and left the room.

He moved closer and held his mother's hand, its brittle, paper-like texture chafing his heart. He kneaded her fingers gently, moving from base to knuckle to tip. Her eyelids twitched ever so slightly at his touch.

"I'm back, Ma. Can you hear me?" He closed his burning eyes, shutting out the image of her grotesque, cancer-ravaged body. He tried to recall his mother in her prime, but everything before Ba's disappearance was a blur. All he could see was his forty-year-old Ma, and her doleful but dignified gaze. His Ba had just abandoned them after a year of laying bricks in Beijing. For weeks, village gossip circled them like swarms of pesky gnats, about his loser of a father who had gotten lonely and frisky in the capital and impregnated a fellow migrant worker, a girl twenty years his junior. His mother, pragmatic and stoic as always, had never mentioned Ba again. Instead, she laboured with a vengeance, plowing, seeding, harvesting the family's small plot of land, letting the sun scorch her once-soft skin to a crisp.

After visiting hours, Dali went back to their bomb-shelter-turned-apartment. The damp, mouldy air filled his nose and prickled his throat as he paced the underground bunker. How could his younger self have tolerated this place? Sucking in big gulps of stale air, he battled the sensation of being trapped in a sinking submarine, racing to the ocean's bottom without a chance for survival. He darted from his room to the kitchen to his mother's bedroom, desperate to outpace the suffocation. Turning on the lights in Ma's room, he gasped. A tapestry of colours graced her south wall, like bouquets of flowers blooming on an annihilating winter's night.

For a decade, his mother had been working a second job at a hanfu tailor shop, but he'd never seen her talent on display. Under the neatly written period labels, elegant dresses made for her wealthy clients hung on a line of hooks—a hundred-bird feather skirt from the Tang dynasty, a moonlight skirt from the Song dynasty, a striped, high-waisted A-line skirt from the Northern and Southern dynasties, a ribboned phoenix-tail skirt from the Qing dynasty. He pictured his haggard mother hunched over a yellow lamp and sewing well into the night, solidifying her ancestors' traditions with fabric and feathers, buttons and beads. He wondered how her works of art would glisten in the sunrays and moonbeams if she'd had a window that led to the open sky.

When he left for America, he had vowed to send her money to rent an above-ground apartment. But years of black-market loans Ma had taken on for his education had buried that dream. He was the reason his mother had languished like a rodent in this tomb, long before cancer hunted her down. And now, he couldn't even say a proper thank-you or goodbye.

HE FELL ASLEEP IN Ma's bed, soaking her pillow with the tears of a repentant son. A ding from his phone roused him: *How r things over there?*

He stared at the WeChat message and tried to reconstruct

his new girlfriend's face, but all he could conjure up was the slimy taste of her tongue when they fumbled in the dark the night before his flight.

*Doing fine, goodnight*, he messaged back and turned off his phone.

Groaning, he straightened his creaking spine. His hands stretched underneath the pillow and felt the presence of a book. He switched on the nightlight: *Legend of the Immortal Woman*. From the deep recesses of his brain, shifting shapes of a temple and a lady saint's benevolent, waxy face floated in and out like a distant dream. He flipped through the pages, soon engrossed in the chronicle of the saint's life—her steady diet of powdered mica, her white lotus that could heal all wounds, her resolve to remain a virgin, her disdain for the rich and powerful. The book was tattered and dog-eared. He wondered if Ma had found solace in reading the story over and over, mapping her own life to the saint's lonesome yet enlightened existence. Perhaps she'd dreamed of breaking free from this suffocating pit and soaring into the sky, like the ancient spirit released from under a pagoda.

At the hospital, his mother was slipping away. He applied for and received an overnight seat at the ward. He spent the days massaging her skeletal limbs and engorged stomach, stroking her forehead, speaking to her constantly, to pull her away from the black abyss. At night, he curled up in a chair and drifted into a few hours of fitful sleep. He dreaded the first few waking moments, when a pang would pierce his chest and radiate with alarming speed to his extremities.

In his dream before Ma's final hour, he saw the Immortal Woman riding cotton-white clouds toward him, a massive lotus blossom in her dainty hands. She wore an elaborate

SU CHANG

crown of orchids and peonies above a pair of inky brows and tiny, crimson lips. Her long and elegant eyes—his mother's eyes—glowed warmly. They were suspended together mid-air for a lengthy stretch of time, gazing at each other wordlessly. Then, with a flick of her arm, she dabbed his forehead with dewy lotus blossoms and mouthed a silent *so long*. Turning away, she started her ascent into the clouds. He breathed in the heady scent she left behind, intoxicating and mysterious. Later, he held on to that image and fragrance, through the medical team's frantic shouts and footsteps, through the nurse intern's panicked sobs, through the last kiss he planted on his mother's forehead, sensing the strong presence of her spirit as she glided toward the bank of the Immortal Stream.

# 3

## *Lin*

It was one of those sunny, perfectly blue-skyed mornings, a common setting for horror stories. She was strolling among the tulip blossoms at Lenny Park, her baby dangling in a sling by her breast. She paused to take in the fragrance, with its evocation of honey and apple-spiced tea. Fluffy parachutes of dandelions grazed her bare skin, a seductive, tingling sensation.

At the nearby playground, a young mother hoisted her infant daughter above her head. "My little cutie pie," she cooed, her face bathed in a maternal glow, her eyes mesmerized by her own creation. The baby let out a ripple of giggles, her fine golden hair framing her tiny head like a nimbus. Her huge blue eyes flashed at Lin before turning back to her proud mother. Lin's heart skipped a beat for the infant's beauty, and for the motherly love she'd effortlessly aroused in her. She hastened past them.

*I'm not my mother.*

*Are too.*

*Am not.*

*Are too. Are too. Are too!*

It had been exactly one month, and Sasha and his friends were celebrating the baby's "monthiversary" at home, but Lin couldn't shake the anxiety. Only in the dark of the night, when Pearl was snuggled in the crook of her arms, would she breathe in her sweet milky scent and feel the rush of affection befitting the title of Mom.

"Don't worry about a thing, honey," the kind, tired Filipino nurse at the maternity ward had told her with a knowing smile. "You baby's your drug. It'll cure all your aches."

Lin didn't believe her, but she had smiled back at the nurse through clenched teeth. In the days that followed, as the pair of pain and fatigue settled in beside her, announcing their long-term intentions, she donned an industrial-strength mask and played mother figure for every visitor and stranger alike, placating them, validating their expectations, reassuring them the baby was the best thing that had ever happened to her. But her heart hardened with the first ray of sunlight every morning, bracing for new revelations of hidden prejudices, the guilt fest that would soon devour her.

THE CARELESS COMMENTS, following typical messages of congratulations, came early and often.

"What a funny-looking thing you are!" Sasha had exclaimed, holding Pearl minutes after her birth. He had the look of a boy discovering a puss moth caterpillar in his backyard for the first time, at once intrigued and repulsed. Gingerly, he planted a kiss on the baby, but Lin felt her heart constricting, waves of failure washing over her.

On that sleepless night at the maternity ward, her absent father sneaked into her addled mind. Her father was dead, Laolao had long told her, but even as a child, she knew that wasn't the whole story. Whoever her father was, he was not the kind to be eulogized. He was not only dead, but also a sinner, a villain, an ugly stain. Robbing her of the exotic beauty her mother had possessed was the least of his crimes. To save themselves from shame—Laolao had warned her with flinty eyes—they must scrub him from their history. On her tenth birthday, Lin had defied Laolao and pressed her mother about her origins. Ma had gasped, burning herself on the birthday candles, and fled into the bathroom. Laolao had followed Ma and the sound of sobbing. "Enough. Don't let that damn rapist ruin you for life." She'd overheard Laolao's exasperation behind the closed door. She never inquired again; she wanted her only surviving parent to live.

Cradling her newborn, she sensed her father's genes lurking in the baby's blood, screaming to be seen, screaming for revenge. The thought of him staring down at them with a triumphant smirk sent goosebumps flaring. She shot up from bed and shut the blinds.

Three days after they brought Pearl home, Nadya arrived with a new perm and shade of auburn to her hair, shaving years off her age. She glanced at Lin with pity and offered her congratulations. "Now let's see the heir!" She marched into the nursery like a hard-nosed inspector.

"Ah, how precious!" Nadya beamed at the sleeping baby, the harsh lines on her face softening.

Lin felt a heavy weight lift off her chest. *Silly me, it's her first grandchild, after all.* She opened the curtain a slit, letting in a narrow sunbeam, and took out her camera. She was composing the perfect picture when Pearl woke up and fixed her gaze on Nadya's face. In her focused lens, the grandmother's Pavlovian response unfurled in slow motion: her gnarled hands rising in the air like a conductor's, the first contact between index fingers and crow's feet, the ripples of sagging skin stretching upward, the blue rocks in her sockets obscured by the narrowing slants. Lin inhaled sharply, dropping the camera. Nadya snapped out of her trance. "Jesus Christ, I didn't mean to—" she started, her face beet-red.

Sasha sauntered into the room, oblivious. "Mom, you want to hold her?"

"I don't know ... Yes, of course, okay."

At her touch, Pearl burst out crying.

"Sorry, sorry!" Nadya plopped her back into the crib.

The baby crash-landed on her belly; a sneezing fit ensued, likely triggered by the grandmother's potent perfume. Tears and snot rained down her face.

Nadya swung around toward Sasha, her eyes pleading for a way out. "I don't think she likes me. I ... *scare* her."

"She's never met you. She'll warm up to you." Sasha wiped Pearl with a tissue and lifted her out of the crib. The baby balanced on his arm like a miniature Buddha.

Watching the pair, Nadya shook her head and turned to Lin, the apology and embarrassment on her face hardening into a cleaving glare. Lin could see it too—the pair's ancestors had not crossed paths for thousands of years. Nadya edged toward her son with a sigh and kissed him on the cheeks. She patted the baby swiftly on the head and left the room.

Later, in her shallow sleep between feedings, Lin arrived

at her mother's house with the baby at her breast. Ma's face materialized behind a glass door, grim, defeated. She peered at the baby and groaned, "Our genes, too strong…"

Lin smashed a fist on the glass. "You want her to hate herself too?"

"If only you didn't burn it all down."

"I'd do it again and again."

"Vicious, vile."

"Destruction—I learned it from the master."

She wanted to shatter the wall, shatter Ma's face, along with the disappointment in her eyes.

"Where's my American granddaughter?" the shrill voice demanded from the other side.

Lin pounded on the glass, over and over, until a siren blared, bent on splitting open her skull. She woke up shaking and stammering in the nursing chair, her mind a whirling cloud of condemnation:

*Thief! Stole a white man's seed and buried it under your own. You've contaminated your baby.*

Her breasts leaked and she fumbled in the dark for Pearl, desperate for the sensation of being suckled, the oxytocin that would blunt the sharp edge of pain.

ON THE MORNING OF the monthiversary, the Fox gang had descended on the rental house they'd recently moved into, bearing food and gifts for the baby.

"Happy to be the honorary uncle or great-uncle or whatever you want me to be!" declared Vlad. He tickled Pearl under the arms and played Humpty Dumpty, letting the baby slap his smooth bald head. Pearl returned his kindness with a cascade of giggles.

By the kitchen island, Sasha was cleaning the mess from breakfast when a new actor Lin didn't recognize ambled toward him and nudged him teasingly on the shoulder. "Best stepdad of the year!" he tittered, prompting the stink eye he deserved.

Lin was already slipping downhill when Paulina made her grand entrance, a showy peacock wearing a low-cut seafoam dress and an extravagantly made-up face. She handed Sasha a large tray of beef lasagna—his favourite—and pecked him on the cheeks. When she spotted Pearl, a look of pity spread across her face, followed by a smug smile. Paulina held the baby to her bare clavicles and let Pearl play with her gemstone necklace, her milky complexion a stark contrast to the baby's yellow hue. Her gaze trailed Sasha around the room. *Is this what you wanted, this coloured little alien?* Lin read the actress's secret messages to him. *Look what you've missed out on. I could've given you the most beautiful offspring, straight from a Renaissance painting.*

Sasha, for his part, averted his eyes. Lin wrenched Pearl from Paulina's arms, tucked her into the baby wrap dangling perpetually around her inflated waist, and stormed out the door. She imagined the startled faces behind her, the murmurs that were sure to embarrass Sasha. She refused to look back.

She ran. At first, Pearl stared at her with alarm, but her undulating steps soon lulled the baby to sleep. The sharp burn in her lungs replaced the heartache, her head lightening with each block she traversed. When she reached Lenny Park, she slowed down and panted for air, before hastening past the tulip bushes and the playground—a minefield of doting mothers with their angelic babies. She reached the narrow trailhead tucked behind a deserted skating rink and stepped into the woods, sighing with relief. The woods were her protector, her sanctuary, an ancient shrine with its intoxicating scent of pine sap.

Late morning sun seeped through the leaves, dripping bright spots by her feet. She traced the narrow path near the creek, chasing the songs of the blue jays until she came to an imposing white oak surrounded by blazing dogwood. She plopped down on the soft earth, adrenaline ceding ground to fatigue, her back easing into the furrowed contours of the tree trunk. She kissed her precious on the cheeks and rocked her, quietly humming "Down by the Bay," a Canadian classic she'd only learned recently, a song that went on and on, loopy and absurd like the postpartum days.

Into the shadows of the ancient canopy, Ma sauntered toward them, followed by Dr. Hong wielding her gleaming knife, her wide-set eyes black and impenetrable. The doctor glided a finger over the baby's forehead, her nails blood-red.

"It can all be fixed," she intoned. "Just leave it to me."

"*No!*" she shrieked.

*Am not. Are too. Am not! Are too!*

"Get the fuck away from my baby!"

Sweat poured down her spine. Her heart leapt to her throat. She clutched Pearl as the lights went down in front of her eyes.

# 4

## *Lin*

The office of Dr. Green, the in-house psychologist at St. Joe's maternity ward, looked more like an indoor playground than a physician's office.

"Excuse the mess," the doctor said as she guided Lin to the back of the room, tiptoeing around plush toys, baby slides, and a ladybug teeter-totter. "Many moms bring their babies with them, so we make sure there's always something for the little ones to do."

The section for mothers had fuchsia walls and pictures of palm trees and vast white-sand beaches. Lin imagined Dr. Green leading other crazy moms through transcendental meditation: *Mind over body; we're in a tropical paradise.*

"I know there's still a stigma out there about postpartum depression, and therapy, but think of our session as your mini vacation from baby duties," the doctor said after they were both seated, her voice syrupy. "The good news is both the cardiologist and the neurologist have given you clearance. So stress is the enemy we'll target here. We'll find coping strategies to prevent a similar episode from happening again."

Lin stared at the doctor's emerald eyes and perfectly coiffed blond bob. She looked like a fairy godmother who could eradicate all the world's problems with a flick of her wand and a chant of "Abracadabra!"

"Let's start with your episode." Dr. Green took out a notepad. "Tell me what happened before you fainted."

"I don't know. I must be too tired."

The doctor only gave her a silent nod.

"The baby didn't sleep well the night before," she tried again. "I barely had any breakfast. Maybe low blood pressure."

"Anything else?"

Lin shook her head.

"I spoke to your husband. He said you stormed out of the house during a social gathering. Can you tell me what was going through your mind then?"

"Don't quite remember," she lied. "Sometimes I get restless. I like to go walking with my baby."

"You keep on doing that. Walking does wonders for new moms' mental health." The doctor's tone darkened suddenly. "But you collapsed in a wooded area. Fortunately, a dogwalker found you two. Next time, you might not be so lucky. We need to make sure your baby isn't at risk."

Lin felt chills along her spine. Before the earth pulled her down, Pearl's tiny face had flashed before her eyes, so trusting and peaceful, and she had put her in danger.

The doctor's gaze weighed on her like a gravestone.

*I've got to give her something, or I'll never get out of here.*

"My husband had some friends over. I got insecure. I was

reminded how small my own social circle is," she said, offering up a sheepish grin.

"Ah, thanks for sharing. That must be so hard." The doctor softened again. "You are definitely not alone in feeling this way." She doled out a string of statistics while rummaging through her drawer, and finally pressed a pink sheet into Lin's palm: a long list of to-dos, from chatting up fellow shoppers in the diaper aisle to signing up for online networks.

"This week's homework—join a mommy group!" Dr. Green said cheerily. "Find other new moms to connect with, those who can fully understand what you're going through. I want you to go at least weekly, and the more the better." She offered Lin another colour-coded sheet. "Any group on this list will do. I'll quiz you on your assignment when we meet again, okay?" She beamed, satisfied with her own helpfulness. "Just kidding, no pressure. Enjoy your new friends!"

Lin thanked the doctor, whose smile was so bright and contagious that she too felt something akin to joy: she had contributed to this woman's sense of purpose! She'd do right by the friendly blonde, copy her irresistible, symmetrical smile and strike up friendships. She'd stop being mental and give nobody an excuse to take her baby away from her.

Lin was buoyed by the fairy doctor's positivity for the rest of the day, until memories of her lonely childhood crashed back at night for a reality check. She'd never learned the art of friendship growing up. She'd always known she was different, that she had a mission, that she was the executor of Ma's Grand Plan. Her schoolmates learned to leave her alone as she tackled set after set of Olympic math challenges and buried her nose in English books far beyond her peers' abilities, rendering her the eccentric, pretentious super-achiever in their eyes. In her teenage years, when a few brave boys pressed their secret notes of admiration into her hand, she'd tuck them away in books or pencil cases. Ma would harness the teachable moment whenever she found the notes, which she always managed to do, as if she truly possessed a sixth sense. "You're so close to that brilliant life in America. Why waste time and get tangled in something that's not meant to last?"

"Of course not," she'd reply, scoffing at the silly suitor. "Not in a million years."

She knew not to get greedy. She had Ma, after all, her most devoted companion.

So it was with great trepidation that she dragged her feet toward the mommy circle at Lenny Park the following Saturday. To her surprise, the newborn at her breast was her admission ticket, no questions asked. The zombie-eyed members were too sleep-deprived to set up a vetting procedure. Her new routine was settled: twice a week, she and Pearl would circle-time with a dozen mother-baby pairs under a puffy willow, sharing nuances of their little ones' nap qualities and poop consistencies, as well as a plethora of problems plaguing the brave new world of a postpartum woman. They were her problems too—a traumatic birth where human anatomy was stretched to inhuman limits, the aches and pains that lingered like a bull-headed domestic abuser, the mission impossible known as breastfeeding, the sleep deprivation that loosened screws in the brain, the swift identity shift from liberated professional to full-time wet nurse. She listened, signalling her support with eager nods, but she didn't get to talk much. Hailey, the indefatigable group leader, complained incessantly about her deadbeat husband and the loss of their once-steamy sex life. There were other dominant voices too, busy offloading their stresses, hungry for extra pairs of attentive ears. Unwittingly, Lin sat with the group's silent faction, who looked on in a daze, fed their babies, and occasionally nodded off for quick naps.

Moms in the popular faction never seemed to recognize her outside the circle time, but nonetheless, she nurtured the nascent feeling that she'd found her people and, more importantly, a tribe for Pearl. She fantasized about the many birthdays and holiday parties ahead, the joint visits to waterparks and the science centre, their group vacation on a far-flung, *real* white-sand beach, the children playing tag and digging for crabs while the mothers massaged sunscreen into each other's backs.

During her follow-up visit with Dr. Green, she rattled off the names of her mommy friends, her voice quivering with joy.

"How wonderful! Making such progress already." The doctor's high-voltage smile returned. "You're doing *so* well that I have a little present for you." She handed Lin a rubber wristband. "The hardest thing for new moms is to stay present. Mommy brains wander endlessly, but staying present is everything. Next time you find yourself drifting, give our friend here a gentle snap and it'll bring you back to the here and now."

With that, she stuck a gold star on Lin's chart, like rewarding a diligent pupil in a kindergarten class. "See how fast things can turn around? Connection, connection, connection! We've seen this over and over in our research. You're one more case of success!"

. . .

CONNECTION, CONNECTION, CONNECTION.

Lin stared at Hailey's fast-moving lips, foamy bubbles at the corners of her mouth, wondering if she could get a word in edgeways today. *The secret to forging long-lasting friendships as an adult,* she'd read in a *New York Times*–bestselling self-help book, *is your willingness to be vulnerable, to open yourself up for others to see.* She didn't know how. Tight-knit interest groups, *cliques,* had been forming in the past three months over things like coffee grinders, pressure cookers, and hair extensions. She wasn't invited to any of these extra-curricular groups since she'd failed the audition, when brand names flew around the main circle and her only contribution was a consistent blank stare.

Her only girls' night, or "inner-circle confab," as she'd come to call them, had ended in awkward goodbyes and a promised follow-up invite that never came. Over glasses of red wine, the women had traded contacts for waxing salons, paleo dieticians, naturopathic doctors who could prescribe weight-loss pills. They'd slapped their bulging midriffs and barked out resolutions in unison ("Time to get our pre-baby bod back!"). She'd had a eureka moment watching her mommy friends away from their babies—their similar body shape built on a near-identical diet since childhood, their light-coloured eyes scanning each other with a primordial recognition. She'd recalled the neighbourhood's appeal when Sasha insisted on renting here: *an Eastern European stronghold, a rarity in the city, familiar groceries, restaurant food like home cooking.* The women had only remembered her at the night's end. "Aren't you quiet tonight?" One patted her arm with a mix of envy and pity. "Ah, you've got nothing to worry about, with your tiny Asian frame."

"Lil' Twig!" another had joined in.

"And hairless!"

Lin had smiled broadly until her cheeks hurt.

She had gone on a more promising art museum trip, and oohed and ahhed with her mommy friends over a roomful of Japanese calligraphy. Afterward, in the sun-dappled museum café, she was as jittery as a hunting puppy, convinced that her reveal-your-vulnerable-self moment had finally arrived.

"Can't wait to start my new hobby tomorrow!" Hailey chirped as she hovered over a velvety box. When exiting through the gift shop, she'd succumbed to the temptation of a calligraphy set meticulously wrapped by Kyoto monks.

Lin took a deep breath. "I once had a calligraphy set as a kid," she started. "My mother used to give me lessons every Sunday morning. I loved them so much. Calligraphy is a lot like meditative dance. So many different styles to learn. Wish I'd continued."

"Why didn't you?" Hailey asked.

*THANK YOU.* She flashed a grateful smile at the group leader.

"My mother got sick. She went a bit mad, in fact."

"Oh my gosh, isn't that just the worst for a kid? A crazy mom?" Ashley cut in. "I had one growing up too, couldn't stand her. Until I had a baby myself. Now I know, moms are so misunderstood. It truly takes one to know one."

"Same here!" Karen echoed. "Had so many epic fights with my mom in my teens. I was convinced she was cuckoo. But since having Archie, Mom and I are besties, for the first time in our lives!"

"My mom was really quite crazy," Lin murmured, but her moment was gone. The group had moved on to trite manifestos on motherhood and female solidarity, and later, the calming effects of the Oriental Arts. She raged in silence for the rest of their date, not so much against the women, but against her stupid self-help book. *What's the secret to long-lasting friendships? Don't be a pain in the ass! No one wants to hear about your messed-up third-world childhood. Keep it light, keep it superficial. Keep on smiling!*

Now, sitting in the mommy circle on a beautiful late-summer afternoon and watching Pearl play harmoniously with her curly-haired friends, Lin was determined to keep on smiling. Hailey had finally paused her speech and was beaming at something outside their circle. Lin turned and saw a rosy-lipped lady sashay toward them on a pair of precarious stilettos like a Stepford wife, her golden hair swishing around her slim waist, a tray of tantalizing sweets on her palm. A little girl, four or five years old in a frilly tutu and a rainbow hairband, tailed her. Lin was intrigued by the girl—she was not a replica of her Barbie doll mother, but she had her own striking features: her big blue eyes belied a hint of exotic origin that Lin couldn't put her finger on. The group went quiet and stared in awe at the mother-daughter pair. Even Pearl craned her head and gawked.

"So sorry we're late, Hailey! Treats from Butternut for all my new pals!" the lady announced in a honeyed voice.

Hailey clapped her hands. "Ooooh, that new bakery on Dundas?"

"Yup, they're keto, paleo, gluten-free!" the lady declared triumphantly.

"I've always wanted to try them! Everyone, I'd like you all to meet my friend of twenty years, Ana. And this is her daughter, Katy."

"Ladies, hi!" Ana greeted the group with an exaggerated wave, jiggling her sizable breasts. "Sorry to crash your party. I know it's meant for new moms, but we just moved to the neighbourhood. What better way to meet new friends, right?" She ambled around the circle and doled out the uber-healthy treats. "You girls are working overtime churning out liquid gold for your babies. Here's a little something to fuel those precious bodies of yours!"

Lin took a piece of lemon bread from the tray. It crumbled in her mouth like sawdust, the artificial sweetener leaving an afterburn on her tongue.

Ana and Hailey hugged rigorously before plopping down on the grass. Everyone munched their desserts in suspenseful silence, as though waiting for a cue from the new leader.

"Traffic's horrific today," Ana said in an intimate tone, as if she were among a circle of longtime confidantes. "I told Katy's dad to be back by three. Took him two hours to get back from the East End."

"Katy's still doing the Saturday lessons?" Hailey asked.

"Oh, yeah."

"What kind of lessons?" Lin asked, sensing the shifting dynamic and a new potential.

"She's taking Estonian with an old friend of mine."

*That's useful.*

"It's just super important to me, you know, as the daughter of Estonian immigrants. Got to pass on the language, the traditions, right?" Ana said cheerily, studying Lin's face with her sapphire eyes. "Are you Chinese?"

Lin nodded.

"Which part of China?"

"Shanghai."

"Ooh, I *love* Shanghai! We went on a vacation last year and had the best time! The most futuristic city I've ever seen. And the food, oof. You must miss your hometown so much."

All the women trained their eyes on Lin expectantly. After months of obscurity, she wasn't used to the sudden attention.

"Yeah, sure," she murmured.

"Ana's husband is Chinese too," Hailey chimed in. "Interesting how Katy has blue eyes, eh? I thought genes for blue eyes are recessive."

"I know. I mean, just by looking at her, you could never tell the kid has Chinese blood," Ashley piped up.

"Hahahaha, the power of my ancestors' genes!" Ana flexed her arms, Rosie the Riveter–style.

The group laughed. Lin felt tiny needles pricking her heart.

"So, you speak Chinese to your baby?" Ana's doe eyes were on Lin again like a pair of stage lights.

*Here we go again. The dreaded question.* The baby-time leader at the library had asked it. The nurse at the hospital had asked it. The Ukrainian granny at the grocery counter had asked it. *You must!* those well-intentioned folks breathed down her neck. *Multilingualism is GREAT for your baby's brain development!* She had to turn away, their earnestness scorching her. She had whispered Mandarin to Pearl on the first few nights after bringing her home. The strangely contrived sounds lingered in the nursery as if they'd come from a performer.

"Not really, not much." She shifted awkwardly on the grass.

"Why not?"

"Hard to explain. Some days I feel I'm stranded on an island alone, English the only thread tethering me to the mainland where my husband and other humans live."

"Ahh, we've got a poet on our hands! Well put—considering it's your second language!"

Ana's patronizing shrill irked her.

"But aren't you bothered that your child will lose her heritage? That it'll all end with you?" Ana looked genuinely concerned.

Pressure was building inside her. She sucked in the humid air. Time to change tactics. "Does your husband speak Chinese to Katy?"

"Not at all. He claims he's too embarrassed by his preschool-level Mandarin."

"But Craig came here when he was a teen, no?" Hailey chimed in.

"Twelve. His parents switched to English overnight when they got here. I really don't understand it. Such a shame when people let go of their heritage."

"Yeah, how sad ..." more voices joined in.

"Keep it up, Ana," Hailey said brightly. "So cute to see your Katy speak her foreign mother tongue."

"*Foreign mother tongue!*" Ashley clapped. "I *love* it!"

"I don't want her to be like her dad, you know? Detached from his roots." Ana's searching gaze was on Lin again.

"And yet, Craig is now chauffeuring your child to Estonian lessons all the way across town every single weekend," Lin said breathlessly, tripping over her syllables.

Ana's smile froze. Raised eyebrows rippled around their perfect circle, silence hanging above them like a menacing cloud. Lin knew what social decorum called for. A change of topic. An olive branch. But she could barely contain the scream inside her: *Naive! Oblivious! Have you SEEN my Pearl? Does she need to SOUND like an "Oriental" as well? Your Katy should learn Chinese indeed! She's won life's lottery! She can conquer the world with her alabaster skin, big blue eyes, and Mandarin skills!*

She had the queasy sensation of lip-syncing with her mother. A leash yoking her firmly to the past while the world moved on. The women sent furtive glances at her hands. She looked down and saw red lashes on her left wrist, her right hand snapping the rubber band with stronger and stronger force.

"Easy, easy, you're going to bruise yourself," Hailey said at last. "You all right? Want me to call somebody for you?"

Lin sensed the murky tide surging toward her again. Before it engulfed her, she shot from the ground with Pearl and darted away from the circle like a mouse. Out of the shade of the willow tree, the sun blinded her instantly, and for a brief moment, she saw a bright, empty field she could scurry into, taking all her petty sorrow with her.

# 5

## *Lin*

The room was suffocatingly still, Sasha's silhouette on the wall motionless. Lin's bedside lamp cast a yellow sheen, rendering everything a shade of tarnished gold.

"Hey," she called feebly to his shadow, rubbing sleep from her eyes.

Silence.

She propped herself up and felt a lurch of pain. Bruises bloomed on her kneecaps like inky flowers. Her chest tightened.

"Where's Pearl? Sasha, what's going on?"

"You're not allowed to take her out by yourself. *Ever. Again.*" His anger-laced voice chilled her.

"Where *is* she?"

"Do you remember anything?"

"Sasha, where is she? Is she okay?"

"In the nursery. You're lucky Hailey went after you,

300

catching you just before you fell. Do you remember any of it?"

She shook her head.

"You know how dangerous it was? What if you'd fallen on top of her? You could've broken her bones! You could've killed her! This is the second, and last, strike! I won't allow it anymore."

To her horror, a cackle leaped out of her. "What will you do? Lock me up?"

"What's *wrong* with you? Ever since Pearl was born, you've been acting like a total stranger. I know things have been hard, but your behaviour is just... I don't know how to live with you anymore!"

"Didn't know my pain was inconveniencing *you* so much."

"We're a couple. Of course what goes on with you affects me."

"A *couple*? When was the last time we were intimate?"

"You had a baby!"

"Four months ago!"

"Do *you* want to have sex?"

"Sex is not the point. There are many ways to be intimate. You're just not interested in me anymore."

"I know I haven't always been a good husband, but haven't I gotten better since Pearl was born?"

*Perhaps. I don't know.*

*Nothing's working.*

"You're off in your head all the time. Always brooding, sad, angry. The first time you put the baby in danger, we had friends over and you just ran off like a maniac. Everyone was stunned. I felt like I no longer knew you!"

"Let them be stunned. I didn't invite them."

"So you'd rather wallow alone in whatever dark pit you've dug for yourself? And drag me and Pearl down with you? You ever think of the impact on the baby?"

*Yes, I'm an unfit mother.*

"You need to pull yourself together. You need to go back to Dr. Green."

"You've never loved me, have you?" She stared down at her engorged breasts, the loose skin around her waist, the clumps of fallen hair matted against her shirt. She couldn't summon an ounce of self-love.

"You need help."

"You married me for my good stable job," she hissed, consumed by a sudden urge to egg him on. "You married me for my swanky apartment, for the prospect of a leading role in my script!"

His face turned crimson. "You've got to be fucking kidding me!"

"You know it, you married me for all the perks!"

"We had a baby on the way!"

"Right, you'd never have married me if I wasn't knocked up. Now you're full of regrets."

He was quietly seething, purple veins bulging at his temples. She took his silence as an affirmation of what she'd long suspected.

"I saw how you were around Paulina."

He threw up his hands. "Is that what this is all about? I almost never see her. She's changed theatres."

*Retreat! Retreat!* a voice urged in her head. But she saw her desperate self rising at dawn to construct her white-resembling mask. She saw Nadya's abhorrence holding her

Chinese heir. She saw the smugness on Paulina's ravishing face. She charged forward as if on a suicide mission.

"But you *desire* her, don't you? You want to lick her marble-white pussy, come inside that firm, sculpted body."

"Obscene! You are a *mother*! You ... *disgust* me."

"That's your buyer's remorse talking. You fantasize about your white beauty, the children she'd give you, the children who'd look like mini versions of yourself. Then you look over at me and Pearl, the aliens you've unwittingly invited into your home."

She felt herself shrinking, becoming unbearably small. All over the world, children were dying, rainforests burning down, glaciers melting in a bubbling cauldron, whole species slipping into extinction, and what was she fighting about? Who was she fighting for?

"Toxic! You and your toxic ideas! Stop projecting them onto me, onto others! I'm so, so sick of this."

*Me too. So, so sick of this.*

He shook his head, blinking hard with bottled fury. Then he made a curious motion with his arms slicing through the air, as if cutting all ties. Stomping around the house, he shoved some clothes into a duffle bag and dashed out, slamming the door behind him.

A WEEK PASSED WITHOUT a peep from him. Days and nights bled into a thick, viscous tunnel entrapping her and her baby. Some nights, she stretched out her hand to peel at the darkness, convinced it was a stage curtain that concealed a sun-filled garden. But there was only dark behind undulating dark. She and the baby nestled in the nursing chair, drifting in and out of consciousness. Only when extreme hunger attacked her would she rise from the chair and ferret through the dwindling supplies in the pantry. Even going out for groceries was a risky business now. The one time she'd ventured out, bleary-eyed in her baggy pajama bottoms, she saw her mommy group at the store, giggling and getting ice cream together. They didn't lift their eyes in her direction, but she was the Bell Witch who haunted them anyway, freezing their smiles and paralyzing their faces. Like a gaggle of geese, they trotted hastily toward the exit. One of them—a mom from the silent faction—turned and peeked at her, eyebrows knitted, mouth pulled down, shoulders lifted in a remorseful shrug. Lin couldn't help but shrug back.

*Sorry to have scared you.*

*All good. Have a nice afterlife.*

The woman gave a sheepish wave before scampering out with her friends. Lin stared at the trail of melted ice cream the moms had left behind. A pair of young siblings were smearing the mess around like paint, coating their white shoes with rainbow stripes. Their mother charged out of the noodle aisle and chastised them, her piercing voice drowning out the noises in Lin's head—the juicy gossip of a ghost sighting among her old friends.

In her dream that night, an orange blob swayed on a match's phosphorous tip, its glow illuminating the dusky jungle of anatomy charts and skeletons. She opened the drawers; journal papers spilled out and beckoned the fledgling flame between her fingers. She lowered the match to the top of the stack. *Facial modifications in East Asia.* The fiery tendrils licked the byline—*Hong Ting, MD*—before caressing the page with a burst of energy. The flame sank into the flesh of the paper, a darkening stain percolating downward and fanning outward, until it clutched the wooden desk and devoured the dry fuel with a beastly hunger. The wood popped and crackled. She jerked her chair back and hopped aside, her heart thumping, her hands grabbing all they could reach—charts and jars and tubes, Caucasian masks, Asian masks. Feed the beast! Feed the beast! With each round of renewed fuel, the flames jigged and jived, a mesmerizing dance. She danced too, her silhouette on the wall a wild blurry dynamo, swelling, ballooning. The women burst in, shrieking. Ma's gnarled hands were on hers, wrestling, killing the beast. Strings of apologies leaped out of Ma's mouth, saturating the thinning air. She couldn't breathe; she had to fight back. But the doctor lunged at her like a White Bone Spirit, whiplashing her with shrill cries: "Psychos! You and your mother—you are both psychos!"

She trembled awake, narrowly escaping the demon's blow.

WHEN SASHA CAME HOME two weeks later, he wore a sombre look and avoided eye contact. He sauntered around the house with a peculiar gait, slept on the sofa in the living room, and left early in the mornings. Every few days, he'd take Pearl for a walk and return with bags of groceries spilling out of the stroller. Most nights he'd come back just before bedtime, reeking of liquor. He'd flop down on the sofa, clasp Pearl to his chest, and hum a Russian lullaby, the melody elegiac and meandering. When Lin did her night feedings later, she could smell on the baby a mix of alcohol and a foreign, inexplicable scent.

She wondered how long they could play pretend. One night, when she was pacing the living room with Pearl suckling at her breast, Sasha's jeans pocket lit up. Flashes pierced the darkness with urgency, transmitting a distress signal. She fished the phone out of his pocket as he snored peacefully. She was calm as she scrolled through the missed calls and text messages—Paulina's salacious push-and-pull and his apparent retreat. She didn't know Paulina could be a good writer too, whose play-by-play recounting of their single night of reunion triggered a flood between her legs.

It was only later, when Sasha grasped her hands and apologized on repeat, that she snapped back to reality. Her hard-earned family—the ruby-cheeked baby flanked by her handsome man and her shyly smiling self—dissolved before her eyes, blown into shards of coloured sand like a Tibetan mandala. Blood rushed to her temples; rage roared in her ears. She didn't remember everything they said happened. Only snippets of the humiliating scene lurked in the cavity of her skull for days after—the hard and fast scratching of her body, the bleeding, the incongruent urge to slap her sex, the siren of an ambulance. And the immense pressure building inside her—not unlike the sensation of giving birth—as if a demon child, full of fury, were burrowing out of her skin.

# 6

## *Dali*

He was amazed at her ability to sleep through the pandemonium. Lin must have been thoroughly exhausted, or perhaps it was the stream of antipsychotics being pumped into her blood. To him, the morning was a parade of sinister shouts and murmurs. The post-breakfast burst of energy ricocheted down the hallway, iron gates slamming, cascading bangs rattling his ears. But Lin slept through it all. She only opened her eyes when the lady next door belted out a song: melancholic, jazzy strings of Hindi verses percolating through the paper-thin wall between them.

"Hey, you," he called out to her in English, honouring their old agreement. But before he could say more, a nurse marched in with a black box. "Electric pump for you, and some Tylenol," she said.

Lin cupped her breasts under the hospital gown. He had to look away.

"I need to feed my baby," she pleaded.

"Time to take care of yourself. Your baby's fine," the nurse said dismissively.

"The baby must be starving."

"You can't feed her anyway, with all the medications in your body. Your husband has lots of formula at home."

*Husband.* The word stabbed him in the heart. He shot from his chair and left the room. But his feet dragged, until he stood still in the antiseptic hallway. An unkempt woman with a rocking head and a pasty complexion floated by, flanked by two weary nurses. The woman gave him a dirty look and murmured obscenities.

*Pull yourself together. Finally, you have a chance to take care of her. Don't let anything get in the way.*

After he scattered his Ma's ashes, with Lemei and her frail mother as his sole witnesses, he'd had the urge to call Lin. He couldn't talk to his new girlfriend when all he wanted to hear was Lin's voice. He hated himself for it, but this proud, stubborn, frustrating girl was the perennial puzzle of his life, the challenge he had grown addicted to. Night after night, he phoned her, pacing around the spot where his Ma's ashes had fallen into the Mother River of Shanghai, momentarily obscuring the neon lights and gleaming skyscrapers. When he couldn't reach her after dozens of calls, he booked a one-way flight to Toronto. He wandered aimlessly through the downtown streets, dialling her number every few minutes until, one morning, a tired female voice came on the line: "CAMH, how can I help you?" He'd run the ten blocks to the psychiatric ward, as if he were a much younger man racing to meet his lover for a fun-filled rendezvous.

*I can't quit her.* He rubbed his face and headed back to the room.

"Am I dreaming?" Lin whispered, her lacklustre eyes fixed on him. "You appeared out of thin air."

He shook his head.

"Oh, right, I forgot you're a spy now." She giggled.

*So the drugs haven't dulled her edges. Or her cruelty.*

"My Ma died," he said.

She shivered, snapped to attention. "Ah, I'm so sorry. I remember her well."

"Yeah, the migrant worker, the dutiful cleaning lady." Bitterness reared its head, until he saw her reddening eyes.

"To me, she was an auntie from the neighbourhood. A gentle, kind soul. I'm sad she passed, way too early."

"Hey, I didn't mean to make you feel worse, especially now." He couldn't help but survey her surroundings again, the no-nonsense ward built for maximum efficiency: the single bed, the bare, peach-coloured walls, the shelf fastened to the floor.

"Yeah, what a fun place," she rasped. "I'm glad you're here." She offered him a smile so vulnerable it melted all his resentment.

THREE TIMES A DAY, a nurse would materialize and inject Lin with a cocktail of medications, which stiffened her gaze and lengthened her vowels, turning her into a temporary zombie. At mealtimes, Dali took it upon himself to feed her, one spoonful at a time, wiping away the liquids that escaped the corner of her mouth. When the effects of the drugs subsided, she'd lean against the bedpost and talk to him in that new lethargic voice of hers. She had switched to speaking Chinese, and he read it as a gesture of gratitude and reconciliation, like she was capitulating in a long-haul struggle between them.

"You sound beautiful," he told her the first time she switched. "Your mother tongue suits you."

She laughed, her facial muscles straining under the drugs' lingering effects. "Mother. Tongue." She repeated the phrase as though puzzled by its sound.

"Do you still read in Chinese?" he asked.

She shook her delicate head, her eyes turning pink. "I do miss it. I remember the classics. *Dream of the Red Chamber*, *Water Margin*, *The Peony Pavilion* ... We had a two-person book club once, me and my Ma."

"What was that like?"

"Like living in the house of a different ancestor every month. Sometimes it was a band of fiery warriors, sometimes pretty maidens, sometimes mischievous spirits. It was like ... *heaven*."

"But it ended?"

"My mother got sick, very sick ... Somebody killed my uncle, I don't know the details." Tears filled her eyes.

"Hey, hey, we don't have to talk about that now—"

"When Ma returned from that cuckoo's nest"—she cut him off, resolute—"she tore our favourite books to shreds so I'd never waste my time reading them again. She crushed my calligraphy brushes, smashed my inkstone, wiped out all traces of our ancestors." Lin clenched her fists, her steely gaze gliding past him and into the open air, as if pleading her case in front of a higher authority.

. . .

FOR DAYS, THEY PASSED the time venting about their shared Shanghai adolescence—the school bullies, the military-style rallies, the stern-faced teachers barely masking their disappointment in life, the endless standardized tests hanging like swords over their heads. Baby Pearl was Lin's other treasured topic. Her face, dull and grey only a moment before, would flicker with a maternal sheen as she narrated the minutiae of her favourite person, while the husband lurked like a shadow in the background.

"How come Sasha never visits you?" Dali asked once, unable to swallow the suspicion that the laowai husband had a lot to do with her current state.

Her face turned hostile and small. "Didn't I tell you we have a baby?"

*Stop making excuses for him.* He held her gaze. *I can be a much better husband and father. When will you see me?*

LIN WAS DISCHARGED FROM the hospital after a week. "Why so soon? She's not ready!" Dali had argued with the attending doctor, selfishly not wanting their time together to end. The hospital had a severe shortage of beds, he was told, and Lin's further treatment—a combination of talk and group therapies—would continue on an outpatient basis.

The morning of her discharge came on a wave of heat and humidity, reminding him of the summer when they sat shoulder to shoulder at the math competition, when he crafted the golden ticket for her departure.

"Sasha is picking me up," she said sheepishly, her frail body barely concealed by a satin camisole.

He nodded, rising to gather his belongings.

"I appreciate your help so much ... Truly ... I wouldn't have survived the past week without you."

He waved to stop her, or he'd have no strength left to face the lonesome bus ride to his hostel, and the thought that he was losing her all over again.

"Your husband and daughter are here," a nurse intern chirped as she entered the ward, a final thermometer in hand.

Dali ducked out of the room without saying goodbye, but a blond man with piercing blue eyes was already at the door, cradling a baby in his arms. They locked gazes briefly before the man looked away. Exhaustion marked his striking face, his cerulean irises enmeshed in a net of red veins, grey hair sprouting at his temples.

*So this is Sasha.* Dali couldn't take his eyes off him.

The man's effect on Lin was swift. Her femininity went on instant display—in the eyes that leaked light, the softening curve of her lips, the gentle tilt of her head.

"I'm so sorry," Dali heard him say. "It was only one time, a big mistake. It won't happen again."

Lin wrapped her arms around herself and trembled like a startled bird.

Sasha drew closer. "How do you feel?"

"I'm okay."

"It's been a shitshow at home without you."

She glanced at his bloodshot eyes and drapey clothes. "You realize you have yellow formula stains all over your sleeves."

Sasha chuckled and leaned into her. "I'm so tired. Let's all go home and take a nap together." She hesitated, and instead of relaxing into him, took the sleeping baby from his arms and smelled her tiny head. Sasha, nevertheless, encircled the mother-daughter pair with his hairy arms and kissed the top of Lin's head.

From behind the door, Dali watched the picture-perfect scene of the family reunion, flames of jealousy scorching his heart. A beast on steroids swelled in him. Suddenly, in Sasha's face he saw all the smug, self-important white men who had debased and crushed him—his cruel, mocking advisor, a devil of a man; the heartless lab mates who had flung him the cold shoulder; the landlord who'd evicted him for the fish sauce smell in his apartment; the band of self-righteous news anchors and pundits with their incessant lambasting of his country. *And now you!* He nearly barged in and hollered at her. *After everything, you still choose him. Why? Just to be close to his whiteness? You think it'll rub off on you? Humiliating!* The beast was on the verge of exploding. Turning on his heel, he stormed down the hospital hallway, salty tears drenching his cheeks.

# 7

## *Lemei*

What got stuck in her head was the trail of dark blood drying across her mother's cheek like a mocking gash, even after the oncologist pulled a white sheet over the dead woman's face.

*But I tucked her into bed last night!* Lemei had seen her Ma's feverish eyes glowing in the nightlight. How could someone cross the threshold of life and death so effortlessly? So *recklessly*?

She sank into the cold metal chair, her body gelatinous, white noise roaring in her ears.

"I'll go type up the report," the doctor said. "Once again, I'm so sorry for your loss." His hand landed on her shoulder and made her jump.

"No, no, not so fast! *You* said—" Her voice was heating up and bounced between the walls. "*You* said my mother was among the luckiest. A year ago, you said it to my face."

"CML is indeed the most treatable type of leukemia."

"You said with the magic pill, she could live out her golden years."

"I don't think I used the word *magic*."

"You sure did!"

"'Targeted drug therapy' was what I said."

"No, you called it the magic pill."

"I may have misspoken in my eagerness to comfort you."

"No, no, you lied! Oh, you put on quite a show too!"

Rage shot up to her throat and choked her. A year ago, the oncologist had presented her with the first slim bag of pills. "The drug normally costs twenty thousand yuan a month, three months' salary for a middle-class family," he'd said with a sly twinkle in his eyes. "But your mother can get it for free since she belongs to the unicorn club—widow of a first-generation revolutionary." Lemei had studied the receipt under her nose, taking in the dramatic accounting trick, the disappearing act of a six-figure number. She'd looked up at the doctor's expectant smile and wondered if she was obliged to shed a few tears or shout a few slogans. In a panic, she'd given a hasty performance, shaking the doctor's hand and singing praises to the Party that had come to the rescue of its most loyal servant.

"I understand your shock, Lemei, but please be civil, be *reasonable*," the oncologist implored. "No one, I do mean *no one*, can guarantee the efficacy of a cancer treatment for an individual patient." He launched into a string of statistics about the medication's potential side effects, but Lemei could hardly listen to him this time, her ruthless mind conjuring up the rest of Diagnosis Day from a year before, when she'd zigzagged through the cramped hospital lobby, through the human maze of migrant workers who had lined up before

dawn to wait for an appointment with a Shanghai special-
ist. The air had been thick with cries, and haggling between
the rural patients and the scalpers who peddled the highly
inflated registration tickets. She had tucked the magic pills
under her arm and practically hurtled out of that bedlam,
wearing her incredible privilege like a badge of shame. *Didn't
you rail against this de facto caste system, you hypocrite?* Those
must have been the exact words bubbling up her throat. *Now
you are its direct beneficiary. Congratulations!*

Next to her, the doctor flipped through notes on a clip-
board. "So, you told the nurse that you and your mother
attended a friend's funeral just two days ago. That could've
been it. A combination of exhaustion and grief overloading
her heart. Heart attacks occur from time to time with this
therapy."

Then, incredibly, that meaty hand of his on her shoulder
again.

"*Or*, you can think of it this way," he intoned, like a guru
ready to impart his profound wisdom. "By witnessing the
return of a body to nature, your mother had caught a glimpse
of freedom beyond her cancer-ravaged shell, and given herself
permission to relinquish the mortal coil."

She shook off his hand, clenching her teeth so she
wouldn't spit at him. She squeezed her eyes shut and hissed
in his direction, "Go to hell."

LATER, AFTER ENDLESS PAPERWORK and a flurry of
calls with the Committee of the Old Cadre, the funeral
parlour, the police station, all facilitated by the oncologist's overworked clerk, she was sent home in a yellow cab
under a starless sky. In the dark living room, her computer

screen flashed and beckoned her. *Ten new messages!* a pop-up window declared. She lunged at her desk and deleted the messages without opening them. She feared the explosion of gratitude each of them contained, the confetti and champagne emojis that would spiral down her screen.

*So it was me who was responsible for Ma's death,* she thought with a shudder. As her mother's sole caretaker, she'd ceded the battleground to sneaky cancer by putting strangers' welfare above Ma's. Ever since her fellow CML activists had scored a momentous win six months ago and the government had agreed to cover most of the costs of the magic pill, she'd buried herself in volunteer work, wading through a flood of applications for their grassroots advocacy group. Those requests had come from all over the world, especially America, from Chinese emigrants who had acquired American passports and, therefore, in the eyes of her government, "defected" to the enemy state. She had given in to her morbid curiosity and let their tales of woe seduce her—the long years of struggle to learn a foreign language and culture, to hold down a job, to raise kids who felt no connection to their heritage, the loss of their jobs during the Great Recession along with their health benefits. Some could no longer support the crushing debt they'd taken on to pay for the magic pill. Some had been off treatment for months, their cancer on the cusp of progressing to the next stage. All were desperate to restore their birth nationality and apply for drug coverage. Eagerly, she'd navigated through the vast machine of Chinese bureaucracy—like the knotty entrails of a mammoth—bearing the emigrants' pleas.

*Who am I to blame the hospital or the idiot doctor?* She stumbled around and tossed into a garbage bag the application binders scattered all over the room—evidence of her crime of neglect. The phone rang and rang, and she suspected it was Li. She couldn't stand to hear his voice now. "Didn't I tell you? Our country is getting better every single day!" he'd exclaimed on their call after the CML win, and he'd followed up with an e-card showing a parade of Party leaders' headshots bobbing and grinning like lucky cat figurines, and sunflowers gyrating toward the rising sun—now an internet meme—accompanied by the popular soundtrack "The East is Red."

For a few weeks after that, he had called her frequently, checking in on her work with the emigrants and praising her for "getting over your family's tragedy." "That grudge you carried has brought you nothing but anguish. So glad it's gone, replaced with pride in our motherland," he said cheerily. She'd been increasingly irked by his official tone, and his relentlessly forward-looking sanguinity, but she couldn't deny it either. That surge of pride whenever she wrote "Welcome home" in her congratulations note, whenever she helped restore another citizenship and secure another drug coverage, like pulling the shipwrecked out of the tentacles of a raging sea. That surge of pride hitting her like its own drug—swelling, euphoric, addictive.

She unplugged the phone line, trudged into her bedroom, and dropped her heavy head onto the pillow.

IT TOOK DAYS FOR her to drag her carcass out of bed, and more days before she discovered the redwood box, her mother's treasure trove. In it, a red Party flag with the golden hammer and sickle blanketed everything underneath, as if Ma, even in death, felt the need to declare her eternal loyalty.

She removed the flag, revealing documents neatly arranged in stacks. Her parents' marriage certificate. Her father's old work uniform, with Ma's meticulous patchwork. A "rehabilitation letter" dated November 1976, informing the widow of her husband's innocence seven years after his death in the cowshed—a non-apology apology. A pile of black-and-white photos with Ma's careful annotations on the back: *Baby Feng's first birthday, Our Happy Girl's 100th day, First family trip to the capital!, Much belated funeral for my beloved.*

At the bottom of the box, she found a stack of Chinese calligraphy with her father's masterful strokes and his personal seal on every page. This was her father's love letter to her mother, in the form of a transcription: *Legend of the Immortal Woman.* She sank to the floor and read the part her Ba had lovingly committed to paper only months before his arrest. She remembered enlisting little Lin's help to complete the transcription years later, when she was still giving weekly calligraphy lessons to her young daughter. But after Feng, she had abandoned the project like so many others in her life.

She reached the end of her father's transcription and ached for more. Rooting around the bookshelf for the original book, she groaned. It must have been destroyed during one of her fits. She'd never made an inventory of the books that were sent to their graves some twenty years ago. Now she knew—the legend of her mother's patron saint was among the victims. She ran her fingers over the unfinished love letter and felt the ancient paper breathing into her skin.

"I'll make it right. I'll start first thing in the morning," she announced firmly, to whoever might be listening.

. . .

SHE ALWAYS BEGAN WITH a cake of jet-black carbon ink, grinding it on her father's plum blossom inkstone. The sweet scent of clove and sandalwood soon seduced her into a trance, until the liquid was rich and velvety-smooth, and she couldn't wait to dip her heirloom brush into it. Closing her eyes, she pleaded for her mother's presence. She prayed too for the skills and strength of her father, who had taught her the art half a century ago. Then she dove in, starting with a neat, highly disciplined seal script that was the hallmark of her father's penmanship. She imagined herself as an extension of Ba, her arms and hands a vessel to resume the work he'd started in another lifetime. As she traversed the terrain of the legend, she saw the Immortal Woman taking the shape of her mother. She chased after her on the bank of a misty stream, as the saint flitted from mountaintop to mountaintop, gathering the finest herbs. Her horsehair brush accelerated, rebelling against the clean, contained squares of her father's script, her strokes flowing into one continuous movement. She lost all poise; the words took on a wild agency, thrusting her forward and closer to Ma. When the saint flew out of sight, she was left panting and staring at her sprawling, eruptive calligraphy, sensing the heavy glacier retreat from her heart, as if she had ingested the magic powder of the Immortals.

SHE WAS HALFWAY THROUGH transcribing the three-hundred-page legend when Dali emailed from Toronto.

*Lin is not well*, he wrote. *You should come.*

That afternoon, after she had booked her visa appointment at the Canadian Consulate, Lemei roamed the streets of her neighbourhood. She passed the dozen 1920s villas in her laneway, which until the early 2000s had been repurposed by the Party and housed scores of cacophonous families in cramped quarters. They now stood like quiet nobles behind the high walls and well-trimmed hedgerows, their new owners—the nouveau riche—replacing the familiar riffraff.

She exited the laneway gate and pivoted onto Huaihai Road. Luxury brands and clothing boutiques flooded her vision with elaborate window displays—sparkling floral pendants, fairies in shimmering qipao, white cranes flying over an enchanted forest, dancing queens in golden robes. She tried to recall the old street scene but was so dizzy with loss that she had to plop down on the edge of the flower bed, newly installed to adorn the sidewalk. A few steps ahead, the new Paramount Leader stared down from the wall with a pudgy, benevolent smile. Men and women in chic attire plodded forward, seemingly oblivious to their towering president.

A group of senior women in bright costumes passed her by. The leader, holding a giant peach blossom fan, flashed her an enigmatic smile. Lemei rose and tailed the group. They headed east and entered Xiangyang Park, stopping under the lush canopy of French wutong. She suddenly felt her daughter's small, warm back pressed against her chest as they rode on a white horse on the royal carousel, watching the king's and queen's golden carriages bob around them in decayed glory. She wandered back and forth along the old strip, Lin's childhood stomping grounds. But everything was gone now—the carousel, the swings, the teeter-totter, the rockery. In their place were meticulously manicured flower beds and a suite of exercise equipment befitting the reputation of her city, a city of and for the future. She could be part of it too, if only she could escape the past.

Behind the flower beds, where the hustle and bustle of city life threatened to spill into the green oasis, her prayer for a miracle was finally answered. A short strip of guard-rail stood, warped and dented, steeped in graffiti. It seemed impossible that it had survived the unremitting onslaught of the city's development. She squatted down, her fingers brushing its grainy surface and tracing every childish stroke of her daughter's handwriting:

*Lin and Mama's Gate*

She closed her eyes and felt the sun setting on her face. Little Lin was about to hitch a ride home on Mama's shoulders, riding tall and haughty, like the proud princess she was born to be.

# 8

## *Lin*

### 2013

*I am terribly sorry*, Sasha had written in his note, placed on Lin's nightstand as he slunk away under the camouflage of night holding a single duffle bag. *Things haven't been working between us, I can't carry on pretending. I did love you, but after all these years, I still don't understand you, the history you came from, the ghosts of the past you keep on your shoulders. Sorry I'm a coward.*

Then, a real reason, a last straw: apparently there had been a call from Mikhail in LA a week before.

*Now that your mom is here to help, Pearl will be in excellent hands. I'll send money once I've saved enough.* Pathetically, he'd written this vow, followed by a final sentence that stabbed into her chest: *Don't look for me, I'm not worth it.*

Lin ripped the note into pieces and tossed a double dose of Xanax into her mouth. She pressed hard on her pounding heart as if she could bulldoze away the ache. There wouldn't be enough time for the drug to hit her bloodstream before the rising heat inside her exploded. Soon Pearl would wake up and, like a ruthless weight-training coach, issue a chain of unceasing demands. Lin stumbled out of the bedroom, jammed her feet into the sneakers by the front door, and bolted out of the house. Her mother would have to get the baby today.

She ran south toward the lake, flew down the stone stairs on Palisades and the long slope at Glenmede, and dashed up the hill into the west forest of Lenny Park. Sweat poured down her back as she darted toward the ravine, panting and pushing away image after image of Sasha. Sasha who could barely breathe holding the phone, listening to the buzzing and humming of a film set behind his old pal, trying in vain to suppress the feeling of injustice, of *disintegrating*. Sasha, once the "it boy" of Fox, who fancied himself the tormented Byronic antihero capable of extraordinary passion and cruelty, lying awake, lamenting how far he'd fallen behind. Sasha, packing in the dead of the night, thanking the Chinese grandmother, thanking the Universe, for giving him one last chance to break free, to become a real artist before his face and body lost their currency. She tore through his mirage, letting loose a string of expletives and screams. The trees, unfazed, swayed above her, splashing their yellow and orange pigmentation onto the canvas of a cloudless sky.

An unleashed dog appeared at the top of the ravine in black silhouette. It charged at her, circling and barking. She barked back, matching its menace, tasting blood on the roof of her mouth. How she wanted to wrestle the beast to the ground, sink her teeth into its shiny, lush fur, and let its claws pierce her skin.

"Chewy, come back! Back here!" the dog's owner yelled and whistled. The beast stared up at Lin and shook its head, as though expressing its grave disapproval of the deranged woman, before springing back to its master. A cackle leaped out of Lin as she met the eyes of the concerned, or perhaps mortified, dog owner. "Fuck you, fuck the whole world!" she hollered, and dragged her sore legs deeper into the ravine.

IT WAS A MIRACLE that she made it home, just in time to hurl herself across the threshold and collapse onto the floor. Her Ma rushed out of the kitchen holding Pearl, applesauce smearing the baby's mouth.

"Old Father in Heaven, what happened to you? You okay?"

"Leave me. Take her for a walk."

"I just fed her—"

"Go! Now! I beg you."

"Are you hurt...?"

"No! *Out!*"

She heard her mother gulp and shuffle past her, the baby babbling her incomprehensible complaints while being strapped into the stroller. Soon, the door closed and she was left alone in the silent house. She lay flat on her stomach, spread-eagled, watching the floating dust motes, wishing exhaustion would obliterate her fevered mind. But there was still so much to do. He had packed light; his stuff was all over the house—clothes, socks, shoes, pillows, combs, razors, shaving cream, deodorant. She needed to prop herself up and drag her bloated sack of aching bones and muscles from closet to closet. She needed to corral his belongings and toss them onto a pile in the backyard. She needed to burn them, or at the very least dump them into the tall garbage bin for the city to pick up. As soon as she got to her feet, she must separate his things from hers and the baby's, expunge him from her home, leaving not a damn trace or scent.

# 9

## *Lemei*

Some mornings, she would lose track of time, when it was still so early that the sky was orangey grey, and she had Pearl nestled on her chest as they slow-danced on the small lawn. The baby's sweet powdery scent, those curious eyes that examined her face with unwavering concentration, would resuscitate her memories of new motherhood, hurtling her back to the days when baby Lin was strapped to her, bathed in the first light of day.

How readily history repeated itself.

Another fatherless daughter, to be brought up by two generations of women, except that in this round, she, the matriarch, was at her daughter's mercy. When she met Sasha, days before he let his cowardice persuade him to leave, she had understood his allure. He was a man who had walked straight out of the American posters in her cramped working closet. Thanks to her years of gospel-like teaching, her daughter had admired, *worshipped*, those men and women throughout her youth, perhaps endowing them with an aura of mythology, extrapolating two-dimensional photos into vivid realms of divinity. She imagined Lin falling for Sasha at first sight, overwhelmed by the collision of myth and reality.

Now that Sasha was gone, Lin's sorrow leaked through her pores and settled on everything she touched like a thick layer of dead skin. Guilt nibbled at Lemei as she followed the trail of her daughter's grief, picking up pieces of her child, her little girl who was long gone. Her once-fervent hopes and ideals had poisoned her daughter's blood, and in her old age, she had to endure the dreadful price of estrangement.

Thank heavens Dali was sticking around. She felt less lonely talking to the old neighbour's boy. She couldn't help but fantasize—a proper son-in-law, who could deliver her daughter from purgatory, who understood their roots and traditions, who might even see her into her golden age. But Lin seemed to look right through him. Did she think she had lived with the gods and could no longer reside among mortals?

Her phone buzzed in her pocket. A WeChat call from Li. She would put a stop to it today, she promised herself. Ever since he'd called her by the wrong name a week ago, perhaps under the influence of too much cognac, she'd known that whatever they had—this fantasy conjured up by her lonely brain and blown out of proportion—was nothing special to him. At her age, she didn't need another man, let alone a *propagandist*, to make her feel disposable.

The baby squirmed in her arms, nuzzling her soft head against her armpit. "I won't let him ruin our moment, my angel." She turned off the phone and kissed the baby's cherubic cheeks, her miniature fingers and toes, the heart-shaped birthmark above her belly button. Holding Pearl for the first time at Toronto Pearson, Lemei had been surprised by her effortlessly Chinese features. She had searched her heart for a hint of disappointment, but all she could find was relief, as if the baby were living proof that all her life's mistakes could still be remedied. Now, she swayed and crooned to the baby, a favourite lullaby from Lin's infancy. Pearl smiled her lethal smile, lifting Lemei's heart out of the darkness.

In her peripheral vision, she saw Lin descend the stairs behind the sliding glass door. Her pulse quickened; she didn't want to surrender the baby to her daughter. She had seen Lin's determination to speak only English to Pearl, pouring the Western tongue like cement into its mould. She recognized her daughter's zeal, inherited from her own wretched self. Or was it out of revenge? Her only child, in cahoots with her new world, would brainwash the baby, fill her little head with a foreign language and culture, and bury the heritage of her blood. Soon, this sweet baby, lying so contentedly in her arms, would examine her with cold, suspicious eyes, the same way she'd look at a mere stranger. She'd lose Pearl too.

"Time to come in," Lin ordered, her voice steeped in a simmering ire.

"Hold on to me tight," Lemei murmured to the baby despairingly.

Then to herself: "You, old master of the Grand Plan, this is your comeuppance."

# 10

## *Lin*

She sat on the sidelines, watching Ma and Dali fall into an easy alliance. Ever since Sasha left, Dali was a changed man—energized, emboldened, *triumphant* even. Every few days, he'd show up at their door with a wide grin and half a dozen bags of groceries, offloading them with a theatrical thud.

"Cannonball!" He charged at Pearl now and launched her into the air. The baby squealed and laughed, her hair wild, a pufferfish in a comic strip. Ma beamed at them, her face transformed from a frozen tundra to a warm pool of light. Lin had to turn away; she couldn't stand the meaningful looks Ma would soon throw at her.

"Why not Dali?" Ma had asked her pointedly a mere two weeks after Sasha's departure.

The chafing of her heart was still raw. She hissed at everything and everyone from under her shell, eager to inflict pain. "A min-gong's child, rural hukou, lower-class.

You never wanted a son-in-law from the countryside."

"You're in Canada now. None of that matters anymore. You have a child and he doesn't even mind. Good with the baby too, a rare gem."

Lin had understood what her mother was really saying. *Your last ship. Climb aboard before he sails away too.*

"Dali is a spy."

"Nonsense! He works to promote Chinese culture in the West. What's wrong with that?"

"Haven't you heard him talk? Like a pet parrot of the Politburo. I don't know how *you* can stand him."

Ma's eyes had shifted.

*Of course, she's long switched camps.*

Lin had heard the sound of a growing chasm on their bleak cross-Pacific calls. Now that Ma was here, the proof was in every subtle sign of disapproval—a raised eyebrow, an averted gaze, a muffled sigh.

Dali plopped down beside her, cutting short her thoughts. He had settled in the antique rocking chair—Sasha's favourite spot—like the true master of the house. "Seen this article, Auntie?" He nudged an iPad toward Ma, on its screen the Mandarin edition of the *New York Times*. "Boss asked me to write a letter to the editor as a rebuttal. A long shot, but I'll give it a try."

"Lao Li can't write it himself?"

Lin cringed at Ma's casual tone reserved for family members, the implication of a life familiar to those two but unknown to her.

"Nah, he's got bigger fish to fry. You should read this: Exhibit A of what we talked about the other day— Western media have no sense of scale when it comes to other countries, especially 'enemy states' like ours."

Lin gritted her teeth. *Here we go again.*

Ma donned her glasses and read the headline aloud: "'China Persecutes Street Vendors in a Bid to Accelerate Urbanization.'"

"People rarely look beyond the headlines," Dali lectured on, his eyes flitting between the two women. "It's about this tiny county two hundred kilometres from Beijing. Some county head hoping to attract developers got a bit harsh with the guys selling knickknacks and mutton skewers. Of course, these days all it takes is some kid snapping a photo of an altercation on his phone. Post it on Weibo, an outrage on the web, blown out of proportion. Next thing you know, it gets picked up by some foreign journalist, and voilà, international news!"

"I highly doubt it's that easy," Lin scoffed.

"I was in the newsroom for decades," Ma chimed in. "The kind of space-fillers on a slow news day—you wouldn't believe."

"But when the *New York Times* does it," Dali continued, "it smears dirt on a country most of their readers have never even set foot in. A low-ranking official's stupidity is now a problem with the whole country, as if the president himself has kicked the barbecue vendors off the street."

"And Lin," Ma said, "your fellow countrymen will laugh at us, say, 'Look at the living hell that is China!' Not fair, is it?"

*Your fellow countrymen*—what an underhanded jibe. She felt dizzy, besieged in her own castle. "I don't think the Western readership is so gullible," she muttered darkly.

Dali snorted. "So you think they'll do their due diligence? They'll research this little town, find out about its geopolitical *insignificance* and the lazy journalist who hasn't learned enough Mandarin to do his own interviews?"

*Back off!* She wanted to shove him out of the house.

"You realize now *you* are the one who's making assumptions," she hissed, barely containing her inner flame.

"Possibly, in this case," Ma said, "but in general, Dali's right. Most American reporters never bother to learn our language and culture, our long, complicated history."

"I recall not too long ago *you* weren't that keen on our language or culture," Lin snarled under her breath.

"So right, Auntie," Dali soldiered on, kissing Ma's behind. "Those Westerners come for an adventure in the 'exotic Orient.' Their editors remind them of the kind of stories that'll sell back home. So they talk to their sources. Not ordinary folks on the street, no, those folks are not exciting, but the few ultra-outspoken critics who will flatter them, make them feel like superheroes fighting a villainous system. You really think they'd be unbiased in their reporting?"

*Look at him go.* Had someone been feeding him the lines? Had he been rehearsing?

But Dali didn't matter, Lin decided. She kept her eyes trained on Ma, who nodded earnestly at his words as if they'd been schooled by the same master.

"That's a super-cynical take, isn't it, Ma? What happened to your faith in America's free press? And everything you taught me when I was growing up?" She was pleading now. She didn't like the sheepish look on Ma's face.

"Guess I was naive then." A hint of remorse flickered in Ma's eyes, but she quickly looked away. Lin knew that was the closest to an admission of guilt, or an apology, she was going to get.

"America's so-called free press? Ideological machines!
So overrated!" Dali carried on, oblivious. "Remember that
attack in Beijing two weeks ago? It's been confirmed—handiwork of the Uyghur Islamic Party! Of course the *New York
Times* bent over backward to justify such a terrorist attack.
When the terrorists are on American soil, they're scumbags,
deserving to be tortured at Guantanamo Bay, but on Chinese
soil? Just admirable activists fighting for human rights!"

*He's not entirely wrong there.* But she couldn't back down.

"Leave the Americans out of it. Let's look at ourselves.
Why are the extremists gaining traction? Maybe, just maybe,
a lack of religious freedom has something to do with it?"

"Religious freedom? Ha, Westerners' favourite talking point!" he cackled, the urge to proselytize warping his
face. "What do the so-called religious leaders want? People's
hearts and minds. CCP's the ruling party, so naturally they
want the same thing. It's all a power struggle. As long as
they don't cross the state, they can have all the freedom
they want. But if they compete with the Party, if they want
separation—"

"So you do concede there's no real religious freedom over
there?"

"Do you have religious freedom here? What would your
Stephen Harper do if a domestic group called for an annexa-
tion in Canada?"

"Uyghurs are not the only Muslims in that area, child,"
Ma interjected in a conciliatory tone. "Lots of Hui Muslims
too. They celebrate their holidays, women wear veils, kids go
to Islamic schools."

"Exactly! Uyghurs have less freedom because of their
separatist tendencies!" Dali cried out.

"But taking away their rights only begets more hatred toward the state, which begets more religious fervour, which—"

"Begets more restrictions, yes. An unfortunate feedback loop." Ma sighed, an exhausted rattle.

"Ma, conditions there will only get worse, a lot worse. Surely the majority of people there are just like you and me, wanting a normal life, raising their kids, not being treated like second-class citizens."

"The new president knows what he's doing," Ma said.

"You've put your faith in the princeling?"

"We have to trust *someone*."

Lin snickered—even the old propagandist couldn't see through the new agitprop. But the lurch of desperation in Ma's voice gave her pause.

"What exactly do *you* propose, young genius?" Dali sneered.

"No one has a silver bullet, but more tolerance is always the better way to go."

"Tolerance?!" he barked. "Not for an extremist group that's declared jihad against China!"

"What about a referendum then? Letting the people decide for themselves?"

Dali and Ma exchanged glances before breaking into an icy, synchronized laugh.

"You've been away from your motherland for too long, child. Completely brainwashed by the West."

*All thanks to you, Ma.*

"A referendum would acknowledge the *potential* for a separation," Ma rasped. "We're one unified people, inter-mingled and intermarried for generations on a united land, handed down by our ancestors. An acknowledgement like that hurts the national feelings of every Chinese person."

*Stop parroting!* Lin wanted to tell her. *That evocation of a mythical past, a country as a mother's body, filial piety mixed with nationalism...* Instead, she quietly took in her mother's wounded gloom.

"Right, of course, you no longer share our national feelings." Ma's voice had broken into shards.

She was now the Other, a defector, a traitor to her country.

*But what about you, Ma? Haven't you betrayed your younger self?*

Her eyes filled. She turned away. They were now utter strangers to each other.

# 11

## *Lin*

In her weekly group therapy sessions, she found the label for her life-long malaise. They called it the "colonial mentality," and confirmed the futility of pills for curing her disease. Instead, they read seminal papers and books like *Black Skin, White Masks* and *The Wretched of the Earth*. She was hooked on the readings; the intimate accounts played out frame by frame before her eyes. The long line of pregnant Filipino women at the altar of the Virgin Mary, praying for their children to have the same light skin and bridged nose as their Holy Saint. The young Indigenous movie buff cheering for the cowboys on the silver screen as they charged into a murderous battle against the Indians. The miserable Martinican boy chastised by his mother for uttering his native tongue instead of perfect French. When the Antilleans refused to stand in solidarity with the Africans, she remembered her own hometown that prided itself on cultural relics from the Concession Era—the French villas and English gardens, the white-tableclothed, fork-and-knife dining, the s'mores and eclairs and mille-feuilles—as if their once-proximity to the whites had "civilized" them, hoisting them above the heads of their fellow countrymen.

They were encouraged to "show and tell" the books of their own heritage too. Lin had roamed the aisles of the last remaining Mandarin bookstores in Chinatown, passing shelf after shelf of splashy cookbooks, Pinyin guides, and bilingual children's books. She felt on her back a pair of observant eyes that belonged to the wiry, silver-haired shopkeeper, who after a long silence sidled up to her. "What exactly are you looking for, miss?" he asked in his Cantonese-accented Mandarin. When she gave the book title, he nearly snickered. "Who still reads that stuff these days? Unless you want Chinese mythology in English? With pretty illustrations? We've got a bunch of those in the children's section. Customers like them, great gifts for their whitewashed kids and grandkids!"

"Thank you for your time." She hung her head and made for the door.

"Wait." He followed her. "Are used books okay?"

She nodded, looking at him with renewed hope.

"Your best bet is to go to my pal in the gay village then, Book Haven on Wellesley. Ask the old Portuguese lady behind the counter. An eccentric. She's got a stack of tattered books in Chinese, her personal collection."

Lin had bowed and thanked the shopkeeper, and ran the seven blocks to a Victorian rowhouse with a peeling, leprous facade. A goth lady in her sixties, with silver nose rings and dark purple lipstick, perched on a tall stool by an oil lamp and stared at Lin with alarm when she walked in. But as soon as Lin mentioned the book, the old woman relaxed her eyebrows and, shockingly, replied in wobbly Chinese: "I've always known someone like you would come through my door one day." She fixed a lunch break sign to the window and led Lin through the cavernous store and up the squeaky stairs to an attic. Under a slanted roof, low shelves of books lined the walls. The aroma of aged paper and old leather bindings mixed with the earthy scent of wooden beams. The woman spent the next hour showing Lin her family trove and recounting stories of her missionary grandfather who had traversed 1920s China. "Now that I'm semiretired, I've been learning Mandarin. Maybe someday, I'll crack the secret code between these covers," she said, and drew a spine off the shelf, pressing it into Lin's palm. "Here, the one you're looking for."

Lin clutched the book with sweaty hands. From its yellowed cover, a rouged lady holding a lotus blossom grinned at her, six long hairs sprouting from the crown of her head.

The Portuguese woman helped her turn the page. "So can you read this? I still can't decipher a word in this *Immortal* series. The cursive characters make my head spin."

"I could try. It's been a long time," Lin murmured.

"Among all the Chinese calligraphy styles, cursive is actually my favorite. So elegant, pulsing, *liquid*. I dream of reading it one day. And even writing it! I bet you know calligraphy?"

*Once upon a time.* Lin thought of the days she stood shoulder to shoulder with Ma, transcribing the *Legend*. She'd long lost the intricate muscle manoeuvres to work a brush.

"Take the book, it's my gift."

"Please let me pay for it."

"Take it. If you truly want to repay me, write me a cursive frame, maybe an excerpt from this *Legend*. I'd like to hang it on my wall."

Lin shook her head in silence.

"Come back and visit, okay? These are from *your* ancestors." The woman gestured around the attic. "Think of this as a home away from home."

*Home.* Lin wrestled with the word, oscillating between a flicker of hope and a sense of futility. "What *is* home?" she blurted, looking into the old woman's smouldering eyes and absorbing their intensity. "What if I run, *crawl*, all the way home and find it's gone up in flames long ago?"

The woman stared back and blinked at her. Undaunted, she held Lin's shoulders. "You can pick up the pieces, child. Start from these pages, you'll see."

LATER, SHE RODE THE train back to the city's West End and ran like a headless chicken in her favourite woods, damp air expanding her lungs, the swirl of sunset-hued foliage blurring her vision. A mourning dove seduced her deeper into the forest with its five-bar melody, and she ended up at the bottom of an unfamiliar basin. Fallen saplings formed the entrance to a deserted stick fort. At its centre, an origami crane made by a child's hands sat on two sheets of paper, its beak bent and wings charmingly crooked. She picked up the sheet with blue polka dots, crinkling it, feeling its ultra-thin texture. Muscle memory flooded through her veins like blood. She watched in awe as her fingers went on autopilot, folding, pulling, rotating, flattening, until the shape of a fairy emerged—faceless, but clear enough to evoke the afternoons of her childhood when Laolao had taught her the art of paper-folding. Together they'd bring forth an army of origami Immortals and spin a vivid saga from a mythical land.

She quivered at the sight of the fairy on her palm, sensing a distant call, a looming shift in the constellation of her stars.

# 12

## *Lin*

NOVEMBER 2013

There wasn't a single guard at the gate, which was a surprise. She had expected young officers in heavy-duty pine-green uniforms with handsome fur collars and earflaps, and behind them a pair of imperial stone lions for added intimidation. Instead, tall steel fences and surveillance cameras stared back at her in eerie silence. She pictured the low-level diplomat on the other side of the cameras, frowning at the grainy footage and logging her physical descriptors: *Female, 28–35, 5′5″–5′6″, medium build, short black hair, purple Columbia jacket and grey woollen scarf, holding white daisies. The suspect has come prepared, camouflaged in a baseball cap and sunglasses.* Her pulse quickened, until chatter in her mother tongue grew louder all around her, the myriad accents and intonations clashing and melding into a colourful soundscape. Safety in numbers, she reminded herself.

342

People were arriving outside the Chinese Consulate of Toronto, bearing flowers and photos. Many knew each other, judging by the familiar way they hugged and shook hands. She searched the crowd for lone figures like herself and there were a few, all shuffling self-consciously, eager for the ceremony to begin. Two white photographers snapped pictures with long-lensed professional cameras, their exposed hands beet-red from the cold. "Is that necessary?" she muttered and pulled down the bill of her baseball cap.

A dissident had died in custody near Beijing. Lin had heard the news on CBC yesterday when she returned from her hideout in the woods, and that elusive sense of peace she'd gained from transcribing her patron saint's legend had evaporated in an instant. The simple labourer had thought it prudent to apply for an event permit to hold a twenty-person memorial on June 4, a tainted day on the Chinese calendar. The police, however, thought he was "subverting state power" and promptly locked him up. His lawyer, himself detained six months later, was understandably incredulous, calling the sentence a mockery of the nation's Constitution.

*You are one naive, brave man*, she mouthed at the labourer's portrait, framed by an evergreen wreath. She felt a kinship, having started writing a story about 1989—a key piece of her family's puzzle. The labourer, with a receding hairline and pockmarked cheeks, wore a sombre look, his eyebrows raised and lips pulled down. His eyes stared straight at her, defiant, unwavering, reproachful.

"You have every right to be reproachful," she said. His fellow countrymen had shown him little sympathy following his arrest, at least on the internet. *Who does he think he is? Going against the government—how foolish and pointless,*

*how arrogant! What foreign government is backing him?
Attention whore—only wants to be famous!*

"Heaven has no internet. Rest in peace."

She bowed and moved away from the portrait, finding
a spot in the second row of the audience. Speakers were
lining up in front of the microphone on a makeshift podium.
Soon, they took turns praising the labourer's heroic struggle,
vowing to carry on the fight. The crowd nodded, echoed,
clapped. In front of her, a ruddy-cheeked preschooler in a
blue toque looked around inquisitively, his mother's hands
pressed on his shoulders. Lin locked eyes with the boy and
exchanged a clandestine smile. *How did you get here—this
patch of foreign land? What ghosts of the past have uprooted
your family from your natural soil?* A familiar Chinese dirge
blasted from the speakers. The boy's mother broke into a
gentle sob. Lin felt her nose tingle; water rose and pushed on
her eyelids. Arms were linking into a wave, strangers' limbs
twining through hers from both sides. She could get used
to this, this warm cocoon of solidarity.

THE HOUR WENT ON, the mood shifting. A wide-eyed
Hong Kong activist seized the mic. "The window is closed
for peaceful democratic transition!" the young man cried.
"For Hongkongers, the choice is clear. The only way is
separation!"

His supporters hurrahed. Lin felt queasy, suddenly
claustrophobic. She wriggled her hands away from her neighbours' and stuck them stiffly in her pockets. The Confucian
ideal—her *mother's* ideal—of a unified, harmonious people,
pounded in her ears like a heartbeat. For the first time, she
noticed the clusters of matching outfits in the crowd, their

signs and banners. *You never know where another Chinese stands!* Ma's advice from long ago echoed in her skull. *Don't be fooled by the water's calm surface; discordance clashes in the undertow.*

"Free Hong Kong! Free Xinjiang!" A chant started like a wailing song. She stood in silence, paralyzed by a mix of sympathy and revulsion.

"Get off the podium, you separatist pigs!" An ocean of blazing red entered her peripheral vision. She let out a shriek seeing Dali at the front of a procession, hair tousled and chest puffed, gripping a Chinese national flag and charging down the street like a battle commander. His companions knocked down the wreaths and pulled the multicoloured cords out of the soundboard. The portrait of the deceased lay by the curb, crumpled by trampling feet and encased in mud.

"Disperse! Stop the illegal protest!" Dali roared, propping up the flag by a roadside planter. "Or we'll send your photos to the authorities!"

"It's *legal* to protest here, Communist swine! Go back to the mainland!" yelled someone to her right. She turned toward the source, only to be thrust forward by the Hong Kong group, who had emerged at the forefront in their black uniforms, interlocking arms to form a human shield.

*Calm down! Don't fight the wrong enemy!* Her inner voice was loud and clear, but nothing could escape her clamped throat. Shoved and bounced between the red and the black, she felt her eyes stinging and sweat pouring down her spine. Above her head, a Union Jack carved the sky and collided mid-air with a Five-Star Red Flag, sending primordial heat surging in her blood. She tumbled toward an opening for a gulp of air, only to slam into a camera.

"Lin? What the hell are you doing here?!" Dali's face emerged from behind the long lens.

She gawked at him, rattled, speechless. Before tears drenched her face, she spun around and ran.

SHE FOUND HER MOTHER napping on the living room sofa, her thin grey hair swept to one side like a giant comma punctuating her balding head. She had to talk to her, not to settle scores this time, but to untangle the knots in her chest. She nudged Ma on the shoulder. Her eyelids flickered, then flew open at the sound of sudden drumming on the door. She looked at Lin, dazed. "Get the door?"

Lin could only shake her head.

"Guess *I'll* have to then," Ma murmured and pushed herself up.

Lin covered her head. *Go away, let me talk to my mother in peace!*

But Dali stormed in like a fighting bull charging a matador. "Why were you there?" He flung his scarf and long parka on the carpet.

"Where *were* you?" Ma followed close behind him, fixing her eyes on Lin.

"She was protesting in front of the Chinese Consulate— for some dissident!"

Ma gulped.

Lin plugged her ears, shutting out the lynch mob.

"What's going on?"

"Talk to us!"

"NOW!"

"I don't know, okay?" she capitulated.

"What do you mean you don't know? Explain yourself!"

"I felt a personal responsibility."

"A *personal*—what are you now, child? A dissident?"

"No, Ma, I'm hardly even a closeted activist."

"Then why were you *there*? In front of the consulate, in front of all those security cameras? I heard they have facial recognition software now. They can track you down and wreck your life if they want to!"

Lin laughed bitterly. "Never mind the security cameras. Dali's taken a bundle of pictures of me."

Ma swivelled around and glared at him. "That true?"

"Auntie, I wouldn't send them to anyone, I swear. I can destroy them right now. But Lin, you've got to stop. Do you know those thugs in the crowd? Do you support the separatists?"

"None of your business," she snapped, though she shook her head instinctively. "Ma, I need to talk to you. I think I understand what you said the other day, about a unified people—"

"Why do you have to be so political, child? Hasn't our family lost enough? Now they're going to get you too!"

"I had my hat and sunglasses on."

"Naive! Naive!" Ma threw up her hands.

"So are we supposed to live in fear forever, wherever we go?" she blurted, helpless in this derailed conversation. "Wasn't that the whole point of going to America, to live in freedom? It's people like Dali who make that impossible!"

"Dali's a good boy. He cares about you. The whole point of going to America was to forget the past, to move on, to start anew—"

"Doesn't work that way, Ma!" Her heart slammed in her chest like a rebellious stallion bent on crashing out of the gate. She stared and panted, suppressing the words bubbling up her throat: *Stop pretending you've forgotten, because you won't, and I won't. Every time I cringe at the sound of my mother tongue, every time I feel the urge to dig into my skin and lift off my alien mask, I remember the poison, the self-hate, you injected into my blood. I remember YOUR past, Ma.* She felt tears surging again, but she couldn't possibly put on a show for Dali.

"We have to talk about your writing too." Dali filled the vacuum. "It's dangerous. You've got to stop."

"He's right. Why are you writing about 1989?"

Lin drew a breath. "How do you know about *that*, Ma?"

"I found your manuscript, asked Dali to translate it."

Lin closed her eyes, a violent sea heaving in her stomach.

"I wanted to know what you're doing, child. Always writing, never tell me anything. How can you write about something you don't even know?"

"That was the year you got sick, wasn't it, Ma?" she said acidly. "The year Uncle Feng died. *You* are the one who never tells *me* anything. What exactly happened then? Why won't you tell me?"

Ma teetered. Whatever ghost she was conjuring threw her off balance. Dali gathered her in his arms and settled her on the sofa.

"Why would Auntie tell you anything," he hissed, like a filial son defending his mother's honour. "So you can write all about it for your white audience?" He screwed up his eyes. "It's your livelihood now, isn't it? Writing dirt about your birth country, your *motherland*, making a spectacle of yourself, profiting from your own people's pain. That's how you make it in this white man's world, isn't it?"

"Yes, yes, I'm the circus monkey begging for eyeballs. Still beats being you, you jingoistic spy!" she spat at him.

"Enough!" Ma pounded on the coffee table. "Dali's right about you. You feed your white audience what they want to see. You confirm their prejudices, flatter them, make them feel morally superior. So *you* can make a living."

"I do my due diligence, Ma. I read so many books ... I write to make sense of *you*, of *us*. This is *our* history!"

Ma shook her head. Her cold laugh said it all: *OUR history? You're not one of us anymore.*

"You're a citizen of an enemy state now." Dali picked up the thread as if tightening a noose.

His meddling words grated on her ears. She pivoted toward him in a fluster. "*Go. Away!* Why the hell are you still hanging around us? Why waste your precious time? Don't you have more important people to spy on?"

He rubbed his face hard. "I'm here for Auntie. Someday even you will realize—"

"*Stop* poisoning my mother."

"Dali is a good man. He's waited long enough for you."

"Ma, stop. Don't be his accomplice."

"Your mother agrees we should be together."

"Tough to be a single mother, child."

"I can't, Ma. You know I can't."

He glared at her with bloodshot eyes. "Maybe I *should* send those pictures to the authorities."

"Don't you dare!" Ma roared.

"Auntie, *someone* needs to teach her a proper lesson. Or she'll never learn."

"Dali didn't mean it. He loves you. He's just hurt." Ma seized Lin's hand and hissed, "*Stop. Fighting. Him!*"

She shook Ma off, her eyes boring into Dali. "Do whatever you want, you dirty spy!"

"You're bewitched by the West! If you'd gone through what I've gone through in America—"

"I *have*!"

"No, you haven't, not even close. It's different for girls like you."

"What's that supposed to mean?"

"You know what I mean. Exotic fruit."

Blood roared in her temples. She pounced at him. "Get the hell away from us! Never come back! Mark my words: I will never, *ever*, love you—"

Her syllables came out long and wobbly, removing the colour from his face bit by bit. His eyes retreated and sank into his sockets like bullets through a deep tunnel. His lips twisted and jiggled and stretched open; his hand thrust into the liquor cabinet. A lupine howl, a death scream, bounced from face to face, wall to wall. Behind him, tears slithered down Ma's cheeks, through the brackets of her laugh lines, and onto their laminate floor.

*Words kill*, Lin remembered with a tremor, smelling salt and despair in the air. *Words kill*.

# 13

## *Dali*

T he chilly night air met him head-on. He stood in the alleyway, shivering in only a thin shirt. He tried to focus on the bottle in his palm, watching his loot reflect the moonlight in its slender elegance. A pungent, grainy fragrance rushed into his nose as he twisted open the cap and inhaled greedily. *That good-for-nothing Sasha does know his premium vodka.* He took a long swig, savouring the creamy liquid that burned a cleansing path down his throat. He squeezed his eyes shut and waited for calmness to wash over him. But looming behind his eyelids was Lin's glare. I will never, *ever*, love you! Her words lashed into him. He doubled down with another gulp. The memory of warmth snaked through his limbs, but peace was elusive.

There was so much he longed to make her see. He was a min-gong's child after all; living in a land where he didn't belong was the perennial story of his life. How naive she was; her Shanghai privileges had blinded her. He'd thought

Sasha's abandonment would be her wakeup call, that she'd finally notice him, and the lost tribe, the Old Kingdom he'd been painstakingly rebuilding.

*You really want to live in a guest house forever? You think they'll count you as their own if you hang around them long enough, saying all the right things? Can't you see? That slippery dignity you yearn for—you'll never find it as long as you turn away from your own people.*

Then to himself: *Why can't I forget her, that dumb, stubborn girl?*

*Meet me by the water.* He heard his mother's soothing murmur. How he had loved living by the ocean as a boy, hunting for a kaleidoscope of rocks and shells, digging for crabs and sea snails, chasing the white, frothy waves as sunrays danced on the surface of the water like a thousand fireflies alighting on blue satin. After his father disappeared, Ma often clasped his hand and trekked far afield on the village beach until they reached their favourite spot—a rock formation resembling a galloping horse. They'd climb onto its back and let gusts of wind caress their skin, pretending they could race across the water toward the horizon, deposit their sorrow, and watch it sink to the bottom of the ocean.

He felt Ma's warm breath on his neck; she was whisper-shouting *Giddy-up!*, spurring the magic horse forward.

*Wait for me. I'm coming.*

He ran south, in the direction of the lake. When he reached the edge of Lenny Park, he stared at the silhouette of the Norway maple in the middle of the grass field, its branches stripped down to their very essence like a wild bouquet of fishbones. His heart throbbed, for the lazy afternoon he'd spent here with Pearl and Lemei, holding the toddler's chubby hands, gazing in awe at her wide, gap-toothed smile.

*Oh, stop.* Lin's callous voice drummed in his ears. *Get the fuck away from us, you dirty spy!*

He picked up speed, crossing the field, the tennis court, the skating rink, straining to outpace the ballooning pain. A black forest rose before him, cutting off his escape route. A narrow trail meandered into the dark belly of the woods, beckoning him.

*No, no, I know better.* He made a one-eighty and scanned the empty field on the other side of the park.

Something crunchy was under his feet. He squatted down and narrowed his eyes: an origami fairy holding a lotus blossom. *It can't be.* He shuddered. His mother used to make the same fairies to decorate their village shack. He felt faint, a world displaced and misplaced, his unruly mind confronted by a physical reality. He looked around. Another fairy lay in solemn prostration a few steps beyond the trailhead. *It IS Ma!* His heart leaped. Ma had finally come to his rescue. He straightened up, took a worshipful swig of liquor, and strode into the woods.

The moon had broken out of its shy camouflage and splashed a coat of silver onto the narrow path. He surveyed his surroundings ravenously, like a nocturnal animal slinking into new territory. Under the moonlight, he could see his mother's fairies scattered on both sides of the path—in the bushes, on the branches, half-buried under the gravel. He came to the edge of a basin, with an expansive red oak slanting by the cliff, its long branches soaring into the night sky like a dancer in a tableau vivant. Two fairies dangled from its main branch, their weightless bodies swaying in the wind.

"I'm here." He set down the vodka bottle by his feet and raised his arms toward the sky. "I miss you, Ma. I'm so, so tired." Spinning slowly on the spot, he beseeched his mother to reveal herself. But the night, with its solitary moon, remained stubbornly still.

An ear-splitting squeal punctured the silence. He ducked down and listened to the fierce battle in the bushes. Glowing red eyes, like rubies embedded in a bandit's mask, cropped up on the edge of the path. A raccoon, with a fluffy squirrel's tail between its teeth, glared at him boldly, as if he were responsible for its escaped meal. "Shoo!" He stomped his foot, and the raccoon dashed headlong down the trail, into a gust of freezing wind that wailed through the forest and sent him into a spasm.

Teeth chattering, he reached for his bottle, craving the liquor's warmth, but it was no longer there. Its silver-blue label glistened a few metres down the cliff, caught between the tree's roots. He cursed under his breath and lay face down with an outstretched arm, the tip of his index finger grazing the bottle cap. He inched downward, clinging to the roots and digging his hands into the soil.

The bottle was in his palm when the earth beneath him gave way. He tumbled down the hill, his skin scraped and lacerated by the branches and rocks. Blood oozed out of a gash on his leg as he skidded to a stop at the bottom of the basin. He seized the vodka bottle shining mercifully beside him and poured the liquor down his throat. The burn undulated through his veins, dulling the pain and dispelling the chill in his bones. In his blurred vision, an ancient structure, a hut of some sort, stood a few steps ahead. As he propped himself up, he couldn't feel his feet and the earth pulled him down with a resolute force. He crawled toward the shelter instead, dragging the bottle with one hand.

Musty dampness shrouded him as he entered the hut. At its centre stood a tree stump and a child-sized stool. An inkstone and a thick brush perched on a pile of calligraphy paper. Incredulous, he unfolded the stack under a shaft of moonlight. His gasp echoed in the dome-shaped structure. In his hands lay the last chapter from the *Legend of the Immortal Woman*—a favourite chapter he had committed to memory. "Ma's penmanship?" he mumbled, slurring his words. The strokes whirled before his eyes—hour-glass verticals, wriggly throws, sassy presses. He fought against an annihilating drowsiness as he read the familiar text—the Immortal Woman preparing for her ascent into heaven, having rejected the earthly riches offered by the evil empress.

Only one last section was missing. He longed for the achingly beautiful poem that described her final journey to the Immortal Stream. Splashing the last drops of vodka on the inkstone, he ground the leftover ink with a stick. It was not the right consistency, but it would have to do. He closed his eyes, the poem reciting silently on his lips, a surprising wave of heat rising in his belly, battling head-on the iciness in his marrow. He rode the burst of vigour and lucidity, his body dancing weightlessly, his brush sweeping and gliding, condensing ink into the tender lyrics of a bygone era, into faces and heartbeats, and people lost and found.

When he was finished, he flung the brush to the ground and collapsed on the tree stump. The world was fading fast into a black cloud. The iciness had come roaring back from its temporary retreat, freezing his lungs, seizing his heart, clenching his throat. His mother's airy touch was on his face at last. She was humming a quiet tune from their village.

Outside, the first snow of the year was furtively falling, erecting a formidable curtain, separating the seasons past.

# CODA

2014

WEIHAI, SHANDONG PENINSULA

L in sat by the window, peering into the pastel-grey sky. The sound of a foghorn, distant and languorous, penetrated the stillness of the night. Dawn would break in two hours, and Ma would rise to make her signature fish and egg buns. Pearl would smack her lips and devour them until her belly swelled like a melon. At the thought of her resilient daughter, she smiled. Pearl had been the subject of much scrutiny when they first arrived at this seaside village, her slowly maturing face flashing signs of a distant land. Villagers would gather around them at country fairs and temple worship, glancing back and forth between the mother-daughter pair, their eyes wells of confusion and curiosity.

"Why's her nose so big?" the neighbour's five-year-old boy liked to hover over their shared fence and ask his grandfather, who would puff on his water pipe and rasp without lifting his grooved eyelids: "The girl's got the white devil's blood."

Lin had lamented her daughter's fate—exotic everywhere, at home nowhere. But to her surprise, the intrigue dissipated after a few months, once the family had settled into their work at the village school and Pearl had picked up Mandarin. It was as if the villagers, having lived by the simple logic of the land, commanded an innate faith in any transplant that could take root in new soil.

Sipping on her longjing, she mentally went over the day's schedule. The two new teachers were arriving at noon—one from Shanghai, no less—along with the TV crew. She and her mother would do their interviews before taking the new recruits to meet the students. Then a stop at the Temple of the Immortal Woman, followed by a village feast.

This day had arrived like a dream, impossible to imagine even a few months ago. By midsummer, it'd seemed as if all their petitions for funding had gone into a black hole, and they'd forever be the only blockheads willing to stay, teaching the village children in a ramshackle cottage and hemorrhaging their own savings. They'd grown so depressed that, night after night, they clung to an ancient tube TV and numbed themselves with relentless cheering and sensationalism. Her mother was hooked on *Chinese Idol* and the season's leading candidate, a quintessential "flower boy" with the most fashion-forward features—a slim face, alabaster skin, smoky eyes, rouged lips, and lithe, shapely legs. He wrote half-decent rap songs, a new fad in Mandopop. His most popular number—a song titled "China Dream"—deftly wove the new president's Thoughts and Visions with internet teen slang, set to a groovy jazz-funk score. The female-heavy audience went gaga as he riffed and rhymed with a haughty air, his soft masculinity on full display. He was a latter-day model of the Communist Youth, coated in a pop idol's skin. Even Pearl would abandon her toys and huff and puff in front of the screen, mimicking the young man's every move.

They didn't see it coming when the newly minted idol dispatched a gilded lifeboat their way. That evening, the show's famous MC was especially unctuous. "Out of this world, Tongtong!" he shrieked after the singer's performance, a grin blossoming on his freakishly young face, which hadn't aged for twenty years. "I sense so much passion from you, young brother. You're one intense fellow, aren't you?"

"Every word of my lyrics has been brewed in my marrow," Tongtong replied in a trendy Taiwanese accent, despite his biography stating he was from Yantai, merely sixty kilometres from their seaside village.

Lin cringed at the overwrought pair and grabbed the remote. Her mother clutched on to the other end, locking them in a silent struggle.

"Tell me, how do you unwind?" the MC asked. "What do you do to come back to earth after flying so high?"

"I have my secret weapon," said the idol, blinking coyly and flashing his killer smile at the camera. "Part of my night-time routine is to watch Grandma Lemei's cooking videos on Weibo."

Lin covered her mouth and let the remote drop.

"The granny runs a rural school with her daughter. Makes her students the most incredible vegetarian food. Bamboo shoot buns, pea jelly, umami tofu, wild strawberry jam. All handmade from scratch, ingredients sourced one hundred percent from her tiny village. Reminds me so much of my childhood."

Lin turned to her mother, who was slack-jawed and frozen in her seat. "You're our saviour." She squeezed Ma's hand.

WITHIN HALF AN HOUR, Ma's obscure Weibo page exploded with traffic and comments. In the days that followed, internet denizens demanded more videos, more recipes, more time to stare at the misty ocean and rolling hills. The cultural critics waded in too, crowning Lemei the "master of repackaging rural lives for urban fantasy," and commending her for "telling the Chinese story one delicious dish at a time." Even their village school was hailed as a "rare oasis for the left-behind children who otherwise lived an orphaned existence." Weihai's tourism bureau chief wasted no time sending in a task force. "We must scale up Granny Lemei's production!" the potbellied leader declared cheerily.

"Profits must flow back to our village school," Lin said firmly.

"If that's what you want."

"And a national campaign. We want migrants' children to have equal access to urban education."

The leader sagged a little. "We'll study the proposal with the chief."

"We've already announced the initiative on Granny's Weibo. Please check out the widespread accolades for your team and the chief himself." Lin grinned, relishing the sight of an official held hostage in the court of public opinion.

ONE YEAR EARLIER, LIN and her mother had arrived at the village, ashen-faced and puffy-eyed, cradling Dali's urn. They had barely acknowledged each other on their planes-trains-and automobiles journey, each consumed by her own guilt and regret. That evening, the ocean and sun had tangled in an epic battle, the former engulfing the latter only to be set on fire in return. Villagers joined them on the beach—timid children clinging to their white-haired grandparents who remembered Dali as a young boy.

The village head, a soft-spoken, small-statured man in his sixties, gestured at the mourning wreaths all around them. "From Dali's childhood buddies. All working in the cities now. Dali used to be the leader of the boys' pack, smart as hell, a prankster too." The elder chuckled, his eyes glistening with nostalgia.

Lin had stood motionless, staring ahead at Dali's black-and-white portrait. The booming sound of the waves entered her pores and liquified her insides, churning up water behind her eyelids, blurring, melting the face of her frenemy into the blazing clouds.

It was after they had scattered his ashes into the Yellow Sea, after the spike fiddles had torn into the sky and delivered his spirit into the ether, when they were all sitting around one long table for the traditional funeral Tofu Feast, that Lin had the epiphany. This was *her* ancestral village too. Where else could she better atone for her sin?

She and her mother didn't speak for another week. Until the village head phoned her one morning, apologetic. "I know you must still be jet-lagged, but our schoolteacher just quit and went back to the city. The third one this year. Do you think you could help out for a couple days?"

Lin had the best time reading to those dark-eyed, lonesome children, who smiled at her with bashful gratitude. At recess, she played the mother hen in a game of Eagle and

Chicks. The midday sun shone on them warmly. She opened her arms wide, laughing and hopping with the weight of the children on her back. But her body had never felt so light. She was practically floating.

That night, lying in their shared bed, she broke the ice with Ma.

"I want to teach here, at the village school." The words lingered in the air. She held her breath.

"I know what you're doing," Ma rasped back at last.

"What am I doing?"

"You're doing this out of guilt."

"That's not—"

"Remember, it was *not* your fault."

"Yes, it was. The *Legend* was found in his belongings, with his mother's signature."

"The Immortal Woman is the patron saint for the whole village."

"That's why he must've recognized it. He must've found my origami fairies, which lured him deeper and deeper into the woods. He even finished my calligraphy ... That fort was like a death trap custom-designed for him."

Ma waved a hand, her sigh echoing against the walls. "A freakish coincidence. The Universe has its own Grand Plan."

"Don't you feel a special energy here? I've only felt this way when I was in that fort, shut off from the world, answering Laolao's call—"

"Laolao? Your Laolao fled the village in her teens for a better life. Never looked back. *She* wouldn't want us to be here."

"Is it her, or you? If it were up to you, you'd ship me away to a foreign land again, wouldn't you? 'Erase yourself, become somebody else, have no memory of our past!' We've tried that, haven't we?" She was yelling now. She didn't mean to yell.

"Maybe we should just not talk. We've held out for a good while."

"To see who would surrender first. This battle we've been in all our lives, neither of us could ever win, can't you see?"

"I didn't think we were always in a battle. I thought we were on the same team. I thought you *wanted* to leave."

*Not with a bruising inferiority complex, a decimated self.*

"I was just a *kid*. Didn't know what to think. And then you took me to that creepy office, that creepy doctor ... I only wanted to run away ..."

A rattling sigh in the dark.

"You and that doctor, spewing poison, playing God, toying with my fate—"

"I'm sorry—"

"Did you know I used to fantasize about burning down her office? So many times in my dreams ... I even took a box of matches with me once."

"*Please*, spare me."

Lin paused, panting, willing the flickering images to dissolve into blackness. Willing the world to go quiet again.

Warm lava sprang and overflowed from the repentant mother, encroaching on the daughter's terrain and wetting her loose strands of hair. "I didn't know what else to do back then." Her mother's voice reverberated in the shadows after a long silence. "First my father, then my brother. My mind was warped—you *had* to leave, become a new person. That was the only option."

"Why didn't *you* leave?"

"Couldn't find a way. And it would've been too cruel to your Laolao ... I thought I could at least save *you*. You could start over in America ..." Ma was trembling, making the bed creak. "You're right. It was all my fault. You have every right to blame me."

Lin could hear the ocean charging and retreating in the distance, a lone seagull cawing over the dark blue sand. They had both lost their place in the world, been cursed by the world, cursed each other. They could keep drifting apart, letting hate eat away at their hearts and poison their brains, until they perished alone like bloated rotten fish washed ashore in different corners of the earth.

"I don't want to blame you anymore." She exhaled the words. "Not anymore."

Ma let out the breath she was holding.

"Let's not run from ourselves again, Ma. Look at these village kids, left behind by the world. Like Dali when he was a boy, still innocent, helpless. We can't walk away now."

"You sure you want to stay?"

"I want to stand still for a while, quit running from myself."

"But *here*? Your Laolao always felt fortunate to get her hukou from the 'Grand Shanghai,' so her children could be city people."

"None of that matters anymore."

"You've seen the world, the alternative. Your birth country may no longer welcome you."

*I know, I know.* She breathed through the pang. "Guess I'll find out. Worth a try."

"So we're back where your grandmother started."

"The Universe has its own Grand Plan. Just go with it."

She heard air rush out of pinched lungs and sensed her mother nodding. She inched closer to Ma. She wanted to hold her and be held, to recover each other's solidity; so much of themselves had been lost to phantom shapes in dusty memories. But there was one more thing standing between them.

She inhaled sharply. "Do you miss him ... Uncle Feng?"

The question hung above them, the key to a universe that was equal parts healing and perilous. The seagull cawed again, circling, circling.

"I didn't dare," Ma said finally. "Had to shut him out. Carrying him, I couldn't breathe, let alone move through life."

"Will you let him back in, someday?"

A chuckle. "Already happening lately, in small doses. Sometimes, we even argue, both of us stubborn as mules. I think we'll grow old together."

She rested her cheek on Ma's shoulder, a little girl once more, even if just for a fleeting moment. "Will you tell me about him? I promise I'll do all the chores around here for the next thirty days. *Please?*"

*WHAT A NATURAL.* Standing on the sidelines, Lin marvelled at her mother's confidence in front of the camera.

*You should've seen her onstage when she was sixteen, before that ocean of people.* Laolao's voice, travelling from her childhood, drummed in her ears. *Your Ma's made for the limelight.*

"Granny," the beautiful reporter cooed in a honeyed voice, "I heard you've been cooking for the entire school ever since you arrived from Canada a year ago. Those kids are so lucky!"

"No, no, *I* am the lucky one. In fact, it was the kids who started my Weibo channel."

"Is that so?"

"Yup. Chinese New Year, their parents came to visit from the city. The kids got smartphones for presents and started following me around with their cameras—in the kitchen, in the hills where I gathered ingredients. For their art class, which my daughter teaches, they edited and posted the videos online, and voilà, the rest is history!"

"Hidden talents in a small village!" the reporter exclaimed, batting her long, fake lashes.

"Absolutely. These rural children didn't win life's lottery, but they're every bit as talented as kids in the city. They deserve a better chance in life."

"Would you say you owe part of your success to Idol Tongtong?" the reporter asked.

Lin rolled her eyes. *Here we go, back to what sells.*

"Yes, thanks to him, we can now afford new teachers," Ma replied calmly, determined to chart her own course. She looked past the reporter and straight into the camera. "We now pay a salary that rivals the best schools in Shanghai. So if you're a young graduate and you want to do something *meaningful* with your life, send us your resumé, pronto! And Tongtong, if you are watching, come by for dinner anytime. I've perfected your favourite dishes—king oyster mushrooms, silk sweet potato, scallion pancakes…"

Lin watched her mother glow in the flood of lights, her warm grin burning through the grime of trauma that'd settled under her skin. Behind the TV crew, on the other side of the school window, the new teachers were squatting by the village children and chatting earnestly, their pale, smooth faces untarnished by the natural elements. She wished for the urbanites to stay, that the inevitable puncture of their rural fantasies—the reality of smelly manure and valiant insects, things conveniently hidden behind the idyllic footage—would not scare them away. But she wouldn't let herself worry today; the pure light in the newcomers' eyes was all the assurance she needed now. She ambled out of the room, following the faint song of copper bells undulating from the hill. The majestic temple glistened in the slanting sun, under a riot of radiant clouds.

She quickened her steps, her heart soaring toward the seat of the Immortal Woman. Running up the verdant hill with precipices hanging over the frothy sea, she sensed her forebears' ghosts and spirits leap out of the rock crevices and latch on to her, their unfinished murmurings seeping into her pores. Her grandmother, once more a young girl with jet-black eyes, ran abreast with her before racing headlong for the cliff, thousands of pieces of her girlhood dreams fanning into the air and crashing into the mirage of a distant metropolis. Her youthful, frightened mother plunged toward hellfire, toward the hollow shape of a brother, only to be inundated by a tsunami of hands—a life spared, but a soul held hostage by its conscience, forever at war with itself.

Her heart thumped the whole way until she reached the temple at the hilltop and touched the feet of the Immortal Woman. The smooth porcelain cooled her fevered body. For a long time, she stood there, breathing in the soothing fragrance of sandalwood incense. She peered into the tender eyes of her patron saint, reading the secret, radical codes she'd been disseminating for hundreds of years, instructing all her children to flee the golden halls and jade chambers, in search of primordial peace.

And then, she let them all go—the ghosts and spirits. Her lips moved to the cadence of the couplets flanking the saint's elegant statue:

> *Store up your essential spirit and live like a fool,*
> *Exquisite being originates from non-being.*

"Yeah, yeah, I'll try!" She bowed to the Immortal Woman and cast her gaze back at the world of mortals. From where she stood, she could see the caravan of the TV crew leaving, the children tailing the plume of dust in a game of chase.

*Home*—the word bopped on her tongue, silent, earnest, irony-free. It could all crumble to ashes tomorrow, she knew, like a mocking phantasm conjured from a nomad's mind. But still, she wanted to go home now, to her mother and daughter, to her village family. Tonight, they'd all be waiting for her.

# Acknowledgements

My inimitable editor at House of Anansi, Shirarose Wilensky, is my Bo-Le (伯乐), who plucked me and my book out of obscurity, who understood my writing in such a visceral way. I will be forever grateful for her belief in this book, her incredible knowledge, wisdom, and insights, and her steady hand in shepherding the book to publication.

A heartfelt thank-you to the entire talented and dedicated team at House of Anansi—Melissa Shirley, Alysia Shewchuk, Jenny McWha, Gemma Wain, Michelle MacAleese, Emma Rhodes, Emma Davis, and Jess Shulman, to name a few.

Special thanks to my agent, Chris Casuccio, for his belief in this project, his kind encouragement, and his tireless advocacy.

I'm deeply grateful to my tremendous mentor Joseph Kertes, for his wisdom and faith and generosity. Humber School for Writers is the most supportive and nurturing program any emerging writer could dream of.

Thanks to the brilliant writers who have helped me in this journey—Alissa York, David Bezmozgis, Lynda Williams,

Kim Echlin, Thea Lim, Kathryn Kuitenbrouwer, Tessa Hulls, and Jessica Westhead, to name a few.

A few notes: In the translated classic poem at the end of Chapter 1, I changed "he/his" to "she/her" to better suit the context. I took liberty with the production timeline of John Logan's *Red* (referenced in Part 4)—*Red* premiered in 2009, five years after its reference in this book. For certain discussions on Chinese politics, especially to maintain a more balanced debate, I was gratefully informed by Daniel Bell's book *The China Model: Political Meritocracy and the Limits of Democracy* and the trove of articles on TheChinaProject.com, especially Kaiser Kuo's column.

I want to thank my small circle of friends and my book club for sustaining me over the years. An immigrant's life can be excruciatingly isolating. Thanks for being there in good and bad times.

Thanks to my beautiful family-in-law (mother, father, brother, sister, nieces, and nephew) for accepting and loving me.

Most of all, I want to thank the following: my parents, for their incredible strength and character through adversity, and their unwavering love for me; my late Nainai, for giving me the world when our lives were so small; my partner and our children, for rescuing me from darkness and filling my heart with endless light.

SU CHANG is a Chinese Canadian writer. Born and raised in Shanghai, she is the daughter of a former (reluctant) Red Guard leader. Her fiction has been recognized in *Prairie Fire*'s Short Fiction Contest, the Canadian Authors Association (Toronto) National Writing Contest, the ILS/ Fence Fiction Contest, and the *Masters Review*'s Novel Excerpt Contest, among others.